— • —

DEAD RECKONING

When Carver finds out Jessica's younger sister, Sabrina, has been kidnapped, he travels to Austin, Texas to help her out.

The police department is short-staffed, and a detective hasn't even been assigned to the case. Time is of the essence. Finding someone within 48 hours of a kidnapping is a matter of life and death.

Carver isn't a detective, but he has ways of getting information and tracking down people. His methods may not be legal, but they do the job just fine. He's also willing to serve as judge, jury, and executioner upon request.

It doesn't take long for Carver and Jessica to realize Sabrina has been kidnapped by sex traffickers. The stakes were already high, but now they're even higher. They have to find Sabrina before she's sold or shipped out of the country.

One thing is certain. The traffickers will have a reckoning if and when Carver finds them. And if he has his way, they'll wish they were dead by the time he's through with them.

DEAD
RECKONING

JOHN CORWIN

OVERWORLD PUBLISHING

BOOKS BY JOHN CORWIN

Books by John Corwin
Want more? Never miss an update by joining my email list and following me on social media!
Join my Facebook group at https://www.facebook.com/groups/overworldconclave
Join my email list: www.johncorwin.net
Fan page: https://www.facebook.com/johncorwinauthor

PSYCHOLOGICAL THRILLERS
The Family Business
AMOS CARVER THRILLERS
Dead Before Dawn
Dead List
Dead and Buried
Dead Man Walking
Dead By The Dozen
Dead Run
Dead Weather Days
Dead to Rights
Dead but not Forgotten
Dead Reckoning
CHRONICLES OF CAIN
To Kill a Unicorn
Enter Oblivion
Throne of Lies
At The Forest of Madness
The Dead Never Die
Shadow of Cthulhu
Cabal of Chaos

STAND ALONE NOVELS
Mars Rising
No Darker Fate
The Next Thing I Knew
Outsourced
Seventh

CHAPTER 1

Sabrina never thought today would be her last day of freedom.

She was too busy looking at the good news on her phone. A text from her science teacher, Mr. Hardin said it all: *My man on the inside just confirmed your full ride to MIT!*

She giggled and showed the text to her friend, Vania. "Can you believe it? I'm in!"

Vania's mouth dropped open. She took the phone and looked at the text. "Are you sure Mr. Hardin isn't just trying to get into your pants?"

"Gross!" Sabrina took the phone back. "He would never."

"You sure about that?" Vania smirked.

"A hundred percent." Sabrina grimaced. "You have such a perverted mind sometimes."

Vania laughed. "I'm just joking." She hugged her friend. "I'm happy for you. It must be nice having a teacher help you out so much."

"I think it's because of his daughter, you know?" Sabrina's smile faded. "She was interested in science too. Then she vanished, like two or three years ago."

"Yeah, maybe." Vania shrugged. "He's practically adopted you. It's kind of creepy and nice at the same time."

"Well, maybe a little." Sabrina grinned. "But I'm not going to complain. Do you know how hard it is to get into MIT?"

Vania nodded. "Like my parents say, it's not what you know, it's who you know."

"So true." Sabrina sighed. "I thought getting perfect grades would be enough. But it's never enough." She turned off her phone screen. "Rich kids have political connections to the administrators, then you've got programs that make it harder for Asians to get available slots."

"Because you're all so sickeningly smart." Vania stuck out her tongue. "Science Asians are the worst."

Sabrina laughed. "No, that would be the math Asians."

"Eh, I'm not sure about that." Vania stopped walking. "Oh, I forgot to get my lunch from the car. Hang on."

Sabrina waited while Vania pulled an insulated lunch bag from her passenger seat. She checked the time. "We'd better hurry. Our kayak reservation is in two minutes."

Vania locked her car. "Okay, let's go!"

The pair hurried out of the parking lot and toward the kayak reservation counter. There was a large party being helped so they had to wait. Sabrina took the time to text her sister, Jessica, about the good news.

My science teacher, Mr. Hardin got me into MIT! I start in the fall!

She didn't expect a response right away. Jessica had already been halfway through college when Sabrina started high school, so the sisters had never been all that close. But she was still family, and she wanted to brag about it, just a little bit.

Jessica had started her own software company only to have it crash and burn before it ever got off the ground. She'd been living at home for a while now, but that hadn't helped Sabrina form a deeper bond with her.

If anything, Jessica had been more withdrawn since returning home. Probably because their strict parents were ashamed of her failure and didn't seem ready to let her forget it anytime soon. It had been enough to make Jessica leave. She'd been gone for weeks now, responding only sporadically to texts.

Vania saw the text. "Still trying to get your sister's approval?"

Sabrina tucked her phone into a waterproof case. "Sometimes I wonder why I even bother."

"Where did she vanish to?" Vania said.

"She won't tell me. She just said she's working on a project." Sabrina stepped up to the rental counter. A cute boy smiled at her. She felt a blush warm her face. "Hi."

"Hi." He looked at his computer screen. "Do you have a reservation?"

"Yes, for Sabrina."

"That's a pretty name."

Vania rolled her eyes. "Can we get our kayaks, please?"

The boy flinched and broke eye contact with Sabrina. "Yeah, sure."

He finished the paperwork and took them out to get their kayak and life vests. He looked like he wanted to talk to Sabrina more, but Vania gave him a look that made him quickly retreat."

"Aw, he's cute," Sabrina said.

"He's not smart enough for you." Vania folded her arms over her chest. "Only rocket scientists need apply."

Sabrina laughed. Another text arrived from Mr. Hardin. *Let's celebrate! How about pizza on me?*

Vania looked at the text and shook her head. "Isn't that weird?"

"He's just a sweet old man, okay?" Sabrina turned off the phone screen. "Let's get on the water."

"How does a high school science teacher even have contacts at MIT?" Vania shook her head. "You're going to study rocket science all the way up north, and I'll be stuck here going to Austin Community College. God, I feel like such a moron."

"Hey, you're not stupid." Sabrina tightened the straps on her life jacket. "You're just not all that motivated. You could have done much better if you wanted to."

"School sucks. Maybe I'll just become a social media star."

Sabrina laughed. "Along with everyone else these days."

Vania pursed her lips. "I have no idea what I want to do. I'll probably end up becoming the secretary to a high-powered CEO who wants to make me his mistress."

"Ew, don't do that!" Sabrina hugged her friend. "You become the CEO and make some guy your mister."

"My mister?" Vania giggled. "Is that what they call male mistresses?"

Sabrina giggled. "I have no idea, but it sounds right."

"I mean, you're the valedictorian, so you know everything, right?"

Sabrina giggled harder. "I wish. Most of the time I feel like I don't know anything."

The two girls caught their breaths and picked up their kayaks. They carried them to the end of the dock and put them in the water. Sabrina slid easily into hers. Vania grabbed the dock for support and managed to get in without too much wobbling.

They pushed off from the dock and started paddling. It was a busy day on the lake. There were lots of paddleboards, kayaks, boats, and jet skis. It was late spring, so the water was still a little cold, but the weather was great for being out on the water.

"Maybe I'll join a row team," Vania said. "Being part of a team would be cool."

"Yeah, that would be really awesome. You could get in shape and make lifelong friends along the way."

"I have to get into a real university first." Vania sighed. "Ugh, I wish it wasn't so expensive."

"Oh, it's horrible. If I didn't have a scholarship, I couldn't go." Sabrina angled toward the bridge and paddled faster. "Let's try to get in five miles today."

"Five miles? I hope you're kidding."

Sabrina laughed and pointed at the dark clouds on the horizon. "A storm is coming, so I think a mile out and back is good enough exercise."

"Yeah. More than enough." Vania paddled hard to keep up. "Slow down!"

"I am going slow." Sabrina checked her phone to see if Jessica responded. Getting into MIT was big news. Maybe she'd reply faster than usual.

Vania seemed to know exactly what she was doing. "Did Jessica reply?"

"No."

"Are you sure she's okay?" Vania stopped paddling and drifted so she could catch her breath. "Do you think she's really working on a project, or do you think she's drinking heavily and doing drugs to forget about her failures?"

Sabrina shrugged. "I don't know. I really don't. She's six and a half years older than me, so we never became friends, you know? I'm just the kid sister she babysat when our parents wanted a break from us."

"At least you have a sister." Vania sighed. "I wish I had siblings."

Sabrina grabbed Vania's kayak and pulled it alongside hers. "You're my real sister."

"I know." Vania squeezed her hand. "But it would be so cool to have a big brother who beat up the bullies."

"Yeah. That would be cool."

Vania sighed and looked down. "It makes me sad that I'll lose you when you go to school."

"I know. That's the one thing I hate about moving away." Sabrina let their kayaks drift apart and began paddling again. "But it's the only school I want to attend, you know?"

"I know but being separated by thousands of miles sucks."

A pair of jet skis zipped past so fast and so close that the wake rocked the kayaks violently.

Vania cried out in surprise. "My God, did you see how close they came to us?"

"How could I miss it?" Sabrina held up a fist. "Slow down, assholes!"

The jet skis circled back. The men riding them leered at them. One stood and grabbed his crotch in an obscene gesture. The men weren't wearing lifejackets. They were both heavily tattooed and darkly tanned. They said something to each other and laughed. Then their faces grew deadly serious.

Sabrina looked around desperately for any help nearby. Most of the boaters were in pontoon boats and were drifting lazily on the other side of the lake.

The two men gunned the jet skis engines loudly, then sped toward Sabrina and Vania. They whipped to the side at the last minute, spraying the girls with cold water. They spun around and leered at them again.

"Puta!" one of them shouted. He said something else in Spanish that Sabrina couldn't understand.

Vania's mouth dropped open. "Disgusting."

"What did they say?"

"What they want to do to us." She grimaced. "Sexually."

Sabrina got a cold feeling in the pit of her stomach. "Let's go back. I'm scared."

"Yeah, me too." The girls turned their kayaks around and paddled hard for the docks.

"You don't think they'll do anything, do you?" Vania panted from exertion. "I mean, there are tons of witnesses out here."

"Yeah, but no one is paying attention to us." Sabrina looked back at the jet skis. The men were still sitting in place watching them. They were laughing and talking. But they weren't coming after them.

The horizon grew darker and the wind picked up. Clouds rolled in, covering the blue sky. A chilly breeze picked up and thunder rumbled.

"Are you serious?" Sabrina looked up at the oncoming storm. "I thought we had more time before the storm got here."

"I'll take thunder and lightning any day over those idiots on the jet skis." Vania shivered. "I'm covered in goosebumps right now."

"Me too." Despite the exertion, Sabrina wasn't hot and tired because she was in good shape. Her parents had paid for tennis and gymnastics lessons ever since she was a little girl, just like they'd done for her big sister. Athletics was supposed to be a fallback career in case she turned out to be too stupid for academics.

She hated gymnastics, but she'd stuck with tennis and picked up cycling too. She enjoyed sports, but she far preferred being a nerd. Just like her big sister. Jessica might not have given her the time of day, but Sabrina had always wanted to be smart like her.

The cold breeze turned into strong wind. Unfortunately, the wind was in her face and not at her back. Paddling wasn't getting them anywhere fast. Lightning flickered across the sky. The thunderstorm was getting closer and closer.

Jet ski engines revved. Sabrina looked back and saw the men on the jet skis speeding toward them. They were probably just trying to scare her and Vania. Hopefully they weren't crazy enough to actually harm them.

Vania gasped in alarm. "They're coming right at us."

Sabrina gripped her paddle, ready to fight.

Another engine sounded. A pontoon boat that had been across the lake earlier was angling toward them. The men slowed and said something to each other. They looked from the pontoon boat to the girls.

One of them stared right at Sabrina and flicked his tongue like he was licking something. He blew her a kiss, but there was nothing sweet about it. They revved their engines and sped up again but veered wide around them.

The pontoon boat pulled up alongside the girls. A middle-aged woman smiled at them. "Need a lift, girls?"

"Oh my God, please!" Vania looked like she was on the verge of tears.

A man with a round belly came over and helped Vania out of her kayak and onto the rear ladder. "There you go, young lady."

Sabrina held onto Vania's kayak. A young boy leaned over the side and grabbed the pull cord on the front of the kayak. He grunted and pulled it up onto the pontoon boat. Sabrina grabbed the ladder and stepped onto it. She held onto her kayak's pull cord and lifted it up so the boy could pull hers onboard too.

She climbed aboard and found two young girls sitting under the canopy. She turned to their mother. "Thank you so much. I didn't think we were going to make it before the storm hit."

"Yep, it's a big one," the father said. "Denise saw you two and got worried, so we figured we'd offer you a lift back." He looked around and found a shirt. He slid it on and patted his belly. "Sorry you had to see that."

Vania and Sabrina giggled.

Denise laughed and shook her head. "Frank, I swear you think you're funny."

Frank grinned. "It's all I've got going for me, honey."

The rain hit a moment later. It was more than rain. It was an absolute downpour. Frank pulled the pontoon boat over to the dock with the kayak rentals so Sabrina and Vania could disembark.

"Thank you so much," Sabrina said. "You really saved us."

"You're our honorary parents now," Vania said. "We just adopted you."

"Aw." Denise smiled. "Jeff would love to have big sisters."

The teenaged boy looked down shyly. "Mom, come on!"

Vania kissed his cheek. "Thanks for helping with our kayaks. You're going to make a woman real happy one day."

He looked up at her with big puppy dog eyes, unable to speak.

Frank snickered. "Oh, man. His first real kiss."

Jeff stared at him in horror. "Dad!"

Everyone else laughed.

Sabrina and Vania got off the pontoon boat and dragged their kayaks through the pouring rain to the rental place. The cute boy from earlier watched them from his dry spot inside the building. He tapped something on the computer and gave them a thumbs up.

They left the kayaks and trudged through the downpour back to the parking lot.

Vania hugged Sabrina. "Want to come over later? My mom is making dinner."

"Yeah, definitely. I'll ask my parents." Sabrina hurried to her car and watched to make sure Vania got into her car. She waved as her friend drove past, then she pulled out and followed her.

They both turned left and drove past the other public docks, then got onto South Lakeshore. They followed it to South Pleasant Valley Road. Vania turned south and

Sabrina turned north toward the bridge. It was raining even heavier, but traffic wasn't too snarled going over the bridge.

Sabrina crossed over and kept going straight. A red light halted traffic. She scrolled through the pictures she'd taken of her and Vania getting ready for kayaking and decided to make a social media post even though the day hadn't gone to plan.

She wrote a caption. *Got rained out while kayaking but still had fun with my bestie!* She selected a picture of her and Vania holding their paddles next to the lake. The light turned green. Traffic started moving. She looked up from her phone and put her attention back on the road.

It was only five PM, but the thunderstorm darkened the sky and made it feel like it was much later than it actually was. Her windshield wipers could barely keep up even on full speed.

The torrential downpour slowed into a drizzle, making visibility better. Sabrina turned right onto a small residential street. A car was backing out of the driveway in front of her, so she stopped. She glanced at her social media post again and hit the submit button. The car backing out of the driveway accelerated in the opposite direction.

Sabrina drove to the next intersection and slowed for a stop sign. She saw the headlights of a car in her rearview mirror growing brighter by the second. There was a slight bump, and her car rocked.

"No way!" Sabrina clenched a fist and growled. "Freaking idiots!"

She was already soaked to the bone, so she didn't mind getting out of the car to inspect the damage. She got out and walked around to the back of her car. The headlights of the car behind her prevented her from seeing who was inside.

It was an old car. It looked like something an old person would drive. She figured a grandma or grandpa was behind the wheel. They were probably half blind or couldn't hit the brakes fast enough when she slowed down.

She looked over her bumper. Her car was old and worn too. There were already dents and scuffs in the rear bumper, so if the car behind her had added something new, she couldn't see it. There was no major damage and that was all that mattered.

Sabrina walked to the driver's side window of the car that hit her. Thankfully, there were no other cars on the residential street, so they weren't holding up traffic. The windows on the old car were so darkly tinted that she couldn't see the driver.

The car's rear door opened. A man got out. A man who looked very familiar. A man who grinned at the surprise on her face. Sabrina opened her mouth to scream because she recognized the man. It was one of the men from the jet skis.

He slapped something over her mouth. A towel or rag. It muffled her scream. It stank of chemicals. She sucked in a lungful of whatever was on the rag and got woozy. Her knees turned to jelly, and she felt herself being dragged into the car.

Men laughed. They spoke in Spanish. Sabrina had no idea what they were saying. She tried to move, but her muscles felt leaden. She tried to scream for help, but the rag was still pressed over her face.

She was vaguely aware that she was lying sideways across a man's lap. The man was grinning down at her. He moved the rag away. He leaned over and licked her face. He licked her lips. He made a disgusting sound with his tongue and said something to the driver.

The car engine revved. It moved. Sabrina tried desperately to do something, anything, but she couldn't. It felt like her muscles were completely numb. She managed to utter one final word before consciousness abandoned her.

"Help."

CHAPTER 2

Carver unfolded a chair and set it in the sand.

He sat down on the chair and sighed with contentment. He opened the cooler and pulled out a bottle of cold beer. He popped off the lid and tossed it into the cooler. He lifted the bottle to his lips and took a long pull of the stout inside.

He closed the cooler and set the beer on top of it. The warm sun beat down on his skin. It felt good to be back in Miami. It probably wasn't the smartest move to come back to this town, but at this time of year, there weren't too many warm beaches stateside.

His burner phone buzzed. He ignored it. It was time to change phones again. Time to get a number nobody had. It was safer that way. Better that way. Too many people had this number already, and one of them worked for a mortal enemy.

He didn't think Alicia would tell Jericho that she had his number. Carver and Alicia had an unspoken agreement. At least, he hoped so. They also had a spoken agreement, but that had more or less ended a couple of weeks ago.

Alicia had helped him with something, then Carver had spent another few weeks with her and Jessica before leaving them to continue their quest. They still had places to go. People to see. Carver just wanted to get out of the freezing cold north and sit on a beach.

Carver's phone vibrated six times in a row. He sighed and picked it up. He had six one-word texts from Jessica.

Carver

Don't

Ignore

My

Text

Please!

Carver texted her back. *Everything okay?*

No. Please don't hate me, but I need your help. I need it bad.

He couldn't imagine any scenario that had him leaving this beach to help her or anyone else. Not even an inbound nuclear missile could make him leave this beach. He'd earned some peace and quiet for once.

Aren't you still with Alicia?

Jessica replied quickly. *Jericho called her back to duty or whatever.*

Are you still handing out duffel bags full of cash?

No. We finished that. This is personal. Can I call you?

Carver sipped his beer and thought about it. The phone vibrated as it rang on silent. He blew out a breath and answered. "Yeah?"

"Carver, my little sister was kidnapped." Jessica was crying. "They found her car sitting at a stop sign. It was still running, and the door was hanging open."

Carver set down his beer and stared at the ocean. "What did the cops say?"

"Nothing. The city cut police funding by fifty percent a few years ago. They told my parents they haven't even assigned a detective to the case because they don't have the manpower."

"They live in Austin, right?"

"Yes."

"I'll help you."

Jessica groaned with relief. "Thank you, Carver. I really didn't think you'd help me."

"You helped me find Liana."

"Yes, but you also paid me."

Carver shrugged. "You went above and beyond what I paid you for. What's the address?"

She gave it to him. "My parents just told me about all of this a few minutes ago, so I'm going to get a flight right away."

"I'll have to drive. I can't fly commercial. Not easily anyway."

"I understand." She sniffled. "You were the first person I thought of. If anyone can help, you can."

"I'll do what I can."

"I know you probably don't want to come, but I—" she broke off in a sob. "I just really need your help."

"I'll see you in a few hours. What's the address?"

She gave it to him. "Thank you, Carver. I know I can never repay you."

"Gather as much information as possible. Can you put your software to work looking for her?"

"I already have. I uploaded pictures of Sabrina and geofenced it to Texas."

"Good." He ended the call.

Carver finished his beer and drank one more after that. He enjoyed an hour and a half in the sun and surf, then packed up his things and loaded them into his minivan. It was a 2013 Honda Odyssey. It was nice, reliable, and gave him a place to sleep on long trips.

His favorite vehicle by far was the Dodge Ramcharger he'd had for a short while before abandoning it in San Francisco. He could never love a minivan like he'd loved that Ramcharger, but he could certainly appreciate what it brought to the table.

Carver stopped at the public showers to wash off. He picked up food and supplies, and then he hit the road. It was going to be a long drive up the Florida Turnpike and over to Texas, but it was no worse than the road trip he'd been on for the past few weeks with Alicia and Jessica.

They'd searched for small business owners impacted by protests and riots over the last month and given them money to help them get back on their feet. More specifically, they'd given them duffel bags packed with a million in cash.

The money had been taken from people who'd been behind the sale of an undercover agent list, among other things. Most of those people were dead or had been transferred to the front lines of the war in Ukraine. It seemed fitting that their ill-gotten gains were being put to good use.

He was rocking along at 80 miles per hour when a semitruck suddenly turned across both lanes and drove onto the median. It was trying to make a U-turn through an official use only turnaround. Carver registered all of that in a split second.

He hit the brakes and swerved, narrowly missing the rear end of the trailer. Idiots like that were why you could never trust other drivers. As a matter of policy, Carver didn't trust anyone except himself and a very small group of people.

He trusted Paola, Leon and Liana. He'd grown to trust Jessica. That was one reason why he was helping her. That and the fact that without her help he never would have found Liana.

It was a twenty-one-hour drive from Miami to Austin, not including pit stops. Carver stopped around the halfway point just past Mobile, Alabama. He found a motel with decent rates and stayed there instead of sleeping in the van.

He woke up at zero four hundred and grabbed food and coffee from a local diner. He took a large to-go cup of coffee with him and resumed the trip. It took him eleven more hours to reach Austin and another fifteen minutes to reach the address of Jessica's parents.

They lived just north of the Colorado River in a neighborhood of narrow streets and small wooden houses. Their house was right at the corner of Navasota Street and an unnamed street that ran behind the houses.

It was smaller than the other homes, tiny, white and square with a gravel driveway and a wooden garage. Carver parked on the narrow street and walked around along the streets near the house to get the lay of the land.

The houses were packed tightly together. The cars parked on the street were packed together even tighter. That was normal for an old neighborhood not far from town center. Despite the way the houses looked, they were probably worth a pretty penny in this location.

Carver went to the door and knocked. Floorboards creaked. He heard Jessica shouting, "I'll get it!"

Jessica didn't answer the door. A young woman with long black hair and Asian features pulled the door open and looked Carver up and down. She was a little over five feet tall, thin, and wearing dark yoga pants. She looked like she kept in shape.

Carver kept quiet and waited for her to speak. She just nodded once and backed away from the door as Jessica swooped in next to her. Now that he saw them side-by-side, he saw the resemblance.

"Sorry, Carver. This is my mom, Angela."

"Angela?" Carver nodded at her. "Nice to meet you."

Angela reached out a dainty hand. He reached out and shook it.

"Pleased to meet you," she said with a faint accent. Her lips trembled. She was obviously trying to hold in a lot of emotion. "Please come in."

Carver noticed the women were wearing thin flip-flops. There was a shoe shelf just inside the door, so he took off his shoes and put them in one. Angela gave him a pair of flip-flops to wear inside.

Angela walked ahead. "Would you like tea, Carver?"

"Coffee or water is good, thanks."

"I will prepare coffee for you."

Jessica grabbed Carver's arm and pulled him into a small dining room. "My mom is freaking out. My dad is trying to hire a private investigator. He's asking the police for the forensic evidence they collected from the site."

"When did she go missing?"

"Sunday late afternoon around five thirty or six. She was supposed to go to Vania's house for dinner and never showed up. Vania couldn't reach her on her cell phone and got worried, so she drove to the house. Along the way, she found Sabrina's car idling at a stop sign a few blocks down. Sabrina's cell phone was still in the car."

"Who's Vania?"

"Sabrina's best friend."

"Where's the car now?"

"The cops took it to dust for prints and all that." Jessica sighed. "My dad's trying to get it back."

Carver leaned against the wall. "Did they talk to Vania?"

Jessica nodded. "Yeah. A cop took her statement, but like I said, there's no detective assigned to the case yet. Or if there is, he's not doing anything. They're severely understaffed."

"I wouldn't expect a police force in Texas to be understaffed."

She laughed hollowly. "Austin isn't like the rest of Texas. The city council voted to cut the police budget in half a few years ago. A lot of cops abandoned ship, and they haven't been able to recruit anyone since then."

"I'm not exactly a detective myself." Carver looked around the small dining room. The wooden table looked old and worn. There was a cabinet filled with porcelain plates. Old people called it China. He vaguely remembered visiting someone's house when he was a kid. A woman was bragging to his mother about her good China.

"I know you're not a detective, but if you could find Liana, then you can help me find Sabrina."

"It would have taken a lot longer to find Liana without you." Carver shrugged. "She probably would have been killed and framed for the Senate majority leader's death before I found her."

"We make a good team."

Carver smelled coffee brewing. He walked through the door connecting the dining room to the kitchen. Angela was pouring hot water onto coffee grounds in a metal filter. The filter was on top of a tall travel mug.

"Jessica says she worked with you on a project." Angela sat down at the kitchen table. "She wouldn't say much about it."

"Because of the NDA, Mom." Jessica shook her head. "We can't talk about it."

Angela gave Carver a pointed look. "Did you pay her well?"

"Well above industry standard." Carver watched the water soak into the coffee grounds. It smelled great. "Your daughter is a genius."

"Aw, thanks!" Jessica blushed.

Angela pursed her lips, never taking her gaze from Carver. "She's smart but not very business savvy. Perhaps you could help her in that aspect, so she doesn't lose everything all over again."

Jessica's smile faded. "Can we not talk about me, please? In case you've forgotten, Sabrina is missing."

Angela's sharp gaze wavered. She was obviously repressing a great deal of emotion behind her stony façade. Carver had seen the same look on his mother's face many times, though it was usually when she was angry with him.

Angela brushed her shirt even though it looked perfectly clean. "Please get Mr. Carver settled. We do not, unfortunately, have a guest bedroom, but we do have an inflatable mattress."

"No, that's okay, Angela." Carver offered her a smile. He tried to make it look genuine. "I'll get a motel room. I saw a place just down the street."

"Uh, the motel prices in these parts are going to be a lot more than you want to pay." Jessica took his arm. "The air mattress is free."

She was probably right, but Carver didn't want to stay in the house. He preferred his privacy. Money also wasn't a problem for the time being.

The front door opened. Carver stepped through the kitchen doorway and looked down the hall. An Asian man stepped inside. He took off a fedora and hung it on the hat rack. He wore a gray business suit that looked a little large for his thin frame.

He noticed Carver and stopped in his tracks for an instant before registering that Carver was probably the man his daughter had told him about. He smiled and walked into the kitchen, hand extended.

Carver shook his hand. "I'm Carver."

"I'm David, Jessica's father. She told us a lot about you." He had a heavier accent than Angela, but not by much. "We thank you for helping our daughter climb out of the deep rut she dug herself into."

Jessica groaned and buried her face in her hands.

"She does great work," Carver said. "You really can't blame her for what happened to her company. She went up against powerful people and they destroyed her company."

"Yes, many mistakes were made." David shook his head. "A great deal of family money was lost. But thanks to you, she has a chance to recover."

"Can we please not talk about me?" Jessica threw up her hands. "Let's focus on Sabrina." She turned to her father. "Speaking of which, where's the car?"

"Still at the impound. They said it was evidence and wouldn't allow me to see it."

Jessica groaned. "They're never going to inspect it. By the time they get around to it, it'll be too late."

"Where's the impound?" Carver said.

"It's not at the main police impound lot," David said. "They told me they put it in an overflow lot but didn't say where it was."

Jessica typed on her phone. "I can't find anything in the maps app."

Carver looked up a phone number on his burner phone. He called it.

A man answered. "Austin Towing."

"The cops had my car towed to some overflow impound lot. Any idea where that is?"

"Yeah, over off Webberville road. But you've got to go to the police department first to fill out some paperwork, then go get a ticket number from the front office at the impound lot. Then you'll need to pay the special towing fee to have a towing company pick up the vehicle and deliver it to you." The man cleared his throat. "If you request our company to do the pickup, we'll refund twenty percent of the special fee."

"How much is the special fee?" Carver asked.

"It's one thousand one hundred and fifty bucks."

Carver whistled. "That's a lot of money."

"Yep. It's money for nothing, but the government does what the government wants."

"Thanks for the info. I'll be sure to request your company for the pickup." Carver ended the call. He turned to Jessica. "Let's go."

"Yeah, let's go." She hugged her parents. "We'll let you know what we find out."

David put a hand on Carver's arm. "Take care of our daughter, please. She's not very good at taking care of herself."

"She's not very good with money either," Angela said. "But she's a good girl and tries her best."

David nodded. "Yes, a good girl."

Jessica groaned. She grabbed Carver's arm and hustled him toward the front door. "I swear to God my parents hate me."

There was a knock on the door. Jessica stopped abruptly and stared at it before slowly reaching forward and opening it.

A middle-aged Caucasian man stood on the porch. He was tall and thin. His dark hair had lost considerable ground to gray hair, and his skin was just starting to get wrinkles. He was probably in his late fifties if Carver had to guess.

The man blinked. "Oh, you must be Jessica."

Jessica stared at him. "And you are?"

"I'm Josh Hardin, Sabrina's third period science teacher." He extended his hand.

Jessica shook it. "Yeah, she mentioned you in her texts. You helped her get into MIT?"

"Partially, yes." He looked worried. "I'd texted her about arranging a phone call with admissions at MIT. It was supposed to be this morning, but she never responded, so I wanted to come by and make sure everything was okay."

"She was kidnapped," Jessica said without preamble.

He blinked rapidly. "I'm sorry, what?"

"She was taken from her car last night." Jessica stepped onto the front porch.

Carver followed her outside and closed the door behind him. The Texas heat was starting to fade in the late afternoon, but it was still brutal.

"No!" Hardin looked distraught. "Taken by whom? When?"

"Sunday early evening." Jessica ran a hand down her face. "We don't know anything else, and they haven't even assigned a detective to the case yet."

"How could they not have a detective on the case?" Hardin's hands trembled. "I—I can't believe this."

Carver wasn't sure why a professor would be so upset about a student. Then again, he'd never been a model student. "Were you close to Sabrina?"

Hardin nodded. "It's not just that. My daughter, Diana, vanished nearly three years ago and the police never found her."

"Really?" Jessica patted his arm. "I'm so sorry about that."

Hardin wiped his eyes. "She's still officially missing, but the detective told me that it's likely she's dead."

"Wow, what a horrible detective."

"I think she wanted me to find closure, you know?" Hardin cleared his throat. "I spent every waking hour looking for her for months. I spent thousands of dollars and offered my entire life savings as a reward, but it was all for nothing."

"That's horrible! I'm so sorry for you and your wife." Jessica shook her head sadly. "I'm feeling now what you must have felt then."

"Is your wife also close to Sabrina?" Carver asked.

Hardin cleared his throat. "Well, that's another story. We divorced seven years ago." He took out his phone and showed them a picture of a pretty Latina girl. "That's Diana."

Jessica looked from Hardin to the picture. "Yeah, you really don't look anything alike."

Hardin blinked. "Diana's mom is Colombian. As you can tell, she got her good looks from her mother and not from me."

Jessica nodded. "Yeah, I can see that."

Hardin frowned like he hadn't been expecting that response. "What can you tell me about Sabrina's disappearance?"

"We don't know much." Jessica shrugged. "It looks like she was kidnapped from her car just a few blocks away. My dad found her car still running at the stop sign. Her cell phone was still in the car, but it was locked, so he doesn't know what's on it."

Hardin looked distraught. "Can I do anything to help?"

Jessica shrugged. "Can you get a detective assigned to the case?"

"I'm afraid I don't have any contacts with the city government."

"Then, I guess there's nothing you can do but wait." Jessica patted him on the shoulder. "Um, thanks for getting her into MIT." She hurried down the sidewalk without another word.

Carver caught up to her and steered her toward the minivan.

She glanced back toward the house. "That was awkward. Did you get weird vibes from that guy?"

Carver shook his head. "Do teachers normally help students get into college?"

"Maybe sometimes, but not normally." She frowned. "Sabrina talked about Hardin a lot. She's obviously his favorite student." She glanced back at Hardin. "This is the first time I've met him, though."

Carver just nodded.

She looked at the minivan. "Where are we going, anyway?"

Carver opened the trunk of the minivan. He shoved aside a duffel bag stuffed with cash and opened another one. He sorted through the tools inside. Figured he had everything he needed.

"I wish I could be as unconcerned with everything like you." Jessica sighed. "My parents drive me crazy. Do you know how much emotional damage my parents have inflicted on me over the years?"

Carver checked the time. It would probably be best to do this after dark, but he wanted to reconnoiter the impound lot first. He realized he hadn't grabbed the travel mug of fresh coffee since Jessica had hurried him out of the house.

"You're the worst." Jessica sighed. "Can't you answer at least one of my questions?"

"I'm going to get the coffee Angela made for me. Then we're going to reconnoiter the impound lot." Carver went back to the house and walked inside. Hardin was inside the kitchen talking to Angela.

Angela smiled and pointed at the travel mug. "You left without your coffee."

"Yeah." Carver removed the metal filter from the top and dumped the grounds into the garbage can.

Angela procured half and half from the refrigerator and opened a porcelain container with sugar in it.

Carver doctored his coffee until he was satisfied. "Thank you."

"Please let me know if you discover anything," Hardin said. "I really wish I could be more help."

David came in from the other room. "Oh, I thought you'd left."

"Forgot my coffee." Carver tapped the mug. He wanted to ask them a few questions about Sabrina but figured that could wait until later. "Thank you." He left and went outside to the minivan. He climbed in. Jessica was already in the passenger seat.

She wiped away the tears in her eyes. "I'm worried, Carver. Sabrina is the obedient daughter. The one who's never home late. The one who does everything my parents tell her to do. Something bad happened to her. I'm just worried someone's going to find her lifeless body in the river."

Carver didn't try to reassure her. She was probably right. Someone had probably kidnapped the girl and done horrible things to her. And in most cases, people like that killed the victim so they couldn't go to the police.

There was very little hope of a happy ending.

CHAPTER 3

Carver drove to the overflow impound lot.

The lot was behind a large industrial building. The signage on the building indicated it was a service and repair center for official vehicles like police cars, firetrucks, and the like. It was shaped like a triangle. It was a couple of hundred yards long and maybe fifty yards wide near the back. It was bordered by train tracks, a creek, and a street.

The official way in was from the gate on the south side of the property. There was a guardhouse next to the gate, and two men inside. Carver parked on the side of the street just across the railroad tracks from the lot. He watched the men from a distance with his monocular.

The men wore gray shirts with a badge stitched to the right breast pocket. The badge simply said *Security*. They weren't cops. They were probably outsourced from a security guard company.

The gated entrance was maybe fifty feet wide. It was sandwiched between the train tracks and the creek. The chain link fence was ten feet tall and topped with Y-shaped braces and barbed wire. It was a deterrent for sure, but nothing insurmountable.

Jessica sat silently in the passenger seat looking at her phone. She'd remotely connected to the servers they'd hijacked at Plum and Associates to see if her facial recognition software had found any matches for Sabrina. The software was great at tracking publicly available photos and videos but unfortunately couldn't access live security cameras.

Carver pulled onto the road and drove parallel to the train tracks.

The south side of the lot didn't have many cars, but the northern side was packed. Some of the cars were caked with grime and dust. Some looked rusted out. Others had clearly been in wrecks and had been stacked in the northeastern section of the lot.

"What does her car look like?" Carver asked.

Jessica opened a social media app on her phone and navigated to her sister's page. She scrolled through hundreds of photos and found several with Sabrina posing next to an old compact car. She handed her phone to Carver. "She bought the car herself because my parents wouldn't."

Carver read the caption next to the photo. "How did she afford it?"

"She's been working part time at a grocery store since she was sixteen." Jessica shrugged. "I did the same thing."

The car was a red 2001 Toyota Corolla. The paint didn't look great, but the car looked like it was in good overall condition despite the age. Sabrina had taken photos from all angles of the car.

There were two teenaged girls in the last photo. The girl on the left looked a lot like Jessica. She was a little shorter with long black hair and an athletic frame. The other girl had curly black hair and looked Hispanic.

Carver read the tags above the picture. "Sabrina and Vania."

Jessica nodded. "They've been best friends since elementary school."

Carver scanned the lot for the red Corolla. He found it parked alone under a canopy. It was probably kept there since it was part of an active investigation. The canopy shielded it from the elements, but not enough if the cops wanted to dust for fingerprints.

Technically, the cops should have already checked for prints at the crime scene, but there was no guarantee. He wasn't about to attempt entry through the front gate of the impound lot. The only way in was with a cop and it didn't seem likely he'd convince one to let him look at the car. It would be best to go in after dark when no one was there.

Carver lowered the monocular. "Where did they find her car?"

Jessica opened the maps app and dropped a pin at a location. "Right at the intersection of San Saba and East Second. She was stopped at the stop sign."

Carver plugged the coordinates into the GPS and drove there. San Saba had stop signs. East Second didn't. "Which stop sign?"

Jessica pointed to the one on the south side. "Mom said she usually takes this route to avoid the traffic."

Carver parked on the side of the road. He got out and walked to the stop sign. There was mud and leaves in the gutter. There were tire tracks in the mud, but no footprints. He looked at the overcast sky. "Was it raining yesterday?"

She nodded. "Yeah, there was a big storm."

"What time was she taken?"

"Sabrina's phone was left in the car. She'd just made a post about kayaking with Vania, so I think she was snatched sometime shortly after that."

"Show me the post."

Jessica opened Sabrina's social media page and pointed to the most recent post made a little over twenty-six hours ago. There were twenty-one comments and almost a hundred likes. Carver looked at the comments.

One comment was from Hardin, Sabrina's teacher. *Two wonderful young women with a bright future ahead of them!*

"Hmm, that's a little strange, don't you think?" Jessica frowned. "Is it normal having a teacher as a friend on social media?"

"No idea," Carver said. He looked at the other comments.

The first comment was from Vania. She'd posted a picture of her own and commented, *Rain or shine we always have fun!* Carver tapped on her name, and it took him to her page. She'd posted six pictures from their outing.

Carver gave Jessica her phone and walked around the area. He examined the tire tracks near the stop sign. The treads looked like something from a truck not a Corolla. Sabrina would have had to drive much closer to the curb for her tires to track in the mud.

He studied the nearby houses. A small yellow house across the road from the stop sign had a camera doorbell. The three houses closest to the stop sign didn't have any cameras. The fourth one down had a camera doorbell.

Carver went to that house and rang the doorbell. A few seconds later, a female voice emanated from the speaker on the doorbell.

"Can I help you?"

"I hope so." Carver pointed toward the stop sign. "A girl went missing near here yesterday evening and I was hoping your doorbell camera might have seen something."

"Really? A girl went missing near my house? Oh my God!" The woman paused. "What does she look like?"

"She was driving a red Toyota Corolla. The car was found at the stop sign but she was gone. If you could look for footage with that car in it, it would be very helpful."

"Absolutely! I'm at work right now, but I'll check the cloud recordings and see if anything is there."

"Thank you." Carver gave her his burner phone number. "Please let me know what you find." He walked across the road to the other house with the doorbell camera and rang it.

The door cracked open until a chain stopped it. A woman spoke "Can I help you?"

Carver told her what he'd told the other woman.

She opened the door and looked from Carver to Jessica. "She went missing? In our neighborhood?"

"Yes. If your camera recorded anything that would be very helpful."

The woman took out her phone and opened an app. She scrolled through images. "Unfortunately, the bushes block the view of the stop sign." She showed Jessica a picture of someone walking down the sidewalk in front of the house. "Anyone passing by triggers the motion sensor and gets recorded. It's kind of a pain, but my front yard isn't very big."

The picture clearly showed a woman walking her dog on the sidewalk. Two bushes and a tree blocked the stop sign and surrounding area from view. The field of view wasn't wide enough to capture anything else on the road.

"Maybe we'll get lucky," Carver said. "If you could find any recordings between five thirty to six thirty, that would be helpful."

"Um, hang on." She scrolled down and turned the phone toward him. "Three recordings."

"May I?" He held out a hand toward the phone.

She hesitated. "Sure."

Carver took the phone and looked at the three recordings. All were of people casually walking down the sidewalk. He gave her back the phone. "Thanks for your help."

Jessica paused. "Out of curiosity, have the police been by?"

The woman shook her head. "No. Should they have been?"

"They should have, but apparently no detectives were available to take the case."

"Oh, I'm sorry. Are either of you related to the missing girl?"

"She's my little sister." Jessica took a deep breath. "Thanks again."

"Wow, I'm so sorry. I hope you find her. You know, sometimes people just run away, especially if they're under a lot of stress."

"I don't think she would have, but thanks." Jessica turned and walked down the steps to the sidewalk.

"Give me a list of the usual suspects," Carver said. "Does she have a boyfriend? Enemies?"

"Hmm." Jessica tapped her chin. "She was kind of dating this guy named Lucas. I don't know if that's still a thing. As for enemies, I don't know of any. Vania would know more than me."

"You lived at home for a while after your business failed right?"

"Yeah, for months."

"But you still don't know much about what's going on in your sister's life?"

Jessica looked down. "I mean, I was pretty self-absorbed and full of self-pity after my company collapsed. She sighed. "Sabrina tried to talk to me, but I wasn't in the mood to listen. I failed to be a good sister, didn't I?"

"I wouldn't know," Carver said. "Maybe you don't like being around your family."

"You heard the way my mom talks to me." Jessica shook her head. "I love my parents, but I also hate living with them. They constantly remind me about my shortcomings and talk about Sabrina like she's got it all figured out."

Carver said nothing.

Jessica frowned. "You don't think her kidnapping has anything to do with what we did in Washington DC, do you?"

"Doubtful." Carver started walking west down the sidewalk. "I don't think we left anyone alive to retaliate."

Jessica laughed nervously. "Yeah, I guess you're right. Plus, they'd come after me or my entire family, not just Sabrina."

"No phone calls asking for ransom? No missed calls from unknown phone numbers since Sabrina went missing?"

She shook her head. "Not that I know of. Is that bad?"

"It's not good, but it might be too early to tell." Carver stopped at the next intersection and turned south. He looked for cameras on the houses. "Sometimes they like to make the family sweat it out for a couple of days. Make them get a good feel for what it's like to miss their loved one. Then they call with ransom demands."

"And if they never call?"

"Then things start looking bad."

"I mean, ransom is already bad."

"Yeah, but it means the victim hasn't been harmed. At least not yet." Carver stopped at a house with a security camera on the front porch. Unfortunately, it was at the wrong angle to capture the street.

"Okay, so it's worse if there's no ransom call?"

"Yeah."

"Can you tell me how?" She shivered. "Explain it to me like I'm a kid."

"I probably wouldn't explain something like this to a kid."

She punched him on the shoulder. "You know what I mean."

Carver stopped walking and faced her. "It means they did something to her right after they took her. Maybe they raped her and killed her afterward. Or maybe they're keeping her alive and abusing her. They might even sell her."

Jessica seemed to swallow a lump in her throat. "I wish I hadn't asked now." Tears ran down her cheeks. "I'm not that close to my sister, but she's still my flesh and blood, you know?"

Carver put a hand on her shoulder. "I know. I'm sorry."

Jessica wiped her cheeks. "Let's keep going. We need to find out what happened."

There were a couple more houses with cameras. One wasn't facing the road. The other one was. Carver went to that house and rang the doorbell.

An old woman answered almost immediately. "I've been watching you two snoop around my neighborhood. If you're selling something, I ain't buying."

"We're looking for a missing person," Jessica said. "My little sister."

The old woman's gaze softened. "Oh, I'm sorry, dear. Are you sure she's missing? Kids these days run off at the slightest inconvenience. My granddaughter tried to run away because her mom wouldn't get her a fancy phone."

"We found her car abandoned at the stop sign around the corner," Jessica said. "We think something bad happened."

"Oh, that's not good." The old woman shook her head. "Not good at all. This area used to be so safe. I knew all the neighbors. Now it's infested with criminals, pedophiles, and rapists."

"I noticed you have a camera aimed at the street." Carver pointed to it. "It's possible that it might have seen something. Can I look at the footage?"

The old woman looked up at the camera. "My grandson installed that so I could watch the neighborhood without having to stand next to the window all day. I don't think it records, though. It's connected to my television."

Jessica looked perplexed. "So, you just sit and watch a live feed of the neighborhood on your television?"

"Oh, yes. You wouldn't believe what goes on here!" She pointed down the street. "I saw a drug deal happening right in front of the Jacoby house."

Jessica looked down the street. "Your camera can see the corner?"

"No, I was standing outside when it happened."

"Were you watching the street yesterday around five thirty?" Carver said.

The woman squinted and looked up. "Yes, there was a big storm, so I sat out front to enjoy the rain and thunder."

"My sister drives a red Toyota Corolla," Jessica said.

"I don't know what that looks like."

Jessica pulled up the pictures on her phone and showed her.

The woman looked at the picture of Sabrina posing with her car. "Pretty little girl. That's your sister?"

"Yes. And that's her car."

The woman nodded. "I don't remember specifically when I was out here." She pursed her lips. "I just got off the phone with Mabel, and that was, oh, about three o'clock. I went inside to use the bathroom." She moved her index finger around as if recounting all her moves. "The storm had been going a little while."

"Did a lot of cars pass by during the storm?" Carver said.

"Oh, no. Maybe a handful." She waggled a hand. "There was the Miller's noisy old pickup truck. Then the Garcia boy and his muscle car. He loves revving that engine until I think my ears are going to burst! Oh, and I remember now. A red car went by a little after that. Yes, definitely a red car. And then a real nice Cadillac DeVille. My husband used to have one of those and we loved it."

"What color was the Cadillac you saw?" Carver asked.

"It was gold. Very pretty."

"Did you see the drivers?"

"No, the windows were dark. Probably tinted, you know?" She tutted. "That shouldn't be allowed. Who knows what they could be doing in there? All sorts of vile things like drugs and sex, most likely."

Carver let her finish her rant and asked another question. "Did you happen to get a license plate number or notice anything unusual?"

She squinted and looked up as if recalling. "I don't recall anything about the license plate."

"Was it following the red car closely?"

She shook her head. "No, not that I recall. It went by a few seconds after the red car."

"Did the car look new or have any scratches or dents?"

"It looked like it was in very good condition, but it was gray and rainy, and I didn't get a close look at it."

Carver showed her pictures of a 2005 Cadillac DeVille. Apparently, that was the last year it was made. "Did it look like this?"

She frowned. "No. Is that a DeVille? It doesn't look like my husband's."

Carver found pictures of the previous generation and showed it to her.

"Yes, yes! That's it!" She sighed. "Ah, what a dream that car was. I still have it, you know?"

Jessica looked intrigued. "Do you?"

"Yes, it's in the carriage house." The old woman pointed to a wooden garage similar to the other ones in the neighborhood. "It's been in there since he passed ten years ago."

"Mind if I look at it?" Carver said. He wanted to lay eyes on it to make sure she wasn't remembering incorrectly.

"Yes, absolutely." She went inside and returned a moment later with a key. They walked to the garage. She removed the padlock on the barrel bolt and tried to slide it open, but it was stuck.

Carver pushed it to the side and opened the double wooden doors. A blue Cadillac was inside. It was dusty but otherwise it looked like it was in prime condition. It also matched the picture of the 1994 DeVille on Carver's phone.

"It's nice." Carver walked around it. "The one you saw looks just like this but it's gold?"

"Yes."

"Not beige?"

She shook her head. "No, it's definitely a brownish gold color." She stared at the wheels and frowned. "I do remember one thing that was different. It had these ugly gold wheels. The kind with all the spokes."

Jessica tapped on her phone and came up with images of custom rims on 1994 Cadillac DeVilles. "Do any of these look familiar?"

"Goodness, yes." The woman tapped an image. "Just like those."

That was helpful. Very helpful.

"Do you know of any other neighbors who are as attentive as you are?" Jessica asked.

"Oh, I'm one of the last originals in these parts," the woman said. "People these days are too tied up in their own affairs to see the world around them."

"True." Jessica smiled. "Thank you so much. This is very helpful."

"I hope you catch 'em and string 'em up!" the old woman said.

"Thank you."

Carver and Jessica left and continued their stroll down the road. They stopped at one more place with a camera in the front, but the homeowner said it had been broken for a while. By the time they finished canvassing the area, it was dark.

The next order of business was to break into the impound lot.

CHAPTER 4

Carver drove them back to the impound lot.

The lot was well lit with streetlamps around the front and sides. The guard shack was dark and empty. There was no sign of any nighttime security guards.

The road parallel to the train tracks didn't have street parking, so he pulled onto a side road and parked there.

"I can see why you like minivans," Jessica said. "No one looks twice at them."

Carver put some tools into his backpack and grabbed it. "You coming with me?"

"Yes, of course."

He gave her a mask and a black ballcap. "Put these on."

She put them on. He pulled on a beanie even though it was a little warm for one. He slid on a mask as well. He hadn't seen any cameras on the lot, but it was best to cover their faces just in case.

They walked down the street and followed the sidewalk north. They waited until there was no traffic and hurried across the road and the train tracks. They went into the tall grass and bushes on the other side.

"I hope there aren't any snakes," Jessica said. "I really don't want to explain a snakebite to my parents."

"I'll tell them it was in the line of duty." Carver followed the chain link fence looking for weak spots or existing holes. He hadn't been able to see this section of the fence with his monocular due to the bushes and trees.

The bottom of the fence was rooted in concrete. The chain link was old and slightly rusty in places, but there were no holes. Carver opened his backpack and took out the wire snipper. He cut along the bottom of the fence and then snipped upward right next to a support pole so the hole wouldn't be too obvious.

He pulled it open so Jessica could get through and then ducked through after her. They kept to the shadows the best they could and then hurried under the canopy where Sabrina's car was being kept.

There was fine black powder on the door car's door handles and inside the car. "Looks like they dusted for prints already." Carver could see where they'd lifted prints from the inside of the driver's side window and from the outside.

Besides the fingerprint dust, the car was clean. No fast-food wrappers, no empty water bottles or other trash on the floorboards. The fabric seats were clean, and the dash and interior didn't have any normal dust.

There were a couple of dark stains, one in the front seat and one in the back. They looked old. They had probably been there before Sabrina purchased the car. She probably tried to scrub them out and couldn't.

"Your sister keeps her car clean."

"Yeah, looks that way."

Carver examined the exterior. The paint wasn't too bad, but it wasn't perfect. There were scratches and a couple of minor dents. He walked around the car and stopped at the rear bumper. He shined his flashlight on something that stood out.

He knelt and examined a tiny spot on the bumper. There were other scratches and blemishes in the paint. The red had faded to orange in some spots. But it was the tiny spot of brown that got his attention.

He looked closely at it. It was a brownish gold. The same color as the Cadillac. That told Carver two things for certain. One, the perps had been in the Cadillac. Two, they'd rear-ended Sabrina on purpose to get her out of the car.

Carver could see it clear as day. "It was raining. Your sister just came from kayaking so she got rained on. She was probably soaked to the bone. She stopped at the stop sign. The Cadillac came up behind her and bumped her gently. Not too hard, not too soft. Just enough to get her a little angry."

Jessica's eyes widened. "She probably got out of the car and went to look at her bumper. She was already wet, so getting out in the rain didn't bother her."

"Yeah." Carver nodded. "The people in the car didn't get out. The windows were tinted, and it was raining so she couldn't see inside. She probably thought an elderly man or woman was behind the wheel, so went to the driver's side door on the Cadillac. Someone got out maybe with a gun or something and forced her into the car."

Jessica stared at the tiny sliver of paint left on the Corolla's bumper. Her fists clenched and her jaw tightened. "What kind of evil people would do this?" She shook her head angrily.

Carver looked over the car but didn't see anything else of interest. He took a closeup picture of the spot of paint. It looked like the local CSI people had examined the car but missed the paint. If they'd seen it, they would have taken the paint and sampled it to see what kind of car it might have come from.

A forensic investigator could sometimes determine the chemical composition of a paint and find out exactly where it came from. In this case, Carver knew it came from a General Motors assembly plant back in the nineties. He knew what kind of car it came from.

Now he was looking for a brownish-gold Cadillac DeVille with gold spoked rims and a tiny spot of missing paint on the front bumper. If he had access to DMV records, he could probably find the car quickly if it was registered in the state.

"Let's go." He headed back for the hole in the fence. They slid through and went back to the minivan.

"What do we do next?"

"Talk to Vania." Carver started the engine. "You have an address?"

"Hang on." She typed a text and sent it. "I know she doesn't live far from our house."

"Call your parents and ask them."

"Let me see if Vania replies." She stared at her phone for a solid minute.

"You really don't like talking to your parents."

Jessica laughed. "Is it that obvious?"

Carver had another question he hadn't asked because it really wasn't relevant, but he asked it anyway. "I paid you a hundred grand for your services and you had thirty duffel bags with a million bucks in each one."

"You want to know why I haven't gotten my parents a new house, or told them that I'm rich?"

"Something like that."

Her phone chimed. "Got the address." She gave it to him.

Carver plugged it into the GPS and started driving.

Jessica turned off the phone screen. "Yes, I kept a million dollars. Alicia kept four million because we ran out of people to help or at least couldn't find anyone else who needed it. Also, I think she had things to do and didn't want to spend more time on the road. So, she said she'd split the rest with me."

"But you only kept a million."

"Only." She laughed. "That sounds insane. But yes, I *only* kept a million. Because unless I can launder it, I can't use it, you know? I don't want the IRS breathing down my neck."

"It's not hard to launder a million bucks. Especially not if you want to start a new company."

Jessica smiled at Carver. "We've killed people together and now you're offering to help me launder money we took from them. That's the power of friendship."

Carver chuckled. "Yeah, I guess it is."

They arrived at the address. Vania's house looked newly remodeled. It was two stories tall and narrowly built to fit on the small lot. There were two Subarus parked in front. One was orange and the other was pastel blue.

The girl from Sabrina's pictures was waiting on the front porch. She ran to Jessica and hugged her. "Have you found out anything? Anything from the police?"

Jessica shook her head. "Nothing. They don't have enough detectives to go around apparently."

Vania looked Carver up and down. "You're really big."

"I'm Carver."

"That's your real name?"

"It's my last name."

"What's your first name?"

"Amos."

Vania's forehead pinched. "Amos sounds old-fashioned. I like Carver better." She shook his hand firmly. "Come on in." Vania opened the front door and led them inside.

The interior was mostly white with a polished concrete floor and minimalist cabinetry and furniture. The foyer was directly connected to the kitchen and dining area. Stairs near the front door led to the second level.

A Caucasian male with blue eyes and blonde hair was cooking at an electric stove. His long hair was tied back in a man bun. A thin Latina woman with glossy black hair and dark eyes stood next to him.

They smiled at Jessica and looked curiously at Carver.

"Mom, this is Sabrina's sister, Jessica and her friend, Carver."

The woman replied with a light Spanish accent. "Hello, I'm Annabella and this is my partner, Todd."

Todd nodded. "Hey, you two. I'm so sorry to hear about your sister, Jessica."

Carver wasn't surprised that Jessica had never met Vania's parents. She probably barely knew Vania.

Jessica smiled wanly. "The police haven't assigned a detective so we're investigating ourselves."

Annabella frowned. "The cops only have time to persecute minorities and law-abiding citizens. They only help the rich. The rest of us are left to rot."

"Yeah, it's a total racket," Todd said. "Honestly, we'd be better off without them."

Carver looked around at the spacious kitchen and high-end appliances. "Seems like you're doing pretty well."

"Todd's tech job pays well," Annabella said. "But we're not rich."

Vania made a raspberry. "My parents make a combined five hundred thousand a year. They have no idea what it's like to be poor."

"We've been fortunate," Todd said. "We can afford to care about our less fortunate neighbors."

"This place would be a utopia without the police harassing everyone." Annabella shook as if visibly angry. "They make me so mad. How could they not assign someone to find your sister?"

"Probably because they cut the police force in half a few years ago," Jessica said. She turned to Vania. "Did the police talk to you yet?"

Vania laughed sarcastically. "No, they haven't even called me."

Todd waved toward a doorway. "You can go in the den and ask her whatever you need to."

"Don't you want to be present for questioning?" Jessica said.

Todd giggled. It was a strange sound coming from a grown man. "You're not the cops. You're friends."

Annabella smiled. "Our little girl has been making her own decisions for years. She has total freedom to answer questions."

"Oh, okay." Jessica looked uneasily at Vania. "Uh, where do you want to go?"

Vania walked past them and down the short hallway to a living room with a large leather couch and easy chairs. She walked through it and to French doors in the back. She opened them and took them to a screened-in back porch with a bamboo table and chairs.

Vania started talking before they even sat down. "I know who did it. I'm almost positive it was some men who were harassing us on the lake."

Carver pulled out a chair and sat down. "Describe them."

"Latinos with a lot of tattoos." Vania remained standing. "They were on jet skis, but they didn't look much taller than me."

"Describe the jet skis."

"They were rentals from another place down the road." Her mouth dropped open. "Oh, wow, I'll bet the workers there might know who they are."

Jessica jolted to her feet and looked like she was about to run out of the door but stopped and checked phone. "The rental place is closed now, but we can check it first thing in the morning."

Carver nodded. Two seconds with Vania and they already knew a lot more than they had moments ago. "Can you describe the tattoos on the men?"

"Well, their skin was tanned really dark, so it was hard to make out the detail. But they had tattoos on their necks and faces. One had a big number 13 on his chest." She nodded to herself. "That's all I can remember."

"Tell us what makes you think they did it," Carver said.

"Well, we were out on our kayaks when they flew past us on jet skis. They came so close to us that they nearly knocked over the kayaks. I shouted at them and then they circled back and started shouting at us."

"In Spanish?"

Vania nodded. "Yeah. I'm half Guatemalan on my mom's side, but the only Spanish I know is cursing. It's really shameful, I know. That's why I understood some of what they were shouting at us."

"You don't speak fluent Spanish?" Jessica frowned. "Are your parents disappointed?"

Vania laughed. "No. They're always super supportive. That's probably why my grades suck and why I could never go to MIT to be with my best friend." Her lips trembled and the dam finally broke. Her body shook with sobs. "And now I'll probably never get to see her again!"

Jessica walked around and hugged her. "It's going to be okay."

Vania pressed her face to Jessica's shoulder. "I've been trying to hold it in, but I just can't anymore. Sabrina is gone. She's my best friend and—and I just don't know what to do."

Tears pooled in Jessica's eyes. "I know."

Carver let them cry it out for a moment then spoke. "Can you finish the story?"

Vania released Jessica, wiped her tears, and nodded. "Yeah. I'm sorry." She took a moment to collect herself and then continued. "We decided to go back to the dock. The men followed us. It started thundering and raining and we were frantically paddling and scared out of our minds. Then a family on a pontoon boat came and rescued us from the storm."

"Aw, that's nice," Jessica said.

Vania nodded. "Yeah, it was. The men took off and I didn't see them again. Sabrina got in her car, I got in mine, and we left at the same time. She went over the bridge, and I stayed on this side."

Carver opened the map app on his phone. "Show me exactly where this dock was."

Vania pointed it out. She traced her finger along the road. "This is South Pleasant Valley Road. Sabrina went north and I went south."

Carver studied the map. "Where's the jet ski rental?"

Vania zoomed in and tapped on the place.

"How much time passed from the time the family on the pontoon boat picked you up until you returned the kayaks?"

"Probably twenty minutes, but I'm not really sure."

"Which direction were the men on jet skis heading when you last saw them?"

Vania frowned and looked up. "Um, they went past us in the same direction, then made a U-turn and went back the other way."

"They could have easily made it back to the rental place, gotten in a car, and driven to the kayak rental place before you and Sabrina got there," Jessica said.

Carver plugged in the two addresses in the maps app and got directions. It was a five-minute drive from one place to the other. "Where on the lake did the pontoon boat pick you up?"

Vania stared at the map. "I don't know. Probably around here." She tapped the map.

There was no doubt that the men could have returned the jet skis and driven to the kayak rental location long before Sabrina and Vania turned in their rented kayaks and got into their cars.

The men could have watched the girls go to their cars. They could have followed them out of the parking lot and onto South Pleasant Valley Road. When the girls drove in opposite directions, they had to decide who to follow. They'd chosen Sabrina.

And then they'd taken her.

CHAPTER 5

Carver knew what to do next.

They needed to talk to the employees at the jet ski rental place. Describe the men and their car to the employees and hopefully find out their names. Unfortunately, they couldn't do that until the jet ski rental place opened in the morning.

"Can I help somehow?" Vania said. "I really want to help."

"You've already helped," Jessica said. "This new information might be exactly what we need to find her."

"God, I hope so." Vania wiped her eyes. "How could this happen here? I've always felt so safe in Austin."

"You're never really safe anywhere," Carver said. "It's an illusion. Always know your surroundings. Don't trust anyone."

Jessica groaned. "Don't make the poor girl paranoid."

"He's right, though." Vania shivered. "My best friend was snatched right in her own neighborhood. That's enough to make me super paranoid."

Carver stood. "If you think of anything else, let us know."

"Sabrina's science teacher, Mr. Hardin stopped by earlier." She bit her lower lip. "He asked if I knew anything and I told him what I told you."

"Sounds like he's running his own investigation," Jessica said. "That seems a little strange." She turned to Vania. "And he's friends with Sabrina on social media."

"Yeah, they're close." Vania wrinkled her nose. "Honestly, it gives me the creeps, but Sabrina seems okay with it."

"Yeah, who knows these days?" Jessica shook her head. "Maybe it's because of his missing daughter."

"That's what Sabrina says." Vania nodded. "That Mr. Hardin thinks of her as his daughter."

Jessica wrinkled her nose. "Ew, that sounds even creepier, doesn't it?"

Vania wrinkled her nose too. "Yeah." She turned to Carver. "Do you think those men might come for me next since I was with Sabrina?"

That was a good question. It all boiled down to one question. Had the kidnapping been an impulsive decision or planned? The men had been angry when Vania yelled at them. But they'd gone for Sabrina. Something more was at play here, that was certain.

"It's unlikely, but the odds are greater than zero." Carver took out his phone and looked up a stock photo of a gold Cadillac DeVille. He showed it to Vania. "The kidnappers were driving a car like this but with gold spoked rims. If you see one in your neighborhood, let us know."

Vania wrinkled her nose. "Ew, that's such a grandpa car."

"Yeah. Makes it easy to fly under the radar. Sabrina probably thought the same thing right before she was taken." Carver gave her his burner number. "Call me if you see anything."

She looked him up and down. "Definitely. You look like you could take on an army of kidnappers."

"But still call the police if it's an emergency," Jessica said. "We might not be able to get here very fast."

Vania rolled her eyes. "The cops here won't do anything. They let criminals off with a warning these days."

Carver had seen that all too often. "We'll be in touch."

"Thanks." Vania led them to the front door and outside. She hugged Jessica. "Please let me know the instant you find out anything."

"I will," Jessica said as she got into the car.

Carver dropped into the driver's seat. "I'll take you home."

"Can I stay in the motel with you?" Jessica gave him a pleading look. "I really don't want to be home alone with my parents."

Carver couldn't blame her. "Sure."

"I just need to get my bags from the house."

He drove her by her parents' house. It took her under a minute to run in and pick up her things. She probably hadn't completely unpacked since returning home from her road trip with Alicia.

Meeting Jessica's parents had stirred some dormant memories. Memories of Carver's parents. They were still fuzzy around the edges, but the feelings associated with those memories weren't pleasant.

Carver remembered the house they'd lived in at one point. It had thick red carpet in the den. The house smelled like the cleaning oil used on hardwood floors, but he didn't remember any hardwood floors.

He remembered a door in the kitchen. He remembered his parents going in and out of the door frequently one night. He remembered his mother telling him not to open the door. Not to look inside.

He didn't know why meeting Jessica's parents had dredged up that memory. Maybe because his parents were strict and overbearing too. Except his parents trained him relentlessly and would punish him if he complained even a little.

Punishment consisted of anything from a hundred pushups to moving heavy stones from one side of the yard to the other. They didn't believe in spanking or beating which was a shame, because getting spanked was a hell of a lot faster and easier than a hundred pushups.

All things considered, Jessica had it pretty easy.

There was a decent motel not far down the road. It wasn't cheap, but it was cheaper than the other nearby places. The room also looked and smelled better than most motels Carver had stayed in.

Jessica set up her laptop at the desk and went to work. Her software had originally been intended for marketing purposes. It indexed publicly available images and videos and used facial recognition to link people with products and services, or something like that.

The company had gone under quickly after major social media companies sued to keep her from using their networks. Probably because they wanted to exploit their users themselves, rather than letting a third party do it.

Carver had hired Jessica to use her facial recognition technology to help him find Liana. Even though it couldn't access security cameras or archives, the prolific use of social media and smartphones made her software the next best thing.

The best part was that it wasn't limited to just facial recognition. Jessica had also modified the software to recognize specific makes, models, and colors of cars. It could index features of a specific vehicle and search for it.

Jessica was busy manipulating images of a gold Cadillac DeVille. Using an editing program, she replaced the stock wheels with gold spoked rims. If there were any publicly available images of the car out there, the software would find them.

Ten years ago, something like this wouldn't have worked. But people were constantly taking photos and videos with their smartphones these days and posting them to social media. Many of them posted publicly for clout. That was the only reason this software worked at all.

Carver took a shower. Jessica was still engrossed with the software when he came back out, so he made a checklist of things to do and went to sleep.

Carver woke up at zero five hundred and saw Jessica asleep with her head down on the desk. He picked her up and put her on the bed. When he moved her, the mouse woke the computer screen, showing the search results page.

There was a picture of a man standing next to a Cadillac. The software bracketed the car in green. It was the same make, model and color as the car they were looking for, but the wheels weren't gold or spoked. The man was also black, not Latino.

The software seemed to realize the wheels were wrong because they were bracketed in red with slashes across them. Jessica told him it was a learning algorithm, so maybe that was its way of learning.

The second image was of a gas station. Someone had posted a video of their friend trying to fuel an electric vehicle with a gas pump. A gold Cadillac DeVille pulled up to a pump in the background. The software placed green brackets around it. A man got out and walked to the back of the car to fuel it.

Carver backed up the video and paused it when the man stepped out of the car. He backed up the video to the beginning and paused it when the Cadillac drove into frame. The wheels were ugly yellow gold. They might have spokes, but it was hard to tell.

The software also wasn't sure about the rims. It put yellow brackets around the wheels it could see and flashed question marks above them. It cropped a static image of the vehicle in a separate window and began enhancing the resolution.

The man who stepped out of the vehicle was Latino. Tattoos ran up his arms and his neck. Carver zoomed in and saw the number 13 clear as day on the left side of the man's neck.

The software finished enhancing the image of the car. The question marks next to the wheels vanished and the yellow brackets turned green. The wheels were definitely gold spoked rims.

The software began beeping and flashing a message on the screen: *Possible match found!*

Jessica groaned and sat up. She rubbed her eyes and squinted at the laptop. She gasped and ran over to it. "It worked!"

Carver moved out of her way. "Yeah, looks like it."

"More specifically, my video search filter worked!" She sighed in relief. "I've been trying to search videos frame-by-frame, but the indexing codec didn't work for certain social media sites because they compress the image."

Carver raised an eyebrow. "So, the video searching is new."

"Not new, just massively improved." She tapped on the keyboard. "I had to create fake profiles for all the social media sites, and manually log them in, because if I didn't, they'd get flagged. I also had to tie in an AI bot to add friends and make fake conversations, so the profile looks legitimate."

"That's a lot of work."

"Yeah, but the more friends the profiles have, the more searchable images I can access." She shook her head. "The problem is, most sites have a limit to the number of friends you can have, so I have to figure out a workaround."

Carver sat next to her. "Where is this gas station?"

Jessica studied the video. "It was posted at three in the morning at a gas station not far from Sixth Street." She glanced over at him. "That's a big party hub in downtown Austin." She highlighted the man's face and uploaded it to the server. "God, please let this be the right guy."

She advanced the video to get different angles on the man's face and plugged them into the search engine. She refreshed the search page and stared at it as if willing something new to appear. "Ugh, the license plate isn't visible."

She yawned and closed her eyes.

"Maybe you should sleep," Carver said. "The jet ski rental place doesn't open for a few hours."

Jessica checked the time. She went to the bed and lay down. "Wake me up if something new appears."

"I'm stepping out for breakfast. Want anything?"

She looked at the time. "At this ungodly hour?" She shook her head. "I'll eat later."

Carver looked at the gas station in the video. He searched for 6th Street on the map. There were options for East and West 6th Street. He searched for party places in Austin and discovered that spelling out Sixth Street brought up the area Jessica had mentioned. It was apparently a very popular place for college students to party.

The map highlighted seven blocks downtown. The gas station in question was near the northeast corner just off Interstate 35. Had the man been in the party district before getting gas, or was it just coincidence?

That all depended on who these kidnappers were. Had they taken Sabrina for their own personal use or were they pros? If they took girls for sex trafficking, then the party district was a place full of targets. It was a lot easier kidnapping drunk college girls than simply taking them of the streets.

The Cadillac driver looked like he was in his late thirties or early forties. He was certainly no college student, nor could he pass for one. Maybe he worked in the area. Maybe he worked at one of the bars. Carver checked the metadata on the video and saw that it was taken about eight hours after Sabrina had gone missing.

If this was one of the men from the jet skis, and one of the men who'd taken Sabrina, then it was good to know that they hadn't left town. They were almost certainly still around.

That meant Sabrina was still probably in town. But was she alive? If she was alive, what were they doing to her? Unfortunately, that second question didn't take much imagination. The man had probably kidnapped her for his own use or for sex trafficking.

The license plate wasn't visible in the video. Cars in Texas had front plates, but the camera only caught the side of the car. That was a damned shame. It would have made tracking the car a little easier, provided he could get access to DMV records.

Carver walked down the street to a diner. Like everything in this city, it was a little fancier than the diners he usually ate at. The food, however, was pretty much the same. It wasn't any worse or better and it filled him up.

He got some breakfast sandwiches and coffee to go. He grabbed a local paper from a newsstand and took it back to the motel. He checked the laptop but there weren't any new results from the search engine. He looked through the newspaper and found a story about Sabrina on the second page.

The picture was grainy black and white. The story was two paragraphs long. It gave some basic information about Sabrina and said the police were investigating. It looked like the story had been cobbled together at the last minute before the newspaper went to press.

Carver checked the website and found the same story. He searched the internet for "Missing Austin girl" and got over a hundred results. Only two of the stories were about Sabrina. The others were about other girls who'd gone missing over the last several years.

Apparently, Sabrina's kidnapping wasn't an isolated event. It wasn't something that happened rarely. In fact, it looked like something that happened with regularity. It looked like hundreds of females under the age of twenty-one had gone missing over the last few years.

The statistics weren't broken down very much beyond male, female and whether they were under twenty-one years old. At least not on any official websites. He looked through several news stories and stumbled across an old-school blog that looked like it had been designed in the late nineties.

While it wasn't fancy, it had compiled data specifically about females who had gone missing from various cities across Texas, including Austin. The number had spiked a few years ago, dropped for a short period and then shot back up. The same thing had happened all across Texas.

According to the nationwide stats, over two hundred thousand females under age twenty-one went missing each year. That was a lot of young women and girls. Granted, those were just missing persons reports. Some of those people weren't really missing, but they'd been gone long enough that a worried parent reported them as missing.

It was the ones that went missing and were never found that fed into another statistic. It was likely that Sabrina was now a member of that statistic, human trafficking. But it was also possible that the men who'd taken her were keeping her for their own personal use and would discard her later.

As with anything else, it was going to be a race against time to prevent that from happening, provided the race wasn't already over and Sabrina wasn't already dead. The next few hours were going to be vital.

The morning had drifted past zero eight hundred. The jet ski place was going to open in a little under an hour and now they had a picture to go with their questions. He nudged Jessica until she woke up.

She squinted at him. "Did you find something else?"

He shook his head. "No, but the jet ski rental is going to open soon."

Jessica pushed up and out of bed. She stumbled and caught herself. "I feel like I didn't sleep at all last night. I kept dreaming that I was talking to Sabrina and then she'd vanish or die. It was a nightmare on loop."

"I brought you breakfast." Carver opened the bag with the sandwiches. "Egg and bacon sandwiches."

"Thanks, Carver, but the thought of food makes me sick."

"You need to eat."

Jessica looked down and sighed. "Yeah, you're probably right. I'm going to shower first."

She showered, dressed, and took a couple of bites from a sandwich before making a face and shaking her head. "Let's go. I just don't have an appetite."

They left. Carver drove to the jet ski place. He parked close to the side building where the door was and waited for it to open. Other cars were also pulling into the parking lot. The people in the cars were watching and waiting for the business to open. This place was going to get real busy real fast, so he'd have to be the first one in line if he wanted to question the employees.

Jessica stared miserably out of the front window. Her eyes were red from crying, and she had bags under her eyes.

She looked over at him. "Sorry."

"For what?"

"I don't know. I feel awful in more ways than one."

"Understandable." Carver his hand on hers. "You can sleep in the back. I'll let you know when something happens."

She shook her head. "No, I'll be fine." She rotated the coffee cup from the diner in her hands. "I just need something better than this motor oil."

About seven minutes after the business was supposed to open, an old Honda Civic parked next to the minivan. A tall kid unfolded himself out of the car and walked toward the building. Carver knew the kid was an employee because he wore a T-shirt with the name of the rental place on it, Ladybird Rentals.

Carver got out of the car with Jessica, and they hurried over to the kid while he was unlocking the door. The people in the other cars were also piling out and hurrying toward the building.

Jessica touched the kid on the arm. "Hey, we need your help finding a missing person."

The teenager blinked and focused on her. "Huh?"

She showed him the picture of the tattooed man. "We think this man might have kidnapped my sister. Do you remember seeing him yesterday?"

The kid looked bewildered. "Sorry, what? Did you say kidnapped?"

Jessica took a deep breath. "Sorry, I'll start over. My sister was kidnapped yesterday. Some men driving this gold Cadillac in the picture probably took her. This is a picture of the car and one of the men."

"Whoa, that's crazy." He peered at the picture. "So, I wasn't working yesterday, but Ashley was." He looked at the time on his phone. "She should be here soon, but she's always running late."

Carver didn't point out that the kid had also arrived late. "Was anyone else working here yesterday?"

"I think our boss was in for a while. He usually comes by for a few every day, but he also manages other businesses, so you never know."

"What's his name?"

"Yohan."

"Yohan?" Jessica's forehead pinched. "Is he foreign?"

The kid laughed. "No. He's a total giga-Chad though."

"Ah, I see." Jessica cleared her throat. "Um, what kind of paperwork do people need to rent a jet ski?"

The teenager glanced at the crowd forming in front of the building. "Um, I kind of need to get to work. Can you hang on while I process these reservations?"

"Yes, of course." Jessica backed off. "What's your name, by the way?"

"Um, I'm Jacob."

"Thanks, Jacob."

"Sure, no problem." The kid went inside and raised the shutter on the window to open the rental counter. A young couple went to the window. Jacob slid waiver forms over to them. He told the other people waiting behind them to come get started on the waivers.

Carver picked up the pad with waivers on it and took one. It asked for name, address, and contact information. He showed it to Jessica. "If they filled out one of these, then we can find them real easy."

"Unless they falsified the information."

Carver watched the other people fill out the info. Once they did, Jacob looked at their identification and typed something into his computer. "Looks like they verify them with an ID."

Jessica's eyes widened. "That's great. Maybe we can look at the waivers that were filled out yesterday."

"Yep." Carver had a feeling Jacob wouldn't let them do that. Not without his manager's approval. But it wouldn't hurt to ask.

And if they were lucky, they'd have the home address of the suspected kidnappers today.

CHAPTER 6

Carver heard an engine revving loudly.

He turned around as a yellow Lamborghini Urus pulled into the parking lot. The driver revved the engine. People turned to look at the car.

"God, what a douche," a woman said.

The Urus pulled into a slot reserved for employees. A Caucasian male a couple inches shy of six feet tall slid out of the driver's seat. He had a goatee and a shaved head. He wore nice shorts and a polo shirt. He looked like he was ready to hit the golf course. It looked like he also hit the gym frequently judging by the bulging muscles under his shirt.

He looked at the people waiting in line and did a double-take when he saw Jessica. "Hey, pretty lady. How are you?"

Jessica blinked rapidly as if caught off guard. "Are you talking to me?"

"Definitely." He smiled and approached her. "If you're waiting on a rental, I can get you one right away. I could even get us a double and you can ride with me."

"Um, I'm not—"

"You work out, don't you?" He looked at her toned legs. "You've got a great physique."

"Thank you, but I'm not here for a rental."

Carver stepped into frame.

The man blinked and seemed to notice Carver for the first time. "Oh, my bad. This your girl?" He looked up at Carver. "Man, you work out a lot, don't you?"

Carver ignored the question. "Are you the manager?"

The man flinched. "Are you having problems?" He glanced at the rental counter. "Jacob, did you screw up something?"

"No, no!" Jessica waved her hands. "It's nothing like that. We just need some help finding someone."

Yohan flinched again. "Uh, finding someone?" His voice seemed to go dry.

"Yes, my sister was kidnapped yesterday, and we think the kidnappers rented a jet ski from here."

Yohan cleared his throat. "Kidnappers on jet skis?" He laughed. "Is this a joke?"

"No, not at all." Jessica dropped her pleasant tone. "My sister was kidnapped, and we think this man had something to do with it." She showed him the picture on the phone.

Yohan stared at it in silence. "You think this guy rented a jet ski here and used it to kidnap your sister?"

"No." Jessica paused and then spoke slowly. "This man and another one rented jet skis here. They encountered my sister on the lake and harassed her. They then followed her in their car and kidnapped her in her own neighborhood."

"Oh." He nodded. "I don't recognize that man and I was here for a while yesterday."

"Okay, but they filled out your waivers. Can we look through them?"

"You want to go through confidential paperwork?" Yohan shook his head. "No, you can't do that. Not without the cops and a warrant. Sorry."

"The cops haven't even assigned a detective to the case yet. We need this information fast before the trail goes cold."

"Look, I get it." Yohan smiled. "I get it, okay? But I could get sued if I just hand out people's confidential information to random strangers."

"No, you don't get it at all!" Jessica shouted.

The people nearby looked their way in alarm.

"My sister was kidnapped and you're not willing to help me find the kidnappers! You can look through the paperwork yourself. I really don't care." She clenched her fists. "Just look yourself and see if there are any names that stick out, okay?"

"Like Hispanic names?" He chuckled. "You realize you're in Texas, right?"

A girl on a bicycle pulled into the parking lot. She wore a shirt like Jacob's. She was probably Ashley, if Carver had to guess. While Jessica continued to argue with Yohan, Carver watched the girl approach on her bike.

She parked it next to the building and got off. Carver walked over to her. "Ashley?"

She looked up at him. "Do I know you?"

"No, but Jacob gave us your name." Carver motioned toward Jessica. "We're looking for some possible kidnappers and hope you might be able to identify them. He showed her the photo of the man.

She looked at it. "Oh, yeah, I remember that guy. He was with another guy who had a lot of tattoos too. They were scary looking."

Yohan hurried over. "Ashley, you can't talk to these people."

"Huh?" She looked confused. "Why not?"

"Because our customer information is confidential. We could get sued."

"Not for questions like this," Carver said. "This is a matter of life or death."

"I mean, those dudes definitely looked like they kidnap people," Ashley said. "They kept looking at me like they wanted to kidnap me."

"Ashely, you need to stop talking right now." Yohan held up a finger. "One more word and you're fired."

Her eyes flared. "You'll fire me for helping them find kidnappers? You can't do that!"

"I can and I will."

"What the hell is your problem?" Jessica lunged at Yohan like she was going to punch him.

Yohan dodged back. He shook his head. "I'm a martial arts expert. Don't come at me like that unless you want to get hurt."

Jessica seemed to barely contain her anger. "I will flood social media with posts about you not helping me. I will stand out here all day long with a sign and tell everyone the same thing."

"I'll call the cops and have them remove you from the premises."

"Good luck with that," Jessica said. "They don't even have enough people to investigate kidnappings these days."

Carver put a hand on her shoulder. "It's okay. We'll come back with a warrant."

Jessica's mouth dropped open. "How are we going to get a warrant?"

"Trust me."

"Listen to your boyfriend, lady." Yohan shook his head and backed away. "Being a drama queen isn't going to solve your problems." He opened the door and motioned Ashely inside. "Get in here before I fire your ass."

Ashely gave them an apologetic look and then went inside.

Jessica stared at Carver like she'd been betrayed. "Can't you do something? Slam him against the building and put a knife to his throat?"

The other customers were openly staring at them. Some had their phones out to record any drama. Carver didn't like being recorded but it was hard to avoid these days. Hopefully they wouldn't end up plastered all over social media.

Carver walked away from the rental building.

"Seriously?" Jessica hurried after him. "Can't you do something?"

"I will. But not now. Not with all these eyes on us." He kept walking. "Plus, I have a feeling about Yohan."

"A feeling?" Jessica frowned. "Like what?"

Carver had noticed several small things about Yohan. His demeanor, his facial tics, his reactions to certain words and phrases. By themselves they didn't mean much but added together said a great deal. "I think he recognized the man in the picture."

"You think he saw him yesterday?"

"I think he saw him before yesterday. I think he's seen him a lot. Maybe even knows him."

She frowned. "You got all of that just from the few minutes we talked to him?"

"Yeah." Carver kept walking toward the minivan. "He's the manager for a jet ski rental shop but he drives a Lamborghini."

"Maybe he's the owner?"

Carver pulled up the website for Ladybird Rentals. He tapped the menu and navigated to the about section. The owner was listed as Bryan Reynolds. Apparently, he owned multiple rental places and was a member of the local city council.

"I recognize him. He's a local real estate bigwig." Jessica shook her head. "I guess he moved into politics."

"The point is, Yohan isn't the owner. He's a manager." Carver pocketed his phone. "Unless he's getting paid the big bucks, there's no way he could afford a Lamborghini on that salary."

"So, you think little muscle man knows the kidnappers? You think he's working with them and that's how he can afford a Lambo?"

"Yep."

"Your theory sounds legit." She scowled. "So, we wait until he leaves and then take him?"

"There's still something that doesn't add up." Carver got into the minivan and waited for Jessica to get into the other side before continuing. "If he knows these guys, then why didn't Jacob or Ashley mention seeing them before yesterday?"

"Jacob said Yohan manages several places. Maybe they don't come here often?" She tapped a finger on her chin. "Also, lake rental places like this only operate during the summer and hire high school students seasonally. So, Jacob and Ashely probably just started working here. They probably wouldn't have seen them before."

Carver nodded. "Good theory."

"Also, if Yohan knows these guys, then they might not even have to fill out waivers."

"Unless he wasn't here when they arrived." Carver took out his monocular and studied the rental counter. The counter and the window ran from one side of the building to the other. The entire place was only about twenty feet long and maybe ten feet wide.

It was a small building. There was one door inside and the sign on the door labeled it as the bathroom. There were no filing cabinets or any place to store paper files. There were two computers behind the counter, and that was about it.

Which meant they didn't keep paper files. At least not onsite. In fact, they probably only held onto the paper waivers until the renters returned the jet skis. They probably threw away the waivers every day, so they didn't have to store them.

Yohan stood behind the counter next to Ashley. He was talking to her. Putting his hand on her shoulder. Squeezing. She nodded several times and looked distinctly uncomfortable. Jacob kept glancing at Yohan with concern plain on his face.

Yohan was probably telling Ashley not to talk to Carver or Jessica if they came back. He was probably making sure she understood what would happen if she did. Yohan touched a pad of waiver forms and said something else to Ashley.

Ashley nodded and pointed toward the back of the building. Yohan nodded and smiled. He said something else and then left the building. He walked around the back of the building. Carver knew exactly what he was doing.

"He's going to look for the waivers in the trash."

"So, they did fill out waivers." Jessica clenched her teeth. "That lying piece of crap."

"It means Ashley looked at their IDs to confirm the information."

Jessica's eyebrows rose. "Do you think she could be in danger because of that?"

"Possibly. We need to get that information before Yohan destroys it." Carver studied the area. "Wait here."

Jessica took a deep breath as if to calm herself. "I really don't want to, but you're the specialist."

Carver slid out of the minivan. Yohan was behind the building so he couldn't see Carver coming. Ashley and Jacob were too busy helping customers to notice him. He circled the parking lot anyway, keeping behind parked vehicles so he didn't stand out.

He walked around the side of the building. There was a large municipal trash can right behind the building. Not far from that was a boat ramp where the jet skis were put into the water. The jet skis were on small rolling platforms so they could be wheeled over to the boat ramp and easily be put into the water.

Yohan had pulled a garbage bag from the trash can and was digging through a mound of waivers. It seemed like an awful lot of trouble to go through when he could simply take the entire bag and burn the contents.

Then again, he probably didn't want to put a garbage bag inside his Lamborghini. It would be better for him to find the two slips of paper and burn them instead of hauling away the entire bag.

Carver counted the jet skis sitting at the dock. They cost fifty bucks for half an hour, seventy-five for an hour, and multiples of that for every consecutive hour. There was a discount for a half-day and full day rental, but it would still cost someone five hundred dollars if they wanted it for eight hours.

Most people probably rented it for an hour due to the cost. There were twenty-five jet skis on the dock, so if they were all rented out hourly, that would add up to a lot of paperwork. Most of the jet skis were designed for two people, so that doubled the number of waivers.

In other words, Yohan was digging through about four hundred waivers, give or take. It was probably going to take him a while to find the right ones. Carver was just fine with letting Yohan doing the dirty work.

He used the wait time to look for cameras and didn't see any on the back of the building. The storage area for the jet skis was protected by a tall fence topped by razor wire but no cameras. It seemed a little odd not to have cameras protecting expensive gear, but maybe stealing a jet ski was more trouble than it was worth.

The thief would need the key for the jet ski, and they'd have to remove the decals and the paint identifying the owner as Ladybird Rentals. Whatever the reason for the lack of cameras, Carver wasn't going to complain. In fact, it was going to work out great for what he had in mind.

Yohan finally stopped and stared at a slip of paper. His eyes lit up like he'd just found exactly what he was looking for. He picked up the next waiver, looked at it, and blew out a sigh of relief.

He dumped the other waivers into the garbage bag and cinched it up. He picked up the bag and dumped it into the garbage can. Carver used that time to sidle up to the side of the building. He came around it nice and slow, peeking around the corner to let Yohan finish cleaning up his mess.

Yohan folded the waivers and tucked them into his back pocket. Carver had a pretty good idea about what was going on now. At the very least, Yohan knew the men. At the most, he was actively working with them.

That gave Carver some latitude in dealing with Yohan. A great deal of latitude. Yohan wouldn't go to the police no matter what Carver did to him. Regardless of how deep his involvement was with the men, he couldn't risk getting exposed and going to jail.

The only people he'd report Carver to would be the men he was working with. Those men would probably come after Carver. And that was fine. Just fine. It would save him the trouble of hunting them down.

With that in mind, Carver stepped around the corner and walked right up to Yohan. The other man stared blankly for a second like a deer in the headlights. His eyes flared and he adjusted his stance, one leg slightly behind the other, knees bent in some kind of martial arts pose.

"Give me the waivers and I won't break your arms," Carver said.

Yohan smirked. "Come get them, big guy. I eat kids like you for breakfast."

"You're working with them, aren't you?"

Yohan turned his fist upright and opened his hand. He waved Carver toward him and grinned. "You have no idea what kind of hell I'm about to unleash on you."

That was true. Carver had no idea how good Yohan was at martial arts. Maybe he really could lay him out flat. But the odds were good that he couldn't. So, he walked toward the other man and watched him closely.

Yohan's weight shifted forward and his right shoulder twitched. He punched right toward Carver's crotch. That was smart. Punching someone in the face was a good way to break your hand. The crotch was a soft target. A solid strike to the testicles would take down most men.

Carver had been punched in the balls more times than he could count, mostly during unarmed combat training. It wasn't pleasant, not even a little bit. But he'd learned to overcome the pain and the reflexive action enough so his opponent couldn't deliver the killing blow.

In this case, he didn't need to take a blow to the crotch. He just gripped Yohan's wrist and used the other man's momentum to twist him around, so his arm was pinned behind his back. He pinched the space between Yohan's thumb and index finger and the other man cried out in pain.

Carver pulled the waivers from Yohan's back pocket and unfolded them with a few flicks of his wrist. He looked at the names and addresses. "Is this where I can find them?"

Yohan whimpered. "You're hurting me!"

"That's the idea. I hurt you until you tell me if these addresses are right."

"I don't know, man! I just send them pics of girls, and they pay me money."

"You identify girls for them to kidnap."

"I had no idea—"

Carver squeezed the nerve in Yohan's hand a lot harder.

Yohan squealed. "Yes, yes!"

"What do they do with them?"

"I don't know, I promise!"

"Lie to me again and I'll break this arm. It won't be a clean break, either. It'll cripple you for life."

Yohan tried to drop to his knees as if that might relieve the pain, but he jerked upright again when it made it even worse. "I've never gone to their place. They always come to me. But they did give me an inside angle to a place. It's an underground club."

Carver knew what kind of club it was without asking. "Where is it?"

"It moves around every week. They haven't sent out invites this week. They usually send them at the beginning of the week."

Carver had a lot of other questions for Yohan, but in a few minutes, Jacob and Ashley would start bringing customers back here to get their jet skis. Yohan might not report him to the cops, but someone else almost certainly would.

"Do you have their contact information?"

"They change numbers at least once a week. I think they use virtual phones or something."

Carver wasn't surprised. "So, you can't tell them to meet me somewhere?"

"No!" He groaned in pain. "I'm telling you the truth. I won't have a number until I get the next invite."

Carver released Yohan's hand and booted him hard in the back. Yohan fell. His face smacked into the concrete. The blow stunned him good because he didn't even cry out in pain. A pool of blood began to form under his face, probably from a broken nose.

Carver hurried around the side of the building and circled back toward the minivan. He had an address. Now it was time to pay a visit.

CHAPTER 7

Carver climbed into the minivan.

He handed Jessica the waivers. Plugged the address into the GPS. Started driving.

"Juan Gonzalez and Jose Rodrigez?" Jessica frowned. "These are super common names. They're the Latino equivalent of John Smith and Joe Jones."

"Yep."

She stared at him as if waiting for him to say more before following up on her observation. "These have got to be fake names. Probably a fake address too."

"Probably, but best to check it out anyway." Carver drove up the ramp to the interstate and headed toward the bridge. Traffic was heavy but moving. They made it across the bridge and headed east into the residential areas.

"How would Yohan know these are the right waivers if the names are fake?"

Carver shrugged. "He probably knows them by their fake names."

"What if Yohan calls ahead to warn them?"

Carver shook his head. "I don't think he can. They use virtual phones and switch numbers every week."

Jessica frowned. "Do you believe him?"

"Yeah. But don't worry. I'll still be careful."

Thirty minutes later they turned onto Perry Road and took a right onto Ventus Street. Some houses were of contemporary design. They looked like concrete cubes randomly stacked together two or three levels tall. Others were much smaller single-story homes with flat but slanted roofs.

The address in question belonged to one of the smaller homes. There was a Chevy truck parked in the driveway beneath the carport. No sign of the Cadillac they'd seen in the videos. Carver parked on the side of the road across from the house and looked it over. No cameras.

Carver decided to just go up and knock on the door. He started to get out of the car.

Jessica held up a hand. "Let me go. They might not open the door if they see you outside."

"Okay, but be careful."

She slid out and walked across the street. She walked straight up to the front door and knocked. A Latino man answered. He looked young. Probably in his mid-thirties. He had good skin and was a little chubby. This wasn't a guy who worked outside or with his hands.

He smiled pleasantly at Jessica and spoke to her. She showed him the waivers and said something back. He took the waivers and frowned. He stared at them for a moment, a troubled look on his face. His reaction seemed natural.

He looked like a guy who'd been going about his day only to have the normalcy broken by a stranger and a mystery. He looked at Jessica and shook his head. He looked back at the waivers and shook his head again.

Jessica held her hand up like she was describing someone's height. She touched her face like she was describing facial tattoos and other features. The man shook his head and shrugged. He looked apologetic, like he wished he could help.

Jessica took the waivers back, probably thanked him for his time, and came back to the minivan. She got in and blew out a breath. "He's never heard of these names or seen the men. Their IDs are fake."

"Not surprising." Carver drummed his fingers on the steering wheel. He started the car and wheeled it around.

"What now?"

"There's another possibility." He told her about the underground club. "Yohan can get us the address."

"How did you get him to give you the waivers?"

"I twisted his arm."

"And you think he's going to help us after that?"

"I probably broke his nose too." Carver looked at the red on the map and took a different route.

"Oh, God, really?" Jessica's mouth dropped open. "What if he reports you to the cops?"

"He won't."

"Because he's connected to the kidnappers?"

"Not just that. He probably paid cash for his Lamborghini. Cash that wasn't reported as income."

"Ah, so he's afraid of the IRS too."

Carver nodded. "If he's smart, he is."

"He doesn't seem very smart." She stared at the traffic ahead. "He looks like a muscle-head."

"Maybe. But I think he's got enough brain cells to avoid the authorities at all costs."

They returned to the rental place. Yohan's car was gone, so Carver got out and went to the counter. In the hour they'd been gone, almost all of the jet skis had been rented out. Apparently, business was good.

Ashley and Jacob saw him coming and gave each other worried looks. Carver leaned on the counter. "Where's Yohan?"

"Uh, he tripped and broke his nose," Jacob said. "He said he was going to get it looked at."

Ashley winced. "We're not supposed to be talking to you."

"Last time I checked it's a free country." Carver met her gaze. "Any idea where Yohan went to get his nose looked at?"

"He said something about a quick clinic." Jacob shrugged. "That's all I know."

Carver checked the GPS and looked for nearby quick clinics. There were two. One was at a national chain drug store. The other looked like it was a standalone building. That one was the most likely destination.

Ashely bit her lower lip like she was trying not to say something. She gave into her impulse and did it anyway. "Did you break his nose?"

Carver shook his head. "Do I look like someone who would break his nose?"

Jacob laughed. "Yes. You look like you could break Yohan in half."

"He's into martial arts." Carver shook his head. "I wouldn't stand a chance."

Ashley narrowed her eyes. "I don't know. You look like the silent but dangerous type."

"Thanks for the info." Carver turned around and went back to the minivan.

"Do they know where he went?"

Carver plugged the quick clinic address into the GPS. "He told them he was going to a quick clinic. There are two nearby. One is inside a drug store. It's probably not set up to handle broken noses. The standalone clinic probably is."

"Sounds like a reasonable assumption."

Carver navigated traffic and aimed toward the clinic. It was only three miles distant, but twenty minutes away thanks to traffic. Carver saw Yohan's Lamborghini from across the intersection when they were almost there.

Jessica chuckled. "A car like that makes him easy to find."

Carver pulled into the lot and parked. They got out and went inside. Yohan wasn't in the waiting room. He was probably getting patched up in one of the back rooms.

The receptionist looked from Carver to Jessica. "Can I help you?"

"My friend said he was coming here. He broke his nose."

"Oh, yes, he went back about thirty minutes ago."

"Great. We'll just wait for him out here." Carver selected a chair on the left side of the room. That way he could watch the patient exit door without Yohan immediately noticing him when he came out.

Jessica dropped into a chair next to him. "Shouldn't we wait outside for him?"

Carver shook his head. "This is fine."

"What if he makes a scene?"

"He won't."

Yohan emerged from the exit a few seconds later. His nose was bandaged. Both his eyes were black and blue, and he looked a little woozy. They might have given him painkillers. He walked to the receptionist and paid. She apparently didn't tell him that his friends had shown up looking for him, because he turned and exited the building.

Carver followed him outside. He followed him to his car and cleared his throat.

Yohan stopped walking and turned around. His eyes went wide. "What the hell?"

"The address was no good." Carver leaned against the Lamborghini. "We're going to need an invite to the next party. You said the invites usually drop today."

Yohan pulled out his phone with a trembling hand. "Uh, I don't have anything yet. It probably won't come until later."

"Okay." Carver held out his hand. "Let's go to your place and wait."

"My place?" Yohan's mouth dropped open. "You broke my nose, man! I don't want you in my crib."

"Crib?" Jessica laughed. "I haven't heard that term since the early two thousands."

"I can break more than your nose, Yohan." Carver gripped the other man's wrist. "A whole lot more."

Yohan gulped. He pulled his key from his jeans pocket and placed it in Carver's other hand. "I guess you're driving?"

"Yep."

"Um, what about our car?" Jessica said.

Carver tossed her the keys. "Follow us."

"You got it." She went to the minivan.

Carver nodded toward the other side of the Lamborghini. "Get in."

Yohan licked his lips and nodded. He went to the passenger side and got in.

Carver climbed into the driver's seat. He dropped the key fob into the cup holder and pressed the start button on the dash. The Lamborghini rumbled to life. He switched the central screen to the GPS and tapped on the home icon. The address appeared. The navigation system painted a blue line on the map and told him where to go.

He followed the directions. Jessica followed close behind in the minivan. They went north of town to the suburbs and turned into a subdivision. The homes were nice but not too nice. There were nice cars parked on the driveways, but none as upscale as the Urus.

If Yohan lived here, it proved he wasn't a complete idiot. Most criminals were caught because they spent unlaundered money on big ticket items like houses and cars and a jealous neighbor reported them to the IRS.

There was a decent chance people in an upper-middle class neighborhood like this wouldn't report someone for a Lamborghini, but it was still a risk most smart criminals wouldn't take. Yohan clearly hadn't been able to resist the siren call of a fancy car.

An iron gate blocked the driveway. Yohan reached over and tapped an icon on the vehicle's touchscreen. The gate slid to the side. He touched the neighboring icon. One of the doors on the three-car garage swung up and open.

Carver pulled inside. A Ducati motorcycle was parked in the neighboring bay. The third bay was empty. He turned off the vehicle and got out. He walked to the buttons on the wall and pressed the opener for the third door.

Jessica drove the minivan inside. He closed it behind her. Yohan watched quietly, apparently resigned to helping them. He put his thumb to the biometric lock on the entry door. The lock disengaged with a mechanical whir. He opened the door and stepped inside.

Carver went in after him. There was a large and mostly empty mudroom on the other side. He figured a guy like Yohan probably had weapons in the house. Probably a fancy gun or two. It was Texas, after all.

"Where are your guns?"

"I don't have any." Yohan held up his hands in surrender. "I really don't."

"You're not going to like it if I find one," Carver said. "You're going to wish you'd told me the truth."

Yohan went silent for a long moment. "I just have a small revolver." He left the mudroom and entered the kitchen. Like most modern homes, it was wide open and connected to the den. He slid open a drawer.

Carver was already standing next to him just in case. There was a snub-nosed revolver in the drawer. It was a Ruger SP101, a sturdy little 357 magnum. He picked it up. It fit neatly in the palm of his hand.

Carver had seen mostly stainless-steel models with a black grip. This one had a ceramic rose gold finish, handle and all. The serial number was all zeroes. In other words, the serial number had been removed and replaced.

Jessica took it from Carver. "Cute gun." She gave Yohan a questioning gaze. "I'm glad to see you're in touch with your feminine side."

"It isn't even mine." Yohan clenched his jaw and winced, probably because it hurt his broken nose. "I got it for my ex."

"You bought your ex a gun?" Jessica laughed. "You're braver than you look."

"You're sure you don't have any other weapons?" Carver said. "Knives, guns, anything?"

Yohan blew out a breath. "Does it matter? Can't we just chill in the den until the invite arrives? You don't need to go taking all my stuff, man."

"I'm just ensuring your survival, Yohan." Carver pushed him toward the couch. "If you try to surprise me with something, you won't live to regret it."

Yohan licked his lips. "I have a gun upstairs next to my bed, and a safe with some collectibles."

"Are they all scrubbed like the revolver?"

He nodded. "I have a guy who can get me anything."

"Have you ever used a gun against another human?"

Yohan shook his head. "Nah, I'm just keeping it chill, you know? I'm not a criminal. Just give me some fine bitches and some coke and I'm all good."

"You're disgusting and a criminal." Jessica wrinkled her nose. "And on top of what you just said, you're helping kidnappers target girls."

Yohan stared blankly at her for a moment, like nothing she said registered. He shook his head. "Nah, that's not true. Those girls are eighteen and over. They're not kidnapping anyone. You ever think your sister just went with them willingly? Like maybe she likes older men?"

Jessica punched him in the nose.

Yohan grabbed his nose and screamed. Blood soaked the bandages. Jessica kicked him in the crotch. His hands went from his nose to his groin. His screams turned into a whimper. He went down and curled into the fetal position, sobbing like a child.

Jessica brushed her hands together. "You're lucky I don't use your ex's pretty little gun on your sorry little ass."

Carver pulled Yohan's phone out of the other man's back pocket. He held it in front of Yohan. "Unlock it."

Yohan managed to press his thumb to the screen. The face lock wasn't going to work with all the bandages on his nose. The screen unlocked. There were dozens of notifications piled up on the screen.

Carver sorted through them. Many were spam emails and phone calls. He flicked those to the side and got to the text messages. There were texts to a lot of women. Most of them were labeled by a first name and a sexual description, like *Brenda with the big ass* and *Rochelle Anything Goes.*

Most of the texts were sent by Yohan to the women. Most of the texts had been sent in the wee hours of the morning and simply said, *You up?* Most of them had gone unanswered, but a few had replied. Carver wasn't surprised to see those were the majority of the texts. He wasn't surprised to see that Yohan had also sent images of his pint-sized genitalia to some of the women.

One contact stood out from the others. It was simply labeled *Unknown*. Carver opened the conversation and found a long string of locations inside. Most of the texts were spaced about a week apart. Sometimes they skipped a week or two.

The most recent text had arrived moments ago during the drive to Yohan's house. It said, *842 Montopolis Place.*

Carver put the phone in front of Yohan's face. "Is this the new invite?"

Yohan stopped whimpering long enough to answer. "Yeah. I wish it would have gotten here sooner before your dumb bitch kicked my balls!"

Jessica growled and reared back her foot as if to kick him again. She stopped herself and shook her head. "You're not even worth it."

Carver looked through the other texts. He found a conversation string with names, addresses, and descriptions of girls, including their ages. They all went to a number with an Oregon prefix. Probably a burner number from one of the many free services that offered them.

Katie Spiegel. 51 Plato Court. Blonde, nice small tits, slim, 15.

Anna Rodriguez, 804 Bowman Street. Black hair, big rack, big ass, 17.

The texts were clearly to the men Yohan had tried to protect. Carver put the phone in Yohan's face. "I thought you couldn't contact them."

"I can't. Look at the history. The number changes all the time."

Carver scrolled up and saw different phone numbers. "How do you keep them all in one conversation thread if the number keeps changing?"

Yohan looked at him with watering eyes. "I use an app. Women have a cat icon. These guys have a bull icon."

Carver noticed the tiny icons at the beginning of the contact names. He'd just assumed Yohan did that himself. "So, I can't text them with this number?"

"No, it's already expired." He touched his nose and winced. "They'll send out a new number that expires in forty-eight hours. The only time a number doesn't expire is if there's a special request that hasn't been filled."

"A special request?" Carver said. "Like a specific girl?"

"Yeah."

"Why do the numbers expire?" Jessica said.

Yohan looked like he didn't want to answer, but he did. "So they can't be traced."

Carver scrolled slowly and found nothing about Jessica's sister. Yohan hadn't sent the men anything about her. Apparently, they'd decided to rent jet skis and find some women on their own.

They probably had several other contacts throughout the city that sent them similar information so they could find girls. The men had sent Yohan pictures and descriptions of women.

Some of the descriptions were extremely specific, right down to clothing size, bra size, race, and a dollar amount. Those must be the special requests. That told Carver something he already knew. These girls weren't simply being kidnapped.

They were being trafficked.

CHAPTER 8

Carver showed Jessica the phone.

She gasped. Her eyes flared. The surprise morphed to anger. "This pure evil! They put bounties on specific types of girls!"

Carver nodded. "You know what this means, right?"

Jessica looked from him to the phone.

Carver let her figure it out on her own. It didn't take long.

Her face went pale. The phone dropped from her fingers and bounced on the floor. "My sister wasn't just kidnapped for a one-time thing. She's being trafficked and sold."

Carver picked up the phone and nodded. He looked through the text string. Yohan had answered several of the specific requests by sending pictures. The traffickers had replied with a thumbs up or thumbs down emoji to the images.

In one text with a thumbs up, there was a message that said, *Deposit sent.* They apparently put a down payment in advance of receiving more information on the target.

There was a recent request sent two days earlier. *16+ blonde, c-cup or larger, slim, small plump ass, pale skin.* Carver searched the internet for a female matching the description. He found a lot of images to choose from. He downloaded a couple from a girl's social media. She was in another country, so he figured she wouldn't mind him using her photos for a good cause.

He sent the image to the phone number associated with the request.

Jessica frowned. "What are you doing?"

"Baiting the hook. If we don't find them at the party, maybe we can bring them to us."

"Ah. We give them an address and lie in wait."

"Something like that." Carver knelt next to Yohan and showed him the address for the party. "There's no date or time."

Yohan struggled to sit up. "They always start at nightfall on the same day the invite is sent."

"It doesn't get dark until almost nine PM," Jessica said.

Yohan glared at her. "Then that's where it'll start, sweetheart."

"I don't like your tone, you nasty perverted piece of human filth." Jessica patted the rose gold revolver. "How about I blow off your junk?"

Carver went to the security settings on Yohan's phone. He changed the passcode. It asked him for the current passcode and a thumbprint. He held it out to Yohan. "Approve this."

"You're taking my phone?" Yohan groaned, but did what he was told. "Man, that case is custom."

Carver removed biometric security from the phone so he could access it exclusively with the passcode. He was going to need access in case the party didn't pan out. "Do I need anything else to get into the party?"

"No. The address is the invite." Yohan gently touched his bloody bandages and groaned. "God, I've got a killer headache now."

"You got painkillers?" Carver said. "Oxy? Opioids?"

"Yeah, of course. Can I please get something to take the edge off?"

"Get up and take me to them."

Yohan struggled to his feet. "Upstairs."

Carver followed him upstairs. They went down the hallway and to the master bedroom at the end. They went into the bathroom. Yohan opened the linen closet. He removed the towels and extracted a box from behind them.

Inside the box were prescription bottles, bags of pills, bags of powders, syringes, and more. It was a complete druggie's toolkit. Yohan pulled out a bottle of white pills. It looked like a generic version of an opioid.

Carver looked through the bottles. "Do you have fentanyl?"

"Nah, that stuff is dangerous. I only use natural stuff."

"Heroin?"

"Nah, that's dangerous too. I don't want some bitch dying from an overdose." He put two pills into his hand. "Oxy treats me right every time."

Carver watched him down the pills. His original plan was null and void without fentanyl. That was okay. There were other ways of dealing with certain issues. "How long does it take to feel relief?"

"Usually twenty minutes." Yohan tucked the bottle back into the box. "After that I'll be right as rain."

"Let's go back downstairs."

"Sure. Let me put this away."

"You can do it later." Carver motioned toward the door.

"All right." Yohan walked out of the room and down hallway. He made it to the top of the stairs.

That was when Carver wrapped an arm around his throat and squeezed.

Yohan made a choking sound. "What the hell?"

"There are a lot of cockroaches like you out there in the world." Carver tightened his grip on Yohan's throat. "But that doesn't mean I won't stomp one out when I come across it."

Yohan trembled violently. "Come on man, I'm just making a living! I haven't hurt anyone!"

Jessica appeared at the bottom of the stairs. She looked up at them. "You've hurt a lot of girls, you sick bastard. You're worse than a cockroach. You're worse than the garbage roaches feed on."

"Please no! I have money! I can pay you!"

Carver put a finger on Yohan's throat. "You feel how fast your heart is beating right now?"

Yohan nodded slowly.

"You feel that terror creeping up from your chest, choking you until you can hardly breathe?"

"Y-yes!" Yohan shook with sobs. "Don't kill me, bro! Don't kill me!"

"Imagine how those girls feel being raped by some old man. Imagine that terror." Carver put a hand on the side of Yohan's head. "Are you imagining it?"

"Yes!" Yohan sobbed violently. "Please, please, please don't—"

Carver twisted his head savagely. Yohan's neck snapped. It was a loud, wet snap. He gently pushed Yohan forward. Let his body tumble down the stairs and land on the hard tiled floors below. His body jumbled up nicely.

Jessica gagged and ran to the sink. She dry heaved a few times and then took deep breaths. "I thought I was ready for that. I wasn't."

Carver walked up beside her and patted her back. "You didn't have to watch."

"I wanted to." She wiped tears off her cheeks. "My sister is living that terror right now, Carver, and that sick bastard is to blame."

"Wait here." Carver went upstairs and wiped off the prescription bottles he'd touched. He emptied out the one with Oxy onto the bed. The CSI crew might think Yohan overdosed and tripped on the stairs, breaking his neck in the fall.

He went downstairs. "Wipe off anything you touched."

"I didn't touch anything."

Carver had let Yohan open everything, so the only thing he'd touched was the steering wheel in the Lamborghini. He grabbed a paper towel and used it to open the door to the garage. He wiped down the handles and the steering wheel in the Urus. He opened the garage door with the wall button and used another wall button to open the gate.

They left in the minivan.

"Where to now?" Jessica said.

"We'll get a late lunch then go scope out the party address."

"Okay. Am I going in with you? Or do you think they won't let a girl in?"

"I don't know. We'll find out." During his time with Scion, Carver had seen all kinds of sex parties. Some involved consensual sex. Most of them didn't. Most of them involved girls bought and sold by the sex slave market.

Scion hadn't been tasked with ending human trafficking. If anything, they'd facilitated it by removing governmental roadblocks and specific people from various law enforcement agencies like INTERPOL.

The mission briefings often gave little to no detail about the reason behind the operations. The targets were often framed as corrupt government officials. Carver had known that wasn't true because he read the local news after several such operations and learned that the targets were actually some of the few non-corrupt government officials.

At the time it hadn't mattered to him. He was just doing his job. Doing what he was told. Scion's faceless handler told Rhodes what to do. She told everyone else what to do and they did it, no questions asked.

Leon was the only one to question orders. He was told to follow orders, or he would not only be scrubbed from the group, but from life.

This was going to be just another sex party. But this time Carver was going in with a whole new perspective. This time he didn't have orders to follow. This time he wasn't tasked with killing the one good guy standing in the way of a criminal enterprise.

He wasn't sure what he was going to do if this was indeed a sex slave operation. Helping Jessica save her sister was the primary objective. If he did anything to disrupt the so-called party, he would almost certainly end up on someone's radar.

The best way to save Sabrina was to come in fast, low, and unseen. But why was he doing this? He didn't have a personal stake in the matter.

Carver glanced at Jessica. He liked her. He considered her a friend. So, in a way, he did have a personal stake in this.

He wasn't out to save the world. He was just helping a friend. That was why he'd gone after Liana when she went missing. That was why he was helping Jessica now. He'd never intended to form relationships. At least not anything meaningful.

It all started with Paola. He'd gone looking for her when he found out a hired killer was on her trail. More recently he'd hunted down Liana's killers only to find out she was still alive. And now he was helping Jessica.

He was forming meaningful relationships. He was risking life and limb to help people he cared about.

It was almost becoming a habit. A very bad habit. One that would probably not only get him killed but keep him far away from a nice beach. He couldn't even pinpoint when he'd decided to start helping people out of situations that were none of his business.

Jessica broke into his thoughts. "Carver, you've got the look of a man who's questioning his life choices."

Carver glanced in the rearview mirror. There were slight wrinkles next to his eyes. A slight furrow to his brow. Nothing too noticeable to most people, but Jessica apparently had a way of seeing his facial tics.

"We can talk about it if you want." She reached over and touched his leg. "I won't think any less of you."

"You probably don't want to hear what I have to say," Carver said.

"It's obvious you don't want to be here doing this." She offered a wan smile. "You left me, Liana, and Alicia without hardly a goodbye so you could get back to the beach."

"What's a good place to eat?"

"Don't change the subject."

"I'm not. I just want to have a destination before we keep talking."

"There's a decent steakhouse about a mile down the road." Jessica raised an eyebrow. "Sound good?"

"Yep." Carver stopped at a traffic light. He turned his full attention to Jessica. "I'm here because you helped me. But there's something more. Friendship, I guess. Kind of like with Liana. I don't like the thought of you having problems."

Jessica laughed. "You must have been a real machine back in the day. No emotions. Just someone who did whatever he was told to do."

"Mostly, yeah." Carver shrugged and looked at the traffic in front of him as it started to move again. "I was raised to do what I was told, no questions asked, or my parents would punish me."

"Where are your parents now?"

"Dead."

"How?"

He shrugged. "I'm not really sure. A cop told me it was an accident. Some old man in a military uniform said they were targeted because of my dad's work."

"And you never looked for answers?"

He shook his head. "I never had the time or inclination. I was orphaned, went through some rough patches, then joined the military the first chance I got. Thanks to my birth records being lost, I was able to get in a couple of years before I was eighteen."

"They didn't know how old you were?" Jessica's stared at him with a half-smile on her face. "My God, you had a really messed up childhood."

Carver shrugged. "It was okay. My parents taught me how to look out for myself. They trained me in self-defense, showed me how to shoot guns, made me run gauntlets every day, and fed me well."

"I mean, you're as big as a horse. They must've given you the corn and beef diet."

Carver thought back to those times. "Yeah, lots of meat and potatoes They took me to a cabin in a forest for a few weeks a year and made me hunt for my own food. Survival training."

Her mouth dropped open. "How old were you?"

"I'm not sure. Old enough to use a knife on a wild boar."

"Your parents were insane!" Jessica stared at him. "Were they raising you to be their own personal assassin or something?"

"No. They just wanted me to be ready to serve in the military." Carver saw a steakhouse and pulled into the parking lot. "At least, that's what they told me."

"Your parents were monsters. But I guess you turned out okay."

Carver said nothing. He really hadn't turned out okay. Not like a normal person, anyway. He'd had trouble fitting in with the SEALs. Not because he wasn't good, but on a personal level.

That lack of personal connections made him a perfect fit for Scion. A perfect soldier who did anything without question. The other members of Scion hadn't cared that he wasn't their friend, their buddy. He was a cog in a well-oiled machine and that was enough for them.

At least until someone up the chain of command decided to burn the entire dark ops system to the ground so they could privatize it. Then Tony Menendez and Sam Rocker had framed him for human trafficking and Scion had been disbanded.

"Hey, it's okay." Jessica leaned over and kissed his cheek. "You might be a monster, but you're my monster."

Carver smiled. "You've got an interesting way of looking at things." He got out of the minivan. Went into the restaurant. He chose a booth in the back corner with a view of the front door.

Jessica got ribs and made a real mess of herself while eating them. Carver didn't mind. He liked that she attacked the food with abandon. He also liked that she didn't talk much while she was eating.

After she finished the ribs, she went to the bathroom and came back out with a clean face and hands. She sat down and sipped her sweet tea. "How are we going to approach this?"

"Carefully."

She rolled her eyes. "Obviously."

He paid the bill in cash and got up. "First, we scope out the territory."

They got back in the car and drove to the address. It was in a poor section of town not far from the interstate. The building in question was behind a motel that looked like it charged by the hour.

The building in question wasn't abandoned. There was an old grocery store that looked like it had been built decades ago and had never been updated or renovated. It was the anchor store in a small shopping center.

That wasn't too surprising to Carver. He'd seen underground events at all kinds of places, even in the basement of a police station and a city hall. The place didn't need to be abandoned. It just needed to be closed to the general public for the event to take place.

Carver parked at the end of the lot and scanned the buildings with his monocular. He spotted a couple of old cameras. The cables were cut on both. There might be cameras inside the buildings, but there wasn't anything operational out here. Nothing he could see, anyway.

He got out of the car.

"We're going inside?"

"Yep."

"Why would they have the party here of all places?" She shook her head. "It doesn't look like a great place to have a secret party."

Carver checked the address again. It didn't specify which building in the shopping center would host the party. It could be any of the other buildings in the shopping center. Maybe that information would be provided closer to the starting time of the party.

It would be ideal to pinpoint the precise location sooner rather than later. That would give him a chance to get setup beforehand. Because if Jessica's sister was here, he was going to need all the advantages he could find to get her out safely.

CHAPTER 9

Carver entered the grocery store.

The tiles were worn and cracked from decades of use. The walls were painted an ancient shade of beige. The metal shelves were relics of decades long past. Despite its age, the store was clean and well-kept.

It was relatively crowded with older folks, mostly Latinos, mostly women. Some looked curiously at Carver and Jessica in passing. Carver walked the aisles. He pushed through double doors in the back and entered the stock room.

Jessica hesitated before following him inside. "Are we going to get into trouble being back here?"

"Not if we're quick."

She laughed nervously. "I can't believe I'm afraid of this after what we just did to Yohan."

Carver inspected the loading dock and the pallets of unboxed inventory. He crossed from one side of the stockroom to the other and didn't see any convenient spots for hosting a party. There were too many pallets to move and not enough space, as far as he could see.

He exited the stockroom on the other side and left the store by the front door. The grocery store was in the middle of the shopping center. He went left. Walked past a nail salon. The name of the place was Viet Nails and the women inside looked Asian. It was a pretty good bet they were Vietnamese.

There was only one customer inside. The other employees were staring at their phones in boredom or talking to each other. They were mostly young women but there were a few older women scattered in with them.

A jewelry store was next door, and next door to that was a mattress store. Carver ducked into the mattress store for a quick look. It wasn't big and the back room was tiny. There were also a lot of windows that would need to be covered if a party was held inside.

A salesperson watched him and Jessica from across the room. "Need help?"

Carver shook his head. "Just browsing, thanks." He left. Walked toward the other end of the shopping center. There was a furniture rental store to the right of the grocery store. He looked through the window but didn't go inside.

"Seems like the mattress store or this place would be ideal," Jessica said. "They could use the existing furniture for their nefarious activities."

Carver's gut didn't agree. He walked past the furniture store to the last shop at the end. A female mannequin stood in the window. Its naked form was painted purple. A fake birds' nest was perched on top of the head.

The display was enclosed by a tall black plastic barrier. At the foot of the mannequin was a sign that said, *Bird Juxtaposed*.

Jessica scratched her head. "What the hell is that supposed to mean?"

The window display stretched for about twenty feet. Another mannequin took up the second half of the space. It was bent over at the waist, the right hand reaching down to pick up the mannequin's left arm which was lying in front of it. A placard in front of it said, *Silent Struggle*.

"Who in the world does this to mannequins?" Jessica shook her head. "If I lost my arm, I wouldn't be silently struggling. I'd be screaming in pain."

They continued to the front door. The glass was painted black with the name of the store, *Visions By Greta*, in green letters just above the door handle. A yellow sticker on the outside of the door said, *Open by appointment only*.

"Visions by Greta?" Jessica laughed. "More like drug-induced hallucinations."

Carver glanced at the display window to the left of the door. A pair of mannequins artfully painted and arranged, took up the space just like on the right side.

"Who in the hell calls this garbage art?" Jessica sighed. "Well, this can't be the place." She made air quotes when she said the last two words. "Maybe there's a building behind this one."

"This is the place." Carver walked to the end of the sidewalk and around the corner.

Jessica caught up and paced alongside him. "Huh? What makes you think this is it?"

"Closed to the public, blacked out windows, and it's an art gallery. Probably a front for laundering money."

She frowned. "How in the world could you launder money through a place like this?"

"Because the price of art is subjective. You can process a lot of cash transactions with art." Carver walked to the back of the building. There was a service road for delivery trucks and parking spaces for business owners. A lot of cars could fit back there unnoticed.

There was a metal door leading into the back of the art gallery. Carver pulled a slim jim from his waistband and jimmied the latch. He gently opened the door and looked inside.

There were no walls in the gallery. It was just a big open space. He looked for cameras and saw none tucked into corners or out in the open.

There were about a dozen mannequins scattered randomly throughout place. They were painted, posed, dressed, and labeled. They were the so-called art pieces. One was called *Standing Tall*. Another was named *Finding Shapes*. It was like someone chose random words from a dictionary and put them on the placards.

Jessica stared in distaste at one of the exhibits. "This place is creepy as hell."

It wouldn't take much to transform this place into a so-called party venue. They could string up a disco ball and call it a day, depending on what kind of venue they wanted to set up. The best way to know would be by keeping an eye on the place.

Carver motioned Jessica to follow him. He went outside and pulled the door to without shutting it.

"You sure this is the place?" Jessica asked.

"Pretty certain." Carver checked the time. "Guess we'll know for sure in a few hours."

"What do we do until then?"

"We prep." Carver went back to the car. He drove it around back and parked it behind the neighboring store. He opened his bag of surveillance goodies and checked the battery levels on his wireless cameras.

It had been a while since he'd charged them and the batteries tended to lose the charge after extended non-use. One of them was at seventy percent, but the others were sitting under fifty. He used a 12 volt to USB adapter and plugged in several devices.

He took the mostly charged wireless camera into the art gallery and looked around for a good spot to conceal it. The place was designed like a loft. There were no ceiling tiles so the air conditioning duct work and wiring was fully exposed all the way up.

The wireless camera was black and had a magnetic base so it could stick to just about anything up there. Unfortunately, he couldn't reach that high and he didn't have a ladder. He motioned Jessica over and pointed to a space in the upper back corner.

"Can you put the camera up there if I give you a boost?"

"Yeah, no problem."

He cupped his hand and bent over. She put her foot into his hands. He lifted her. She grabbed the metal rafter for balance, but she wasn't quite high enough. Dust drifted down into her face.

She coughed and sneezed. "Man, it's dirty up here." She muscled herself up and onto the rafter and balanced on top. More dust drifted down as she shifted sideways and placed the camera.

Carver checked the feed on his phone. "Angle it down slightly and a little to the right."

She adjusted it until he had a good view of the entire room. He had motorized cameras but none of them were fully charged. This would be just fine for now.

Jessica hung from the rafter. Carver reached up and eased her down. He looked at the floor. The dust from the rafters was barely noticeable on the dark concrete, so he brushed it around with his hand to disperse it more and then just let it be.

He checked the camera feed one more time and then put it into motion sensor mode to conserve battery life. "Let's go."

They walked to the back door. Carver wiped down the inside handle, closed the door, and wiped down the outside handle. They went back to the car. One of the cameras was at sixty percent charge, so he pulled it off the charger and looked around for a good place to put it.

He stuck it to the side of a metal junction box on the back wall of the neighboring store. That way if it was noticed, someone wouldn't think much of it. He adjusted the angle until he had a good view of the back door to the art gallery.

Jessica looked through his bag of surveillance equipment. "You got some really good stuff from Plum and Associates, didn't you?"

"Yeah. Top of the line equipment."

"I can tell it makes you happy. At least now I know what to get you for Christmas."

Carver chuckled. "Surveillance equipment?"

"Maybe. Although I'll bet you'd be real happy to get a drone equipped with missile launchers or something crazy like that."

Carver nodded. "Yeah, that would be a real thoughtful gift."

She laughed. "Okay, so we wait and watch?"

"Almost." Carver got into the driver's seat and drove the minivan to the front of the shopping center. "We need to go shopping."

She frowned. "For guns? Missile drones?"

"What kind of clothing did you pack?"

She looked confused. "Summer dresses, gym outfits, maybe a pair of shorts. Why? Do I need bulletproof armor?"

"Nope. Just some new outfits." He looked at the maps app. "You need something trashy, and something classy. What's a good place to find those kinds of outfits?"

"Probably a mall." She took his phone and typed in a name. The GPS mapped the route. "It's a little bit of a drive, but that's one of the few malls left that has everything."

Carver followed the route. It was only twenty miles away, but it took them an hour with traffic. The mall was huge. There was a movie theater, some large department stores, and bougie restaurants. The parking lot was packed.

He found a spot near the back, and they walked to the nearest entrance. Jessica inhaled deeply, as if smelling the place. She released the breath and smiled. "Wow, this brings back memories."

Carver frowned. "A shopping mall brings back memories?"

"Yeah. We used to hang out here all the time when we were just teeny boppers. We'd hang out with friends, go see movies, and eat in the food court. We could spend the entire day here." She shook her head. "Places like this hardly exist anymore. Everyone shops online now. Mall rats are a dying breed."

Carver knew teens liked to go to shopping malls to hang out, but only as a matter of fact. He'd never experienced anything like it during his childhood. The closest he'd ever come was when his mom told him to follow a teenaged boy for them. The boy had gone to the mall and played video games all day.

Carver had watched him and not without some jealousy. He'd really wanted to play video games too. But he hadn't. He'd done his assigned task and eventually followed the boy to a motel, apparently where his father was staying.

Carver's parents had told him he'd done a good job, then left him at home that night. They never told him why they wanted him to follow that boy, but in retrospect, he had a gut feeling it hadn't been good for the boy or his father.

Jessica took his hand. "I know just the place to go."

Carver let her lead him. They took an escalator to the second floor, went back in the opposite direction, and turned into the third store on the right. There was mostly women's clothing inside.

Jessica browsed the racks. Carver looked for a place to sit down and couldn't find anything even resembling a seat. A man standing behind his wife gave Carver a nod of solidarity as if they were both enduring a common trauma.

"Ah, this is good." Jessica picked a dress from the rack and held it up to her. "Classy enough?"

Carver studied it. It was a black body conforming dress that reached halfway down her thighs. "I think so."

She picked up a red dress and held it next to the black one. She stared at them for a moment then put the red dress back. She took Carver's hand and led him to the dressing rooms entrance. He caught a look from the woman in the back that told him he couldn't go any further, so he stood his ground and waited.

Jessica came out a moment later. Her long black hair framed her face and hung over her shoulders. Her athletic figure filled out the dress nicely. She turned in a slow circle. Carver nodded. She looked good. Real good.

She smiled and blushed. "Hey, tone it down, mister."

Carver nodded. "Looks classy enough."

"Not the way you're looking at me." She winked and went back into the dressing room. After she changed back, Carver bought her the dress, and they went to another store. This one had clothing that was the opposite of classy.

Most of the clothing looked like it had survived a warzone. Shirts and pants were torn, patched, and ripped. There were no dresses, only skirts that left very little to the imagination. Jessica picked out an outfit and went back to the dressing rooms.

The attendant didn't bat an eyelash when Carver went back with Jessica. He closed the room door and sat down on a chair. Jessica stripped down to her underwear and put on a short skirt, torn netted stockings, and a low crop top.

She turned in place. "Looks really slutty, doesn't it?"

"It works."

She sat down next to him. "What kind of scenarios are we looking at, Carver? Like, what's the classy scenario?"

"Might be an auction with upper-middle class men and women looking for young girls. Might be just wealthier men looking for something taboo. In that case, the girls are usually dressed up to get a higher price."

"Seems like they'd dress them up like this." She ran a hand down the short skirt.

"You'd think, but in these cases, a look of innocence is preferred."

Jessica scowled. "Why don't they just hire prostitutes?"

"Because there's something about despoiling a young girl that those kind of men like. It's why they like virgins."

She clenched her fists and closed her eyes. "Okay, so what are the slutty clothes for?"

"It might just be a meat market similar to a brothel." Carver shrugged. "In either case, we'll go in like a couple who are into that sort of thing."

"Makes sense." She took off the outfit and changed back to her normal clothing. Carver bought the outfit, and they went to a store to see to his needs.

They stopped at a suit store. He tried on several and had to go with an extra-large suit jacket just so it would fit around his shoulders and arms. He went with black to match Jessica's dress and tried on the entire ensemble.

Jessica looked him up and down then smacked him on the butt. "You look good enough to eat."

Carver bought the suit. He didn't need to buy alternative clothing because his cargo pants and t-shirts would do just fine for a casual affair.

"So, what's next? We wait and watch?"

"Yep." Carver went back to the car. He checked the camera feeds. Nothing was happening at the art gallery. Sundown wasn't for another couple of hours. "Let's eat."

"Yeah, we don't want to go into battle on an empty stomach."

"Hopefully it won't come to that."

Jessica looked worried. "What's the best-case scenario?"

"We find your sister there, snatch her and leave without incident."

"And worst case?"

"Best not to think about that." He found a pizza place with good reviews on the maps app. "Is pizza okay?"

"I don't care." She shivered. "I imagined about a dozen worst case scenarios and lost my appetite."

Carver took her hand and squeezed it gently. "Hey, it's going to be okay."

"You're just saying that."

He nodded. "True. But it's best if you go into this with a positive mindset. You need to make yourself believe that this is going to go flawlessly. That's the only way to approach it."

She looked at him with worried eyes. "Maximum confidence?"

"Exactly. And a full stomach."

Jessica managed a smile. "Okay. We've got this. We'll have my sister home tonight."

"Yep." Carver didn't believe that. Not even a little bit. He was fully confident that he'd find out something about Sabrina tonight, but it wouldn't be pleasant. It might be worst case, it might be marginally better than that. But one thing was certain.

This wasn't going to have a fairytale ending.

CHAPTER 10

Sabrina woke up with a shout.

She felt groggy and weak. She felt like she wanted to throw up, but something was stuck in her mouth. She tried to look around, but something was covering her face. She could barely make out light and shapes through fabric.

Sabrina felt something else. Something cold and metallic. She tried to touch it, but her wrists were strapped down. She felt clothed, at least partially on her upper body. But her lower body felt bare and exposed.

Soft but strong hands touched her bare legs. She tried to struggle, but her legs were strapped down and completely immobile.

A man spoke. "She's awake." He had low raspy voice. The voice of someone who chain-smoked multiple packs a day.

Another man spoke. "It doesn't matter. Best not to keep them too drugged anyway. You know the clients hate getting damaged goods."

The raspy voice spoke again. "So, what do we have?"

Sabrina felt hands probing her privates. She tried to scream. Tried to struggle and resist, but between the drugs and the straps she could hardly move.

The other man spoke. "Hymen is intact. The coloring is very nice. Very pink." The hands left her. "She's an excellent specimen. Should bring top dollar."

The smoker wheezed with laughter. "How are you so clinical with such a tempting target right in front of you?"

"I've seen more vulvas than you can imagine. I've seen healthy ones, diseased ones, clean ones and dirty ones." He made a disgusted sound. "Nothing about them is tempting to me in the slightest."

"You gay or something?"

"As a matter of fact, yes."

"Oh, well, that's why you don't like them."

"Yes, but even if I were straight, I've seen enough disgusting genitalia to make me swear off sex."

"Man, how do you live without sex?"

"Look, this is a very personal discussion that I'd rather not have with you, okay?"

"Hey, you're the one who brought it up."

"No, you're the one who asked me how I resist. Now you know."

The smoker laughed a raspy laugh. "Maybe that's why Jaeger chose you. He knew you wouldn't sample the goods."

"I'm a professional first and foremost."

"But you lost your medical license, doc. How'd that happen?"

The doctor sighed loudly. "Look, I have a dozen other girls to inspect. Can you just keep quiet and let me do my job?"

"Hey, have at it." There was a metallic clicking sound like a cigarette lighter sparking. The odor of tobacco smoke drifted into Sabrina's nose. "I'll just sit here and look at the pretty merchandise."

Sabrina shuddered at the thought of the smoking man staring at her exposed body. She struggled as hard as she could. The gag in her mouth muffled her screams.

She felt a presence. Smelled strong cigarette breath. Felt a hand on her bare stomach. "Calm down, girly. Don't make me put you under again. We want you nice and fresh for tonight."

Sabrina shouted muffled curses at him.

He laughed and kissed her on the stomach. "You're feisty. Someone's going to love that."

She shuddered in revulsion. His hand was rough, and he stank like alcohol and smoke. He was rubbing her stomach but not going any lower. Apparently, he wasn't going to spoil the merchandise, her womanhood.

His hand left her, and his presence receded. She heard him talking from across the room. He wasn't talking to the doctor. It sounded like he was on the phone.

Sabrina took a deep breath and calmed herself. She recalled the list of things she was supposed to do if kidnapped and wondered if any were applicable. One item on the list was how to break duct tape or zip ties if her hands were bound in front of her. That didn't apply in this case, unfortunately because her wrists and ankles were bound to the sides.

She wriggled her left arm and then her right arm. She did the same for her legs. Her wrists and ankles were strapped to the table. There were straps on her upper legs as well to keep them from moving. Her legs were also elevated and spread wide, like she was on an examination table. There was plenty of context to support that theory.

Her upper arms weren't strapped down. That gave her just a little bit of extra mobility, but not enough to make a difference.

She concentrated on her other body parts. It felt like something was holding her waist down. Something else was holding her head in place. She could move it back and forth, but not very far. Probably an enclosed headrest.

There was something else. Something touching the fingertips on her left hand. She pinched it between thumb and forefinger. It was a nylon strap. One side was rough, and the other was smooth. Like Velcro.

It felt like there was some slack hanging over her hand. She couldn't feel the same thing on her right hand. She pulled up on the slack. She heard and felt the hooked side peeling up from the loop side.

She wriggled her arm, but it didn't feel any looser. She bent her wrist as much as she could to grip the strap a little further back. She finally managed to grip it and tugged. She felt it peeling away but only a little bit.

The smoker shouted from seemingly across a room. "Hey, Doc, you almost done?"

"Twenty more minutes."

"All right. Rodrigo's on the way to start cleaning and boxing them up for tonight." He paused. "Probably be here in five."

"As long as he stays out of my way, I don't care."

Cold fear wormed through Sabrina's stomach. They were coming to get her. She didn't have much time. She pinched the slack between her fingers and pulled again. It didn't peel away any further. She tried to grip it further back but couldn't bend her wrist any further.

She tried pulling up but that didn't do anything. She took a deep breath and imagined the strap. Pulling up wasn't doing anything. What if she pulled sideways? She pinched the loose end and pulled sideways by twisting her arm.

The strap went slack around her wrist. She gasped in surprise. Her first instinct was unstrap her other arm and get out of there as fast as possible. She resisted the frantic urge to flee and forced herself to listen to her surroundings instead.

Sabrina heard the smoker distantly to her left. She heard the doctor clear his throat from maybe fifteen feet away. An air conditioner hummed to life and cold air drifted over her. She kept listening for a count of ten then acted.

She slowly pulled her hand free from the loose strap. She kept her arm close to her body and slowly moved it toward the other hand. She didn't want any sudden movement to catch the doctor's attention.

She felt around for the end of the strap and slowly tugged it free to minimize any noise. Her right hand came free. Her heart started beating faster and harder. She took a deep breath, but it did nothing to calm her.

Sabrina inched a hand toward her head and found a cloth hood. She pulled it up. Bright light blinded her for a moment before her eyes adjusted. A gag was strapped over her mouth. She pulled it down and gulped fresh air.

The smoker man was still talking from somewhere across the room. Sabrina raised her head above the headrest and saw him in a doorway at the end of a long row of metal tables. She saw rows of bare legs in examination stirrups. Nearly every table had a female on it. She could tell by the size of some of the legs that the females were probably very young girls.

The doctor was maybe six tables down from her. He was white with thick black hair and thick glasses. His big head perched on a scrawny body. He was closely examining another female's crotch and seemed to be writing something on paper.

Sabrina looked to her right and saw more tables and women. She noticed thin rods with colored flags raised above each table. Some flags like hers were green. Some were blue. Others were yellow or red.

She looked back to the left and saw that only the girls the doctor had examined had colored flags. It didn't take much imagination to know what they stood for. Green probably meant virgin. Blue was probably a step down from that. Age might be a consideration as well.

None of that mattered. All that mattered was finding a way out of this horrible place. The smoking man was tall. He was big and wide. His face was gnarled up like old tree roots and he had big meaty hands.

He was still talking on his cell phone. Still smoking a cigarette. He was leaning against the doorframe, his profile visible but he wasn't looking into the room. Sabrina could probably get past the doctor, but the smoking man would be a big problem.

She looked around for another exit. There was a window, but it was blacked out with tint. She couldn't see what was on the other side. The wall across from her feet was blank. The wall behind her wasn't. It was lined with transparent boxes.

They looked like plexiglass coffins. No, not coffins. Display cases. Each one had a thin hose attached to the top. The hoses hung to the sides. It was obvious they were meant to pump in air. Maybe oxygen. Maybe sedation too. If she didn't get out of here, she was going to end up in one of those boxes.

Sabrina removed the strap from her waist. She removed the straps from her thighs, leaving only her ankles strapped down. How much time had elapsed since the smoking man said Rodrigo was five minutes away? At least three minutes. Which meant she was almost out of time.

There was no choice but to risk it all right now. She sat up and quickly removed the straps from her ankles. The doctor was too busy examining another crotch to look at her.

She slid off the metal table and ducked. She scurried behind the tables to the right of hers and went to the window.

The window was the kind with a crank handle that slowly opened it. She turned the handle. The bottom of the window angled outward. She saw the worst possible scenario on the other side of the window, a long drop to concrete.

There were no sounds of traffic or other familiar city noises outside the window. Just the hum of an AC unit. The wall outside was gray concrete. She glanced back to see if the open window had been noticed, but the smoking man was gone, and the doctor was busy with the next woman.

Sabrina heard tires crunching on gravel and leaned her head out of the window. She couldn't see where it was coming from, but it was almost certainly Rodrigo and the men who were coming to put her and the other women in boxes.

Her best bet might be to run past the doctor and into the hallway. Maybe the smoking man was outside meeting his men, and she could find another way out. She craned her neck to look up and around the window. There was another floor above this one, but the lip of the window was pretty far up.

She might be able to jump up and grab it, but that was too risky. Running past the doctor and into the building was better. She kept low and moved as quickly as she could between the heads of the tables and the boxes. She touched one of the boxes just to confirm it had the plastic feel of plexiglass.

She heard a gasp. The doctor raced around a table and jumped in front of her. He shouted, "Jerry, we've got a problem!"

Sabrina stood and stared at him. "Let me go, you monster."

The doctor smirked and shook his head. "Sorry, but you're not going anywhere."

"Why are you doing this?" Sabrina's fists clenched and anger heated her face. "What kind of sick, twisted person could do this to another human being?"

"Oh, spare me the anger, princess." He pulled a syringe from his coat pocket and removed the plastic cover from the needle. "You're getting exactly what you deserve."

"Why do I deserve to be inspected like an animal and boxed up?"

"Don't play innocent. Pretty girls like you bully everyone, especially kids like me who never stood a chance with you."

"But you're gay!"

He shrugged. "That's beside the point."

"So, you do this because you like the idea of us being treated like animals?"

He stepped toward her. "Very well put. Now, go back to your table and lie down, or I'll make you do it."

Sabrina had already decided she was going down swinging. She ran straight at the doctor. He'd clearly expected her to give up because his eyes flared wide with surprise. He apparently had no idea what to do because he threw up his scrawny arms in defense.

Sabrina was thankful for once that her parents had put her through gymnastics, sports, and other forms of torture because it made her a muscular girl. A girl with a dense muscular mass. She might not be able to beat most men in a fight, but the doctor wasn't most men.

She plowed into him. He cried out in panic. His head slammed the corner of the metal table behind him, and his cries went silent. Sabrina had been so focused on the doctor that she hadn't heard the other sounds in the room.

Those sounds were the muffled cries for help from the other women and girls bound to the tables. Cries that tore into her heart because there was nothing she could do for them right now. Their best bet was for her to escape and come back with help. But it might already be too late for that.

She grabbed the syringe from the floor where the doctor had dropped it. The doctor lay on the floor, his eyes glassy, a pool of blood spreading from his head. "Burn in hell, you sick bastard."

Sabrina ran toward the door. She sprinted into the hallway. It continued straight and went left and right. She had no idea which way to go but going left felt like that was away from the front of the building. She wanted to find a back door. But which way was that?

She went left. She passed by other rooms. There was nothing in most of them, but she was too focused on making it to the door at the end of the hallway to notice much of anything. She became aware of her bare feet smacking against the floor and that she was in nothing more than a hospital gown.

Running outside was going to be painful if she didn't find shoes. That was okay. She could deal with pain as long as she got away. Flashes of color caught her attention as she ran past a room near the end of the hallway.

She stopped and looked inside. The room was filled with racks of clothing. There were dresses of all kinds, from long and flowy, to tight body conforming dresses, to short skirts. There were schoolgirl outfits, slutty looking clothing and more.

There was no doubt that the men who were boxing them up would probably dress them in those clothes so they could be properly displayed in their boxes. Sabrina ducked into the room and grabbed a pair of flat sandals. She tried them on. They were a little small, but they covered the bottom of her feet and strapped on just fine.

She put them on and quickly looked over the other clothing. Nothing else looked much better than the hospital gown, so she went back to the doorway and peeked into the hallway. She heard male voices echoing from somewhere. She heard the smoking man's distinct voice and laughter.

He was coming back with Rodrigo. In a few minutes, they'd enter the examination room and see the dead doctor. They'd see that she was missing. Then the search would begin. If she didn't get out of this building, there would be no escape.

Sabrina ran to the door at the end of the hallway. It opened into a stairwell. She ran down the stairs. It felt good to have protection on her feet even if the straps bit into her skin. She made it to the bottom level. The only door there didn't open to the outside. It opened into an underground parking lot.

There were high-topped windowless vans parked there, all lined up in neat rows. There were several moving trucks too. They were smaller moving trucks, like the ones people rented. But they were big enough to transport a lot of those plexiglass cases.

If she didn't get out of here, she was probably going to be put into one of those trucks.

Sabrina ran along the rows of vans toward what she hoped was the front of the building and the exit. She finally saw the ramp leading up and out of the parking lot. It was just a few hundred feet away. Despite running all this way, she wasn't breathing too heavily. Once again, she gave silent thanks to her parents for being so hard on her.

She ran up the ramp. A metal rollup door blocked the exit. She frantically searched for a button to raise it but there was nothing but a keypad. She looked for a normal door and found one in a recess to the side. But that door was also locked, and a keycard was the only way out.

Shouts echoed from the other side of the garage. The smoking man was shouting orders.

"Look everywhere. She might be hiding down here."

Sabrina stared helplessly at the closed door. She had nowhere to go. She was trapped.

CHAPTER 11

Carver watched the camera feed.

There was movement behind the art gallery. A box truck had pulled up to the back door. A man got out of the driver side door and walked around to the back of the truck. Another man slid out of the passenger seat and did the same.

The driver pushed up the rollup door at the back of the truck. He opened the back door to the gallery. He climbed into the box truck and disappeared for a while. He rolled a tall box onto the liftgate with a hand truck, went back, and returned with another.

The boxes were five or six feet tall. They were maybe a couple of feet thick and three feet wide. They were nearly the same physical dimensions as a coffin and wrapped in black cloth. There was no doubt that the boxes had human occupants.

Jessica watched intently. "Is my sister inside one of those boxes?"

"Maybe." Carver kept watching.

The man lowered the liftgate. The other man wheeled the boxes inside with the hand truck. Carver switched to the internal camera. The man placed the boxes a few feet inside the back door near the wall.

Jessica gripped Carver's arm but said nothing.

The men unloaded six boxes and left them lined up against the wall inside. Then they put the dolly back into the truck, closed the rollup door, and folded up the liftgate. The driver and passenger got back into the truck and drove off.

"That's it?" Jessica jumped up. "They deliver them and leave them there like regular cargo? Do those men even know what's inside those boxes?"

"Probably." Carver didn't know for sure, but he doubted the traffickers would hire just any old delivery guys.

"Let's go get her." Jessica pointed at the screen. "No one is there. We can just waltz right in."

"Okay." Carver grabbed the car keys and his phone. It wasn't sunset just yet and wouldn't be for another twenty minutes. He'd expected the girls to be brought in a little early, but he hadn't thought they'd be in boxes or left completely unguarded.

He'd encountered plenty of operations that used boxes and coffins for transport of humans, but they were normally unboxed and freshened up before being shown to prospective clients. Maybe this wasn't going to be an auction or a showing. It might just be a cattle operation.

That was what they called it when the girls were brought in so men could pay to have sex with them. They weren't shown to buyers or sold. They were just used. It was the worst-case scenario for trafficking victims. Not that any of the scenarios were good, of course, but this was the bottom of the barrel.

The girls were usually sedated to keep them docile. Random men would come and use them however they wanted. No condoms. No protection. They were practically guaranteed to be infected with sexually transmitted diseases in short order.

The traffickers didn't care. They'd make their expenses on the first night.

Carver and Jessica hurried to the minivan. He pulled out of the motel parking lot and gunned the engine. The bag with their optional clothing was in the back seat. It looked like they wouldn't need it now.

"I still want to kill those assholes who took her," Jessica said. "I want to make sure they can't do this again."

Traffickers were like weeds. Killing the ones who took Sabrina would barely put a dent in overall operations. That was fine. Carver was happy to put a few tiny dents in the operation if he could.

"Okay. After we get her and make sure she's okay, we'll find them."

Jessica reached over and squeezed his hand. "Thank you. We're saving all the girls in those boxes, right?"

"Yeah." Carver was already thinking about logistics. They could fit six women into the minivan, but if they were sedated, he'd have to carry them out and strap them in. It would take time. Probably twenty minutes, depending on how hard the boxes were to open.

He wouldn't know anything until he cut the cloth off the outside of the boxes. They might be wooden. They might be polyethylene or some other kind of hardened material. They might be latched and locked, or they might be unlocked.

Without that information he couldn't make an informed guess about how long the rescue would take. He had tools that could deal with locks and latches. He had bolt cutters and the like. He had a torch too, but it would be too risky to use.

Jessica stared at the phone. She'd activated the cameras manually. "No one else has shown up yet."

"Probably won't be long." Carver checked the time. "It's nearly sundown."

"What's the plan?"

"I'll open the boxes and get the girls. You stand watch with a gun."

"Okay. Like a pistol or a rifle?"

"Whatever you're comfortable with."

"How about your MP5SD?"

"Sure."

Jessica unzipped the bag in the floorboard behind them and rummaged through it. She pulled out the submachinegun and set it next to her seat. She grabbed two magazines from the bag and set them next to her seat as well.

"You comfortable handling that?" Carver said.

She nodded. "I might be Asian, but I was still raised in Texas."

"Yeah, but you can shoot, right?"

"My friends and I went to gun ranges or out into the country to shoot." She bit her lower lip. "I'm comfortable shooting inanimate objects, but shooting people is different."

Carver reached the shopping center. He whipped around the back and pulled up to the door. He hopped out and hurried to the door. It took him a couple of seconds to jimmy open the latch. He pulled it open and rushed inside.

He assumed Jessica was standing at the corner watching for incoming. That was where they'd come from. No one would come through the front door. The traffickers and the customers would park in the back and come through the back door.

Assuming someone was doing something wasn't smart. He should have told her what to do. He should have told her not to hesitate to shoot someone if there was immediate danger. Rushing in unprepared like this was a good way to get killed.

Carver decided to take his chances and hurried to the nearest box. He ran a hand over the material covering it. It wasn't cloth like he'd thought. It was more rugged than that. It felt like a thick tarp material. That was fine. His knife would cut through it just the same.

He slashed vertically down the front then horizontally along the bottom so he could get a better look at the box. He kept cutting until he was able to slide off the tarp and expose the entire box. It was plywood. He could tell by the edges that it was just a quarter of an inch thick. That didn't seem sturdy enough to protect whatever was inside.

It might just be a protective shell. There might be something else underneath it. It might also be nailed onto a sturdy frame like two by fours. There were three latches on the side of the box. They were normal padlock latches but there were no locks, just thin wire threaded through the hole.

Carver cut the wire. He pulled it out and released the latches. He tried to open the lid but something else was holding it shut. He slid the knife under the lid and worked it up and down to pry it open.

If every box took this much effort to open, he was going to run out of time. The party organizers would show up and all hell would break loose. He wondered if having Jessica stand watch was a good idea. She wasn't trained in combat. He hadn't even shown her how to use the firing selector on the MP5.

The shop's front door rattled. Carver pulled up his mask and drew his Sig. The door opened an instant later. A young woman with green hair and multiple piercings stepped inside. A man in a suit and a woman in a nice dress stepped in after her.

Carver had already ducked into the back room. He watched for a moment before slipping out of the back door. Jessica hurried over from her position at the corner.

"What happened?"

"They came in through the front door."

She frowned. "I thought you said there was no way they'd do that."

Carver watched the camera feed on his phone.

The girl with green hair stared at the partially opened box. "I think the delivery men tried to open it!"

"Looks like it," the man in the suit said.

"I'm sorry. I need to check the goods." The girl with green hair went into the side room and returned with a small pry bar. She worked it back and forth and opened the box. She pulled out foam padding and paper and then reached in and tugged. "Stop resisting, you bitch!"

Jessica bared her teeth. "We need to go in there now!"

"Hang on." Carver put a hand on her arm.

The man stepped up to help. Together they pulled out a stiff, rigid feminine form. It wasn't alive. It had never been alive. It was a mannequin, not a human.

"Thank you." The green-haired girl looked it up and down. "I ordered these from France. They're top of the line Jean Claude Auclair creations."

"Beautiful," the other woman said.

The green-haired woman smiled and motioned toward the other mannequins in the gallery. "These are my latest creations. Please look around and tell me if there's something you'd like."

Carver turned off the camera feed. He shook his head. "I was wrong. This isn't the place."

Jessica stared blankly at him. "After all that the mission is a bust?"

"No." Carver walked across the service road to the minivan. He looked down the service road and saw several cars parked a few stores down. They hadn't been there earlier. "The party is at this address but not in this suite."

He checked Yohan's phone. A text from the party organizers had arrived just a moment ago. It gave a suite number for the address. Carver didn't need the suite number. Judging from the number of cars parked behind the shopping center, it was clear which place was hosting the sex party.

He aimed the monocular at a car that had just arrived. An older Caucasian man stepped out. He was probably in his sixties. He was overweight and walked with a slight limp. He wore gray slacks, a polo shirt, and sneakers.

He pulled out a wad of cash and gave it to someone who was standing on the other side of a dumpster. Most of the lights at the back of the shopping center weren't working. It looked like someone had shot them out, judging from the broken glass, but there was a single working streetlamp above an area where most of the cars were parked.

Jessica stood next to him. "That's the place?"

"Looks like it."

"Let's go."

Carver looked down at his cargo pants and t-shirt. He figured it was proper attire for the event. Proper enough, anyway. He watched another car pull up. Watched a middle-aged man in shorts and t-shirt walk inside.

It certainly wasn't a formal event. It looked like it was the worst-case scenario party. Probably a room full of drugged women and men having their way with them. They'd probably wonder why he showed up with a girl of his own. They might not let Jessica in.

"You'll probably have to wait outside."

"It's bad in there, isn't it?" She gripped his arm. "They're probably tied to posts or beds or something. I've seen movies about this kind of thing."

"I won't know until I see inside. It might be best if you stay out here and watch my back." He took the MP5SD from her and showed her the firing selector. "Keep this on single shot. It's better for accuracy."

She blew out a breath. "Okay."

He walked her over to a dumpster that was diagonally across the service road from the entrance. There was no sign above the back door, but Carver knew it was the nail salon they'd seen earlier.

A Vietnamese man was standing at the back door taking money from the men who went inside. Carver couldn't tell how much money they were paying the man, but it didn't look like much.

He walked straight up to the door. The doorman blinked and flinched, probably because Carver just appeared out of the darkness and not from one of the cars parked under the streetlamp.

"How much?" Carver said.

"Fifty," the man said with a heavy accent.

Carver pulled a wad of money from his pocket and counted out fifty bucks. He gave it to the man. The man knocked on the door. A metal latch slid aside with a snick and the door opened. Two large Vietnamese men stood inside.

He walked past them. He stood in a large open space, the backroom for the nail salon. The air was heavy with perfume and body odor. There were probably twenty men mostly Caucasian mingling with scantily clad Vietnamese women. He recognized some of them as the women he'd seen working in the salon earlier.

There were young women who looked old enough to be daughters and women who looked old enough to be mothers and grandmothers. The male clientele seemed interested in women of every age. A man who looked like he was in his twenties was all over a woman who was probably in her sixties.

There were small stalls with curtains along one side of the room. A man gave one of the girls money and they went into a stall. The curtain closed and it didn't require much imagination to know what happened next.

This was indeed a sex party. But it was nothing like what Carver had expected. And one thing was certain. Sabrina wasn't here. This wasn't the kind of sex party Carver had expected to find.

One of the girls approached him with a big smile on her face. "You want fun?"

"How much?"

"Good money for good fun." She bit her lower lip and rubbed his crotch. "More money, more fun." She had a strong accent. She probably didn't speak much English.

She was short, so Carver leaned down a little. "Are you here of your own free will? Are you being forced to do this?"

The girl backed away from him like he'd slapped her. She turned toward one of the big men in the room. "Hey David, we have a problem." Gone was her heavy accent, replaced by perfect English.

The man was big by Vietnamese standards, but he was two heads shorter than Carver. He put a hand on a gun at his waist. "You causing problems?" He had a heavy accent, and he probably wasn't faking it.

Carver raised his hands. "Just making sure she's not being forced into this."

"You a cop?" The man drew his weapon and held it low.

"No."

The other customers were staring at them, concern on their faces. The women were watching them too.

"It was a simple question," Carver said. "No need to get upset about it."

"It's a question cops ask," the girl said. "I don't think we can risk it. Get him out of here and shut down the venue."

"No need," Carver said. "I'll show myself out."

"I don't think so." The man raised his gun.

Carver gripped the man's wrist and squeezed. The gun dropped to the floor. He twisted the man's wrist hard and spun him around. He booted him in the back and sent him sprawling. Girls shouted in alarm. Customers panicked and ran toward the door.

The men guarding the back door were suddenly overwhelmed by the rush of clients trying to get out. Some of them stampeded over the curtain stalls, knocking them down and revealing couples in the middle of the act.

The backdoor guards pushed through the crowd, guns drawn. It was time to get out of there before the shooting started.

— • —

CHAPTER 12

Carver looked for an escape route.

He ran toward the door at the front. It was unlocked. He opened it and stepped into the nail salon proper. It was empty and closed. He went to the front door, twisted the thumb lock open, and ran outside.

He texted Jessica. *Meet me at the van.* He jogged down the sidewalk, glancing back to see if the guards were following him. They weren't. They probably had their hands full with the fleeing clientele.

Carver ran past the art gallery and the end of the building. He found Jessica waiting for him around the corner. She breathed a sigh of relief.

"What in the world happened in there? Was my sister there? Did something go wrong?"

Carver shook his head. "Your sister wasn't there. It wasn't even the right kind of party." He got into the van and cranked the engine. Turned on the air conditioner to cool down.

Jessica got in and stared at him. "What happened?"

"Nothing good." He told her what happened.

She sighed. "You did the right thing asking that girl if she was there of her own free will. I can't believe she was faking her accent."

"I guess the clients like it." He stared out the windshield. "Tonight was a complete failure."

"Yeah, but we have Plan B, right?"

Carver nodded. He unlocked Yohan's phone and scrolled to the text where the kidnappers had requested a young blonde girl. His reply to the text remained unanswered. The original request had been sent two days ago so someone might have already filled it. If they sent another request, he'd be quicker with it.

Jessica ran a hand down her face. "All that preparation for nothing. I feel like we're getting nowhere fast."

"It happens." Carver shifted into drive and headed for the motel. He wasn't an investigator. Hunting down perps wasn't his specialty. In the SEALs, someone else usually did the groundwork and someone else put the pieces together. Then they assigned resources to handle the task.

Carver had been one of those resources. They gave him a mission. He did it. They pointed him at a target, and he killed it, kidnapped it, or destroyed it. He hadn't been assigned to investigate and gather facts.

Scion had been a little different from the SEALs. He'd been tasked with gathering information from specific targets, be they human, computer or otherwise. Finding clues and solving crimes was another matter altogether.

He'd tracked down Liana, but with help from the NSA. Trying to track down Sabrina without any outside help was starting to look like a hopeless task. He needed help from someone who had more experience in the field.

Liana was still on sabbatical and hadn't returned to the NSA. Even if she had, sex trafficking wasn't exactly part of the NSA's core mission. The FBI was better suited to such investigations, but he didn't have any contacts on the inside.

He still had blackmail material on Rachel Evans, the deputy director of the NSA. He could probably use that to gain access to agency resources. But that would risk stirring up a hornet's nest. He was off their radar for now and preferred to keep it that way.

The timing was a big problem. Once twenty-four hours passed, a case like this became harder to solve. At least that was what he'd heard once from a TV show. Maybe it was true, maybe it wasn't. Maybe he should just ask a seasoned detective for advice.

He drove back to the motel and went inside. He sat on the edge of the bed and ran things back through his mind. He made a mental checklist of what they'd done and what they should do. They hadn't missed anything big. All the boxes were checked as far as he knew.

"I got a text from the people with the doorbell camera," Jessica said. "They sent a link to the footage." She sat down next to him and showed him the video of the incident.

It went down how Carver thought it had. The Cadillac rear-ended Sabrina's car. She got out, looked at her bumper, and then went to the car that hit her. The back door opened. A man got out and yanked her inside.

"It happened so fast." Jessica replayed it over and over again. "She never had a chance. Hell, I never would have had a chance when I was her age." She took the phone to her laptop and copied the URL to the video.

She downloaded it from the cloud and paused when the man stepped out of the car. She used her software to analyze his face. "This is the second guy. I'll add the new images to the search."

Carver sat back on the bed and watched her work. She seemed to lose awareness of anything else around her while she manipulated the image and pulled slightly grainy footage into sharper focus.

After Sabrina was yanked into the back seat by the man, the Cadillac backed up then steered around her car and turned right. The video ended a few seconds later. Jessica buried her face in her hands and seemed to deflate.

She turned to face Carver. "I don't know what to do except sit back and wait."

"Start the video over again," Carver said. "Maybe we missed something."

"We didn't miss anything."

"Play it again."

Jessica dragged the mouse cursor to the play button and clicked it. The video started when Sabrina's car triggered the motion sensor. The Cadillac came up behind her seconds later. Only Sabrina's silhouette was visible in the car.

She opened the door. The interior light blinked on, casting her in shadow. The windows on the Cadillac were blacked out with a dark tint. When the back door opened, the Cadillac's interior light didn't come on. If not for the streetlamp, the man's face wouldn't have been visible when he stepped out to grab Sabrina.

"Again," Carver said. "Half speed."

"I would have seen anything important."

"It's not like we have anything better to do."

Jessica replayed it at half speed. Sabrina pulled up to the stop sign. The Cadillac hit her. The reverse lights on Sabrina's Toyota flashed as she put it into park. Light reflected off a bumper sticker.

Sabrina got out of her car in slow motion.

"Pause it," Carver said.

Jessica paused it. "What?"

"Back it up four seconds."

She backed it up four seconds.

"Play it back at quarter speed."

Jessica played it. The Toyota stopped. The Cadillac bumped it. It was hardly more than a nudge. The Cadillac backed up a couple of inches. It was less than a foot away from the Toyota. Sabrina's silhouette moved as she put the car in park.

The reverse lights flashed. Light reflected off the bumper sticker.

"Pause it."

Jessica paused it. The reverse lights were still on. The light from them was reflecting off of something on the Cadillac and onto the silver bumper sticker on the Toyota.

Carver got up and sat next to Jessica at the computer. He pointed to the bumper sticker. "That light isn't coming from the Cadillac's headlights. The cars are too close."

"The light is reflecting from a surface on the Cadillac." Jessica zoomed in on the reflection. "The bumper sticker is also slightly reflective." She cropped the image and ran it through a filter. "I'm glad the doorbell camera is ten-eighty p resolution. Otherwise, this would be way too blurry."

Carver knew what 1080p was. It used to be considered high definition. Things had progressed significantly to 4K and 8K resolutions, but most security cams hadn't gone above 1080p mainly because of battery life and storage limitations.

Jessica watched the image sharpen pixel by pixel. The source of the reflection from the Cadillac became visible. It was the front license plate. It was white with black lettering. Two letters and two numbers were visible. They were blurry, but legible.

Jessica gasped. She jumped up and raised her hands above her head. "We have a plate number!"

"A partial," Carver said. "Coupled with the car type that shouldn't be too hard to narrow down." He shook his head. "We'd need someone with DMV access to plug it into a computer and put an APB on it too."

Jessica sobered quickly. "So, it doesn't really matter if we have the plate or not."

"It matters, but we need someone on the inside to help us."

She blew out a breath. "A local cop."

"Yep."

Jessica drummed her fingers on the desk. "Maybe they've assigned someone by now."

"It's possible." Carver took off his shoes and socks. "We'll go to the station in the morning and ask to talk to someone. Give them the info we have."

"Okay. But what if they don't have anyone who can help us?"

"We'll figure it out." Carver pulled off his shirt and went into the bathroom to take a shower. "Best thing to do is get some sleep."

She stood up and stared at the computer screen. "What do you think Sabrina is going through right now?"

"Nothing good."

Jessica looked at him. "You're supposed to reassure me."

"Am I?"

She blew out a breath. Stared at the laptop for a long moment. Closed the lid. "I feel so powerless."

"We're doing what we can."

"I know." She ran a hand down her face. "I feel like a hypocrite. I hardly even know my little sister. I don't even have a good relationship with her. But I feel horrible. I feel guilty."

"She's your sister," Carver said. "Doesn't matter if you love or hate her, you want to save her."

"Yeah." She nodded to herself. "I feel like she's the favorite daughter and it's going to destroy my parents if I don't save her."

"You don't have to explain yourself to me." Carver shrugged. "I won't judge you."

"I think I'm explaining it to myself more than anything." She walked over to him and hugged him. Pressed her face against his bare chest. "Thank you."

Carver patted her back. He wasn't very good at consoling people, but patting a back wasn't too hard.

Jessica looked up at him with big eyes and smiled. "You're horrible at making someone feel better, you know?"

"Yep."

She sighed. "I'm going to take a shower and go to bed."

"Okay." Carver had been going to take a shower first, but he didn't mind waiting. He lay down on the bed and looked at his texts. Still no reply to his text he'd sent the traffickers. They must have already found a woman matching the requested description.

Jessica didn't take long in the shower. He cleaned off after she was done and went to bed. She curled up next to him and went to sleep without so much as a good night. He couldn't blame her. She was probably emotionally and physically spent after all they'd done today.

###

The next morning after breakfast they went to the police station. There were several different precincts listed on the map, but they went to the main headquarters downtown. Carver figured the odds of finding someone to talk to were higher there.

He didn't much like walking into a building with lots of cameras and ways to record and take pictures of him, but there wasn't much choice.

The station was a big building that dominated a couple of city blocks. There was a tall black iron fence around it and multiple gates around the perimeter. The fence didn't look particularly hard to scale because the top was flat. There was no razor wire, no spikes, not even a curve at the top to keep people out.

Then again, most people weren't looking to break into a police station. Carver wasn't most people. He thought about breaking into places a lot. Not because he was necessarily planning on doing it, but it was always good to know a building's weaknesses just in case.

He counted four exterior cameras around the front entrance. A person could circumvent them by climbing the fence on the side of the building and hugging the wall to the entrance. There were two cameras guarding the service entrance at the back and cameras watching the entrances to the attached parking deck.

He stopped across the street from the parking deck and pegged it as the best way in. There was a ten-foot gap between the top of the deck and the roof to one section of the building. There were stairs leading to large air-conditioning units and a maintenance door.

Jessica paced alongside him as he continued prowling the perimeter. "Are you always this thorough before you go into a building?"

"I like to know my options before exposing myself to the cops." Carver continued to the front of the building. "Maybe things will go smoothly or maybe someone at the NSA decided to leak my picture to law enforcement to make life difficult for me."

"Do you really think Rachel Evans would do that?"

"Maybe not her. Maybe someone else who's not a fan of my work." Carver walked across the road. He went up the stairs to the courtyard in front of the police station and went through the front doors to the main lobby.

The lobby was cramped and lined with the kind of seats usually found in airport terminals. These didn't have cushioning. They were hard vinyl. Most of the seats were taken. There were tired-looking mothers with children running around, women who looked like they lived hard lives on the street, and a smattering of old men and young boys who looked like they were waiting on someone.

Carver went to the front desk. A woman behind bulletproof glass looked from him to Jessica as if trying to piece together what brought them in to bother her today. She pressed a button to activate the mic and speaker built into the window.

"How can I help you?"

Jessica spoke. "We have important information about my sister's kidnapping. We need to talk to a detective."

The woman tapped on her computer keyboard. "Which detective is assigned to the case?"

"I don't know."

"Name?"

"The kidnapped girl is Sabrina Sato. I'm her sister, Jessica."

The woman typed on the keyboard for a moment. She stared at the screen. "It was assigned to Detective Piker. Let me see if they're available."

Jessica looked surprised. "Thank you." She turned to Carver. "I had no idea they finally assigned someone."

The receptionist tapped on her earpiece and spoke for a moment. She glanced at Jessica and nodded a couple of times. She passed a clipboard through the slot at the bottom of the window. "Fill out the visitor forms. They'll be down in a moment."

They filled out the forms. It didn't ask for an ID, but Carver didn't use an alias. He didn't have a bulletproof fake ID and didn't feel like risking it. But he used messy handwriting so his last name looked like Carter instead of Carver.

The receptionist took the completed forms and handed them back generic visitors passes a moment later. Carver was surprised a place like this didn't print passes with names on them. Then again, if the budget cuts to the department had been severe enough, maybe this was one way they saved money.

There was a steel door with a card reader on the left side of the room. There was another similar door on the right side of the receptionist desk. Having walked the perimeter of the building, Carver figured the one on the right led to the rear parking deck and the service entrance.

He watched the door on the left because it was connected to the three-story section of the building. That was almost certainly where the detective would come from. He looked for a seat, but the only open ones were right next to a woman with four kids that were running wild around her.

Carver opted to stand against the wall.

Jessica stood next to him and stared at the others in the room. "What do you think they're waiting on?"

"Probably a family member who was brought in for one reason or another." Carver shrugged. "Just a guess."

The metal door opened a moment later and a woman pushed through it. She narrowed her eyes and looked around the room. She had short hair, a round face, and the rosy skin of someone who either drank too much or smoked.

She wore jeans, a dark oxford, and a suit jacket that didn't match either. Her gaze swept across the room but never made it to the wall where Carver stood. She wasn't wearing a badge on her shirt, but Carver pegged her as a detective. Probably Detective Piker.

Jessica started to move, but Carver put a hand on her arm. "Just wait a minute."

The woman obviously wasn't finding what she was looking for. The receptionist had probably given her a physical description. Someone like Carver would stand out. She finally looked all the way to her right and saw Carver.

She didn't smile or say hello. She just waved them over. "Follow me."

Carver looked for a badge under the jacket but didn't see it. "Detective Piker?"

She stepped into the hallway and let the door close behind them. "Yes, I'm Piker."

"Thank you for seeing us," Jessica said. "We have some important information—"

Piker waved off whatever she was going to say next. "Are you a detective?"

Jessica paused. Shook her head. "No."

"Have you been trained in investigative techniques? Do you know how to question possible witnesses?"

Jessica frowned. "Why are you—"

Piker scowled. "I need you to go home and stop trying to play detective. You and your boyfriend here obviously think you know what it takes to be a cop but all you're doing is getting in the way and confusing a lot of people. So, I want you to go home and let the professionals do their jobs."

She opened the door and motioned them out. "Now, go home!"

CHAPTER 13

Carver didn't budge.

"We have a partial license plate and video."

Piker stared at them. "I gave you an order."

"An order?" Jessica stared back at her. "We don't work for you. You're supposed to be helping us find my sister!"

"All we need is a license plate check," Carver said. "Then we'll be out of your hair."

Piker scowled. "Do you know what it's like to question possible witnesses after a couple of amateurs have already tainted their testimony? Do you know what it's like having everyone ask why I'm questioning them when they think the cops have already been by?"

"We never told them we were cops," Jessica said. "I was told that no detective was available to take the case, so I took matters into my own hands. This is my sister we're talking about!"

Piker looked Carver up and down. "I suppose you think you're qualified, don't you? Are you one of those testosterone-fueled steroid junkies who thinks he can do anything?"

It was obvious the detective was extremely territorial. She seemed to take great offense to civilians doing her work. It wasn't the first time Carver had seen someone fly off the handle when someone else stepped onto their perceived territory.

He tried an approach that sometimes worked. He held up his hands. "Hey, I'm sorry. I guess I'm being that guy. But we did get lucky and got a partial license plate. We can give it to you and get out of your way. You're the expert."

Piker's gaze cooled slightly. "Give it to me and I'll see what I can find out. But don't expect me to share the information."

"Just as long as you can use it to find the bastards." Jessica trembled with anger. "Do you want me to write it down?"

"Yes. Let's go to my office." Piker let the security door close and walked down the hallway. She took them into an elevator and hit the button for the third floor. They rode up in silence.

Jessica gripped Carver's hand tight. It wasn't the grip of someone looking for support. It was the grip of someone trying not to punch a police detective. Carver understood completely. People like this detective were everywhere in the military. He'd done his best to avoid them whenever possible.

The elevator opened. There was a receptionist desk with two dark-haired women behind it. Carver couldn't help but note they were both very attractive and both dressed in body conforming dresses.

They smiled brightly at Piker.

One of them spoke with a heavy Spanish accent. "Hello, Detective Piker. Can I get you coffee or anything?"

"Aw, Carla, you're so sweet. Maybe in a few minutes." Piker leaned against the desk and openly stared at the other woman's cleavage. "You look very nice today. Dark blue suits you." She smiled at the other woman. "I like the red on you too, Flora."

Flora smiled but it looked a little forced. "Gracias, Miss Piker."

"That's thank you, Special Detective Piker," Piker said. "I might have to give you some private English lessons later."

"Thank you Special Detective Piker." Flora struggled with the pronunciation.

Jessica frowned and looked from one woman to the other. Then Piker walked past the desk, and she followed her.

They walked into the hallway behind the receptionist desk. There was another receptionist desk at the foot of a short flight of stairs. There were two attractive Latina women sitting behind it. A big metal sign next to the door at the top said, *Commissioner Linda Reid.*

There were several offices with the names of special detectives on the doors, an office for a police lieutenant, and one for a police captain. Carver had seen the inside of a lot of police stations. Most detectives had desks, but they were out in the open. Usually only the administrators were given offices.

Maybe these special detectives were the only ones with offices. Maybe the regular detectives were on the second floor in a shared space. Maybe Austin just did things differently. It was hard to know without seeing more of the building.

Piker's office had a sign on the door that read *Special Detective Quinn Piker.* Apparently, she was one of the top dogs in the detective department. Maybe the best of the best. Or maybe just someone who knew how to kiss ass. In government it usually wasn't what you knew, it was who you knew that got you into good positions.

Piker went behind her large wooden desk and dropped heavily into the leather seat. Jessica and Carver sat down on the leather couch across from the desk.

Piker clasped her hands on the desk and smiled at them. It wasn't a friendly smile. It was a condescending smirk. "Tell me what you have besides this partial plate number."

"A video of the incident." Jessica opened the video on her phone and turned it toward Piker.

Piker motioned her over. "Bring it to me."

Jessica stood and brought it to her. Piker took the phone and watched it. She tapped on the phone, probably to watch it again. She grunted. "Modern forensics already told me how it went down. The video is good supporting evidence that I would have gathered. I take it this is from someone's security camera?"

"Yes, a doorbell cam."

Piker pursed her lips. She typed something on the phone. "I opened your email app and entered my email address. Send me the video and anything else you have."

"Okay." Jessica took the phone back. She added several files to the email including the picture of the license plate. She tapped the send button. "Okay, it's sent."

"Good." Piker's condescending smile returned. "Now what you've just sent me is evidence."

Jessica looked confused. "Okay."

"It's not the kind of evidence you think it is," Piker said. "Sure, there's evidence of a crime that we will look into, but there's also evidence of another crime. Obstruction of an official investigation."

"I'm sorry, what?" Jessica jolted up from the couch. "Obstruction? All we've done is help!"

"Official investigations don't just happen, little lady. They take time to start. You and your guy here jumped the gun. You spoke to witnesses and tainted their testimony. You took official evidence as if you were working in an official capacity."

Piker rose from behind her desk. "You not only obstructed an official investigation, but you impersonated officers of the law."

"We did no such thing!" Jessica shouted. "What the hell is wrong with you?"

Piker smirked. "I'm just letting you know that if you stick your noses into official police business again, you will both be getting a jail cell." She paused as if for effect, looking from Jessica to Carver. "Am I clear?"

Jessica raised a fist. "You piece of—"

Carver stood and gripped her arm. "Let's go."

She stared at him in confusion. "Are you kidding me? I'm reporting this so-called detective to her bosses."

"Go ahead." Piker crossed her arms. "Try it."

"Let's go." Carver put an arm around Jessica's shoulder and steered her for the door.

Piker stood there and watched them. "That's right. Go."

"What the hell, Carver?" Jessica wormed free but kept walking toward the elevator. "Something's wrong with that woman!"

Carver looked into the other offices as they walked. They were dark and empty. Aside from the four receptionists, there didn't seem to be anyone else up here. He paused next to the receptionist desk.

"Is the commissioner in today?"

Carla looked uncertainly at him. "I'm sorry, sir. I cannot give you this information."

Carver turned to Flora and spoke in Spanish. "Have you worked here long?"

Flora smiled and shook her head. She answered in Spanish. "No, sir. I am with a special work program."

Carla reached over and squeezed the other woman's leg. Carver could see it because of his height. Flora winced and stopped talking. The two women smiled uncomfortably at him and remained silent.

"You're here of your own free will?"

Carla didn't answer right away. She forced a smile and nodded. "Yes. Of course."

"Thank you," Carver said. "Have a good day." He went to the elevator and punched the down button.

Piker came out of her office. "Flora, honey, come see me right now, okay?"

Flora turned at the sound of her name but looked confused. Carla said something too quietly for Carver to hear. Flora abruptly stood and brushed off her dress even though it was clean. She walked toward Piker's office and went inside. The door closed behind her and the blinds snapped shut.

The elevator door opened. Carver and Jessica stepped inside. She hit the lobby button. "Carver, what in the hell is going on in this place?"

Carver looked at the camera in the upper right-hand corner of the elevator. "Business as usual." He hit the second-floor button, and the elevator stopped. The doors opened to a large room with lots of desks positioned head-to-head with each other.

There were no offices to be seen. Just a wide-open area cluttered with desks, filing cabinets, and extra chairs. There were plain-clothed detectives at most of the desks, and officers in uniform at others.

Carver figured there had to be a hundred desks jammed into the space. More than half of them had nothing on them. No file organizers, no random paperwork, and no personal effects. They looked empty and unused. Some of them had piles of folders on them, but they were probably overflow stacks from other detectives using whatever real estate they could.

He looked around and spotted a man just past his prime. A man with gray in his hair, wrinkles on his face, and a no-nonsense expression. He was staring intently at a spread of papers on his desk and slowly sorting through them.

Carver walked right across the room like he was supposed to be there. Jessica followed his lead. He glanced at the name plate on the desk. *Detective Frank Hancock.* The man seemed to sense someone was coming and looked up when Carver was a few desks away.

"Hello, Detective Hancock. We were told to come to you and give you some evidence for a case."

Hancock rose and extended his hand. "And you are?"

"Carver." Carver shook his hand and noted the firm and calloused grip. Hancock wasn't a desk jockey.

"I'm Jessica." Jessica extended her hand and Hancock shook it.

"All right, have a seat." He sat down and leaned back in his seat. "I wasn't told about anyone bringing me evidence. If I'm being honest, they've been winding down my case load because I'm retiring in two months."

"Oh, they didn't tell us." Carver shrugged. "We have a video and a partial license plate. I guess they figured you'd want it."

Hancock nodded. "All right. Give me what you got."

Jessica showed him the video. "This is my sister, Sabrina, being kidnapped."

He watched it intently, his face growing grave. He backed it up and watched it again. "I'm sorry, Miss. That must be real hard for you to watch."

"It is, but it's evidence that could help you, right?"

Hancock gathered the papers spread on his desk and neatly stacked them and put them in a folder. "I don't recall being assigned to this case. I'll need to talk to the duty officer first so I can get my bearings. I'm truly sorry I haven't reached out to you or your family yet. I must have missed the case assignment."

"Can you look up this license plate?" Carver wrote down the partial and description of the car on a sticky note and handed it to him. "That would at least get us on the right track."

Hancock looked from Carver to Jessica and back to Carver. He leaned back in his seat and steepled his fingers. "I see what this is. I haven't been assigned a case, have I?"

Carver shook his head. "No. But we need your help."

Hancock nodded. "The victim's family hired you to help them because we haven't been responsive, have we?"

"More or less," Carver said. "I'm helping for free."

"Well, that's mighty fine of you, Mr. Carver."

"Just Carver is fine."

Hancock blew out a breath and sighed. "I have been strictly forbidden from helping any private investigators. The higher-ups claim it makes us look bad. But what makes us really look bad is this."

He waved a hand toward the empty desks around the room. "We've been at maybe thirty-three percent of capacity for years now, but they haven't hired a single replacement in all that time."

"Look, we just want to find my sister," Jessica said. "We're desperate, okay?"

"I understand." Hancock typed on his computer. "But I have been strictly forbidden from helping you." He kept typing. "They threatened to take away my pension if I did."

"I'm sorry to hear that, but we need help." Tears filled Jessica's eyes. "Please help us, Detective Hancock."

"My best friend Ray Ferguson retired three months ago." Hancock stared at his computer screen. "He had a real nice nest egg saved up. He and his wife were finally going to tour the world like they wanted."

He looked away from the computer screen. "They died in a car wreck on the way to the airport."

Jessica wiped her tears away. "That's horrible, but I don't know what that has to do with my sister."

"He was a real good man." Hancock bit his lower lip. "The best of us." He hit a button and the old printer on his desk hummed to life. "He was also a real jokester. He loved to play tricks on us. He would find out the login of other officers and file fake cases with them."

Hancock laughed. "He had Mike Johnson believing he was supposed to arrest a party clown. Can you believe it?"

Jessica shook her head. "I don't know why you're telling me this."

Hancock pulled the printout from the printer and gave it to her. "No reason. But he sure had the login information for a lot of detectives. A lot of them have long since resigned or moved on, but it's nice being able to login to the various computer systems as them so nobody knows it's me."

Jessica looked at the printout. Her eyes widened. "Is that what you did?"

He nodded and handed her a business card. "Now, I don't know what's happening with your case, but I will ask around. Maybe I can get someone assigned to it. It probably won't be me, though."

"I have a confession to make," Carver said. "We were taken upstairs and reamed out by Detective Piker."

Hancock scowled. "Understood. In that case, I won't be making any inquiries. I wish I could do more, but my hands are tied."

"We don't want you to get in trouble," Jessica said.

"I appreciate that." Hancock stood and walked around the desk. He smiled kindly at her. "I really wish there was more I could do, but the higher-ups just tell us to put on a happy face and toe the company line."

"Not surprising," Carver said.

Hancock gave him a business card with a handwritten number on the back. "That's my private cell if you need any other under the table assistance."

"Thank you." Carver took it. Carver didn't usually take to people easily, but this old timer seemed okay.

"You're welcome."

Jessica hugged him. "Thank you."

He patted her back. "You hang in there, okay? If I hear anything else, I'll try to pass it along."

She backed away from him. "I appreciate that."

Carver walked back to the elevator. Jessica handed him the printout. It had a name and address on it. Specifically, the name and address for the owner of the Cadillac.

They were back in business.

CHAPTER 14

Carver and Jessica left the building.

Sticking around wasn't a good idea. If Piker found out they'd detoured to the second floor, she'd probably have them thrown in jail. They went to the minivan and got inside. It felt like it was a hundred degrees in the cabin. Carver turned on the engine and blasted the AC.

He took the printout from Jessica and studied it. The first page was a list of vehicles matching the partial tag number. Only one of them was a gold Cadillac DeVille. The second page had the registration for the car.

There was a lot of information on the registration, but the only parts that mattered were the name and address. Carver plugged the address into the GPS. It was a thirty-minute drive. There was just one problem. The name on the registration wasn't a man's name. It wasn't even a Hispanic name.

Jessica took the registration back and shook her head. "Who's Ramona Brennan?"

"Might be the wife of one of the men. Might not even be connected to them. The car might be stolen." Carver pulled onto the road and followed the GPS. The destination was just five miles away, but traffic was going to make it a crawl.

The route took them to the northeast part of town. There were a lot of new houses in the area. A lot of big houses. Some of the original homes were still there. They were tiny shoebox houses with vinyl siding and narrow driveways. Most of them had probably been torn down to make way for the wave of gentrification.

Jessica looked at her phone and whistled. She pointed to the for-sale sign in the yard of one of the original homes. "They're asking five hundred thousand. There's an open lot down the road going for even more. That's insane."

Carver didn't know or care much about home prices. He slowed down and parked in front of one of the original homes with the for-sale sign in front. He took out his monocular and aimed it toward the address on the Cadillac registration.

The home on the property was definitely a rebuild. It was two stories tall with painted brick and an entrance that looked like a castle tower. It had a nice green lawn and a black iron fence guarding it. The driveway was long and wide with a motorized gate keeping out unwanted visitors.

Some of the homes had similar fences and gates and others didn't. Carver figured the gated homes had been built when the neighborhood still had most of the original homes and inhabitants. Recent newcomers probably trusted their wealthy neighbors and didn't feel the need to build a fence.

At least, that was Carver's theory.

He looked at the cars parked in the driveways of the nicer homes. One home had a Jeep Wrangler, a Dodge Ram TRX, and a Tesla Model X. Another home had two Audis and a BMW SUV in the front.

A large home next door had an aging Toyota Camry and a minivan. Another had no cars parked in the driveway because they were probably inside the three-car garage. There was a wide variety of visible vehicles, some luxury class and others economy class.

Some people might have all their money tied up in their expensive house, so they had to get a cheaper car. It was possible that Ramona was in the latter category and had an older Cadillac since she couldn't afford anything newer.

Who was she to the kidnappers? A wife? A relative? A girlfriend? About the only way to answer that question was by knocking on the front door and asking. Breaking in and searching the house would work too, but this would be faster.

Carver got out of the minivan and crossed the road.

Jessica walked alongside him. "What's the plan?"

"We knock on the front door."

"What about the gate?"

"There's a callbox on the side." Carver walked up to the callbox and pressed the doorbell button.

"Hello?" A female voice crackled over the speaker.

"We're here to ask about a Cadillac DeVille," Carver said. "Is this Ramona?"

"No." She went silent for a moment. "Have you located her?"

Carver glanced at Jessica. "No. May we speak to you in person?"

There was a hum and gate rolled slowly to the side. Carver and Jessica stepped through and went to the front door. Latches scraped open and the door swung inward. A middle-aged woman stood on the other side.

"I'm Carver and this is Jessica."

The woman didn't offer to shake hands. She looked from one to the other and nodded. "What's this about?"

It seemed best to keep details to a minimum until Carver knew more about the situation. "We're looking for Ramona to ask her about her gold 1994 Cadillac DeVille. Judging from your response it sounds like you don't know where she is."

"No, I don't." The woman sighed. "What has she done now?"

"Ma'am, I don't know of any wrongdoing by her. We just know that some men were driving her car recently."

"Are you cops?"

Carver shook his head. "No." The woman had the defeated posture and attitude of a parent who felt like they'd failed at parenting and had given up on the child. Carver had met plenty of parents like this.

Most were rich. Most raised their kids by proxy with nannies or other surrogates. Most thought money could give them freedom from raising children while also raising their children. It was the sort of absentee parenting that a lot of wealthy families indulged in only to find out that their children had turned into spoiled little monsters.

Maybe he was wrong, but he probably wasn't. He didn't much care if Ramona was like that, but he most certainly wanted her current whereabouts. He already had a clear visual on how the Cadillac had ended up in the hands of the kidnappers.

Carver pulled up a picture of one of the kidnappers. "Did you ever see her around this man?"

The woman's eyes widened slightly. "No."

He showed her the picture of the man driving the Cadillac through the gas station parking lot. "That's her car. He must have met her at some point."

"I-I've never seen him before."

It was a lie. The woman barely kept her face straight when she said it and her voice wavered.

"I'm looking for these men, not your daughter. You don't need to protect her from us. We just want to find the men."

"I'm sorry, but I can't answer your questions." The woman closed the door.

Carver put his foot out and stopped it.

The woman's eyes flared. "Go away! Get off my property!"

Carver pushed his way inside. He grabbed the woman by the arm and motioned Jessica inside. Jessica had already followed him in and closed the door.

"She's lying like crazy," Jessica said. "She knows something."

"Yep."

"I don't know anything!" The woman tried to jerk her arm free. "Let me go or I'll scream!"

Carver guided her through the foyer and into the den. He pushed her down on the couch. "Go ahead. Scream."

She didn't scream.

This house didn't have an open floor plan, but it didn't really need it. The den was huge. The ceiling was probably twenty feet high with stained wooden beams. A large chandelier hung from a black iron chain. The fireplace was all natural stone.

Jessica walked through the doorway to the kitchen. She came back with a pile of mail and dumped it on a coffee table. She held up a piece of junk mail, the kind that looked like a newspaper. "Fran Coker."

She kept sorting the mail and held up what looked like a bill. "This is to Martin Coker." She looked through the others. "No other names. Just Fran and Martin Coker."

Carver stared down at Fran. "Ramona is from another marriage?"

Fran folded her arms and stared sullenly back at him. "I'm going to call the cops and you're going to spend a very long time in jail."

Carver nodded at the cell phone in her hand. "There's the phone. Do it."

She didn't do it. She bit her lower lip and dropped the phone at her side. "What in the hell do you want? Who are you?"

Jessica pulled up the video of the kidnapping on her phone and showed her screen to Carver. "May I?"

Carver nodded.

"My sister was kidnapped by the men using your daughter's car." Jessica showed her the video. "We want to find them. We don't care about your daughter."

Fran watched dispassionately. Like she'd seen something like that a dozen times. "She's not my daughter. She's Martin's. Martin and Ramona's mother split up when Ramona was four. I met Martin when she was five. She was already a spoiled little brat by then and it only got worse."

"She got angry and bored," Carver said. "She spoke out, got in trouble at school."

"Yes, exactly." Fran laughed hollowly. "You have a child of your own?"

"No, but I know how the story goes. She fell in with some bad people and you haven't heard from her in a while, right?"

"She became involved in an activist group that wanted to stop the use of oil. She and others would block streets and get arrested like clockwork. The cops never pressed charges, though, because the local politicians didn't want to look bad for going against climate activists." Fran shrugged. "It slowly spiraled out of control from there. She traveled the country with different groups basically taking up any cause that came her way."

Fran sighed and rolled her eyes. "Martin kept that old Cadillac because it was the first luxury car he ever owned. It was a personal collector's item for him. She knew the combination to his office safe and took the ten thousand dollars he had inside. She also took the car title, forged his signature on the back, and transferred it to her name so he couldn't claim it was stolen."

Jessica shook her head. "She sounds like a real nice person."

"Oh, she knew taking that Cadillac would hit Martin right where it counted. He was furious and devastated at the same time when he found out." Fran looked down at her hands. "That was months ago. We haven't seen her since."

Jessica frowned. "How did he not notice all the money and title missing?"

"He rarely opens that safe. It's just a place where he stores keepsakes and a little bit of emergency cash."

"Where is Martin now?"

"He's in California finalizing the process of relocating his few remaining businesses from San Francisco and Los Angeles to Austin."

Jessica nodded. "So, you're transplants from California?"

"Yes. We moved here several years ago to escape the taxes and congestion. It's taken several years to move the businesses though."

"Do you have any idea where Ramona might be or any way of finding out?"

Fran shook her head. "She might have sold the car or given it away for all I know."

"Does she have any close friends who might know her whereabouts?"

"I have no idea. I tried to befriend her when I married her father, but she hated me then and hates me now." Fran bit her lower lip. "I just stayed out of her way, you know?"

"Would Martin know anything?"

"No, but his ex might. She got two of their houses, alimony, and a lot of money in the divorce." Fran waved a hand around the house. "That's why we're still slumming it years later."

"This is slumming?" Jessica laughed without humor. "What are his other houses like?"

"Bigger." Fran waved it off. "Anyway, his ex, Delilah, is living it up in California. I can give you her number if you want to ask about her spoiled little bitch of a daughter."

Jessica frowned. "Is Brennan her mother's maiden name?"

Fran nodded. "Yes."

"I assume Ramona uses social media," Carver said.

"Oh, of course. My God she didn't go a moment without recording her every little feeling in a video and posting it on the internet."

"I don't suppose you're connected to any of her accounts, are you?"

"Heavens no." Fran scoffed. "I just don't want her legal troubles to spill over onto us, okay?"

And there it was, the honest truth. That was why she'd been so reluctant to talk about it in the first place.

"Look, Martin's divorce from Delilah cost him a lot of money. It ruined two of his successful businesses because he foolishly gave her a controlling interest in two of them back when they were so in love." Fran said the last part with a healthy dose of sarcasm.

Carver held up a hand. "It's okay, we don't need to hear anything else. Whatever happens, we promise not to get Ramona in trouble if we can help it. In return for that, you need to let us know if you find out anything in the meantime."

"You know what? I'm fine if you get Ramona in trouble." Fran ran her hand down her face. "Maybe it would be good if she had to do hard time. All she ever does is make trouble. She does everything she can to make our lives miserable."

"We just want to find my sister," Jessica said. "Before it's too late."

Fran managed to look a little sympathetic. "I'm sorry about your sister. If I come across any information that might be useful, I'll contact you."

Carver gave her his burner phone number. "Thanks. We'll leave now." He and Jessica walked to the front door.

"Wait!" Fran caught up to them. "I think I have one thing that might help." She went up the tall stone staircase and vanished into an arched hallway on the right. She returned moments later with a tablet computer and handed it to Carver.

Carver tapped on the screen, but the device was dead.

"It just needs charging," Fran said. "Ramona has a dozen of these things."

"It looks ancient," Jessica said. "Why are you giving us this one?"

"Because it's so old that it doesn't have a passcode or any security." She nodded at it. "Once you charge it, you should have access to her social media accounts."

Jessica took it and looked at the bottom. "Wow, I haven't seen that kind of charge port in a while."

"Hold on." Fran vanished upstairs again and returned a few minutes later with a tangle of cords. "One of these works."

Jessica extracted a cable with a wide plug on the end. "This is it." She took a charging block from another cable. "Thank you, Fran. This could be very helpful."

"You're welcome. Just try to keep our names out of this." Fran looked worried. "Someone tried to sue us because of things Ramona did, and Martin's named got dragged in the mud because of other incidents. We just want to avoid all of that."

"We just want my sister back." Jessica squeezed her hand. "I promise."

"Okay." Fran smiled weakly. "Good luck."

"Thank you."

Carver turned to leave but Fran grabbed his arm. She stood on her tiptoes and pulled on his arm. He leaned down because it was clear she wanted to say something.

She got close to his ear and whispered. "If she is in with bad people and something happens to her, that would be better for the family. It might be worth some money." She released his arm.

Carver nodded but said nothing. He and Jessica left. They went to the van.

Jessica stared at him. "What did she say to you?"

"That she wouldn't mind if Ramona stopped breathing." Carver started the car. "She hinted that allowing something to happen to Ramona might be worth something."

"My God." Jessica shuddered. "I would say she's evil, but I'm not sure I blame her, given what Ramona has put them through."

Carver plugged the tablet charger to the same 12 volt to USB adapter he used for the wireless cameras. They didn't have anything else to do except wait for it to charge, so they went back to the motel.

By then, the tablet was charged enough to start. They took it inside and plugged it into an AC outlet since that would charge it faster.

Jessica turned on the tablet and waited for it to start up. The main screen was filled with icons. There were icons belonging to social media apps Carver had heard of, and icons for apps he was unfamiliar with.

Jessica tapped on several of them. Some had automatically logged out after not being used on the device for a long time. She was able to use cached passwords to log into some of them, but others required two-factor authentication, including two of the most popular apps.

"Damn it!" Jessica blew out a breath and looked at Ramona's profiles on the apps she'd been able to access.

There was nothing recent on any of them. She started going through the other less popular apps. One called RingRang finally had something recent. In fact, it looked like she posted frequently to it.

Right at the top of her profile was a picture of a girl in her early twenties. She had red hair and fair skin. Her hair was tangled into dreadlocks. She had a nose ring and multiple other piercings. She had colored feathers clipped to her dreads. She was posing with a helmet and what looked like a riot shield.

Jessica wrinkled her nose. "God, she could be so pretty if she got rid of all that metal."

Carver read the caption under the picture. "Gearing up to fight for our fellow humans. Notify us on ICE Block if you see any criminal government activity, and we'll be there."

"What the hell is ICE Block?" Jessica said.

Carver searched the internet and found it. "It's an app that people use as an early warning system for when immigration and customs enforcement is coming. It looks like Ramona and others will show up to those locations to block officers."

"Are you serious? Won't they get arrested for that?"

"I don't know. What I do know is that now we can find her." He downloaded the app and looked at it. "All we have to do is watch for a notification to pop up and we go to that location. Odds are, she'll show up."

"Oh my God, you're right." Jessica stared at the screen. "Do you think she'll know who has her Cadillac?"

"No idea," Carver said.

But he was going to find out.

CHAPTER 15

Carver watched and waited.

The app tracked all notifications nationwide and categorized them by region. He filtered results to show only local notifications. There were dozens of them for the area, but they'd become less frequent over the last week.

Even so, it looked like it averaged two alerts a day, so they were bound to get something. The only question was whether Ramona and gang would show up.

Jessica pored through all the apps. She downloaded pictures of Ramona and fed them to her search engine. "She doesn't share location in her videos. She's smart enough to know that law enforcement can find her that way."

She turned to her computer and typed on the keyboard. "She uses RingRang a lot because it's a new app and apparently is very popular with the activist crowds. She's also active on Shoutout for the same reason. Using her account, I'm also indexing all the pictures her friends take. Maybe we'll get lucky and get an identifiable location from one of those pictures."

Carver studied the ICE Block app. Apparently, it allowed anyone with the app to create an alert that immigration officers had been spotted. It was as simple as long-pressing on the map and then typing in a description. A notification would go out to anyone else with the app.

They might not have to wait for a new alert at all. They could simply create one of their own and have Ramona and gang come to them. Of course, all it would take was a cursory look for them to realize ICE wasn't in the vicinity. They might drive past and never stop.

He looked at the local news to see where immigration had been most recently. It looked like they went to big box hardware stores and places where day laborers gathered. He looked at the location history in the ICE Block app. Alerts had gone out for many of those places.

According to the news, many of the usual hangouts for the undocumented were now being avoided. That was why the number of alerts had dropped so quickly. The underground community had either abandoned the area or were finding new places to wait for work.

Carver searched for other hardware stores and places that seemed likely hotspots for illegals to look for work. He found a couple of hardware stores further north, but they were out in the suburbs and probably not good places for day laborers.

He cross-referenced the search terms *day laborers* and *Austin* and found several articles pinpointing popular locations. He cross-referenced those results with the alerts in the ICE Block app and found two places without alerts.

That didn't mean they hadn't been hit by immigration enforcement, so he looked for mentions of those places in the news articles. Neither one had been recently mentioned. The newest articles were a couple of years old and were apparently praising the steep rise in the number of day laborers present in the area.

One article was about how people were saving lots of money by hiring undocumented workers since the cost of local labor had risen so much in recent years. There was a picture of a Caucasian woman, a short Latina woman, and two girls who looked ten to twelve years old in front of a large house with a four-car garage.

Below the image was the caption: *"My old house cleaner charged two hundred bucks to clean my five-thousand square foot home. Anna and her two daughters clean it for sixty dollars. It's a win for both of us. And her husband does all our landscaping and home repairs too!"*

There were several more similar articles. Carver skimmed through them and marked down any mention of local hotspots for day laborers and the illegal immigrant community. He narrowed it down to three good spots to sound an ICE alert.

Out of those three, Hamilton Home Supply seemed like the best candidate. It was a big warehouse-style store that had everything from construction supplies to home appliances. Large crowds of day laborers had been seen there as recently as last week. It looked like low-hanging fruit for an ICE raid.

But for some reason it had never been visited by immigration enforcement. A few quick searches told Carver why. The owner of the store was close friends with bigwigs in the state government. He donated large sums to the governor and members of the state legislature. He'd also donated heavily to federal representatives.

Even the most hawkish pro-law enforcement politicians would bend the knee to large sums of money. It looked like the store owner had bought himself protection from raids. Like the saying went, it wasn't what you knew, it was who you knew and how much you could bribe who you knew to look the other way.

Or maybe it was just coincidence. Carver doubted it. He really didn't care either way. He just wanted to use the place to lure Ramona out into the open.

He located Hamilton Home Supply on the map in the ICE Block app. He long pressed on the location for a couple of seconds and a pin dropped. A screen opened requesting information. It wanted to know how many agents, whether the location was actively being raided or whether they were just staging for the raid.

It also asked the user to confirm that the agents were immigration and not DEA, FBI, or other agencies carrying out non-immigration raids. It asked for pictures confirming the report, noting: *Due to thousands of fake reports from bad actors and government boot lickers, we have to verify the information before sending the alert.*

Carver used a photo of a raid from earlier in the year to satisfy that requirement. He entered the other information as well. The app then requested to know his location so it could verify he was actually on the scene.

That was clever of the developer. If he was nowhere near the reported incident, then it would assume the report was fake. That was fine. He needed to be there anyway to wait for Ramona.

He pocketed his phone. "Let's go."

"Huh?" Jessica looked away from her laptop. "I'm still compiling images for the search engine."

"We can make Ramona come to us."

She frowned. "Did someone post an alert?"

"No, but we can." He explained the process and showed her the location he'd selected.

"What happens if she shows up and sees there's no raid?"

"We'll watch for her or her friends and follow them back to wherever they call home."

Jessica tapped a finger on her chin. "I guess it's better than what I'm doing. Despite uploading hundreds of images, I still haven't gotten a hit on any images that give me a location. It turns out that RingRang and Shoutout don't collect locational metadata like some of the other social media apps."

"None of them are supposed to collect that information."

She laughed. "Most social media apps track information they're not supposed to even if you opt out of location sharing and private data collection. They found a loophole in the law that allows them to clean that metadata from images and posts after the information is already collected."

"So, the data is there for a moment, then deleted?"

"Exactly." She shook her head. "But even when they delete it, it's never really gone. That's because the deletion method they use is called de-indexing. In other words, they remove the index that points to the data. There's software that simply rebuilds the index and the information is still there."

Carver wasn't surprised. Many laws had loopholes built in so political donors could keep doing what they were doing by exploiting the loophole while the politicians could claim they'd fixed the problem, but bad actors were abusing a flaw in the system. Both sides covered each other.

Jessica packed her laptop in her backpack. Carver grabbed his bags and put them in the minivan. He drove to Hamilton Home Supply and circled around the parking lot. There were probably a hundred day laborers milling around in a shaded area right next to where pickups pulled in to pick up large loads of lumber and other supplies.

The laborers weren't just men. There were women too. They weren't just Latinos either. Some looked like they were from sub-Saharan Africa and the Middle East. It was such a large crowd that it seemed impossible for immigration enforcement to not know about them. That just reinforced Carver's suspicion that they were protected by their friends in government.

"I don't think day labor is the only thing being sold here." Jessica pointed to a group of women in skimpy clothing. "Looks like other services are available as well."

A man in a big pickup was talking to two of the Latinas. They smiled, nodded, and seemed to come to an agreement. The women got into the pickup cab, and the truck drove away. Not twenty feet away was a black and white SUV with *Austin Police* emblazoned on the side.

The cop inside was drinking coffee and watching everything that was going on. It was strange. Real strange. Or maybe it wasn't. Maybe he was positioned there to keep an eye on things and run interference if federal agents showed up.

Carver opened the ICE Block app and entered the information again. He shared his location with the app and it confirmed he was onsite. Then he submitted it. The app accepted the report. A message popped up on the screen.

Alert is being validated.

"They must have gotten thousands of fake reports," Jessica said. "If they were smart, they could use image search and an AI checker to validate submitted photos and make sure they're not AI generated or downloaded from the internet."

"Let's hope they're not that smart yet," Carver said.

A good twenty minutes passed during which time four more prostitutes found clients and eleven day laborers climbed into the backs of pickup trucks and were whisked away to a jobsite while the cop watched.

ICE Block came to life with an alert using a klaxon sound effect. It was hard to miss. The alert was not for Hamilton Home Supply. It was for a roofing supply store several miles south of their location.

Carver mapped the route. It would take them twenty-five minutes to get there.

Jessica looked at the alert. "What now? Do we wait here or go there?"

"There's no alert here. It might not have passed validation."

Seconds later, a klaxon sound effect wailed from his phone as a new alert arrived, this one for Hamilton Home Supply.

"Great." Jessica groaned. "Just great! Now we don't know where they're going to go."

"Check Ramona's social media," Carver said. "Maybe she'll let us know."

Jessica took out the tablet. She opened RingRang and Shoutout. Ramona hadn't posted to either of them. She set the tablet on the dashboard so they could watch it. "The other place might have a real raid happening. Maybe we should go there."

Carver opened the alert for the roofing company. There was a picture of the store with a black SUV parked in front. On the side of the SUV was a logo with ICE next to it. There were two other pictures of the area. No day laborers were visible in either of them.

That told him one of two things. Either there had been no illegal immigrants there to begin with, or they'd all seen the ICE vehicle arrive and had run for the hills. There also seemed to be only one ICE vehicle present. It certainly didn't look like a major raid.

He searched for the name of the roofing company and saw that a raid had happened there two weeks prior. A follow up article said that the parking lot remained empty of day laborers ever since the raid and that some employers were angry that their source of cheap labor had evaporated.

Carver leaned back in his seat and watched the area.

Jessica watched him. "You don't seem worried."

"I think they'll come here. The roofing company got hit a couple of weeks ago. ICE probably sent a couple of people to look around." He showed her the pictures. "That's not a raid."

"Okay. So, they'll come here?"

"I think so."

The Austin cop got out of his SUV. He walked over to the crowd of workers and started talking to them. He looked Latino, so the odds were good he spoke Spanish. Members of the large group gathered around and listened to him.

They nodded. Spoke calmly to him. Nodded some more. Then they began to disperse. There was no panic. No running. They just walked off the property and over to the neighboring strip mall.

Jessica stared in disbelief. "Am I imagining things or did that cop just warn them to leave?"

"Looks like it," Carver said.

"Wow, that's crazy." She shook her head. "Do you think Ramona and friends will still come?"

Carver nodded at the tablet on the dashboard. "Looks like it."

A new post from Ramona had just appeared. It was a live video of her and others climbing into what looked like a high-top Mercedes Sprinter van. The camera shifted around but didn't show much of the surrounding area.

"We're going to fight ICE!" Ramona said. "They haven't shown their ugly faces here in a while, but now they're back. We won't let them disappear anyone or kidnap innocent children. We'll do whatever it takes to fight them."

She climbed into the van. "We got two raid alerts, but one of them isn't a raid. It looks like we're off to Hamilton Supply. The owner is a big supporter of immigrant rights, so we want to help them fight off the fascists."

The others in the van raised their fists and chanted, "Fight! Fight! Fight!" The video ended.

"I wish she would have given us an ETA," Jessica said. "What now?"

Carver started the van and drove it to the parking lot entrance. There were two entrances, but he could see both from this location. There was a back entrance leading to the loading dock, but it seemed doubtful that Ramona and friends would enter that way.

Within minutes, the area where the day laborers had been was completely empty. They'd scattered to the four winds and probably wouldn't be back until they were sure the coast was clear.

It was also clear that there was no ICE presence whatsoever. It was a fact that hadn't gone unnoticed by the cop. Carver watched him with his monocular to see what he was up to. It looked like he was typing on his phone. It seemed doubtful he was connected to the protestors, but there was no telling.

An unmarked police car with a magnetic flashing light mounted on the top and sirens wailing was coming down the road. The heavy traffic parted like the Red Sea so the car could pass.

It zipped past them into the parking lot and skidded to a stop next to the patrol car. The officer in the patrol car got out. The person in the unmarked vehicle got out to meet them. Carver had caught a glimpse of the driver as the car drove past.

It was Special Detective Piker.

CHAPTER 16

Carver watched Detective Piker through the monocular.

"What in the hell is she doing here?" Jessica slouched in her seat as if Piker might see her from all the way across the parking lot. "Since when does a detective fly across town sirens wailing to talk to a random cop in a parking lot?"

"They have the app," Carver said. "They both got the warning."

"Let me rephrase," Jessica said. "Why would she come all this way just because there's a possible ICE raid?"

"No idea." Carver saw more police lights in the opposite direction. He focused the monocular on them and saw a patrol car pushing through traffic. Behind it was a Sprinter van. Not just one van. A whole line of them.

"What do you see?" Jessica leaned toward him for a better view. "More cops?"

"A cop escorting Sprinter vans," Carver said. He handed her the monocular. "It looks like Ramona's group is getting a police escort through traffic."

Jessica peered through the scope. Her mouth dropped open. "That's insane. Are you sure those aren't police vans?"

"No markings." Carver shrugged. "I could be wrong, but we'll find out in a couple of minutes."

Despite the police escort, it took a few minutes for the convoy to reach the parking lot. The police escort made a U-turn a hundred feet before the parking lot entrance, causing traffic to halt in both directions.

"Looks like they don't want to be seen escorting the vans," Jessica said.

The vans pulled into the entrance across from Carver's location. That end of the parking lot was mostly empty. The vans parked, the back doors opened, and people spilled out. One of the vans only had a driver because the back of the van was full of equipment.

Polyethylene containers were pulled out and opened. One person pulled signs from inside them. Another person handed out face shields, helmets, and transparent riot shields that looked identical to the ones police used.

Ramona was easy to spot with her red dreadlocks spilling out from under her helmet even among the fifty people Carver counted. Once everyone was equipped, they hurried across the lot toward the place where the day laborers had been.

More vans appeared but these carried news crews, eager to report on a looming conflict between ICE and the anti-ICE protestors. Some sent drones into the sky to get an aerial view of the action. A young woman in a red business dress and heels ran toward the protestors.

Detective Piker met the protestors about halfway across the parking lot and spoke to a tall man. Carver zoomed in and tried to read her lips, but he couldn't see her mouth from that angle. He could tell that the tall man and his followers were angry at whatever Piker was telling them.

The tall man yanked off his helmet and tucked it under his arm. It looked like he said, "It's fake," to Piker. She nodded in reply. He threw up his hands, turned around, and said something to his followers.

It looked like they were all sorely disappointed. ICE wasn't here. It had been a false alarm. The female reporter spoke to the tall man and walked away looking just as disappointed as he was. There would be no clashes today.

The protestors were clearly well funded and supported. It also looked like Austin PD was directly helping these people. Maybe even supplying them with riot shields and helmets, because their equipment looked no different than what riot cops used.

The protestors walked slowly back to the vans. They handed their equipment to the driver of the equipment van. He put everything back in the polyethylene chests and loaded them into the back. Minutes later, they began to leave.

Carver waited until they left the parking lot before pulling out onto the road and following them. He didn't need to be close to them because the high roofs on the vans made them stand out from the rest of the traffic.

"This is so strange." Jessica took the monocular and looked at the vans. "They got a police escort and then a detective met them in the parking lot. Why would the local cops help protestors?"

"No idea." Carver glanced at her. "But it might indicate why Detective Piker is so reluctant to help us."

"Because she agrees with the protestors?" Jessica pursed her lips. "I guess it makes more sense than thinking she's part of a sex trafficking scheme."

"Anything is possible." Carver shrugged. "Let's just hope that Ramona has useful information and is willing to help."

"What if she's not willing to help?" Jessica bit her lower lip. "What if she's so hellbent on her mission that she refuses to tell us anything?"

"We'll burn that bridge when we get to it." Carver shifted to the left lane because the vans were turning at the next traffic light. He reached the intersection just as the light turned yellow and made the turn.

"I have a feeling that Ramona willingly gave that Cadillac to those men." Jessica stared out the window. "Maybe she's sleeping with one of them."

"Possibly. Or they stole it from her." Carver had already considered multiple scenarios and couldn't decide which one fit the best. Ramona probably gave the car to the men or gave it to someone connected to them. The men got the car directly or indirectly from her. It seemed unlikely that they'd have to steal it from someone like Ramona.

The men were most likely in full possession of the car. The video of one of them going to the gas station seemed to prove that. They hadn't just stolen the car or borrowed it for the job. But that didn't mean they associated with Ramona regularly or that she knew anything about them.

Traffic was snarled, probably because the police escort had made everyone move out of the way of the vans moments ago and caused the congestion to worsen. They worked their way north to a toll road with a speed limit of eighty-five miles per hour. There was no way to go the speed limit or anywhere near it because traffic was so heavy.

The convoy continued north by northeast and exited into Round Rock a few miles north of Austin. They drove past several subdivisions and turned into a commercial area not far from the highway.

The vans drove toward a large warehouse-style building that could have once been a wholesale store. Carver got that impression because the exterior used the fake stone concrete blocks that were popular with those kinds of stores.

A double-wide rollup door opened as the first van approached. The vans pulled inside, and the door quickly rolled back down behind them. Carver stopped on the side of the road near the entrance to the parking lot of the large building.

He surveyed the area with his monocular. There were no cameras. There was no fence or gate guarding the approach. The parking lot was just a strip of asphalt around the building. It certainly wasn't large enough for a wholesale store to accommodate very many cars.

There was a regular entry door near the rollup door, and another set of doors on the left side of the building. They were probably emergency exit doors. There were probably more of them all around the building. They might provide a good way in, as long as they didn't have alarms.

"So, this is their secret lair." Jessica stared at her laptop screen. "I just got several hits for Ramona's face at the hardware store. She and her friends posted to social media the moment they arrived."

Carver took out one of his charged wireless cameras. He still needed to recover the ones he'd left at the jet ski rental place, so he didn't run out. He attached the camera to a light pole and aimed it at the warehouse. There was no other way out of the parking lot so any traffic would have to come this way.

"What now?" Jessica said.

"We wait for dark and go in, or we wait for Ramona to come out to us."

"I'd be willing to bet that they don't have to come out of the warehouse." Jessica closed her laptop and leaned back. "They probably have food and everything inside." She narrowed her eyes. "She and her friends are a fast-response protest unit. They can get anywhere in town fast, especially with a police escort."

"Yep." Carver turned the minivan around and headed toward the highway. He'd noticed several restaurants on the side of the road and figured one of those would be as good a place as any to wait for nightfall.

He chose a steakhouse and got a table inside. They ordered food, ate, and had a couple of beers to pass the time. Carver kept an eye on the camera feed but there was no activity outside the warehouse.

"Should we contact Detective Hancock?" Jessica said. "Tell him what we've found so far?"

"Let's see how this goes." Carver looked over Ramona's social media feeds on the tablet. She'd posted an angry video about the fake ICE Block alert and admonished the creator to implement better preventative measures.

The video had probably been made inside the warehouse, but Ramona had recorded it in front of a white wall. He rotated the tablet to Jessica. "See how bright the light is?"

She nodded. "Ramona is probably using a halo lamp and an influencer booth. That's why the wall is so white and smooth and close behind her."

"Very professional."

Jessica nodded again. "Yeah. Everything about this group is professional. They're either well-funded or very dedicated."

"Probably a lot of the former and a little of the latter." Carver glanced at the camera feed. "Money goes a long way toward making someone committed."

"Yeah, but I think Ramona is the real deal." Jessica sipped her beer. "She's so desperate to feel relevant that she'll take up any cause no matter what it is."

"Maybe. Or maybe she just needs attention from her parents."

Jessica laughed. "That sounds odd coming from you."

Carver looked out the window. It was dark enough to go in. He paid the bill in cash and went to the bathroom since it was never a good idea to start a mission on a full bladder. He and Jessica went to the van.

He drove it to the property neighboring the warehouse. A wide strip of trees separated the property and concealed the minivan from sight. They changed into their black clothing, masked up, and put on gloves.

"I should go alone," Carver said. "It'll be easier for me to get in and out unseen."

"I want to go." Jessica gripped his hand. "I can hang back and let you do your thing, but I want to go inside, okay?"

Carver had a sidearm on, but he'd left the big guns in the car. This was Texas so someone inside was bound to have a gun. If he was spotted, they might not think much of a man in black with a sidearm because the protestors dressed in all black too. If they saw an M4 hanging on his back, then their reaction might be much different.

He went to the back door and gently jimmied the latch. He eased it open a crack and extended a small dental mirror inside to see if there was an emergency exit door alarm. There wasn't one, so he pulled the door open all the way.

There was a dark hallway on the other side. He went in and scouted the area while Jessica waited just inside the door. There were empty offices, bathrooms, and a water fountain but not much else, so he motioned Jessica to come to him.

She hurried over and stacked up next to him. "See anything?"

Carver looked around the corner. The hallway continued to a set of double doors. "There's light coming through the crack under the doors." He went down the corridor and gently pushed the door handle. It clicked faintly but even that sounded loud in the hallway.

He opened the door. No one was on the other side, just an empty space and rows of refrigerators. They were lined up back-to-back with each other. Sale tags hung from the handles. There were yellow arrows on most of them, each arrow pointing out cosmetic imperfections.

"Looks like a scratch and dent appliance warehouse," Jessica said.

The lights were off in the back half of the warehouse. The front half was fully lit. Voices and music emanated from somewhere up there. Carver couldn't see anything because of the way many of the appliances were stacked on top of one another.

It looked like the appliances that had once been spread out around the warehouse had been moved into the back section to clear out the front. Carver slowly threaded his way between them until he reached the front half of the warehouse.

The floor space was wide open in the middle. There were eight Sprinter vans parked in a neat line facing the rollup door at the front, ready to go at a moment's notice. There were rows of green field tents to the left and the right of the Sprinter vans.

Behind the tents were elevated bathroom pods. They were six feet long and four feet wide and stood on thick foldable legs to elevate them four feet off the ground. Carver didn't have to see inside them to know what they looked like because he'd used units like them before.

There was a showerhead and a toilet seat that folded against the wall. Underneath the unit was a collapsible drainpipe that connected to the seat. There was also a foldout sink on one wall. It was a relatively lightweight contraption that could be packed in a vehicle and deployed by two people.

The elevation allowed gravity to drain the water through the adjustable drainpipe underneath. A large vinyl water bladder attached to the top. Once it was filled with water, turning on the faucets, the shower, or flushing the toilet simply used gravity.

The most cumbersome part about the entire contraption was filling the bladder with water. It had flexible wires in the lining to give it rigidity, but someone still had to hold it open while another person filled it with water.

Carver had seen variations of these mostly in semi-permanent forward bases and refugee camps. Seeing them deployed in a former warehouse store that already had plumbing and fixed bathrooms was strange.

The only reason they had a setup like this was because they could pack it up and move out quickly. Carver saw a man coming out of the bathrooms at the front of the store, so it looked like they were also utilizing the onsite utilities.

There were several long foldout tables arranged in the middle area. There were electric griddles on one of them. There were several refrigerators next to the foldout tables. Long extension cords ran past the tents and presumably to power outlets on the other side.

There were shelves stocked with potato chips, cereals, and other snacks next to the fridge. A few people were cooking what looked like hamburgers on the electric griddles.

"Looks like a military camp," Jessica whispered. "Do these people have a life outside of protesting?"

"I think this is their full-time job." Carver poked his monocular around the corner of the appliances and swept the area for the primary target. He only saw about fifteen or so people out and about. Ramona was probably in one of the tents.

Most of the protestors had swapped their black clothing for casual attire like shorts and dresses. Aside from the paramilitary vibe of the camp, they looked mostly normal. There were young people, old people, and people of every age in between camping out in the abandoned scratch and dent warehouse store.

One thing was certain. Carver and Jessica couldn't just blend into this crowd. No one was wearing masks, and all the protestors seemed to know each other. Probably because they'd been doing this together for a while now.

This was going to be a tough nut to crack.

CHAPTER 17

Carver needed to locate Ramona.

She was the only reason they were here. Hopefully she hadn't already retired to her tent for the night. If she had, he'd have to wait until everyone was asleep and then go from tent to tent looking for her.

That wasn't ideal either because the field tents had heavy-duty zippers on them that could be secured from the inside. He'd have to unzip every tent and look inside with the night vision on the monocular.

The tents all faced the center area, so even if all the overhead lights were turned off at bedtime, he'd be exposed and in the open. There was also no guarantee that the lights would be turned off. There really was no need to since the heavy tent fabric blocked the light.

Carver walked behind the appliances to the right until he had a good angle on a tent that was open. He looked through the monocular to see what the sleeping arrangements were like inside. There were two cots, one on each side of the tent.

He looked into another tent and confirmed the layout was similar. It wouldn't take long to ID someone inside provided he could unzip the flap and look inside without waking the occupants. That was going to be the real trick.

Jessica crouched next to him. "What do you think?"

"I think that this isn't going to be easy." Carver listed his observations about the tents and the overhead lights.

Jessica pointed to the portable bathrooms behind the tents. "What are those things?"

"Bathrooms."

"Well, we know she'll have to go at some point, right?"

"Yes, but we have to find her first."

"Done." Jessica pointed toward something.

Carver followed her finger. Ramona and an older man were coming out of a tent. They looked sweaty and disheveled. The man was adjusting his pants. Both of them were rosy-faced and smiling.

"Wow, that dude looks old enough to be her dad." Jessica grimaced. "And they were outside in the hot sun in black clothing probably sweating up a storm before they got back. Can you imagine what that tent smells like?"

Carver figured it didn't smell any worse than any of the tents he'd ever been in during deployments. He'd experienced unwashed bodies, farts, smelly feet, and even rotting corpses. Ramona's tent probably smelled good by comparison.

The man was the same tall man that Piker had spoken to at the supply store. He might be the leader of the protest group.

Ramona and her friend went their separate ways. The man went to another tent, and she went to the food. She spoke to someone who was cooking on a griddle. They pointed to a refrigerator. She went to the fridge and pulled a box from the freezer. Carver made out the words veggie burger on the side of the box.

Jessica watched him. "What are you thinking?"

"Ramona is going to cook dinner. She's going to eat it. She's going to take a shower after she eats. That's when we take her."

"Do you really think thoughts in short punchy sentences?"

Carver ducked behind the second row of appliances and walked to the other side of the room. Ramona's tent was unfortunately near the front of the row. There was some cover between the portable bathrooms and the tents but if anyone walked back there, the only place to go was to the side of a tent or the bathroom.

The organizers had spaced the tents about six feet apart so the gap between them also had to be considered. There would be lots of chances for exposure and they couldn't rely on covering their faces for a disguise since no one else was.

Carver lined himself up near the front of the tents so he could keep an eye on Ramona. She cooked her veggie burger and ate it. The man she'd been with earlier came out of his tent with a guitar and started strumming it.

They sang *We Shall Overcome* and some other folk tunes Carver vaguely recognized. Someone stood up and gave an inspirational speech about not giving up even though the day hadn't gone as planned. Others chimed in with their own thoughts and feelings.

"Well, they certainly seem committed," Jessica said.

Carver was just glad they'd eaten and emptied their bladders before coming here. It looked like it was going to be a long night. On the upside, he had plenty of time to think about how to pull this off.

He didn't want to use heavy sedation because he wanted to question Ramona immediately. He didn't want to put her to sleep in a chokehold for the same reason and because it was risky. The movies depicted all kinds of ways to knock someone out quickly and easily but most of those ways didn't work in the real world.

Scopolamine had become Carver's favorite drug of choice because it could induce a zombie like state. It inhibited free will and made individuals highly compliant. You could take their hand and lead them around like a child.

Unfortunately, Carver hadn't been able to get his hands on more of the drug. He wasn't even sure the kind they used in the United States was the same kind that they used to rob tourists in Colombia. Without that wonder drug, his options were limited.

He could use nitrous oxide, but that required a mask and a cannister. He'd have to strap the mask on her face and support the cannister while he carried her. That just wasn't going to work. He had to pick her up and spirit her away across about fifty feet.

That left him little choice but to use fentanyl. Instead of a normal knockout dose, he'd use a microdose. That should be enough to make her compliant but not enough to knock her out for hours.

She was about five feet, five inches, and thin. She probably weighed between 115 to 130 pounds. It wouldn't take much of anything to put her on her ass. He'd have to be precise with his measurements. Thankfully, he had a lot of practice.

About an hour later, Ramona stood and stretched. She hugged the woman next to her and then went to her tent. A moment later she emerged from her tent with clothing bundled under her arm and walked around her tent toward the portable bathroom unit.

It was time.

Carver turned to Jessica. "Wait here."

She nodded. "Good luck."

He stood and walked through the narrow spaces between the portable bathrooms and the tents. He walked normally past the gaps, averting his face. The guitar player had just started playing again and most people were sitting in a circle and looking at him, and not the tents.

A man walked around the corner of one of the tents and passed within five feet of Carver without ever looking in his direction. Carver slowed to let him pass, then kept walking. He kept track of the elapsed time in his head so he'd know how long it would take for him to go back the other way with Ramona.

There were hoses and electrical cables strung between the tents and the bathrooms. The pipes from the portable units all connected to one main drainpipe that also ran through the same space Carver was walking. It was only three inches wide, but if he took a wrong step, it could trip him up, especially when carrying a load.

It took him twenty-six seconds to cross the distance. The bathroom door faced the warehouse wall and not the tent, so he turned left at Ramona's tent and went up the ramp to the bathroom entrance.

The entrance was only secured with a zipper like a tent flap, so he quickly unzipped it and stepped inside. Ramona was already unclothed and standing under the shower head facing away from him.

She'd bundled her hair into a shower cap, so it didn't get wet and was pulling on the cord to let water flow from the bladder into the shower head. The guitar and singalong outside covered the sound of his entry, but the portable bathroom wasn't built to be rock solid.

It must have shaken slightly when he came in because Ramona suddenly looked around like she'd felt something. That was just fine because Carver was already right behind her. He had a small dropper in his hand.

It was the same kind people used for drops of medicine, eye drops and more. In this case, it had one drop of fentanyl inside of it. Since he only wanted to administer a tiny amount of the drug, this device would work better than the small spray bottle he used to knock out people for long periods of time.

Ramona was just starting to turn around when Carver yanked off her shower cap, gripped her hair, and yanked her head back. She reflexively gasped. Carver squeezed the rubber top of the dropper. The fentanyl went into her mouth.

He pushed her mouth closed and clamped a hand over her mouth. She struggled and tried to scream, but it was muffled. Her struggles weakened within seconds as the fentanyl took hold. It usually didn't take long when the liquid was absorbed into the thin membrane beneath the tongue.

Her eyes went glassy, and she slumped against him. The next problem was that she was wet and naked. Thankfully, she'd brought baggy shorts and an oversized T-shirt to wear to bed. Carver pulled her out of the shower to the dry part of the floor and eased her down.

He pulled on her shorts then propped her up and put the shirt on. He looked around the room and realized there was another problem. She hadn't brought her phone with her. Sometimes questioning a person wasn't as revealing as reading texts on their phone.

She must have left it in her tent. It was too valuable to leave behind, so he left her lying on the floor and looked outside. No one was there, so he went down the ramp and walked around behind the tent. He pulled out his survival knife and sliced a nice clean slit in the back of the tent.

He looked through the opening. No one was inside. The phone was lying on top of a cot. He ducked inside, grabbed it, and pocketed it. He went back around the portable bathroom and hurried up the ramp inside.

He lifted Ramona's torso to adjust her shirt. She didn't weigh much so it was easy. It meant carrying her wouldn't be too difficult either. He could carry her one of two ways. Either sling her over a shoulder or cradle her.

If anyone saw him carrying her slung over his shoulder, they'd immediately know something was wrong. If he cradled her, it might look like something else was happening. Something possibly romantic and not sinister. Cradling someone was usually interpreted as helping and caring whereas a shoulder carry looked like a kidnapping in progress unless he was a firefighter carrying someone out of a burning building.

Cradling required both arms and left him open and vulnerable. A shoulder carry left one arm free in case he needed to use his gun. He looked outside and didn't see anyone. It was going to take him a minimum of twenty-six seconds to cross back to the cover of the appliances. He decided the cradle carry was the best option.

Carver cradled Ramona. He put one of her arms around his neck and tucked the other one against his torso, so it didn't flop around. Her face rested naturally on his chest. Her eyes were big and glassy because she was still conscious but just high as hell.

He walked down the ramp to the floor. He walked briskly but resisted the urge to run. He walked toward the appliances like he was supposed to be going that way and supposed to be carrying Ramona.

The same man he'd nearly crossed paths with earlier emerged from the building's bathrooms and nearly bumped into him. He saw the two of them and grinned suggestively. "Someone's about to have some fun."

"You know it." Carver winked at him and kept walking.

The man continued back toward the sing along in the middle of the room without even slowing down. He probably wasn't the most observant fellow in the world since he didn't seem to realize that Carver wasn't one of them.

Maybe these people weren't as tightly knit as he'd thought.

He'd just reached the appliances when the guitar playing and singing abruptly stopped. A male voice shouted, "She's doing what? With whom?"

Maybe the man was more observant than Carver gave him credit for. Ramona's guitar-playing boyfriend was about to come hunting for him and he probably wouldn't be alone.

Jessica was waiting behind a stacked washer and dryer combo. She turned and ran for the side door they'd used to enter. Carver jogged behind her. She held open the door for him, then ran ahead through the strip of trees and to the neighboring parking lot.

She opened the van's sliding door. Carver dumped Ramona on the second-row seat and ran around to the driver's side door. Jessica got inside. She closed the sliding door and buckled Ramona down with two seatbelts since she was lying across the seat. Then she hopped in the passenger seat.

Carver spun the van around and headed for the parking lot exit. Anyone coming out of the warehouse wouldn't see them thanks to the trees separating this parking lot from the other one. They might see the van once it got on the street even though he had all the lights off.

He pulled onto the street and looked at the warehouse. No one was outside. The guitar man was probably running around looking for Ramona and the strange man she was with. It wouldn't be long before someone started to realize that something was wrong.

Ramona was going to be long gone by the time that happened.

Carver drove out of town. He'd already picked out a nice, secluded area where he could freely interrogate Ramona. Hopefully he wouldn't need all that privacy because she'd answer his questions quickly and willingly. If she didn't, then all that seclusion was going to come in handy.

Twenty minutes later he pulled off the highway and onto a dirt road leading through the arid countryside. He followed the dirt road for a mile and parked outside an abandoned farmhouse. He could see the city lights to the east but there were no lights in the other directions. The nearest house was miles away.

He and Jessica masked up. Ramona might have glimpsed him before she was drugged but she hadn't gotten a good look at his face. It was best that she never had the chance to see it, not just for Carver, but for her own sake.

They took her inside the old wooden house and sat her on a metal chair inside. Carver strapped her ankles to the legs of the chair but didn't otherwise secure her. He set a battery powered lantern on the table. The place was still in decent shape. It didn't have utilities, but it did have well water.

He took her phone out of his pocket and turned on the screen. It prompted him for a passcode. He held it in front of her face. Nothing happened. It didn't even give him an error. He tried again. Again, nothing. Apparently, she didn't have face lock activated.

He tried using her fingers one at a time to unlock the phone. They didn't work either. It looked like she only used a passcode. That was smart, but it probably wasn't because she'd thought of it. The leader of her group probably told everyone to only use a passcode since biometrics were easy to break if the cops caught you.

Ramona was finally starting to come out of her fentanyl-induced sluggishness. "Where am I? What's happening?" Her words were heavily slurred, and she was drooling, but it was a good start.

Carver showed her the picture of the man with the Cadillac DeVille. "Tell us where these men are and we'll have you back with your friends in no time."

She slowly wiped the drool off her mouth and stared for nearly thirty seconds straight at the image. Then she scowled angrily at Carver. "I'll never help you assholes! I'll die before ICE makes me talk."

CHAPTER 18

Carver didn't like how this was going.

Ramona thought they were with immigration. He set the record straight right away. "We're not with ICE. We're looking for these men because they kidnapped our friend."

Ramona blinked and slowly looked from Carver to Jessica. "Who are you people?"

"Like I said, we just want our friend back and these men took her using your Cadillac. Tell us where they are and you can go."

"Nuh uh. This is a trick."

"It's no trick." Jessica took out her phone and turned to Carver. "Can I show her?" He nodded.

She showed Ramona the video of Sabrina being taken. "Your car was used in a felony kidnapping. Tell us who has the car and where they are and we'll let you go."

Ramona's gaze hardened. "You'll never get anything from me, you fascist bootlickers!"

"Are you serious right now?" Jessica's eyebrows rose. "My sister was kidnapped, and you won't help us find her?"

"That's clearly AI. You're trying to frame innocent men just because they're immigrants." Ramona spat at her. "Go crawl in a hole and die."

"No, it's not AI! This is a real video!" Jessica's mask moved like her mouth was hanging open beneath it. "They have my sister!"

"Even if you showed me a real picture of them with your sister, I wouldn't help you. This is indigenous land and we're going to take it back from the colonizers." Ramona tried to spit again but most of it went down her chin.

"My God, she's completely brainwashed." Jessica turned to Carver. "Either that or she's just so filled with hate that the kidnapping of an innocent girl makes her happy."

"You have no compassion for what your people have done." Ramona's eyes filled with anger. "You want to wipe us out and kill us. This isn't hate. It's war."

"She's insane." Jessica's eyes filled with defeat. "She's completely insane."

Carver had seen this plenty of times before. Indoctrinated people were often irrational and difficult to reason with. It was why seemingly normal people could be driven to do horrific acts.

Being irrational wasn't the same as being insane. Irrational people could be reasoned with. Insane people couldn't. Ramona was a spoiled kid from a rich family. She was just looking for a cause so she could rise above her feelings of self-loathing and doubt. She wanted to be more than she was.

But like so many people, she was looking for causes in all the wrong places. She wasn't really risking anything by doing what she was doing. It was all performative. That was why she was being so brave right now.

Carver took her hand and pressed down on the nerve between the thumb and index finger. He did it just hard enough to cause discomfort. The fentanyl was still probably dulling the pain so it wasn't nearly as bad as it could be.

Ramona gasped in pain and tried to jerk her hand away, but she couldn't.

Carver pinched a little harder.

She screamed. "Stop it! Let me go! This is torture! It's against the Geneva convention!"

"Do you really think fascists follow the Geneva convention?" Jessica laughed. "We don't have rules."

Carver released the nerve. "Tell us what we want to know, or it's going to get worse."

"No!" Ramona yanked her hand back and folded both hands under her arms. "You'll never get me to talk."

Carver went to the old cast iron sink and pumped the handle. He filled a bucket with water.

Ramona bared her teeth at him. "What are you going to do, waterboard me?"

Carver walked behind her and tipped the chair over backwards. Ramona screamed and tried to move, but her ankles were strapped to the chair legs, so she couldn't move. Carver pinned her to the floor. She was a small, thin girl so it was no problem at all.

Ramona screamed bloody murder and flailed wildly. Carver gripped her wrists and strapped them together. He pushed them down. Jessica took over and pinned Ramona's arms down to her lap.

"Stop! Stop!" Tears poured down Ramona's face. "You can't do this! Call the police! Call the police!"

Jessica burst into laughter. "You can't be serious."

"You're violating my human rights!"

"Imagine how my sister feels right now," Jessica said. "She's powerless and probably being abused by those friends of yours."

"Burn in hell you fascist dickheads!"

Carver poured the water onto Ramona's hair. He poured a travel-sized bottle of shampoo onto her hair and started lathering it. She screamed louder and harder.

"What are you doing to me!"

Carver poured the water onto her hair to rinse it. This was a form of psychological torture he'd learned from Jericho. For some people it worked better than physical pain. It might work on Ramona, or it might just drive her into a blind rage. He was going to find out.

"Not my locks!" she screamed. "Leave my locks alone!"

Carver pulled out a metal comb and waved it in her face. "Tell us what we want to know, and you can go."

She sobbed uncontrollably. "Not my locks! It took me two years to get them!"

Carver worked the comb into the end of one of her dreadlocks and started untangling it.

"Stop! I'll tell you!"

"Tell me first, then I'll stop."

"Antonio is the guy with my car. I met him when I ran away. We dated for a while. I told him that I would never let the fascists remove him and his people from our country, so I joined the movement and let him keep my car."

Carver kept working at the dreadlock. "What's his full name and location?"

"I don't know his last name."

"You dated the guy and don't know his last name?"

"Life isn't about names!" Ramona wriggled. "Stop combing out my locks!"

Jessica showed her the picture of the man at the gas station. "Is this Antonio?"

"Y-yes."

Jessica showed her the picture of the other man. "Who's the other guy?"

"That's Mateo, his brother."

"Did you date him too?"

Carver overrode the question. "Give us their location."

"They move around a lot. I don't remember all the addresses."

"Are they on your phone?"

She blinked. "Maybe."

"What's the passcode to your phone?"

"Ten dash nineteen-seventeen."

"October nineteen-seventeen?" Jessica frowned. "Is that a significant date?"

"Date of the Bolshevik Revolution," Carver said as he punched in the code.

"It's the day of the Great Socialist Revolution," Ramona said. "A day that we will repeat so all humanity will be freed from the chains of capitalist oligarchs."

"Your head is just full of buzzwords and garbage." Jessica looked at Carver. "See anything?"

Carver found a string of texts between Ramona and Antonio. There were lots of them going back over a year. It looked like they'd met when she was still living at home and not when she ran away. It looked like Antonio and her brother had come over several times while Ramona's parents were out of town.

Most importantly, there were two addresses where they'd met as recently as a month ago. He showed them to Ramona. "Did you regularly meet them at either of these places?"

She looked at them. "A few times." She wriggled. "Now, stop wrecking my locks!"

Carver stopped combing her hair. It probably would have taken him hours to comb any of them out. The hair was hopelessly tangled, matted and filthy. It didn't look like she'd washed her hair in over a year.

He skimmed through her other texts but didn't find any with Mateo. Everything had come from Antonio. There were texts from her parents asking her to come home. Texts from what looked like regular friends.

There were no texts from the protest organization she was with, but she did have Signal on her phone. It was a commonly used encrypted messaging app. He opened it and it prompted him for the passcode. He used the same code that unlocked her phone, and it let him in.

There were only a few texts inside the app. Nothing from Antonio or Mateo. Only texts from someone with a number for their name. Probably the protest organizer. There probably wasn't much need for texting since the protestors apparently lived and travelled together all the time.

Carver stood and put his foot on Ramona's hair.

She winced. "What are you doing? I told you everything!"

"Did you tell us everything?" Carver knelt. "I feel like you're leaving something out. Something important. Which means we're going to have to hold onto you until we verify everything."

Jessica pulled a pair of hair trimmers from her bag and held them up. "If we have to come back, I'm shaving you bald."

"No!" Ramona shivered. "There's just one small thing I didn't mention. I promise."

"Tell us this small thing," Carver said.

"There's another house they took me to before. A big ranch east of town."

Carver nodded. "I'm listening."

"There were a lot of armed men there."

"That's not a small thing," Jessica said. "In fact, that's a really big thing. What the hell was happening at this ranch?"

"I don't know."

Carver scrolled back through the texts with Antonio. He found dozens of photos of young girls from a few months back. He read the texts from around then and it became clear what was going on back then.

"You took photos of girls and sent them to Antonio." Carver put the phone in front of her face. "And you helped lure them to him. Then they took them to this ranch. That's why you were there."

Ramona shivered. "Yes."

"Do you know a man named Yohan?"

She nodded again. "Yes."

Carver wasn't surprised. "Did he help you find and lure girls as well?"

She nodded. "Yes, but he lured the girls himself."

Jessica gasped. "My God, you're one of them, aren't you?"

"The children of colonizers deserve to be prisoners. They deserve to be punished."

"You evil piece of shit." Jessica's eyes filled with tears. "Is that what happened to my sister?"

"You and your sister can burn in hell." Ramona screamed and wriggled. "I told you everything, so let me go!"

Carver looked at the dates on the messages. "How long have you been with the protest group?"

"Why do you care?"

"Just tell me."

"Nearly a year."

"That's a lot of overlap. Is your group helping Antonio or people like him find girls?"

Ramona glared at him. "We do anything we can to get rid of people like you."

"They're not just protestors," Jessica said. "They're helping traffickers take away kids."

"I've told you everything, now let me go!" Ramona thrashed helplessly.

Carver had seen this kind of thing before. If you couldn't kill the adults, you went after the kids. You destroyed the next generation. Going after the kids didn't mean killing them. It meant indoctrinating them to hate their own people. It meant using other means to get rid of those they couldn't reach or convert.

What was interesting was just how well funded this operation was. He sensed larger forces at play. Probably Enigma or something similar to it. Despite the dents he'd put in the organization, it hadn't gone away.

Carver yanked Ramona and the chair upright. He nodded at Jessica. "Shave her head."

"What?" Ramona screamed. "No! You promised!"

Carver pinned her shoulders to the chair. "I said I wouldn't comb out the locks."

"You filthy liars!"

"That's rich coming from a spoiled little rich brainwashed moron like yourself." Jessica went to town with the clippers, and she wasn't gentle with them, leaving scratches, scrapes, and blood on Ramona's pale scalp.

"Usually there's a side that's willing to accomplish a goal by any means necessary," Carver said. "A side that thinks the ends justify the means." He stepped away to look at Jessica's work. "Then you have the other side that wants to play by the rules. They don't want to stoop to the other side's level."

"My hair!" Ramona wailed. "You ruined it!" She started screaming and screeching uncontrollably.

"The side that plays by the rules usually loses because the other side will say anything and do anything to win. " Carver walked over to Ramona and ran his finger through the blood trickling down her scalp. "I should know. I used to be in that line of work."

"Technically, you still kind of are," Jessica said.

Carver shrugged.

Ramona continued crying and screaming, completely consumed by her shorn locks.

Jessica walked behind her and picked up the shaved dreads. She dropped them into her lap. "Maybe you can glue them back on."

Carver grabbed Ramona by the throat and put four drops of fentanyl into her mouth. Her cries subsided to dull moans. They soon faded to silence.

"My ears and sanity thank you for that." Jessica sighed and stared at Ramona. "What's next?"

Carver had been thinking it over. They had a single objective. Find and rescue Sabrina. They had three locations to check out. The ranch would have to be the last one because it would be guarded.

It seemed extremely doubtful that Sabrina would be at either of the other addresses, but likely that Antonio or Mateo would. Those men were the next step toward achieving the objective.

"Um, can you tell me what you're thinking?" Jessica shook her head. "I swear you still seem to think you're alone most of the time."

Carver was aware that he had a problem sharing information. So, he shared what he was thinking. "We find those men and use them to find out where Sabrina is."

"Okay." Jessica nodded at Ramona. "What about her?"

There were a couple things they could do with Ramona. The best thing to do was to get rid of her because returning her would trigger a reaction. She would immediately contact Antonio or Mateo. She would warn them about what had happened. Then they would be prepared. Carver couldn't let that happen. Ramona deserved to die for what she'd done.

But he really didn't want to kill her. Probably because she was just a small frail thing and she was brainwashed.

That put him in a tight spot. He could conceivably drop her off at her parents' place. Maybe they'd finally do something with her, like have her committed to a mental institution or get her out of the country.

Jessica watched him. "You don't know how to handle this situation, do you?"

"I know the best way to handle it. I just don't feel like doing it."

"Like killing her?"

He nodded.

"Well, as much as I hate her, I can't do it either." She looked at Ramona and tsked. "What are we gonna do with you, girl?"

Carver removed the straps holding Ramona to the chair and hefted her. He tossed her over his shoulder. "Odds are she'll be reported kidnapped or missing if she hasn't already."

"You think her protestor friends will do that?"

He nodded. "They obviously know Piker, so I don't think they'll hesitate."

"Where does that leave us?"

"We take her with us." He turned off the lamp and picked up his bag with his free hand.

"Take her with us to where?"

"To visit her boyfriend." Carver went to the minivan. He put the bag inside then placed Ramona in the third-row seat on her back. He strapped her in with two seatbelts. He'd given her a decent dose of fentanyl this time, so she was going to be out of it for hours.

Jessica hurried outside with the other bag and climbed into the passenger side. "Honestly, this is probably the best decision we could have made."

Carver cranked the engine and put an address into the GPS. It was just past 22:30 hours. The night was young, and they had a lot of work to do.

CHAPTER 19

Carver stopped down the street from the first address.

He pulled on his black cap and masked up. He slung his MP5SD over his back and put some tools into his waist bag. "Wait here."

"Can you use the earpiece?" Jessica opened the small charging case and handed him one.

Carver pushed it into his ear. It was a proper micro earpiece like the ones he'd used in Scion. He turned it on. "Can you hear me?"

"Loud and clear." Jessica put a hand on his shoulder. "Be careful."

The address was just outside northeastern Austin about twenty miles from the abandoned house where they'd interrogated Ramona. It was nothing fancy, just a wooden house with a rusted tin roof and a cracking driveway.

The metal garage behind the house was what caught Carver's attention. It was probably fifty feet long and had a nice wide driveway going to it. It was in much better shape than the house and looked like it could hold a lot of vehicles and equipment.

If it had been a ranch or farmhouse, then it wouldn't have stood out so much. But as a regular house on less than an acre of land, it looked out of place. Maybe there was nothing to it. Maybe there was a lot to it.

Carver decided to check it out first. He had a couple of good reasons for that. First, there were no lights on inside the house. Second, light leaked from beneath the single rollup door on the right side of the garage. It was strange having only one rollup door for such a long garage.

The single window in the front of the building was blacked out with tinfoil, presumably so people could do whatever it was they were doing inside without anyone noticing. There were no outside lights around the perimeter. Aside from the faint moonlight, it was pitch black.

He studied the house and the garage with his monocular. There were no cameras on the outside of either building. The presence of cameras would probably look suspicious to anyone with a keen eye given the derelict state of the house.

Carver skirted through the scrub brush and trees and got right up next to the garage. There was a steel entry door on the side and a window which was also blocked off with tinfoil. He looked at the back of the building. There were no windows or doors there but there was a small air-conditioning unit that wasn't running.

He walked along the back of the building and got a look at the other side of the building. No windows or doors there either. That was typical of metal garages like this. They were meant for holding cars or equipment and didn't need lots of windows.

Carver put an ear against the metal. He heard something inside, but the sound was faint. It sounded like someone talking, but he couldn't be sure. It might be a television or other device. The sound was muffled as if it had to pass through a thick wall.

Places like this usually had thin metal walls with maybe an inch of insulation at most. That didn't seem to be the case with this garage. It sounded like the walls had thick insulation or sound deadening material on the inside.

A click, a hum, and a whirring fan told Carver that the air conditioner had just turned on. The unit behind the building rattled loudly. Maybe that was why the building was heavily insulated. Maybe Antonio and his brother lived in the garage.

Carver walked around to the side entry door and tested the handle. It was locked. With the air conditioner making such a racket, it seemed safe to attempt entry. The door had a deadbolt and a bottom lock.

He jimmied the bottom lock and felt the latch give way. The door didn't budge because the deadbolt was engaged. He had a snap gun that could probably work open the deadbolt latch, but he wasn't sure if he should risk it.

The air conditioning unit was loud on the outside, but the heavy insulation inside the building probably blocked a lot of that sound. Which meant something snapping in the deadbolt lock might be audible to anyone on the inside, especially if they were close to the door.

He shifted his MP5SD to the side so he could quickly bring it to bear and decided to risk using the snap gun. He could pick a lock but even under the best of circumstances, it could take one or two minutes to accomplish.

Snap guns made it simple. They were small devices with a thin rod coming out of the front. The user inserted the rod into a lock. The user then pressed the trigger on the snap gun causing the rod to bump up against the bottom pins in a lock cylinder.

Then one of the laws of physics, the transfer of energy, would take over. The force would travel through the lower pins and into the top pins. The top pins would bounce up while the bottom pins would remain down, thus freeing the cylinder to turn.

A faint clicking sound would be audible to anyone on the other side of the door. Then again, the insulation in the garage might prevent anyone on the inside from hearing it unless they were right next to the door.

Carver inserted the rod and snapped the trigger while keeping a moderate twisting pressure so the cylinder would turn the moment the pins cleared it. It could take anywhere from two to ten pulls of the trigger to make that happen.

But that didn't happen at all. He heard a faint snick, a click, and the door swung inward, yanking free of the snap gun.

"Yeah, I got it! Extra pepperoni this time," a man said as he stepped out of the door.

Carver pressed his back to the left side of the doorway. The man stepped out and pulled the door shut behind him. If man looked slightly to the left, he might see Carver's silhouette against the building, but it was so dark outside the odds were good that he wouldn't even notice him.

The man turned on a cell phone screen and dialed a number. In the short time he'd been visible in the light, Carver noticed that the man was Caucasian, dressed in jeans and a T-shirt, and had a sidearm holstered on his right leg.

He had a tattoo sleeve on his right arm and a single large skull tattoo on his left bicep. His hair was long, greasy, and unkempt. Last but not least, he spoke with a southern accent and a slight lisp.

He was holding up his cell phone and looking at the signal bar. The signal slowly increased from zero bars to four. That told Carver that there was a lot more going on with the garage than just sound deadening. It seemed to be built like a faraday cage to block cell phone signals.

This might be an innocent civilian who simply came outside his sound-deadened and faraday cage garage to order some pizza. He might just be a paranoid type who wore tinfoil hats to keep the government from reading his mind.

But Carver doubted it.

He came up behind the guy before he could dial the pizza place and sprayed him in the face with fentanyl. The man was looking at his phone screen and caught completely unaware by the mist. He sucked it in and started spitting.

"What the hell was that?" He looked up and around as if he thought it was raining. Then his knees wobbled. "Whoa, dude." He braced himself against the side of the garage. "Something ain't right."

The man should have gone down fast and hard. It looked like the dose was affecting him, but not very much. Probably because he was a regular fentanyl user. He'd probably built up a tolerance to the drug.

Carver wrapped an arm around the man's neck and squeezed hard. The man flailed and struggled, but he was uncoordinated with the fresh dose of fentanyl in his system. Drug resistance or not, he wasn't in any shape to fight back.

He went limp a moment later, unconscious but not dead. Carver checked for a pulse just to make sure. Then he looked at the man's phone and went through the texts. Most of the recent texts had times and locations but no other accompanying information.

The man had responded simply with a thumbs up emoji after receiving the information and then a hand emoji with thumb and index finger giving an OK sometime later. Which meant the man had gone to the location and retrieved whatever he was supposed to retrieve.

There was nothing else on the phone, not even social media. There were, however, dozens of phone calls to a pizza place and others to a Chinese restaurant, probably to order takeout food. The time stamps on the phone calls were mostly in the evening and the time stamps on the texts were mostly late morning and early afternoon.

That meant this guy spent his days doing pickups and then came here at night to stay in the garage. He was probably bringing the items he picked up to this garage. And he wasn't alone because he'd said something to whoever else was inside.

Carver eased open the door to see who else was inside the garage. He saw a couch about fifteen feet away from the door. Two men were on the couch, one at either end. It looked like someone was lying sideways between them but the high arms on the couch made it difficult to see.

There was a television on a stand in front of the couch. The men were watching something on it with the volume on high. The walls were lined with spray foam which explained the sound deadening. The high volume explained why Carver had been able to hear the TV faintly through the thick barrier.

A crude metal lattice was laced throughout the spray foam. That was the Faraday cage that blocked wireless signals and isolated the interior.

There was a kitchenette on the back wall with a microwave, refrigerator, a sink, and cabinets. There was an old white van parked near the rollup door and there were some ATVs parked near the entry door where Carver was.

The interior was dimly lit, but he could see all the way to the other end. There were no other cars parked in the garage and now he knew why there were no other rollup doors. That was because the rest of the space was used to hold cargo.

Human cargo.

The room was filled with cages made from chain link fencing. He could see movement in the cages but couldn't make out the details in the dim light. The television and a shelf blocked a clear view of them.

The back of a female's head rose near the far end of the couch. The man on the far end slapped her on the top of the head. "I didn't say you could stop, bitch."

She cried out in pain and then her head disappeared. It didn't take much imagination to realize what she was doing. That realization helped Carver make a few decisions he'd been holding back on.

The men were preoccupied with the television, so they didn't notice when Carver slipped inside and ducked behind an ATV. The loud volume masked Carver's footsteps as he low walked behind the vehicle, so he was completely out of the line of sight of the men.

There were cameras all over the place inside. They were angled down to keep an eye on the cages. Only one camera was positioned to watch the area where the television and kitchenette were.

There was a table next to the kitchenette with a fiber internet modem and a laptop on it. Most modern cell phones could use wireless internet to make phone calls. They probably had a firewall blocking things like that which was why the man had gone outside to call the pizza place. The internet connectivity was probably just for remote monitoring of the cameras.

There was a power over ethernet switch connected to the fiber modem. Cables from the switch ran up the walls and presumably to the cameras. In other words, the ethernet cables carried power and network connectivity to the cameras.

Carver made his way around the back of the room toward the kitchenette. He got a better view of the inside of the first cage opposite him. He could see the silhouettes of several people inside and what looked like mattresses on the floor.

The place smelled ripe, like body odor and urine. He didn't see a bathroom in the place. It might be on the other side of the cages. Judging from the smell, they didn't let the occupants out to use the toilet very often.

He was tempted to scan the area with his monocular, but the cameras took priority. Depending on how actively these cameras were monitored, the next few actions would need to take place quickly.

Once he reached the other side of the kitchenette, Carver pulled the plug to the power over ethernet switch. The small LED lights on the cameras went out. He drew his Sig and walked up behind the couch.

The man on the right side cursed and slapped the back of the woman's head again. "Stop using your teeth or I'll tie you down and pull them out one by one. Got it?"

The woman whimpered but said nothing.

Carver got right behind the men. He looked down and saw that the woman wasn't a woman at all. It was a girl. He resisted the urge to do what he wanted to do, which was to break the man's skull.

The man on the left was short and thin. He weighed maybe a hundred and eighty pounds. The guy on the right was short, chubby, and probably a little north of two hundred pounds. Carver tapped him on the top of the head with the butt of the Sig.

The man cried out in pain.

Carver put the gun to the back of his head just as the guy on the left registered what happened. The girl gasped and looked up at him.

"Are you okay?" Carver said.

She stared blankly at him for a second and shook her head. Tears filled her eyes.

"Come stand by me, okay, honey?" He spoke in a gentle voice and used words that other people used when trying to comfort a kid. Words like honey and sweetheart worked well and made kids a little less afraid of him.

She stood slowly. Her eyelids were drooping and her eyes looked glassy. She was drugged. She walked around the couch and stopped next to him.

"Who the hell do you think you are?" the man on the right said with a heavy Spanish accent. "Do you know who you're messing with?"

"Looks like a couple of sex-trafficking pedophiles to me."

"You really don't have a clue, do you, hombre?" He laughed.

Carver got to the point. "Where are Antonio and Mateo?"

The other man glanced nervously at his companion and then at Carver but said nothing.

Both men were strapped with sidearms but sitting on the couch made it awkward to draw them. They seemed to know that going for their guns was a bad idea.

The guy with Carver's gun pointed at his head tried to act casual. He shrugged. "Man, you better make sure you run fast, because you're on candid camera. The people we work for are gonna make you suffer for screwing with us."

"Answer my question." Carver looked at the guy on the left. "Tell you what, whoever answers first gets to live."

"Where's Freddy?" the guy on the right said.

"He's sleeping. If neither of you answer me, I guess I'll have to show him your bodies and see if he's more willing to answer."

"I ain't saying nothing, pendejo."

Carver grabbed him by the back of the neck and squeezed until he heard bones cracking. The man screamed in pain. The other man looked like he was contemplating going for his gun, but a look from Carver dissuaded him.

Carver kept squeezing. He dragged the man over the back of the couch and dumped him on the floor. He kicked him in the ribs and felt something break. The man screamed. The man's pants were halfway down because of what he'd been making the girl do.

"Stop! Stop! I'll tell you!"

"Too late." Carver stomped on his arm and broke it. He stomped on a knee until he felt it give. The man writhed and screamed but he wasn't going anywhere with all those broken bones.

The girl's eyes widened. She looked up at Carver and back at the man. Carver nodded. "Do what you want, honey."

She kicked him in the side and winced because she was barefooted. She was also in little more than underwear.

Carver turned to the other guy. "Talk or suffer."

"Antonio was here earlier. He didn't say where he was going. I know they got another place but they don't tell us everything."

"Did he ever bring a girl named Ramona here?"

The man nodded. "Yeah."

"He showed her the people in the cages?"

"Yeah. She laughed and said they deserved it."

"Did he bring an Asian girl here the other night?"

The man frowned. "Two Asian girls passed through here this week, but they're both gone."

Carver didn't like the way he said that. He didn't like it at all. Because that usually meant they were either dead or sold.

CHAPTER 20

Carver was getting tired of the screaming.

He put his foot on the downed man's throat while maintaining eye contact with the guy sitting on the couch. "Does gone mean dead or sold?"

He shrugged. "Man, I don't know. Antonio and Mateo deal with that. I just sit here and babysit."

"You don't know anything else?"

"No, I swear."

Carver nodded at the girl next to him. "Antonio lets you play with the merchandise?"

"The girls who end up here are low tier trash. They don't care what happens to them."

"Good to know." Carver took his foot off the man's throat and stepped over him. He walked toward the other man and stood behind him. "I appreciate you answering honestly, so I'm going to do you a favor."

The man relaxed slightly. "You'll let me go?"

"Yep. Painless release." Carver drew his knife and slit the man's throat in one easy swipe.

The man gurgled for a few seconds, but he died with a minimum amount of pain. The girl watched in fascination like she'd seen something like this before. Carver figured he probably should have told her to cover her eyes first, but he wasn't very good with kids.

"Wait here, okay, sweetheart?"

The girl nodded.

Carver went outside and dragged Freddy to the couch. The other guy had about screamed himself hoarse and was just moaning now. "I'm glad you invested in such good sound-deadening," Carver said.

"They gonna kill you," the man rasped. "I hope it's painful."

"Like this?" Carver slashed the knife across the man's exposed genitals.

The man screamed in renewed agony.

Carver took the girl aside. "What's your name?"

She stared numbly at him. Her eyes were glassy. She was definitely drugged. She tried to say something but only mumbled incoherently.

He went back to the screaming man and knelt next to him. "Who should I be afraid of? Who's going to kill me?" These were questions Carver probably should have asked before breaking the man's bones and slicing up his privates, but he had no regrets.

The man's cries grew weaker. He was bleeding heavily from the groin. It looked like Carver had nicked a major blood vessel. Maybe Freddy would have answers for him when he woke up. In the meantime, he needed to see who else was being held here.

Jessica spoke over the earpiece. "My God, Carver, it sounds like a freaking massacre in there. What's happening?"

Carver realized this was the first time he'd heard her talk. "You didn't hear it earlier?"

"My mic was on mute. I just realized it a moment ago. I thought you weren't answering me because you were running silent. And there was some kind of interference breaking up the signal too."

"Probably the faraday cage. I think I disabled it when I unplugged the router."

"They have a faraday cage in there?"

Carver looked around. "Drive the van up to the building and come inside. I'm going to need your help."

"I'm on the way."

He walked to the wall and found the light switches. The dimmer switch was set on low. He cranked it up to full brightness and drove away the shadows. Carver walked between the cages. The girl followed him like she didn't know what else to do.

Most of the cages were empty of occupants but full of dirty mattresses and discarded clothing. They had large pails for urination and defecation. What Carver had thought were heads and faces were pillows that had been pushed up against the chain link fencing.

There was a toilet and a shower stall on the other side of the cages. There was a water hose with a sprayer attachment on it too. The men probably hosed down the prisoners when they wanted to clean them.

The only prisoners were two girls in separate cages. The cages were padlocked shut. He went to the man who'd been screaming. He was dead now and had been for at least a minute. His pants were down around his ankles, so they weren't soaked with blood. Carver dug in the man's pockets and pulled out a wallet and keys.

The wallet had cash inside and a Las Vegas driver's license. That didn't mean the man lived there. It was a common place for the undocumented to get a driver's license. They'd pay someone a few thousand to get a fake address they could use for registration. It was an entire cottage industry in places like that.

Carver knew that because he'd gotten a fake license from Vegas after he'd lost an expensive forgery. The man who'd sold it to him was part of a local mafia. He'd told Carver the undocumented driver's license business brought in hundreds of millions in revenue a year. It sounded like a pretty good racket.

The name on the license was Jorge Gonzales. It might be the man's real name, but there was no way to tell. He was, after all, probably undocumented. People like him could cross the border and make up their names and backgrounds.

The other guy also had a Vegas driver's license. The name on the license, Thomas Johnson, was definitely fake. The man Carver had drugged earlier, Freddy, had a legitimate Texas driver's license in his wallet. He had a local address, too.

He had loads of membership cards, punch cards, and more from various local restaurants and businesses. It looked like he ate out a lot and had a favorite massage place. His wallet was stuffed with singles. Probably for the strip club whose punch card only needed one more hole for a free table dance.

Freddy's cell phone only used a passcode. No biometrics. The same held true for the other men's phones. There might be useful information on the phones, but it seemed doubtful. They'd probably be similar in nature to the texts on Freddy's phone, just names, locations and emoji responses.

Carver sorted through the keys on Jorge's key ring. One went to the van. Another probably went to the entry door. Several small ones went to the padlocks on the cages. He went to the cages with occupants and tried several keys until one worked.

The girls in the cages were Caucasian and in their early teens. Probably thirteen or fourteen if Carver had to guess. They were conscious but drugged like the other girl. They seemed to be in an almost zombie-like trance. He didn't know why they were considered low-tier trash by the traffickers.

"Come here," Carver said.

They obediently walked over to him. That kind of mindless compliance meant they were possibly dosed with scopolamine. They were in raggedy sweatpants and T-shirts. He found a set for the first girl and dressed her so she wasn't in her underwear.

Jessica burst in through the side door and gasped at the pool of blood on the floor. She gasped again at the blood-soaked body on the couch. Then she saw Carver with three girls huddled around him.

She dodged around the pool of blood. "How many are there?"

"Three." Carver pushed the girls gently toward Jessica. "Go with her to the van."

The girls walked to her and waited without saying anything.

"What's wrong with them?"

"Drugged," Carver said. "Take them to the van. I'll be out in a minute."

"What are you going to do?"

"Look around for anything useful." Carver went to the refrigerator and opened it. It was well stocked with beer and liquor. He looked in the top freezer and found air-sealed bags filled with frozen white flowers.

They were called angel's trumpets because they resembled trumpets. He didn't know what the scientific name was. He did know they were used to make a powerful version of scopolamine that was widely used in Medellin, Colombia, especially on gringos.

He didn't know how it was made, but someone here apparently did, or they wouldn't have imported the flowers from Colombia. He looked through the rest of the fridge and finally found what he was looking for in one of the cabinets.

There was a small plastic vial with white powder in it. It was labeled *Scope* on the outside, most likely because it was scopolamine. There wasn't much of it, but it didn't take a lot to put a person into a compliant state. These men had been using it on those little girls, the ones Jorge referred to as low tier trash.

Freddy started to wake up. The man must have built up quite a resistance to fentanyl to be recovering so soon. That was good. It gave Carver a chance to talk to the man and find out if he knew anything useful.

Jessica came back inside. "The girls are buckled in. They're so doped up, it's horrible."

Carver showed her the scopolamine. "This stuff will turn anyone into a zombie in seconds. They probably put it in the girls' water."

"Looks like you took care of business. Did you find out anything about Sabrina?"

"The guy on the couch said there were two Asian girls here, but they moved them."

"Who moved them?"

"Antonio and his brother." Carver slapped Freddy's cheeks. The man groaned. He slapped him harder. "Wake up, sleepyhead."

Freddy blinked slowly and smiled dopily at Carver. "Man, this hallucination is wild."

Carver stood and yanked Freddy upright. He took him to the bathroom on the other side of the cages and propped him up on the toilet. He picked up the hose and turned on the faucet. Then he sprayed Freddy in the face.

The man batted the water weakly with his hands. He sputtered and tried to turn away but only managed to fall off the toilet. Carver walked right up to him and kept spraying him right between the eyes.

Freddy shouted, "Stop! Stop! What the hell, man?"

Carver relented and saw that realization was starting to set into Freddy's eyes.

Freddy blinked and looked up at Carver. "Who the hell are you, man?"

"I'm looking for a young Asian girl by the name of Sabrina. Antonio and Mateo brought her by a couple of days ago. I want to know where she is."

"Sabrina?" He wiped water off his face and frowned. His movements were clumsy and sluggish because of the fentanyl. His brain was probably just as sluggish. "Yeah, I remember two Asian girls. Nice bodies, man, real nice. Primo stuff. They got transferred upstream. Antonio said Japanese girls are top tier, so he was sending them to the big boys, you know?"

"Where are these big boys? Are they at the ranch?"

"Ranch?" He blinked and rubbed his face. "Man, I can't feel my face. What the hell did I take?"

Carver snapped his fingers in the man's face. "Hey, tell me about the ranch."

"Oh, um, you must be talking about Jaeger's place. They don't let us errand boys into Jaeger's place."

"Is Sabrina there?"

"Uh, I don't know." Freddy rubbed his eyes. "Usually, they go to the big house first. They get cleaned up and evaluated. Then they decide where to send them. Jaeger makes those decisions."

Carver showed him the address for the other place Ramona had mentioned. "Is this the big house?"

"Huh?"

Carver opened street view on his phone and showed it to him. "Is this the big house?" Freddy squinted. "Yeah, that's it."

The big house was, indeed, a big house. But it wasn't a place where people normally lived. It was a church. It looked like a traditional old-school church. It was made of wood, had a steeple, and was painted white. It was medium sized for a church but easily double the size of a normal house.

"How many girls pass through here in a week?" Carver said.

Freddy took a long moment to think about it. "About twenty-five to fifty. Depends on the time of season, you know? Even though it ain't a seasonal business." He giggled. "Men are always looking for some hot little thing."

Carver didn't think there was much else of use to get out of the man. He considered giving him an overdose of fentanyl, but in the end, it was easier to just push the knife into his neck and let the bleeding do the rest.

A shocked look crossed Freddy's face when the blade pierced his skin. He was still high, so he didn't even seem to realize he was bleeding out at first. Then he touched his neck and looked at the blood. "Whoa, what the hell?"

He tried to say something else, but his words became slow and slurred. His mouth kept moving but nothing was coming out. Then he slumped and his eyes became vacant. It was an easier death than he deserved.

Jessica gagged and hurried away. She waited for him at the door. "What are we going to do with Ramona?"

Carver already knew. "We'll put her in a cage." He went to the van and pulled her out of the back seat. The three girls were still there. They watched blankly as he dragged out Ramona and took her inside.

He put Ramona in the dirtiest cage and locked her in. It seemed doubtful that anyone would come by anytime soon and find this mess. If things went according to plan, then Antonio and Mateo wouldn't be alive to come by here.

Jessica was waiting next to the car when he came outside.

"Did you throw up anywhere?" he asked.

She shook her head. "No, I managed to hold it in. I'm just not cut out for killing, you know?"

"That's good." Carver put a hand on her shoulder. "You shouldn't have to be."

"So, I just let people like you do all the dirty work?" She shook her head. "Doesn't seem fair."

Carver shrugged. "I like it okay."

Jessica's forehead pinched with concern. "Doesn't that worry you?"

"Nope." He went to the driver's side door. "But it should worry the people who get in my way."

She laughed. "Damned straight."

He got back on the road. One of the girls finally broke the silence. "Where am I?"

"Oh, honey." Jessica turned around and took her hand. "How much do you remember?"

The girl started crying. "Where am I? Why don't I remember anything?"

"You got kidnapped." Jessica gripped her hand. "But we saved you, okay? We're going to get you home."

The girl shook with sobs. "I can't remember anything!"

"What's your name?"

The girl stopped crying for a moment and thought about it. "I'm Iris."

"Where do you live?"

Iris's tears stopped flowing as she thought hard about the answer to that question. The scopolamine was wearing off, but it was still affecting her memory. "It's Julius Avenue, Round Rock. I don't remember the number."

Jessica looked it up. "That's thirty minutes away. How do we handle this? Do we take them home or to the police?"

"Definitely not Austin PD," Carver said. "Most of the cops might do the right thing, but I wouldn't trust the higher-ups like Piker."

"Good point. Maybe Round Rock police?"

"Can't be us that takes them in. We need an intermediary to insulate us from the fallout." Carver gave it some thought. "Better do it now. They won't remember much about us while they're drugged."

"How about a hospital emergency room?"

Carver nodded. "Good idea. Somewhere not in Austin."

Jessica plugged an address into the GPS. "Saint David's isn't far from here." She zoomed out. "It's a few miles outside the Austin city limits." She tried to lean the phone on the center console so he could see it.

A number appeared on her phone. Someone was calling. Jessica frowned and answered. "Hello?" She blinked. "Mr. Hardin?" She put him on speaker phone.

"Jessica, have you discovered anything?"

Carver looked at Jessica and shook his head. He put a finger on his lips.

Jessica nodded. "No, sorry. How about you?"

"Nothing useful." Hardin sighed. "I've been at this nonstop since yesterday. I made countless phone calls and I'm on my way to meet with someone who might know something."

"Who would that be?"

"He's a former coworker with something of a sordid past." Hardin cleared his throat. "It will probably amount to nothing, but I'm willing to try anything at this point."

Carver chimed in. "You're just her science teacher. Would you do this for any student?"

"No, probably not." Hardin went silent for a moment. "She's a bright young woman who deserves a future. Is there something you're trying to accuse me of?"

Jessica gave Carver a confused look. "No, sorry. It's just been a very long night and we're worried."

"Well, I am too." Hardin cleared his throat. "So, you have no idea about why Sabrina was kidnapped yet? No ransom requests, nothing?"

"No."

"Well, if I discover anything, I'll let you know," Hardin said. "Unless your friend thinks I have an ulterior motive."

"We don't think that Mr. Hardin. We're all on the same team here."

"Yes, we are." Hardin blew out a breath. "Please keep me apprised of anything you discover." He ended the call.

Jessica looked at Carver. "Why did you say that to him?"

Carver shrugged. "Just a gut feeling."

"Because he's concerned about Sabrina?"

"He's not her parent. He's just her teacher."

"Well, teachers often go above and beyond for their students. Especially if it's their favorite student."

Carver had never been anyone's favorite student. He hadn't been in one school long enough to connect to anyone because military life kept his family on the move.

Jessica situated the phone on the center console so Carver could see the GPS. He took the next turn as instructed.

Iris had listened to everything. "Something happened to your sister?"

"Yes. We think she was taken by the same people who took you." Jessica ran a hand down her face. "We're taking you to the doctor. You're going to have to be a big girl and take your friends into the emergency room with you. Tell them you were kidnapped and escaped and need medical attention. They'll call your parents, okay?"

"Is something wrong with us?" Iris said. "I can't remember hardly anything, and these other girls can't even talk."

"You were drugged. That's why we need to take you to the doctor. Do you understand what you have to do?"

Iris nodded. "Yes. But we didn't escape. You and that big man got us."

"You can't tell them about us," Jessica said. "Just tell them you escaped and can't remember anything else, okay? It's very important that no one knows about us because very dangerous people will want to hurt us."

Iris' eyes became big. "I don't want you to get hurt. I promise I won't say anything."

"Thank you, Iris. I need you to be strong for all of us, okay?"

Iris straightened her shoulders the best she could. "I will be. I'll get us all to the doctor."

About fifteen minutes later, Carver saw the emergency entrance to a small hospital. An ambulance was parked in the back, but it didn't look like much was happening at the moment. He pulled to the side of the road.

They were outside of Austin and in unincorporated Travis County. Most importantly, they were outside Detective Piker's jurisdiction. Maybe she was working with the traffickers. Maybe she wasn't. It was best not to take chances.

Jessica got out and opened the sliding door. "You can walk from here?"

Iris nodded. She took the hands of the other girls and pulled them out after her.

"You two follow Iris, okay?"

The other girls nodded.

The one Carver had first encountered walked over and hugged him. She looked up at him with big eyes. "Thank you, big man."

Jessica knelt in front of her. "You can talk now? Do you remember anything?"

The girl shook her head. "Thank you." It seemed to take a lot of effort for her to say that.

"Okay, go to the emergency entrance, find a doctor or nurse, and don't say anything about us, okay?"

The girls nodded. Iris took their hands and led them to the entrance. Carver watched until they were inside. He saw a nurse stop what she was doing and run over to the girls. Then he wheeled the minivan around and started driving to the next address.

They were going to the big house.

CHAPTER 21

Sabrina huddled in the back of a van.

She could still hear men shouting and running in their hard-soled boots. After finding the parking deck exit closed, she'd tried the door handles on all the nearby vans and found one with an open back door.

She'd climbed inside and locked the door behind her. It was hot and muggy inside even though the parking deck seemed to be partially underground. That meant she still had to be in Texas somewhere, right?

Maybe it didn't mean anything. It was summer. It was hot everywhere in the United States this time of year. But considering the doctor had been evaluating her and the other girls, it stood to reason that she hadn't been shipped to her final destination.

She had no idea how human trafficking worked except that it involved moving people from one point to another. Some went willingly and others like her were kidnapped and sold like slaves.

There was no telling how long it had been since she'd been kidnapped. It could have been hours ago or days ago. It seemed like she would have woken up several times if days had passed. It seemed like she would have vague memories or dreams about being moved around.

She really wanted to open the van door and breathe fresh air. But the men were still nearby. She listened to them talk. They weren't talking in English. It sounded like Spanish, but she couldn't say for sure.

She wasn't even sure she was still in the United States. The men who took her were Hispanic. Maybe they took her into Mexico. It wasn't that far to the border. The American doctor might be a disgraced doctor living in exile. Except he wasn't alive anymore. She'd killed him.

The shouting faded noticeably. Sabrina considered going to the front of the van so she could look out of the windows, but she didn't want to do anything that would make the van move or shake.

Sabrina waited. Sweat trickled down her face. It was so hot she could barely stand it. What felt like an eternity passed and the silence persisted, so she unlocked the back door and opened it. She quietly lay down on the polished concrete floor and looked under the other vehicles. She didn't see any legs or feet.

She was alone in the garage. A sigh of relief escaped her lips. The concrete felt cool against her body, so she lay there for a moment to cool down despite the rapid beating of her heart and the adrenalin pulsing through her veins.

Her mind raced through the chain of events that took her from the examination room to the parking deck. She couldn't recall seeing any other way out of the building. There was surely a front entrance, but it would be a level above her and guarded especially now that they knew she was loose in the building somewhere.

The fact that the men had left meant there were other escape avenues that they were searching. She was surprised that they hadn't searched all of the vehicles in the garage. Maybe they thought all the vehicles were locked and that there was no way she could get into one.

Maybe someone went to fetch the keys for the vehicles and was on the way back to search them. That thought shocked her back into action. She had to get out of there. She closed the van door and jogged over to the closed exit.

She examined the metal rollup door. She tried slipping her fingers underneath the rubber on the bottom, but it was pressed tight against the concrete. She tried opening the normal entry door, but it didn't budge either. She tried several combinations on the keypad but none of them worked.

Sabrina made a circuit around the garage looking for any other exits. She found the door leading back upstairs and a pair of double doors on the other wall. She heard voices on the other side of the doors. They were getting closer.

She ran behind a van and ducked just as the doors swung open. She lay down flat next to the tire and saw the legs of two men walk past. They were just a few feet away from her. Chills ran down her spine. She clamped a hand over her mouth to stop herself from gasping.

The men spoke in what sounded like Spanish. One of them laughed. The alarm system on a van two spaces down from her chirped and the blinkers blinked. More chirps echoed in the garage. The alarm in the van she was hiding behind also chirped.

One pair of legs walked away from her position. The other came toward her. She watched the legs coming her way. They stopped next to the neighboring van. Doors clicked open and slammed shut.

The man shouted something. The other man shouted back. Sabrina crab-walked around the side of the van using the tips of her toes and her hands to keep her body off the ground. That way she was able to watch the man's movements and adjust accordingly.

She glanced in the direction of the other man. She saw his feet on the far side of the garage. He got down on his knees. He was about to look under the vehicle. If he glanced this way, he'd see her.

Sabrina kept from panicking. She gripped the handle on the van's sliding door and slowly pulled her knees up to her chest as if she were practicing on the gym bars. The handle was barely large enough for both of her hands to grasp so her right arm was bearing most of the weight.

Her arm started to shake. She couldn't hold herself up much longer. She heard the man say something from across the room. The other man responded. His voice was just on the other side of the van from her.

She heard his boots scraping. Heard his pants scuffing the floor. He was getting down to look under the vans as well. The muscles in Sabrina's right arm were screaming in pain. She couldn't hold herself up another second.

The man's clothing rustled and the rubber soles on his boots squeaked. It sounded like he'd stood back up. Her arm was shaking. It couldn't keep this up any longer. Sabrina lowered her feet to the ground and repressed a sigh of relief.

The door on the other side of the van opened. The van shook slightly as the man got in and looked around. The door closed a moment later. Sabrina dropped to her stomach and saw the man nearest her walking to the next van over.

She scuttled sideways so she could see the other man. He was also walking to another van. She didn't know if they planned to look under all the vans or if that single look had been enough for them.

Something buzzed. Metal clattered. She peeked out from the side of the van and saw the garage door rolling up. It was all the way across the garage from her but so tantalizingly close at the same time.

The men searching the garage hurried to the driveway between the vans and stopped to watch whatever was coming through the rollup door. Sabrina considered ducking back inside the building while the men were preoccupied with the opening door. Maybe she could go through the doors they'd come out of.

But going into the building was dangerous. There might be more men waiting just inside. Even if there weren't, she'd have to get to the first floor to find an exit. Maybe there was a side exit she could use. Maybe she could find a map of the building.

Another idea occurred to her. Well, two ideas, actually. One was to run behind the rows of vehicles on the left until she was close to the door. Then she could duck through the door right after the vehicle entered.

The rollup door was already open. She could already see the grill of a van just outside. She made a split-second decision and crouch-walked to the left. She kept close to the wall and sprinted past trucks and vans until she reached the front of the parking deck.

The van engine rumbled. It pulled inside. The men searching the garage shouted and the van stopped. There was a sign on the side of the van. It had a circle with a rainbow, a fish, and some other shapes she didn't recognize inside of it.

Next to the circle it said *Rainbow Road Presbyterian Church*. Beneath that it said, *Missionary Outreach*.

She had no idea what a church van was doing here. She looked more closely at the row of vans across from her and saw that some of them had the same sign on them. Some had the names of other churches on them. There were signs for Missionary Baptist Church, Lakefront Church, and more.

The garage door was rolling shut. She didn't know why the men searching had stopped the van, but she knew that if she didn't make a run for it, the door would shut, and it would be too late. She looked under the van she was hiding behind and saw that the incoming vehicle was nearly blocking the exit.

The only way out was to squeeze past it and duck under the closing door. She looked toward the men who were searching the garage. They were holding up their hands in the universal stop gesture. They'd made the van stop to block the exit just in case she was there and tried to make a run for it.

There was a slight chance she could get past the van in time, but they'd see her. They'd open the door and chase her down. Her best bet was to stay here and hide and wait for the heat to die down.

Despite knowing that, it took all her willpower not to make a run for it. There was a real sense of urgency to find safety and not just because she was scared. It was because of simple biological needs. Needs that would prevent her from hiding indefinitely.

She needed food and water. She would need to use the bathroom. There was sure to be food and water in the building, but getting to it without getting caught would probably be extremely difficult. She could use the bathroom anywhere, but the odor would probably attract attention.

The two men were so focused on the incoming van that it seemed like her best bet was to go back inside the building and find a better place to hide. The life and death aspect made the decision much harder to make.

Which decision would lead to her capture, and which would lead to her freedom? She calculated that her chances of escape were abysmally low. Probably less than ten percent considering the variables.

Would she rather die of dehydration or starvation than become a sex slave? That was a very grim question to consider. She might be sold to someone who was into abuse and humiliation. Maybe even someone who was into killing or other awful things.

She knew more about this kind of stuff than she should have because she loved to read about anything and everything, no matter how horrible it was. Knowledge was good even if it was frightening.

No matter which choice she made, the odds weren't in her favor.

Going back into the building offered her a chance to find an alternative route. Without a keypad code, she wasn't getting out of the parking deck. With that in mind, she hugged the wall and hurried back to the far side of the garage.

The garage door clanked shut. Vehicle doors clicked open and slammed shut. Men spoke to each other in rapid, urgent tones, none of it in English. The smoking man had spoken to the others in English earlier. Did these people understand it or had he mistakenly addressed them in the wrong language?

She examined the signs on the vans and trucks as she passed them. She'd been so panicked when she first entered the garage that she hadn't even noticed them. Now she was making a point of it. She found the names of five different churches, each one a different denomination.

They all had brightly colored logos. They looked so innocent and friendly. Like they were being used to transport church goers to family-friendly events. No one would ever think they were being used to traffic young girls.

Sabrina stopped at the end of the vans and stared at the doors the men had exited earlier. She wanted to get closer. Maybe open the door a crack and look inside. There had to be another way out of this place. But it was far too risky.

She got down on her stomach again and watched the men. She noticed something protruding from behind the back tire of the next van over. It was just a tiny little silhouette, but she hadn't seen it moments ago when she'd been here.

Sabrina crawled to the other van and reached behind the tire. She felt something hard and plastic. She picked it up. It was a key fob. One of the men must have dropped it when they started waving at the incoming van.

There was a label on the fob and a string of alphanumeric characters on the label. It probably corresponded to a specific vehicle. She examined the side of the van, crouch-walked around it, and looked for a label.

She didn't find one. Then she reached the back of the van and realized why she hadn't found a label. The string of characters was from the license plate. This one matched the license plate of the van across the middle aisle from her. A van that had already been searched.

Something else occurred to her. Something she should have thought of when she was hiding in the van earlier. How did the incoming van open the garage door? Did they have a wireless remote for it? Or was there a keypad on the other side?

An ember of hope sparked in her chest. She hurried to the driver's side of the van and looked through the driver's side window. She looked at the visors and the dash. She didn't see a remote. The door probably didn't use one. The keypad was the only way to open it.

Which meant she hadn't found a way out. Not yet. But she had a plan now. If the keypad was the only way to open the door, then she just had to hide and watch until someone left. If she saw what buttons they pressed, then she could escape anytime she wanted.

She looked at the men talking next to the stopped van. There was one major problem with that plan. The keypad was on a console to the left of the garage door so the driver could lean out of the window and easily use it.

When the driver stopped to punch in the code, she had no way of seeing his hand or the keypad except from the side. Watching from the side would make it much harder to see what buttons were being pressed.

But it was something. His hand would move up and down and side to side. It would help her narrow down the combination by a lot. She would also know how many key presses it took. It might be just four or it could be a lot more.

She also had a key fob to one of the vans which gave her a place to hide in the meantime, provided the men didn't realize it was gone.

So, she waited. The arriving van finally parked. The two men who'd arrived in the van went into the doors on the other side of the garage and returned with two foldout wheelchairs. They pulled two girls from inside the back of the van and put them in the wheelchairs. They rolled them inside.

The other two men finished their search and started pressing buttons on the key fobs to lock the vans. They didn't notice the missing fob probably because there were at least twenty vehicles parked in the garage.

They went through the same double doors they'd come out of earlier. Sabrina went to the van she had the fob for and pulled on the door handle. It was still unlocked. She got inside. Another row of vans blocked her view of the door the men had gone in, but they would pass by her van when they returned.

She waited and watched. She had no idea how much time had passed but it felt like hours. It didn't seem like anyone was going to leave this place. At least not tonight. And what if they decided to take the van she was in? What if they noticed the missing key fob?

That made her worry a lot. She counted the number of vans and trucks in the garage. There were thirty-one. They were parked in three rows of eight and one row of seven. That meant her van had a little more than a three percent chance of being chosen.

Then she realized that the church names on the vehicles might be tied to different geographical areas. So, if the next departure required a specific church vehicle, then the odds of hers being chosen might be much higher or lower. Or maybe since the key fob was missing, the odds were zero.

She couldn't help doing the math in her head. It was the only thing that kept her sane and kept her from panicking again. She thought back to when the van entered the garage. Had she seen daylight coming through the door?

Sabrina closed her eyes and envisioned it. There hadn't been any outside light. It had been daytime when she looked out of the window in the examination room. Maybe it was dark outside. Maybe it was nighttime, and the criminals were all snoozing in their beds.

In other words, no one would be leaving for several hours. That presented her with several problems. Her mouth was dry, and her lips felt like they were cracking. She was very thirsty, and very hungry. And to make matters worse, she had to go to the bathroom.

Which meant unless she could figure out the keypad code now, she was going to have to go back inside the building to hunt for supplies.

Then another thought occurred to her. Maybe there was another way out. A way without the keypad. And if everyone was asleep, she might have an excellent chance to escape.

Sabrina hopped out of the van. She ran to the rollup door and rapped her knuckles on it. It felt relatively sturdy, but the rattle and movement told her the metal was thin. She pushed on it and felt it give slightly. That was even more promising.

She did the math in her head. Tried to calculate the odds of success but couldn't arrive at an answer without knowing all the variables. That was fine. She knew enough to wing it. Like Vania often said, "I have no idea what I'm doing but I'm doing it anyway."

Sabrina got in the van. She pressed the start button. The engine rumbled to life. It sounded awfully loud in the garage. Hopefully everyone was asleep somewhere on the upper floors and not sitting just outside the doors to the parking garage.

She shifted the van into reverse and backed it into the center aisle. She backed all the way up until the bumper touched the back wall. She was lined up with the garage door. Sabrina put the van in drive and put on her seatbelt. She backed the seat up enough to give her plenty of space between her face and the airbag because she didn't want it knocking her out if it deployed.

Sabrina gunned the engine. The van lumbered forward. The engine certainly wasn't built for speed, but it managed to hit forty-eight miles per hour by the time it reached the rollup door. It smashed into it.

Metal screeched. The front of the van bent the metal slats and punched through them. There was another loud screech, and the van jerked to a halt, caught like a giant metal beast in the web of bent metal.

Sabrina's body rocked forward from the arrested momentum. The airbag exploded from the steering wheel simultaneously. Her face bounced off it. The impact was like being slapped, dazing her slightly.

She saw the concrete ramp leading up and out of the parking garage. She saw the night sky above. But the driver and passenger doors were pinned on both sides by the bent slats of the rollup door.

Sabrina hopped into the passenger seat. She slid it all the way forward then shifted her back down and her feet up. She pulled her knees to her chest then kicked out. Her muscular legs delivered the impact she needed.

The windshield cracked and puckered. She kicked once more, and the safety glass crumbled. Sabrina stood in the seat and pulled herself through the opening. She slid off the short front of the van and hit the ground running.

She ran up the ramp and found herself facing a tall concrete wall. It was at least eight feet tall. Too tall for her to reach the top no matter how hard she jumped. The wall continued in both directions.

This was the same service alley she'd seen from the doctor's window. It was below ground level, meaning there had to be a ramp leading up and out of it. That ramp might be just around the corner. She had to get there before the men in the building woke up.

She heard shouting inside the garage. It sounded like the men were fully awake and fully aware that their quarry was still on the loose. The rollup door was blocked, but they could exit the garage through the normal door next to it.

Sabrina saw black skid marks on the concrete. It looked like they turned toward the left side of the building. That was probably where the van had come from. She sprinted left just as the garage entry door banged open.

She turned the corner and stopped dead in her tracks. The concrete wall cut across and connected with the building.

This was a dead end.

Chapter 22

Carver stopped down the street from the church.

It looked just like it had in the maps app. It looked like a nice, quaint house of worship. It looked like a lot of churches he'd seen all over the world. Unfortunately, the façade of safety and religion was often used to hide horrors.

The sign outside said Rainbow Bridge Presbyterian. The marquee next to it said, *Everyone welcome! Come in and find salvation at the end of God's rainbow!*

It was late and the church was dark. Carver doubted they kept prisoners in the sanctuary. There was an annex behind the church. The three-story building looked like it had seen better days.

Most of the windows were boarded up. The paint was peeling on the wooden exterior and the concrete foundation had large cracks in it. There was also a chain link fence stretched across the front door.

The church itself looked just fine. The paint was good. The siding and foundation didn't have any problems. It was an interesting contrast from the annex. It basically told him everything he needed to know.

Carver put in his earbud. "You know the drill."

Jessica raised an eyebrow. "Wait here?"

He nodded.

"You know the drill too, right?" Jessica squeezed his hand. "Be careful. Scream like a girl if you need help."

Carver slung the MP5SD across his back. He buckled on his hip pouch and holstered his Sig. He sheathed his survival knife and pulled on his black cap and mask. He double-checked the items in the pack to make sure everything was in order. Everything looked good.

There was a playground next to the church. It had a metal slide, a metal merry go round, and several spring horses. There was a swing set made from metal tubing and chains, and a jungle gym of similar construction.

The chain link fence around the playground was leaning to the side in places and the gate hung open. An old florescent streetlamp bathed the place in dim yellow light, revealing peeling paint and rust on most of the equipment.

The whole place had an eerie quality to it, especially given what the church was being used for. Carver skirted the chain link fence and kept to the shadows. He crossed through the field of overgrown grass between the playground and the annex.

He scanned the building with the monocular using night vision and infrared. He caught heat peeking out of the cracks around the boarded-up windows. The place definitely wasn't as abandoned as it looked.

There was a small house behind the annex. It was a shoebox house with wooden sides and a wraparound porch. Probably the preacher's house. The front porch light was on, but the rest of the house was dark.

There was a detached two-car garage next to the house. The doors were closed. That made Carver curious to know what was parked inside. Was Ramona's Cadillac in there? Were Antonio and Mateo here somewhere?

Most importantly, was Sabrina here?

Carver looked for exterior cameras. He didn't see any. They probably had cameras inside like the last place. He considered his options and decided to check out the house first. It looked well maintained so someone was almost certainly living there.

He tucked away the monocular and slid on his night vision goggles. They were great for hands-free vision but didn't have the high zoom capabilities of the monocular.

He crept up to the garage and found an entry door on the side next to the house. He tested the door handle. It was unlocked. He turned the doorknob and opened the door. A Chevy Suburban was parked right inside.

It looked black, but it was hard to tell with night vision. The windows were tinted too dark to see through. It had black steel wheels. The same kind found on government vehicles. It might not be government issue, but it sure looked like it.

He walked to the front of the vehicle. It had a Texas tag with no government markings on it. It was just a lookalike. But a lot of people wouldn't know that just from looking at it. They'd assume it was an official vehicle.

Something else was parked in the neighboring bay. It was a long sedan, but Carver couldn't tell what kind because it had a cover over it. He walked over to it and lifted the front of the cover.

It was a Cadillac DeVille. He took out his small flashlight and shined it on the paint to confirm the color. It was gold, just like Ramona's. He lifted the cover a little further and saw the gold spoke wheels.

Carver spoke softly. "I found Ramona's Cadillac."

Jessica gasped. "Really? Does that mean Sabrina is here?"

"I don't know. I'm going to check out the house first."

"Please let her be here." Jessica whimpered softly. "I'm so scared for her."

"I'll let you know as soon as I find something." Carver pulled the car cover back to free the front doors. He pulled on the handle and the driver's door opened. He looked inside. The keys were on the dashboard.

He slid inside and opened the glove compartment. There was a snub-nosed Smith and Wesson revolver buried under napkins and discarded wrappers. The serial numbers looked like they'd been burned off with acid. It was a classic Saturday night special, good in a pinch and practically untraceable.

Carver left it where it was and closed the glove compartment. He opened the center console and found a bag with small vials inside. They were plastic do-it-yourself vials. You could buy them online or at a medical supply store, fill them and cap them yourself.

Empty vials had been discarded in the console, but the ones in the bag were filled about halfway with clear liquid. Carver tucked the bag into his hip pouch. There was another baggie of capped syringes next to it. He took those too even though his pouch was getting crowded.

The back seat of the DeVille was dirty and stained. Carver used his flashlight sparingly even though it was doubtful anyone would see the light from outside. Some of the stains were blood. Others looked like they could be semen, but he wasn't sure.

The car stank of marijuana, body odor, and God only knew what else. It was obvious the brothers had used the vehicle a lot in the short time since Ramona gave them the car. A black light would probably reveal stains beyond counting. About the only way to clean this car was to set it on fire.

He got out and pulled the cover the rest of the way off. He popped the trunk. It was empty aside from a box of painter's plastic. Some of the plastic had been used to cover the carpet in the trunk. It wasn't to protect it while hauling groceries. It was probably to keep bodies from staining it.

He closed the trunk and covered the car. It was best to cover his tracks just in case things went south. He was wearing gloves, so fingerprints weren't an issue, but it was best to make the place looked as undisturbed as possible. That way if he had to bail, there was a chance they wouldn't know anyone had been there.

Carver looked around the rest of the garage but found nothing else of interest, so he left it and moved toward the house. He avoided the front porch and ducked around to the back. The wooden stairs looked well maintained, but he didn't want to take any chances by just casually walking up them.

He tested the first step with his weight. It creaked faintly, but not loudly enough to wake anyone sleeping inside. The second step didn't creak at all. He skipped the third step and tested the porch itself. No creaks.

The back door was locked. He jimmied the bottom latch and tried to open it. He expected the deadbolt to be engaged, but it wasn't. The hinges were apparently well oiled because they didn't make a sound.

Carver stepped inside and into the kitchen. There was a gas range with a stainless-steel hood over it. There was a stainless-steel microwave and fridge. The cabinets looked new and modern with large metal handles.

The hardwood flooring wasn't actually made of wood. It felt like porcelain tile and as such, didn't creak in the slightest when he walked on it. The same tile was in the neighboring rooms too. He couldn't determine the color with the night vision, but it wasn't all that important.

The den had a long leather couch and a big-screen television. There were stains on the couch and the floor. There were also padded handcuffs and a ball gag on the floor next to the couch. It didn't seem like the kind of thing that belonged in a preacher's house, but maybe things were different in this day and age.

The place had a strong perfume odor to it, like a deodorizer had been liberally sprayed to cover other unpleasant aromas. The scent grew stronger as he neared the couch, as if the leather itself was soaked with the stuff.

Carver went down the hallway. There was a bathroom on the left and a bedroom on the right. The bedroom had a mattress on the floor and piles of assorted leather straps and restraints. The next bedroom had a regular bed in it but no one was in it.

The last room on the left was a larger bedroom. Probably the master suite. There was a king-sized bed inside with two occupants. Carver walked in quiet as a ghost and looked at the larger of the two occupants.

The one on the left was a Caucasian male, probably five feet and seven inches tall with skinny legs and arms, but a big, round stomach. Probably late forties or early fifties. He was sleeping on his back and snoring gently.

The figure on the right side of the bed was much smaller and female. She was huddled under the covers, but a long slender chain ran from under the covers and to the metal bed frame. She was probably cuffed.

There was a large, framed poster above the headboard. It said,

This is the MASTER'S Chamber.

You will do what the MASTER commands.

You will feel pain or pleasure by the MASTER'S hand.

It went on and on for about ten lines that he didn't bother to read. It told him everything he needed to know.

Carver wanted to question the so-called master, but he also didn't want to make a lot of noise. Someone from the annex building might come back this way and hear unusual sounds. Or maybe the man would scream and raise the alarm.

At the same time, he also didn't want this man to go gently into that good night. So, he went to the den and picked up the ball gag from the floor. He adjusted the strap to fit a grown man and went into the room with the leather restraints.

He collected a few and went into the bedroom. The windows were outfitted with blackout cellular shades. They were the kind built into frames so no light could get in and no light could get out. That was convenient.

Carver pulled the covers off the girl on the other side of the bed. She was a small Black girl. He couldn't guess her age, but she was a minor and the bruises and markings on her body told him she'd been abused. The cuffs on her wrist and the headboard were buckled shut and secured with a tiny padlock.

He used his survival knife to cut through the buckle on the headboard because he didn't want to risk cutting her wrist. Her eyelids opened slightly like she couldn't open them any further. Probably because she was drugged.

Carver lifted her from the bed and took her into the guest room with the normal bed. She tried to lift her arm but could barely move it. He put a hand on her forehead. She felt a little cold.

He leaned down and whispered in her ear, "Stay here. I'm here to help."

She moaned softly. It was such a tiny sound, but it made Carver's blood boil.

He went back into the bedroom where the man was still slumbering peacefully. The peace was about to be broken. Carver pushed the ball gag into the man's mouth and strapped it on. The man moaned but didn't wake. Carver took the man's right wrist and cuffed it. He secured it to the metal bed frame but didn't pull it taut just yet.

He pulled off the covers. The man was sleeping in what looked like leather bikini bottoms and nothing else. Carver cuffed the man's right ankle and secured it to the metal footboard. He did the same for the left ankle.

The man started to moan and stir. Carver walked to the other side of the bed and cuffed the man's left wrist. He strapped it to the left corner of the headboard and pulled it tight. A muffled shout of surprise told Carver the man was now fully awake.

Carver yanked the man by his left ankle to pull him closer to the center of the bed. It was like dragging a sack of rocks. The man had skinny extremities, but that belly of his was something else.

The man struggled, but all Carver had to do was pull the restraints tight. He stood to the side of the bed and met the man's terrified gaze. "I'm looking for an Asian girl. Her name is Sabrina. Is she here on the premises?"

The man's eyes bugged. He tried to talk around the ball gag and couldn't.

"A simple nod or shake of the head will do."

The man shook his head.

"Was she here?"

The man approximated a shrug the best he could with the tightened restraints.

"How could you possibly not know that?" Carver put the tip of his knife against the man's stomach.

The man struggled and made muffled cries.

"You're obviously someone who should know what girls are coming in and out of here." Carver pursed his lips and pretended to think. "I'm going to loosen the ball gag so you can tell me what I want to know, okay?"

The man shivered and nodded his head.

"If you try to shout for help, I'll start cutting body parts off of you. Understood?"

The man's eyes flared. He nodded.

Carver loosened the ball gag and lowered it.

The man spoke in a whimpering voice. "I'm just the minister. They brought me in to give sermons and put on a good front for the public."

"You're a real minister? A man of God?"

"Y-yes." The minister shivered.

"How many kids are they keeping in the annex building?"

"It's never constant. They bring them here one day and they're gone the next."

"Yeah? Did they give you that girl?"

"I assure you that this is an affliction I've been praying about every night, but I keep giving into temptation." Tears pooled in his eyes. "I promise to never do it again if you don't harm me."

"Answer the question."

"Yes."

"Did you go into the annex and choose her?"

"No, they have certain girls that are considered undesirable or very common."

"What makes them undesirable?"

He gulped. "I don't know. They just let me choose from that group."

"You know Antonio and Mateo?"

Recognition passed flashed in the man's eyes. "Yes."

"Are they here in the annex?"

"I don't know. They really don't tell me very much at all. I only do what I'm told." His eyelids fluttered. "You see, I'm just as much a victim as anyone else here."

"Yeah." Carver had heard enough. He shoved the ball gag back into the man's mouth and tightened the strap. "You wait here, and I'll go check the annex."

Relief filled the man's face. The relief didn't last very long because Carver pushed the razor-sharp blade of his knife into the man's underbelly. He slashed it open. The man's innards began to spill out.

The minister's face turned bright red. He tried to scream. Tried to struggle. But all he did was push his insides out of the hole. The man's internal organs were choked and covered in visceral fat.

Carver looked down at the minister. "It's going to take a long time for you to die. Maybe not as long as a bullet to the stomach, but still, you're going to suffer for at least thirty minutes. Maybe you'd better start praying for forgiveness."

The minister sobbed and looked like he was trying to beg, but the ball gag was very good at silencing him. Just like he used it to silence his victims.

Jessica spoke over the earbud. "Carver what did you do to him?"

"I helped him lose weight." Carver checked the restraints one more time to ensure they were all good, then he left the minister to die in agony. He went to the bedroom and found the girl lying there. He turned on the bedroom lights since the blackout shades on the windows would hide the light from anyone on the outside.

The girl was naked and bruised all over. She had choke marks on her neck and one of her eyes was black and blue. She was a slight little thing. Completely helpless. Memories flashed through Carver's head. They were old memories buried deep. Memories he didn't even know he had.

He was the helpless thing. His parents claimed they were training him. Molding him into something special. He remembered that now. They'd tied him up and given him an hour to escape. If he couldn't, then they'd beat him. Torture him.

Jessica's voice broke through his thoughts. "Carver are you going to answer me?"

"I'll be out soon," he said.

The memories faded to black, and he was standing next to the girl again. He'd seen dead kids, tortured kids, sexually abused kids and worse many times before during his time in Scion. But he'd never had flashbacks like this.

Why now? What had changed? He thought about his entire reason for being here. He was helping a friend. This wasn't something he would have done years ago. But now he was. Now he was hunting down human traffickers instead of enjoying time on the beach.

And that was bad news for anyone who got in his way.

— ¦ —

CHAPTER 23

Carver took the girl to the van.

Jessica was already outside with the sliding door open. She gasped when she saw the girl. "My God, you poor thing!"

Carver gently put the girl in the second-row seat. "I'm going into the annex next."

Jessica put a hand on his arm. "I hope that bastard suffered."

"He's still suffering and will be for the better part of an hour." Carver put his hand over hers. "I'll be back."

She nodded mutely and watched him go.

Carver skirted the edge of the playground again and went around the side of the annex. He looked around the corner at the back door. There was a metal barrel, a small, round table, and four chairs.

There were cigarette butts on the ground and the slight odor of garbage emanated from the direction of the barrel. This was a break area. A place where the people working for the traffickers came outside to enjoy a smoke.

Four chairs probably meant four guards, but it was best not to assume anything. There might be five guards. Maybe even six. Maybe only four guards could take a smoke break at the same time.

It was late and some of the guards might be asleep. Depending on how many people were inside, it might be best to keep things fast and clean. If Sabrina wasn't here, it meant she was probably at Jaeger's place. The ranch.

On the other hand, these men might know more than the ones at the last place. Maybe he could keep one alive. If Rhodes was in command, she'd want a couple of the targets drugged so they could be questioned later.

But this wasn't a team mission and Carver didn't have time to waste. If Sabrina was inside, then he didn't need to leave anyone alive. But if she wasn't, he needed more information. He needed to know more about Jaeger and the ranch.

He tested the back door handle. It was locked. He jimmied it and gently tried to open it. The deadbolt was engaged. He pulled the snap gun from his hip pouch and got it open in thirty seconds.

Carver eased open the door. It creaked loudly but there was no helping it. He looked inside with night vision and saw a utility room with a gas water heater, a washer, a dryer, and shelves with detergents and cleaning agents. There was a flight of concrete stairs against the left wall and a door at the top. This was apparently the basement.

He stepped inside and closed the door behind him. It squeaked the whole way closed. He locked the deadbolt and waited next to the bottom of the stairs in case someone came down them.

After two minutes passed and no one appeared, he looked around the large basement space to make sure no one was sleeping down there. It was empty, so he walked up the stairs, grateful they were concrete and not wood.

Carver had just reached the top when the door handle began to twist. The door was a left-hand inswing, so it opened toward the metal railing and not the wall. He swung himself over the railing, keeping his feet on the stairs, and hung onto the railing.

The door bumped the fingers on his left hand. It didn't feel great, but it didn't hurt too much either, so he kept quiet. He nodded his head upward to disengage the night vision goggles just as the lights were switched on.

A man walked past him. The man wasn't Antonio or Mateo. He was a short Latino with a gun on his hip and a cell phone in his hand. If he'd turned to close the door, he would have seen Carver right away.

As it was, he only turned when he heard Carver's shoes scraping on the concrete as Carver swung himself back over the railing and came up behind him. The man barely had time to open his mouth and no time to shout in surprise before Carver's fist landed on the bridge of his nose.

He tumbled down the hard, unforgiving stairs like a rag doll and rested in a boneless heap at the bottom. Carver went to the bottom and checked for a pulse. It was there but fading fast. The man's neck was broken. So were most of the other bones in his body.

Once the man was a hundred percent dead, Carver went back upstairs and turned off the light. He listened for sounds of movement and heard faint talking from somewhere down the hallway.

The hallway led to the right. There were several doorways along it, presumably to former Sunday school classrooms. A light was on in the room down the hallway. Male voices drifted from within.

The floor was carpeted, and the subfloor was concrete. Carver knew that because the basement ceiling was concrete. It was why he hadn't heard the man's footsteps outside of the basement door.

He walked to the first doorway on the right and looked inside. There was a corkboard with bible verses on it and chairs arranged in a circle. There was a heavy layer of dust on the chairs, so it was obvious the room hadn't been used in a while.

Carver worked his way down the hallway, clearing the other rooms as he passed them. They were all in similar shape to the first one. There was a flight of stairs in the middle of the hallway. They led up to the next floor.

There was a steel door at the top that was locked from this side. It was clearly there to keep people upstairs from getting out. He put his hand on the first step and pushed down. The subfloor here was wood, not concrete.

The voices in the room at the end of the hallway weren't coming from a television. They had the ebb and flow of a normal conversation. It sounded like three or four men speaking in Spanish. He couldn't make out what they were saying.

The men weren't talking loudly enough to cover any sounds he made while walking up the stairs. He used his hand to test the second and third steps and felt them buckle slightly. The plywood decking would almost certainly creak when he put his full weight on it.

It would be best to take care of the men first and then go upstairs. Besides the possibility of creaking stairs, there were a couple of reasons to do it in that order.

The upstairs door was locked from the outside. It seemed highly unlikely that any guards would want to be locked upstairs with the prisoners. That meant all the guards would almost certainly be down here on the first floor. Taking them out would probably give him the run of the building.

Carver walked down the hallway, sliding his MP5SD around to the ready position. He could probably get the drop on these guys and get some answers. It was at least worth a try. Because he was going to have to deal with them before finding out if Sabrina was here.

Carver reached the doorway. He listened for a moment. The men were talking about pickup trucks. Something about modifying pickups with lift kits. One of them said he was too short to climb into a lifted pickup and the others laughed.

They were having a good time. Enjoying a moment of levity. He figured now was as good a time as any to introduce himself. He peeked around the edge of the door and saw the men sitting around a table. One of the men was facing the doorway. His eyes widened with surprise.

So much for the element of surprise. Carver stepped into the doorway, MP5SD aimed and at the ready. "Stay in your seats. I have some—" He didn't have time to finish the sentence because the man who'd seen him was already raising a sidearm to fire.

Carver put a bullet right between his eyes. The man flailed and fell over backward. The other men jumped up. Their chairs fell over backwards. Some had guns in hand, others reached for them. There were five men. Not three, not four.

That made six total, including the man Carver had pushed down the stairs. That was why it was never safe to assume things even if there might be some evidence to support it. The men were in an enclosed space. A Sunday school classroom with kid's drawings on the walls and a big picture of Jesus on the wall.

Jesus was looking down and smiling at a group of children. The children were petting lambs and smiling up at Jesus. Carver had never been to Sunday school. This was technically his first time, and it looked like he was learning all the wrong lessons.

He pulled the trigger and put a hole in another guy's forehead. The other three men were facing away from him, so he shot the first guy in the back, dead center in the spine. The next guy was already halfway turned so he put a bullet through his temple.

The last guy had the right idea and was diving to the side while drawing his sidearm. While the idea was right, the execution was all wrong. His legs got tangled in the chair and he was having trouble swinging his oversized magnum revolver around.

He was a short guy. Probably the shortest one out of all the short men in the room. He was probably the one who said he couldn't climb into a lifted pickup. Carver made sure he never had to worry about that again and put a bullet in his rib cage right where the heart was located.

The short man dropped his gun and flopped dead on the floor about a second after the 9x19mm supersonic round traveling at subsonic speeds ripped through his internal organs and bounced around his insides.

It was over fast and almost quietly aside from the shouts of surprise near the end. None of the men had gotten off a shot. The bodies hadn't made much noise hitting the carpeted floor. If there were more guards in the building, they might not have heard anything.

One thing was certain. None of these men were Antonio or Mateo. They had tattoos and piercings but nothing like what the brothers had. The shortest guy had a hairdo that looked like a bird's nest and a flaming skull tattoo on his bicep. His dead friends had the same tattoo. It was almost certainly gang related.

Carver checked for signs of life and found none. Then he went into the hallway and began clearing the other rooms on the floor. The last two rooms had bunkbeds in them. One room was empty. The next room had a guy snoring peacefully on a top bunk.

He was short but muscular. He had the same skull tattoo on his bicep and lots of tattoos on his face. Tattoos were fine and dandy if you were an average law-abiding citizen. But they were dumb to get if you lived a life of crime because they made a person much easier to identify.

Face tattoos were the worst. They were front and center on a part of the body people rarely covered. People noticed facial tattoos. A person with them stood out from the crowd and not in a good way. Maybe that was the point. Maybe tough guys wanted to be seen.

It worked because Carver saw this guy. He yanked him off the top bunk and let him fall to the floor. The man hit the carpet with a dull thud. He groaned and pushed himself into a sitting position. He seemed to think he'd rolled off the bed himself.

Then he saw Carver's feet. He blinked rapidly and looked up. He shouted and tried scoot backwards but his back was against the bottom bunk. Carver pointed the gun at him and smiled.

"Hi."

The man spoke rapidly in Spanish. Carver understood bits and pieces, but it was a strange dialect. Spanish, like English, had lots of dialects. Some were harder to understand than others. It was like an American trying to understand someone from Liverpool or Newcastle, England.

Carver spoke in Spanish. "Talk slower."

The man spoke slower but his Spanish was still hard to understand. "Who are you?"

"I ask the questions. Are there more guards upstairs?"

The man narrowed his eyes and bared his teeth. "I say nothing."

Carver put the muzzle of the MP5SD on the man's forehead. It was probably still a little hot from all the shooting. The man winced but didn't try to duck away. Carver raised an eyebrow. "Answer me."

"No."

Carver pulled out his knife. "I can cut pieces off of you until you answer."

The man said something Carver didn't understand. But the tone was clearly defiant. Like many gang members, he'd probably had a hard life. Judging from the tears tattooed under his eyes, he'd probably killed a lot of people and survived.

There were scars under his tattoos. There was a long white slash under the metal chain around his neck. This guy had survived a lot. He wasn't afraid to die. Hell, it might even be a relief for him. Most likely, he knew he was dead no matter what he said.

On that count, he was right. Carver could respect that. But that was as far as his respect went. This guy sex trafficked minors. He abused kids who had no chance at defending themselves. And he thought that made him a badass.

There really wasn't time to give the guy a true lesson in pain. But he didn't want to give the guy a completely painless death. So, he shot him in the stomach. The man cried out in pain.

He started calling out names. "Jorge! Alfredo!"

Carver grabbed him by his thick head of hair and dragged him down the hallway to the break room. He dragged him through the blood of his downed coworkers and dropped him. He leaned down and picked him up by the neck and slammed him on the table.

Jessica spoke over the earbud. "Carver, what are you doing?"

Carver didn't answer. He spoke to the dying man instead. "Jorge and Alfredo have already moved on to the next life."

The man started coughing up blood. Apparently, the bullet had bounced around and nicked a lung. With blood filling his lungs, this guy wasn't going to be sticking around much longer. But as much as Carver wanted the man to suffer, he couldn't leave an active threat on his six nor could he take the time to watch and wait for the man to die.

So, he looked the man in the eyes and said, "You're lucky I'm in a hurry." Then he stabbed the man in the heart with his survival knife. It only took a few seconds after that. Carver checked for a pulse, found none, and moved to the stairs.

"Carver, answer me," Jessica said.

"I'm terminating the guards." Carver took a moment to remember why he was there. He was letting emotions control his actions. Yes, these men deserved to suffer, but he was here to complete a mission.

He needed to get in, clear the building of threats, and get out. One bullet per target if possible. Don't waste time questioning uncooperative combatants. It had been a long time since an operation got into his head like this.

In the long run it wasn't good for his health or his odds of survival. He took a deep breath. Cleared his head. Got himself back into the zone. There might be more guards upstairs. He couldn't let himself slip, not even a little bit.

The locks on the upstairs doors were hand twist deadbolts. No keys were necessary from this side. There were no cameras in the hallway or rooms on the first floor. He hadn't seen a monitoring station for cameras either. It seemed safe to assume that there were no cameras upstairs.

It had seemed safe to assume there were only four guards and not six. He would have been wrong. Dead wrong. There might be more guards upstairs. Carver had learned the hard way to always err on the side of caution. Assume the worst, not the best. He would visually verify if there were cameras or not. He would verify there were no guards upstairs.

Assuming too much was a good way to get killed.

Carver felt clearheaded again. He felt ready to move upstairs and handle any threats that might be there. Hopefully Sabrina was onsite. Hopefully, this would be the end of it.

But he had a feeling this was only the beginning.

CHAPTER 24

Carver tread gently on the stairs.

They buckled and creaked faintly. The men in the break room would have heard him for sure if he'd tried to do this earlier. Anyone upstairs would almost certainly hear it too. If there was someone upstairs.

The door was a bottleneck. There could be someone right on the other side. Someone pointing a gun at the door because he'd heard the commotion downstairs. Maybe he'd called for backup. Maybe this place was about to be flooded with armed men.

Carver walked along the right edge of the stairs to minimize creaking. He hugged the railing, ready to turn sideways if someone emerged from the door. A smaller profile made for a smaller target. It didn't seem likely anyone would try shooing through the steel door, but you never knew.

He reached the top and slowly twisted the top deadbolt. There was also a deadbolt where the doorknob would normally be. He gently twisted it open. The lock scraped and clicked loudly in the silence.

Since the door locked from this side it also opened to this side. Carver thought about the best approach. He could stay behind the door while opening it. If someone was waiting on the other side, they might open fire right when it opened.

If they were smart, they'd go prone and wait until Carver tried to enter before shooting. The door was a bottleneck, so anyone with half a brain cell would aim their gun at the door and wait. They had the upper hand no matter what.

Carver could mitigate some of the risks, but not all of them. A flash grenade would come in real handy, but he didn't have any of those. So, he turned off the hallway light and pulled down his night vision goggles.

There was no light leaking from beneath the door or around the edges. It probably had a good seal so he wouldn't know if there was light on the other side until he opened it. He went downstairs and removed the belts from two of the dead men. He buckled them together and went back upstairs.

He hooked a buckle onto the lower deadbolt twist handle. He lay prone on the stairs out of line of fire and yanked on the belt. The door opened. No gunfire erupted. No bright light blinded his night vision.

It was pitch black on the other side. He noticed something else. The door was heavily padded on the inside. It was the same kind of padding used on sound isolation rooms. The kind used in any situation where absolute silence was necessary.

Carver low-crawled up two steps and peered into the darkness. He saw nothing. There was so little ambient light that it was like looking into a void. He rose to a knee and kept his weapon aimed and ready.

He switched on the infrared illuminator on the goggles. It was basically a flashlight for night vision, so the goggles worked without ambient light. The problem was, it was visible if someone was looking straight at it. It almost defeated the purpose of night vision. But it was still better than turning on the lights.

Carver saw a wall with the same heavy padding on it dead ahead. He kept low and peered around the corners. He was in an upstairs hallway similar to the one downstairs. There were doors all up and down the hallway, just like the floor below. There were no other adjacent or intersecting hallways just like the floor below.

The walls had the sound-deadening foam on them like the door. He stopped moving and listened. All he heard was dead silence and a faint ringing in his ears. He examined the ceiling. There was overhead lighting. There was a light switch on the wall to the left. There were no cameras in the hallway.

He left the light off and examined the first door. There was a doorknob and a deadbolt just above it. Like the stairway door, the twist locks were on the outside, not the inside. There had probably once been wooden doors here, but they'd been replaced with steel exterior doors. They were the only things in the hallway not covered in the sound deadening foam.

A small sign hung from the doorknob. It was the kind of sign you found in a hotel. The side facing Carver said, *Pets Inside. Do Not Disturb.* He took it off the doorknob and looked at the other side. It said, *No Pets Inside. Please Clean.*

There were pictures of dogs and cats frolicking on the signs. It was cute. Real cute. Especially considering it was probably referring to human occupants and not animals. It was how the traffickers knew which rooms were occupied and which ones weren't. He imagined the thug who picked out the signs had a real good laugh about it.

Carver went down the left half of the hallway first. Most of the rooms were occupied according to the signs. The rooms were probably covered in sound-deadening foam like the hallway because he couldn't hear any noises from inside.

He checked the other end of the hallway. Same deal. It was nearly a full house. Hopefully Sabrina was inside one of these rooms. Hopefully she was okay and hadn't been abused too much yet.

There was something else about the door signs that Carver noticed. There were stickers on them. They were different colors, but he couldn't tell what colors they were with night vision. The hallway was clear of guards and cameras, and there were no windows in the hallway, so he decided to turn on the lights.

Carver turned off the IR illuminator and the goggles. He flicked them up and turned on the light switch. Old florescent tubes blinked on. The light was dim and yellow, but he was able to see just fine.

The sticker on the door sign near the light switch was green. All of the neighboring stickers were also green. There was one green and four blues across the hallway from those. He went to the other half of the hallway. Same thing there. Greens, blues, and one yellow.

They were color coded for quality. It was a system commonly used by sex traffickers. Green was for young pristine virgins. Blue was for slightly older virgins. Yellow was young but not a virgin. At least that was one version of the rating system. This one might be different.

Carver felt the anger rising again. He tamped it down. Cleared his head. It was time to start opening doors. He chose the door with the yellow sticker first since it was at the end of the hall.

The door opened outward. The inside of the door was covered in sound-deadening foam. He looked inside and didn't see any cameras. The walls were also covered in sound-deadening foam except for a notch cut out for the light switch. A bed was situated dead center with a small form beneath the covers.

The foam was to keep anyone outside the building from hearing any screams for help. The light switch was a smart switch. It could be turned on or off remotely from a phone. The app would show which lights were on and which ones were off.

Turning on the light when you weren't supposed to would notify the guard with the app. The guard would probably come upstairs and punish whoever dared turn on their light. As if being kidnapped and imprisoned wasn't already punishment enough.

The guy who controlled the lights was most likely dead in the break room, so Carver turned on the light. He saw the small form under the covers move. A small face peeked out. A terrified face.

The girl's eyes widened. Her lips quivered. She didn't cry, probably because she was all cried out. Carver figured he probably looked tall and scary, so he knelt next to her bed.

He pulled down his mask so she could see his face. "I'm here to help you. What's your name?"

The girl shivered and spoke in a quavering voice. "Emma."

"My name is Jack." He didn't want to use his real name. "The bad guys are gone, okay?"

"They are?"

He nodded. "Yes. I'm going to free you and the others and we're going to walk out of here, but I need you to be brave for me. Can you do that?"

She nodded. "Yes."

"How old are you?"

"Ten."

"Did the men do anything to you? Touch you anywhere?"

She nodded. "They touched me a lot. Like my daddy does."

Carver understood why she was rated yellow. He felt his temperature rising. Felt the rage deep in his gut. He turned it off. "Maybe after this is over, I should talk to your daddy."

"He's in jail now."

"I'm sorry, Emma." He pulled the covers down. She was in a nightgown. She wasn't cuffed to the bed. Carver took her little hand and helped her out of bed. "Can you walk?"

She nodded. "And I can be brave."

"Good." Carver heard quiet sobbing and realized it was coming from his earbud. "Jessica?"

Jessica answered between sobs. "I-I can't handle this. I'm sorry."

"It's okay. Can you come to the building and help?"

"I'm already on the way."

"Who are you talking to?" Emma asked.

"A friend. She's coming to help. We need to unlock all the doors and get everyone out, okay?"

Emma nodded seriously. "Okay."

Carver went across the hallway and unlocked the door. He opened it. Turned on the lights. Found another girl inside, maybe a little older than Emma.

Emma ran to the girl's bed. "This is my friend, Jack. He's freeing us!"

Carver went down the hallway unlocking doors, opening them, and turning on the lights. He let Emma go to the girls inside and get them. It seemed less threatening that way.

Jessica arrived moments later. She saw the girls and started crying again. "My God. I hope you ended every last one of the assholes responsible for this."

"All the ones I've found so far." Carver put his hand on her shoulder. "You can do this."

She looked up at him. "You're not usually one to offer words of encouragement."

"I know. But we need to do this fast and get out. I don't know if anyone else is going to show up here."

"You're right." Jessica took a deep breath. "Get it together, girl."

Emma looked up at her with big eyes and took her hand. "You can be brave too."

Jessica laughed and cried at the same time. "Thank you."

They worked their way down the hallway. Jessica's eyes filled with hope at every door only for the hope to die each time. The girls here were minors. All of them ten to thirteen years old. Sabrina wasn't here.

Jessica kept up a brave front. She took the girls out to the van through the basement door. These girls were in much better shape than the girl from the minister's house. They didn't show signs of being drugged. They weren't bruised and beaten.

At least not on the surface. Mentally, they were going to be bruised and scarred for life. Trusting men would be difficult for most and impossible for many. Maybe they'd block it out like Carver had blocked out chunks of his childhood. Maybe that would help them recover.

Maybe, but probably not.

They packed the twelve girls into the minivan. Thirteen including the girl from the minister's house. Five in the third-row seat. Five in the second-row seat. The last three managed to squeeze into the floor space in front of the second-row seats. Carver figured he'd need a bus before this was all over.

They were just inside the Austin city limits, not far from a hospital. It would be much faster and easier to drop the girls off nearby, but Carver still had reservations. Piker might be involved with the traffickers. It was best not to take chances.

Since Sabrina hadn't been at the so-called big house, there was only one place left to look. Jaeger's ranch. Carver plugged in the address. It was named Eastpoint Ranch on the map. There were reviews for it. Pictures of hunters posing with dead deer, elk, and even bison that they'd hunted on the property.

The place was on a hundred acres of land. Satellite view showed arid, hilly terrain with lots of scrub brushes and small trees. There was a creek and a couple of lakes too. The house was located about a quarter of a mile from the highway.

The main house was big with a circle drive out front. Behind it was a long square building with a wide driveway and concrete pad. It looked like a detached garage. There was a barn, a long rectangular building near the barn, and another square building about a hundred yards away from everything else.

The place was set up like a hunting lodge. Thin symmetrical lines around the entire property indicated the presence of a physical barrier. Street view showed a stone wall. The stone was pale and grayish white. Probably limestone. There were no other roads with street view available, but it looked like the stone wall extended along the entire property line.

Miles of fencing was one thing. A miles-long stone wall was something else entirely. Building something like that had to cost a small fortune unless the labor was from humans smuggled in from South America.

Carver zoomed in on one of the lakes. The water looked blue and pristine. It wasn't a natural lake. It was a quarry. The stone must have been sourced from there and used in the wall's construction. It must have been done long ago before the quarry was allowed to fill with water.

The place looked like a fortress, and it probably was. There were a few hours left until dawn. It might be possible to breach the perimeter and go in for a closer look. First, Carver had to deliver the girls to a hospital in a jurisdiction he trusted.

He opted to go back to the same hospital they'd used last time. It took fifteen minutes to reach thanks to the lack of traffic. There were several Travis County Sheriff cars parked near the emergency exit this time.

No one was outside, so Carver stopped in the same place he had last time and told the girls what to do. "Find a nurse or doctor. Tell them you escaped on your own. Don't mention us, okay?"

The girls looked confused but nodded. Aside from the girl in the minister's house, these girls hadn't been heavily drugged. Carver had put his mask back on and Jessica had done the same, but the odds were good that one of the kids would give a description of them.

Emma nodded. "We won't say anything, I promise."

"I promise," another girl said.

"Why not?" another asked.

"Because the bad guys will find out who we are and kill us," Carver said. "There are more girls just like you being held in other places. We can't save them if we're dead."

The girls gasped, mouths dropping open. Emma squeezed Carver's hand. "I promise we won't, Mr. Jack."

This time everyone promised, and no more questions were asked. The girl from the minister's house wasn't able to walk on her own, so the other girls helped her. They made their way toward the hospital.

Jessica sighed heavily. "My heart can't take this much longer. How many girls have these monsters taken?

"You don't want to know." Carver pulled his mask down. "They're kidnapped off the streets here or trafficked across the border from other countries. It's an endless flow."

"As usual, you do a lousy job of making me feel better." Jessica pulled down her mask. "What—" She didn't have a chance to finish that thought.

Blue lights flashed behind them and a siren whooped. They were caught.

CHAPTER 25

Carver resisted the urge to hit the gas.

It was best to evaluate the situation before fleeing. There might be nothing to it. Maybe a cop wanted to know why they'd illegally parked on the side of the highway. Maybe a taillight was out. The minivan couldn't outrun a police interceptor anyway, so Carver didn't really have a choice.

At least, not yet.

The minivan wasn't registered in his name, and he didn't have a valid driver's license on him. If the cop asked for documents, he had none to provide. If and when that happened, he would make a run for it. The cop would have to run back to his car first, and that would give them a head start.

The cop was a Travis County deputy. He was a tall black guy in a beige shirt and black pants. His vehicle was a silver Ford SUV. He'd turned off the flashing lights before exiting the vehicle, which was odd. It was unusual enough to put Carver's instincts on high alert.

He drew his Sig and held it in his lap with the barrel facing the door. The bullet would go right through the thin metal and into anyone or anything standing outside of it. He untucked his shirt and pulled it out to cover his hand.

Carver rolled down the window and looked at the deputy when he arrived at the window. The deputy's right hand was down by his side and slightly behind him. His gun holster was empty. The way he was walking told Carver that he was already on guard and ready for trouble.

Carver looked toward the hospital and scanned the environs. He saw more silver Ford SUVs parked further down the street. He couldn't see the lettering on their sides, but he didn't need to. Coming back to the same hospital had been a mistake.

Or had it? He looked around and saw cameras on a nearby building. They'd probably recorded the van earlier. It was now a known vehicle. A vehicle that could be tracked with traffic cameras.

It might have been spotted on a camera when they were coming back this way. The cops probably figured it was headed back to the hospital, so they'd set up just a few minutes in advance.

The deputy stopped about four feet away from the window. His hand was down by his side, the sidearm visible. "Good evening, folks." He smiled, but it was obviously a practiced smile. A false indicator that everything was A-OK. The gun told Carver otherwise.

Carver read the man's gold metal nametag. "No need to put on a show, Deputy Marvin. Why are your people moving in on us?"

Marvin's face went taut. He raised his gun. "I need you out of the vehicle, now."

Carver glanced in the side view mirror. Two more deputies were running down the sidewalk. They'd reach the van in under a minute. "What are your intentions, deputy?"

"You're under arrest for human trafficking."

"You mean for rescuing victims of human trafficking?"

The deputy smirked. "You've been causing quite a commotion tonight. A lot of people are very unhappy."

Apparently, just getting out of Austin hadn't been enough. Carver should have taken the girls to another county entirely. "You're actively helping the traffickers. You're in league with Piker."

Marvin didn't seem surprised. "Piker mentioned you two. She thought you might be involved in tonight's activities. But now it's over."

"And the girls?" Jessica leaned forward so the deputy could see her. "What are you going to do with them?"

"That's not my business." Deputy Marvin raised the pistol a little higher. "They wanted you alive, but if you don't get out of the van now, I'm happy to deliver you dead."

"How did you know we were coming back here?" Carver already figured it was because of the traffic cameras, but it was best to know for certain.

"We have cameras everywhere." The deputy shook his head like he thought Carver was an idiot. "We just got lucky you decided to come back to the same place."

Carver pulled the Sig's trigger. The gun barked. The bullet traveled through the thin metal and struck the deputy right in the beltline. Marvin screamed in pain and dropped his gun before toppling over. Clearly, he'd never been shot before.

Carver hit the accelerator. The minivan didn't quite jet out of there, but it managed to squeal the front tires a little. One deputy rushed toward his fallen comrade. The others sprinted back toward their interceptors.

If this turned into a typical police chase, the minivan was going to lose. Except it probably wouldn't be typical. Just because a few cops were bad didn't mean everyone in the department was bad.

In other words, they wouldn't be calling for backup, at least not from the good cops. The bad cops would try to catch Carver themselves, so they didn't have to explain anything to the good cops.

They had about a thirty second head start, a highway, and countless suburban neighborhoods to duck into. They had to ditch the minivan, that much was certain. But then they'd be on foot with a lot of equipment.

Jessica was already thinking ahead. She plugged an address into the GPS. "Go here."

Carver glanced at the line on the map and cut left to follow it. "Where are we going?"

"My ex-boyfriend's place."

He gave her a sideways look and nodded. "Is this the guy who stole your source code and made millions off of it?"

"Yes."

"And you think going to him is a good idea?"

"It's just an idea."

Carver shook his head. "Look for a car repair shop with a lot of old vehicles in the parking lot. We can hide the minivan there and steal a new ride."

"My ex-boyfriend posts a lot of videos on social media to show off his wealth. I know that right now he's on vacation in Europe. I know that he has four houses around the US, one of which is here in town."

Carver snaked the minivan through a subdivision and emerged on a highway on the other side. He didn't see any flashing lights in the rearview mirror or signs of pursuit, but that could change in a heartbeat.

He checked the traffic lights for cameras. So far, he hadn't seen any. They usually reserved cameras for the busiest intersections and the route he was taking through neighborhoods avoided those.

He hadn't seen any car repair shops with lots of old cars in the parking lot. Most well-run shops didn't allow that to happen, but plenty of repair shops accumulated old cars that couldn't be repaired. They were good places to ditch a hot car and find a temporary replacement.

He just needed something to get them by until he could get a better replacement. He continued to follow the general direction the GPS wanted him to take while avoiding the highways.

Thirty minutes later, he was in a rich neighborhood on the shores of Lake Travis. He stopped at the address and looked at the big iron gate guarding the driveway. He turned to Jessica. "Yeah, this isn't going to work."

"Hang on." She hopped out of the car and walked up to the keypad next to the gate. She put a sticker over the camera and punched in a code. The gate slowly opened inward. She got back in the car and nodded. "Let's go."

Carver drove up the driveway. It wasn't paved with concrete but with what looked like limestone pavers. They were multicolored, ranging from almost white to a beige sandstone color. It was probably the most common kind of stone in the area, but that didn't mean it was cheap. The driveway alone probably cost more than most regular houses.

The house was down a short slope right near the shore. The landscaping hid the house from the road with a variety of native plants that relied heavily on cacti and other prickly bushes he didn't recognize.

It was called defensive landscaping. It was a technique used regularly by wealthy home-owners to make it difficult to breach the perimeter by placing specific plants around the fence and other entry points.

In this case, it would certainly hide their presence from anyone passing by on the road. Only someone on the lake would be able to see lights on inside the house. They could mitigate that risk by simply not using lights on that side of the house, provided they could get inside without raising an alarm.

There was a four-car garage ahead of them. It was attached to a large Mediterranean-style house at a forty-five-degree angle, so the two buildings surrounded a court-yard with a fountain in front of it.

The buildings were constructed of slightly darker stone than the driveway, and dark gray clay roof tiles. The place had to be at least ten thousand square feet. Carver had seen plenty of mansions just like it, but it was still impressive.

All four garage doors were closed. There were cameras on all the corners and a camera doorbell too. There was no way they were getting inside without being picked up by one of the cameras.

Carver hit the brakes before they got too close, but it was probably too late if the cameras were on motions sensors.

"Keep going," Jessica said.

Carver pointed out the cameras and the closed garage doors. "This isn't a good idea. The cameras are going to activate, your ex-boyfriend or a security company is going to get a notification, and the cops are going to be here in a hurry because it's a rich neighborhood."

Jessica tapped on her phone screen. One of the garage doors began to open. She swiped on her screen and showed Carver what she was looking at. "Confession time. I hacked his smart home devices, so I have complete control over everything, even the cameras."

Carver looked at her phone. On it were multiple camera feeds showing the inside of the garage and the house. "Are you going to delete the footage of us?"

"I disabled recording, so there is no footage."

"Good." Carver pulled up to the garage. Even though it had four doors, it was large enough inside to accommodate probably twenty vehicles comfortably.

It was packed with a wide variety of vehicles ranging from exotics like Ferraris and McLarens to pickup trucks and electric vehicles. Most impressive was a vehicle that looked like a pickup truck merged with a semitruck.

It occupied most of the first bay all by itself. If not for the extra tall garage doors, the thing wouldn't have even fit inside.

"That's an International CXT," Jessica said. "Ford makes a similar one called the F-650. I always wanted one when I was younger because they look so cool."

"You don't strike me as a big truck kind of person."

She shrugged. "I have my quirks."

"So I've noticed."

Jessica grinned. "After Roy made his millions from my source code, he bought that thing and sent me a picture. Just to rub it in, I think."

"Roy? I thought your ex was Chinese."

"That's the American name he took so people would think he was a cowboy."

Carver never understood the desire to be a cowboy at least in the old sense of the word. They were basically glorified cattle herders. Then again, he'd never been allowed to watch westerns when he was a kid and he'd never had the desire to watch them as an adult.

Jessica tapped her phone screen and the garage door closed behind them. "I can tell you're judging me right now."

"Why would I judge you?"

"Because I hacked my ex's house." She blew out a breath and turned toward him. "Look, after I lost everything, I was really angry with myself, with Roy, and with a lot of things. I was also insanely bored, so I started poking around in his personal business."

Jessica bit her lower lip. "I found out he was using a Minerva home hub to network all his smart home devices. They're top of the line devices used by a lot of rich people so they're very popular targets for hacks. I found a vulnerability on the dark web and used it to gain access."

Carver held up a hand. "You don't have to explain. I'm not judging you. But you could have told me up front that you chose this place because you had access."

She frowned. "Yeah, I suppose I should have led with that. But I wasn't thinking clearly after you shot that cop and took off. I was in panic mode, you know?"

Carver got out of the minivan and walked around the garage. He looked at the various vehicles while Jessica went straight for the CXT. It had large cylindrical fuel tanks on the side beneath the cab like a semi-truck. She stepped up on one and tried to open the door, but it was locked.

"Hey, we could use this." She pointed to a box on the wall. "The keys are in there. We could probably smash right through the wall around Jaeger's ranch and drive right up to the house, guns blazing."

Carver shook his head. "A vehicle like that sticks out. Everyone would notice it. And it has a loud diesel engine. People would hear it coming from a mile away."

"Yeah, but it'd be sweet revenge to smash this thing up and leave it at a sex trafficker's house. Maybe they'd think Roy is a client."

He held up his gloved hands. "Put your gloves on so we don't leave fingerprints."

"Yeah, good idea." Jessica retrieved her gloves and put them on.

Carver checked the time. They had a few hours before dawn and then they'd have to wait until nightfall again before moving on the ranch. "When we dropped those girls off at the hospital, the Travis County Sheriff's department was called. The wrong people answered that call and realized something had happened to Jaeger's trafficking operation."

Jessica nodded. "So, they'll be on guard."

"Yep." Carver kept looking at the cars in the garage. They needed something that wouldn't stick out too much. "We just dropped off thirteen more girls from the church. So now they know for certain that their operation is under attack. Which means if we don't try to get into the ranch tonight, we might not have another chance."

"What if we got the feds involved?"

"Too slow and too risky." Carver shook his head. "If they keep girls on the ranch and they think it might be targeted, they might try to move them."

"We could wait until they try to move the girls and ambush or follow them."

"The risk is that they eliminate the girls instead of moving them." Carver had seen that happen way too many times. "It's best if we go in tonight."

"Whatever you think is best." Jessica squeezed through a row of motorcycles to reach him. "So, what's the plan?"

Carver was looking for an ordinary vehicle that they could take but so far hadn't found anything that wouldn't stick out. There was a Dodge Ram TRX with a rainbow vinyl wrap on it that made it sparkle like the Fourth of July. There was a GM pickup with a lift kit that required a ladder to get in.

Jessica sighed. "We almost have too many choices, don't we?"

"Not really. Everything here is loud and extravagant." Carver saw the perfect vehicle hiding behind one of the jacked-up pickups. He walked around the Dodge Ram and found a black Sprinter van. This one had all-terrain radials on it and looked like it was modified for camping.

He went to the key box, found the key fob, and opened the van. It had a small bed, a kitchenette, and a lithium camping battery. "This will do."

Jessica looked inside. "We could live here if things go south."

Carver moved their equipment from the minivan into the Sprinter.

"You have a thing for vans, don't you?"

"They're good utility vehicles." Carver looked at the vehicles obstructing the van's path to the garage door. "We're going to have to move the CXT and other pickups to get it out."

Jessica rubbed her hands together. "So, I get to drive the CXT after all?"

"Yep."

She grabbed the key, climbed into the cabin, and started the big truck. The diesel engine rumbled loudly. She leaned out of the window and said something.

Carver cupped his ear. "What? I can't hear you over the engine."

Jessica shouted, "God, you're right. This thing is way too loud." She pulled the truck out of the garage. Even with fifteen feet of clearance, it barely fit through the garage door. She left it idling and went to get more keys.

They moved the Ram and other pickups and got the van outside, then put the minivan where the camper van had been. When the trucks were back in place, the minivan was almost completely hidden.

Jessica stared at the CXT. "That thing is awful to drive. I could barely hear myself think over the engine." She sighed. "In retrospect, I'm glad I never wasted money on one."

Carver didn't comment. He was thinking about the time they had left before sunrise. They had a little more than three hours of darkness left. Three hours to breach the ranch's perimeter and find Sabrina. Now that the heat was on, this was risky. Real risky.

But they had no choice.

CHAPTER 26

Carver needed a plan.

He didn't have one for the ranch. Not even the outline of a plan. The main entrance was just off the highway. There were no roads, dirt, paved, or otherwise, that led cross country to the ranch. At least none that showed up on the maps app.

He switched to satellite view and zoomed in until the image was blurry. There were trails and dirt roads inside the perimeter. They led to different sections of the property. If the reviews were accurate, people could pay big money to hunt "strange and exotic" animals on the ranch.

One guy had killed a wildebeest. Another hunted bison and elk with a bow. It didn't sound all that exciting or worth the price which some reviewers said was over ten thousand dollars. It was almost certainly a cover for money laundering or other nefarious activity.

Herds of different animals were visible in satellite view, so it looked like the ranch raised most of them rather than importing them from other countries. There were disclaimers stating that all exotic animals qualified for exemptions from exotic animal laws in Texas.

Jessica turned her phone screen to Carver. "Does that look like a trail?"

He looked at the image. There were faint tracks in a section of soil, but they were too narrow to be car tracks. "Look like motorcycle tracks maybe."

"They must have a back door in the wall, right?" Jessica scrolled along the wall. "Every villain's lair needs a back way out in case the coppers come calling." She said the last bit with a British accent.

"I think you're right," Carver said. "But we'd have to ride around the entire perimeter to find it."

Jessica frowned and tilted her head sideways as if trying to see something from a different angle. "Hey, see this creek?"

Carver looked at the creek. "Yep."

"It's a mile behind the property and just comes out of nowhere."

"Probably from an underground source."

"Exactly." She followed the creek downstream. There was what looked like a boat ramp, a metal garage, and a dirt road. She zoomed in on a rectangular outline. "Does that look like a van to you?"

Carver took her phone and looked closer. It was definitely a van. A high-topped van with a white roof and some kind of sign on the side. The image wasn't clear enough to make out much more than that.

He followed the creek back up to where it appeared from what looked like a cliff. It was hard to tell because the top-down angle distorted it. From there it was about a two-mile hike to the stone wall around the ranch.

"You think the back door is here?"

Jessica grinned and nodded. "Yep." She scrolled over to the quarry and zoomed in on the eastern cliff face. There was a dark spot on the image. "I think that's an opening into a cave tunnel. I think the quarry is the source of the creek."

"But quarries usually fill with rainwater, right?"

"Water is constantly being pumped out of quarries, sometimes because of rain but mostly because of groundwater like natural springs." She tapped the image. "Sometimes the flow of water is strong enough to require an outlet, so they'll dig into the side of the quarry and make an artificial canal to get it out. In this case, they might have dug a long tunnel before reaching a place where it could flow across the landscape."

"So that's an artificial tunnel."

"Yep." Jessica watched him closely. "I think that's how they bring girls in and out of the place. It's a lot more covert than bringing them in the front door."

"Agreed."

She bit her lower lip. "Could that be our way in?"

"Yeah." Carver put a pin on the map to mark the boat ramp because the dirt road didn't have a name or a way to navigate to it. The GPS mapped the route from Roy's house to the pin. It was a forty-minute drive. They weren't going to have much nighttime left when they arrived, so he put the van in gear and started driving.

Jessica put a hand on his arm. "Wait, don't we need a boat?"

"If they're using that place to ferry in girls, then they probably have boats stored onsite."

"Yeah, that makes sense." Jessica tapped on her phone. "Sunrise is three hours and fifteen minutes away. It's supposed to be cloudy and overcast. Eighty percent chance of a thunderstorm."

"Good." Carver liked thunder. It covered up the sound of gunfire. He didn't see any way to avoid using guns in a place like the ranch. There were almost certainly bound to be guards and the place was built like a fortress.

But every fortress had a weak spot. Maybe this quarry was that weak spot. He just had to get there with time to spare. If they reached the boat ramp on the creek in forty minutes, and if the creek went through an underground tunnel to the quarry, that would take another twenty to thirty minutes.

That would give them two hours to hike from the quarry to the house. Maybe less, depending on if they made good time up the creek or if it was slow going. It depended on what kind of boat was stored in the boat house there.

"What's the route out of the quarry and up to the house?"

Jessica looked at the image. "Looks like the road goes straight up and out of the quarry. They must have dug it out after the fact because quarry roads usually spiral up and out."

"How far from there to the house?"

Jessica dropped pins on the map and calculated the distance. "From the start of the quarry road to the house is three quarters of a mile."

Carver added another fifteen minutes to the trip. He rounded up to twenty minutes since the quarry road probably had a steep slope. He sped up to ninety miles per hour since there was no traffic and nothing but darkness on the country highway. They needed to shave every minute off the drive that they could.

"Hey, there's a metal shed next to the start of the quarry road." Jessica showed it to him. "I thought it was just a shadow, but I think it's a building."

Carver glanced at it and nodded. "They might keep ground transportation in the shed."

"I hope so." Jessica blew out a breath and looked at the empty road ahead. "God, I hope she's there. If she's not, I don't know what I'm going to do."

"There's nowhere else she could be," Carver said. Not unless she'd been moved out of the state.

"Look at these outbuildings." Jessica showed him the satellite view again. "It looks like there's a concrete wall around this one. They must be keeping prisoners inside there, right?"

Carver didn't look. He was going too fast to divert his attention from the road. "We'll find out when we get there." He had other worries too. What if this place had motion sensors and cameras everywhere? They might be spotted the moment they got on the property.

He didn't have time to stop and scan the terrain every few hundred yards. But it was better to be safe. The enemy already suspected they were coming. But they were expecting them from the front, not the rear.

The element of surprise was still on their side, but Carver had to ensure they preserved it. If they set off a motion detector or camera, then it was game over. He'd need help from

Jessica. The house and environs were too large for him to run into without eyes and ears on the outside.

He nodded towards his duffel bag. "There's another monocular inside. It's in a small rectangular hard case. Pull it out and I'll tell you how to use it."

Jessica dug around for a moment before finding the case. She opened it and pulled out the monocular. "I think I've watched you use yours enough to figure it out." She put her eye to the rubber eyepiece. "I can't see anything."

Carver tapped the monocular. "You have to take off the cap first."

She grinned sheepishly and pulled off the cap then put her eye to the device again. She switched through the modes from normal to IR to night vision. She turned on the IR illuminator and jerked her eye back from the eyepiece.

"Whoa, that reflection about blinded me."

"Don't use the illuminator unless you have to. It's visible from a direct angle."

"Okay." She turned it off and put the cap back on. "Will I be watching your back?"

"I need you to help me find cameras and guards."

"Do they patrol the grounds like you see in the movies?"

"Sometimes they do, sometimes they don't." Carver slowed as the van approached a turn. "Sometimes a patrol scares off potential intruders. These days they rely a lot more on cameras with motion detection because manpower is expensive."

He turned onto the dirt road leading to the creekside dock. He killed the headlights and relied on night vision for the final stretch. They arrived ten minutes ahead of schedule. That was good, but they still had a long way to go to reach the ranch.

A long metal garage with three doors faced the road. Behind the shed was a boat house. They probably used flat-bottomed boats to ferry cargo up and down the creek. There was no need for anything fancy or fast.

If he ran an operation like this, he'd use a metal fishing boat with a small motor and a canvas roof to hide the passengers from satellite surveillance. The garage and boathouse concealed loading and unloading operations. The boat needed to do the same.

There was no good place to conceal the van, so Carver drove right up to the garage and parked on the left side out of sight. If someone was inside, they would have heard the engine, so he got out quietly and hustled to the entry door.

He tested the handle. It was unlocked. He swung the door inward. It was dark inside. He crouched and peered around. There was a large open space inside. No boats, no vans, just a couple of offroad motorcycles and a side-by-side ATV, all lined up on the far wall.

To the right of the vehicles was a ten by fifteen feet space enclosed in fencing. It wasn't chain link fencing, but it was heavy gauge all the same. Metal poles embedded in the concrete floor supported the wire fencing and a metal door. It was a cage for humans.

Carver left the lights off and walked toward the rear door. "Nothing inside," he said into the earbud. "I'm going to the boathouse."

"Affirmative," Jessica said. "Over and out."

The rear door opened into a corridor about six feet wide and twenty feet long. It looked like a cattle corral except it was used for herding humans from one end to the other. The metal door at the other end was unlocked.

He opened it and went into the boathouse. The building was completely enclosed with no other entrances or exits except for rollup doors for the boats. Just as he'd expected, there were two flat-bottomed metal boats moored in the left bay.

There was also a right bay, but there were no boats in it. They were probably in the quarry. Crank handles opened the rollup doors for the two bays. He tested the crank handle on the left side and the door rose just above water level.

The boats were longer and wider than normal fishing boats. They had had six rows of seating, canvas roofs, and small outboard motors. They would probably pass as tour boats if not for the metal rungs welded onto the seats and the chains coiled on the floor next to the seats.

The victims were obviously chained to the boat for the ride to the quarry. Even if they managed to escape the boat and get into the water, there really was nowhere for them to run. The motorcycles and the side-by-side were probably used to catch runaways.

The chains were small and slender. They didn't need to be thick and heavy to hold someone prisoner long enough to get up the creek and into the quarry, especially not if that someone was a little girl.

The keys to the boat motors were in the boats. Carver turned on the ignition and pressed the starter button. The motor thrummed to life. He hit the kill switch to turn it off. This kind of ignition system was easy to bypass if the keys weren't available.

"Can I come in?" Jessica asked over the earbud.

"I'm coming out." Carver hurried outside to the van. He strapped on an ammo belt with magazines for the MP5SD and put on a hip pouch. He pulled out an M4 with night vision scope and gave it to Jessica. "How are you with rifles?"

"I grew up in Texas, Carver. Me and my friends went to the shooting range regularly. This one guy even had a fifty cal he let me shoot." She nodded grimly. "I can shoot someone if I have to." She winced. "I hope."

"Good."

Jessica flipped up the cap on the scope and held the rifle up to her shoulder. "Is this right?"

Carver nodded. "Yep. I don't necessarily need you to be accurate, but I might need you to lay down covering fire if something goes wrong."

"Do I go full auto? Spray and pray?"

"No." Carver flicked the rifle to single shot. "Aim in the general direction of an enemy and gently squeeze the trigger once. See what they do. If they go prone or take defensive action, then you've done your job."

"I can do that."

"Do you understand trigger discipline?"

"Of course." She put her finger across the top of the trigger guard. "My friends said not to put your finger on the trigger unless you're ready to fire."

"Yep."

She smiled. "Do I have a license to kill now?"

"If you're comfortable with it."

"You really don't get movie references, do you?"

Carver shook his head. "Nope. Show me how you load and unload magazines."

She pressed the release button, popped out the magazine, and shoved it back in slowly. "Like that, right?"

"Yep. Just don't forget to pull the charging handle." He showed her.

"Oh yeah, I guess that helps."

"It is if you want a bullet in the chamber." He showed her how he aimed and a couple of other tricks just in case her friends hadn't taught her.

Jessica did what he said. "This is quite the crash course."

"It's all we have time for." He strapped an ammo belt around her waist along with a hip pouch. He tucked her monocular inside and figured that was everything she needed.

She inspected herself. "Not going to lie. I feel like a real badass."

Carver strapped a small survival knife around one thigh and strapped a sidearm holster on the other. He put a G19 in the holster. "You know how to use that?"

"I thought my comment about growing up in Texas answered that question already."

"Okay. If you get rushed, use the knife to reach your handgun. Use your handgun to reach your rifle."

"Huh?"

He demonstrated. "If someone grabs you, use the knife to create space. Stab them anywhere you can. That should give you enough distance to pull the handgun. Shoot them if you can and run."

"And that gives me space to aim the rifle, right?"

"Yep but running might be better."

Jessica looked herself over again. "I feel so powerful right now. Like I could take on the world."

"Don't let it go to your head." Carver closed the van. "Let's go."

Jessica toyed with the M4 strap trying to get the rifle situated. Carver angled it so it hung the right way. He went to the garage since it was the only way to the boat ramp. Then he heard something in the distance. A faint humming.

It was a boat motor. And it was coming their way.

CHAPTER 27

Carver hurried around the garage and to the creek.

"Is that a boat motor?" Jessica said.

"Someone's coming." There were thick reeds and cattails in the shallow waters near the creek bank. Carver crouched and scanned the creek with the monocular. He zoomed in on a hot spot a short distance away.

Jessica crouched beside him. She looked at her phone. "Hardin texted me again."

"He's still awake?" Carver glanced at the text but didn't read it.

"He's tried calling four times in the last hour." She stared at the call log. "Do you think he found something?"

"Doubtful. Ignore him for now. We don't have time for distractions." Carver spotted the incoming boat. It was the same design as the ones in the boat house. He counted nine heat signatures. Five of them were seated near the front. The other four were in the back row near the motor.

The ones in the back were larger than the ones in the front. He felt reasonably certain that the five in the front were girls and the ones in the back were men.

"Wait here." Carver hurried to the van and grabbed the parabolic microphone from his equipment bag. He went back to the creek and put on the headphones, then aimed the mic at the oncoming boat. The motor thrummed loud in his ears.

He scanned from left to right until he heard one of them talking in Spanish.

"The van will arrive soon. Put them in the cage for now. We'll take the other two boats back with us to get the others."

Another man spoke. "Why are we doing this?"

"They said there might be a raid, so we need to transfer the merchandise for safekeeping. We have to get it done before sunrise."

"A raid?" The other man laughed. "Who would dare raid us? Jaeger owns this town."

"They don't give me the details. I just keep my mouth shut and do what I'm told."

A two-way radio crackled. A male voice spoke in English. "Transport is enroute. ETA twenty minutes."

The man on the boat answered in accented English. "Acknowledged."

The boat was much closer now, maybe a hundred yards distant. Carver hurried back to the van and put the parabolic mic inside. He got in the driver's seat and drove the van behind the garage, so it was hidden from view from the road.

The boathouse and the corridor connecting it to the garage hid the van from the north side. If a boat went past the boathouse, then the occupants might see the van in the dark, but the odds were good they wouldn't.

He went back to Jessica who was crouching in the reeds. "They're definitely evacuating the ranch. We've got incoming from the creek and from the road."

"How many?"

"Four bogies in the boat. The ones coming from the road will probably be driving cargo vans. I don't know how many are coming."

"So, what's the plan?"

"Good question." Carver considered the options. Jaeger was doing them a favor by bringing the girls to them. If they were lucky, Sabrina would be on one of those boats. If they were extremely lucky, she'd be on the first boat.

He mulled over the logistics and ran through the scenarios in his head. The men on the boats would deliver the girls and lock them in the cage inside the garage. The driver of the incoming boat would pilot that boat back to the quarry. Two of the remaining three would pilot the other two boats back.

That would leave one man to guard the girls. That was all they really needed since the girls would be locked in a cage. The driver would arrive in the van. If it was a high-top cargo van, then he could fit a lot of girls inside.

The vans could hold 15 adults. Twenty girls could probably be crammed inside one. That was assuming all the so-called cargo consisted of small minor females. Once they were inside, the driver would presumably take them to a predetermined location.

The men were in a hurry so the chain of custody would be stretched thin and weak. It would present a prime opportunity to take the girls off their hands without anyone being the wiser until it was far too late.

What if Sabrina was in the first batch? Carver considered the risks involved in rescuing all the girls in Jaeger's compound. The mission goal was Sabrina. But stopping with her would be criminal. If he played his cards right, all the girls would be brought right to him. He wasn't going to stop with just Sabrina. He was going to make sure all those girls got out.

Even if the risk was ten times greater.

It was strange to find himself thinking like that. He was emotionally vulnerable when it came to this, whether it was from some forgotten childhood trauma or just because this was about innocent girls being sold, traded, and abused.

"Carver?" Jessica put her hand on his arm. "What's the plan?"

"The driver." That was the best link to exploit. "Once the girls are loaded in the van, we take out the driver and take the van."

"That definitely makes it easier." Jessica bit her lower lip. "I can drive the van away from here."

"Not back to Austin." Carver opened the map and tapped on the road leading west. "What's a good town to take them to?"

"Elgin. It's right outside Travis County."

Carver calculated the distance. "This dirt road winds all over the place, so it's about a thirty-minute drive."

"That's fine. I'll drive slowly." She ducked lower as the boat went past. "How many vans do you think are coming?"

"No telling."

"Carver, I want to save them all even if we get Sabrina out first."

"Same." Carver listened to the boat engine thrumming in the hollow interior of the boathouse.

"You're really okay with that?"

He nodded. "Sit tight and let's see what happens next."

The boat engine went silent. A man shouted. Small female voices cried out in fear and pain. Carver's hand tightened around the monocular. He didn't like hearing their cries. Not one little bit. But he had to be patient and let this play out. It was the only way they were going to save anyone and survive.

Fifteen minutes ticked past before the boat engine started again. Two more engines started in short succession. Three boats left the boathouse and headed back toward the quarry. The girls were probably in the cage and just one man was guarding them.

Carver aimed the parabolic mic at the garage and picked up a girl talking. "Please, just a little water. I'm so thirsty."

"Shut it, puta!" Metal clanged like the butt of a rifle being struck against the metal fencing inside. Girls shrieked in terror.

Carver gritted his teeth and kept listening. There was a hiss of static and then someone spoke over a two-way radio. "ETA five minutes."

The man inside answered with a Spanish accent. "Copy."

No mention was made of how many vans were coming. Carver figured since they had all four boats operating and each boat could carry about twelve passengers, they'd need three or four vans total.

Then he thought of something he hadn't seen. He hadn't seen the fourth boat yet. Presumably, it would have been loaded with kids and sent on its way shortly after the other boat arrived.

It probably took fifteen minutes to reach the boathouse from the quarry. That meant thirty minutes had passed since the boat left the quarry, dropped off the cargo, and then headed back to the quarry for another load.

But the fourth boat hadn't arrived. Which meant either a fourth boat didn't exist, or it was out of order. Maybe the three boats would have the last of the kids when they returned. It was impossible to know, really.

One thing was certain. Three boatloads would be a lot of kids, anywhere from thirty to fifty depending on how many they could cram onto each boat. The first boat probably only had five kids because those were the ones they could load the fastest.

They needed to get the other two boats as quickly as possible, thus the big rush and the smaller number of passengers on the first boat. That almost guaranteed the next arriving boats would be full to the brim.

Headlights bounced around the corner as the van hit the ruts in the dirt road. A Sprinter van stopped in front of the garage. It turned around and backed up to the first rollup door. A man hurried out of the entry door. The driver got out of the van and met the other guy.

Carver aimed the parabolic mic at the pair.

"Yo, Renaldo." The driver bumped fists with the Hispanic man. "You ready for me to load up?"

"Hola, Benji." Renaldo shook his head. "Not yet. We want to pack the van full. All the cargo should arrive in about twenty or thirty minutes."

"Enough time to have some fun while we wait?"

Renaldo laughed. "I wish. These girls are already spoken for."

"Yeah, I figured." Benji sighed. "The other drivers aren't far behind me."

"We're going to fill them up completely."

Benji grunted. "What about all the vans onsite? Why aren't we using those?"

"The garage door is broken. We can't get them out."

"Broken?" Benji laughed. "How did that happen?"

"A girl tried to escape and crashed a van into the door."

Benji laughed again. "Escaped how? I thought you kept them sedated and strapped down from start to finish."

"No idea, man. Somehow, she got free from the examination room. The doctor tried to stop her, but she plowed right into him. He fell and hit his head on an examination table."

"He let a girl run him over?"

"Oh, more than that. She killed him." Renaldo laughed. "His head hit the corner of the table very hard."

"Jesus!"

"Crazy, right?"

"What about the girl. You caught her?"

Renaldo nodded. "Jaeger said he caught her."

"What did he do to her?"

The Hispanic man ran a finger across his throat and grinned wickedly.

"Really?" Benji shook his head. "Seems like a waste of good product."

"Jaeger wasn't happy." Renaldo shrugged. "It's his property, man."

"I guess losing the doc to a girl must hurt." Benji shook his head. "I never would have seen that coming."

Renaldo laughed. "The doc was a real pendejo, but he's going to be hard to replace."

"I don't know about that." Benji shrugged. "There are plenty of disgraced doctors who will do anything for money."

"Yeah, but he was a lady parts doctor. I don't know how you say in English."

Benji howled with laughter. "Gynecologist."

"Yeah, that." Renaldo patted his crotch. "Kitty doctor."

The pair kept talking. Carver listened in case they said anything else of interest, like the names of certain girls or the total number that would be coming. They never got that specific, but it was obvious they were expecting a lot.

"What are they saying?" Jessica asked.

Carver told her.

"A girl escaped and killed their doctor?" She pumped a fist. "Hell yeah."

"Doesn't sound like it ended well for her."

"Since when does it ever end well for sex trafficking victims?"

"Good point." Carver slowly scanned the area with the parabolic mic. He heard crickets, birds, coyotes yipping, and the faint sound of car engines coming their way. He didn't hear any boat motors.

Within fifteen minutes there were three vans parked in front of the garage. Renaldo and Benji greeted the other drivers, a short, plump man named Jamar and a thin woman named Hattie.

"Wow, a woman is helping those bastards." Jessica bared her teeth. "Can I shoot her?"

"No." Carver planned to take them down silently. The problem was the drivers and the guard remained out front talking. Apparently, they were just going to keep talking until the other boats showed up.

The plan had been to take out the first driver after his van was loaded and hijack the load of prisoners. Then they could wash, rinse, and repeat with the other vans. But it looked like all the girls were going to be loaded at once and then taken away.

That meant there would be three van drivers, three boat drivers, and one guard standing in the way. Six men and one woman. All of them carried sidearms on their hips. Renaldo had a scoped M4 slung across his back. The drivers probably had rifles in the cabs too.

Carver studied the three vans. Benji's was parked facing him. The others hadn't backed up to the garage and were parked at different angles, giving him a view of the sides and backs. The vans had front and back windows but none on the sides.

Four rows of seating were visible through the windshield on Benji's van. The others were probably similar. These were passenger vans, designed like hotel shuttles or other large-capacity vehicles.

All three had the same magnetic sign on them from Lakeview Church. Apparently, this operation favored using churches as cover. It was certainly a good way to explain why they were transporting so many kids.

Maybe that church was their next destination. Carver looked it up on the GPS. It was all the way over on the west side of Austin near Lake Travis and a little north of Roy's mansion. It was a big church that looked like it could hold a lot of people.

The sanctuary was designed like an auditorium with stadium-style seating. There were multiple outbuildings, each one large enough to accommodate hundreds of people. The place even had its own paved airfield named Heaven's Runway.

"Wow, that's one big church," Jessica said.

It was a big church on a big chunk of land. There was a large airplane hangar next to the runway. It was the perfect setup to smuggle people all around the country and internationally. Church planes could often get missionary clearance to go places other civilian flights couldn't.

The drivers and Renaldo were still talking outside the building. Carver kept listening to them hoping one of them would talk about their plans for the girls. Would they temporarily hold them at the church, or did they plan to put them on a plane and spirit them somewhere else?

It was becoming clear that his plan wasn't going to work. Not without serious modifications. He ran through multiple scenarios and concluded that waiting for the boats to arrive with the passengers wasn't going to cut it.

Jessica peered through the reeds at the group. "What are they saying?"

Carver didn't answer. He was picturing a series of events that didn't end with him full of bullets or severe collateral damage.

He envisioned the boats arriving. The girls being loaded into vans under the watchful eyes of the guards. The drivers would get into the driver's seats. The guards would get into the passenger seats so they could keep an eye on the cargo.

There would possibly be a brief opportunity to act while the guards and drivers were preoccupied with loading the girls into the vans. But he couldn't see any scenario in which taking out the drivers and guards didn't result in lots of bullets flying and lots of girls dying.

There were three garage doors. Would the vans back up to all three doors or would they take turns loading up at the door nearest to the cage inside the garage? He pictured that scenario and concluded it would end no better than anything else.

There was only one way to avoid mass casualties. Only one way to force the odds closer to his favor. It wasn't even remotely close to ideal, but it was much better than allowing the girls to be taken to another secure location.

He was going to have to act right now.

CHAPTER 28

Carver told Jessica the plan.

She didn't object. She agreed with his assessment. "The only thing I'm worried about is the execution. Specifically, me shooting live targets."

"Just aim through the scope and pull the trigger." Carver pulled the M4 around to her front. He ensured the silencer was securely fixed and pulled back the charging handle. He switched from safety to single shot and turned on the night vision scope. "This is no different than the shooting range."

"Except these are living humans."

"Pretend they're paper targets."

She took a deep breath. "I can do that. These people are monsters. They're inhuman trash."

"Exactly." Carver remained crouched and crab-walked to the edge of the reeds. He knelt and got into his shooting stance. "Aim, pull the trigger. Wash, rinse, repeat."

Jessica steeled herself. "I can do it. I won't hesitate, I promise." She knelt next to him and aimed.

"You go right to left. I'll go left to right. Nice and easy." Carver put a hand on her shoulder. "Ready?"

She nodded. "Give the word."

Carver noticed her hand was shaking. That was to be expected. She was nervous. Probably a little scared about ending a human life no matter how vile or deserving the person was. He just had to make sure he hit enough people before they had a chance to shoot back.

The MP5SD wasn't exactly a great long-range weapon, but this was a thirty-yard shot at most. That shouldn't be a problem for him. He considered taking the M4 since he could definitely hit every target with it from this distance, but he needed Jessica to hit at least one target. She might not be able to hit anyone with the submachinegun.

Carver aimed at the person on the left of the group. He mimicked pulling the trigger, aiming at the next, pulling trigger and so on. Three drivers, one guard. Four bullets. As long as Jessica hit one of them, he could handle the rest.

Carver aimed at the thin female driver, Hattie. Jessica aimed at Renaldo on the far left.

"Three, two, one, fire." Carver pulled the trigger. A red dot puckered on Hattie's temple. She was just going down when Benji's temple caved in and a hot mist burst from the other side of his head. He heard three coughs from Jessica's rifle in the same space of time. She'd probably missed the first shot, but he couldn't worry about that.

Carver aimed at Jamar, but the fat man was already dropping to the ground right next to Renaldo. They weren't dropping to take cover or aim their rifles. They were dropping like rag dolls because Jessica had vacated brain matter from their skulls.

Five shots. Four bodies. He held up a fist and scanned the area to ensure there were no surprises like someone waking from a nap in the back of a van. There were no shouts of surprise. No one jumped out of the vans to find out what happened to their comrades.

Carver glanced at Jessica. "I guess you weren't all that nervous."

"I just imagined them abusing little girls and my nerves settled down." She shrugged. "They barely reacted even when their friends' brains exploded from their heads."

"They were caught completely off guard." Carver squeezed her shoulder. "Impressive shooting."

"Thanks." She grinned.

Carver scanned the area with his scope. "Wait here."

"I can cover you."

"Okay." Carver moved up quickly, rifle at the ready. He reached Hattie's van first. He opened the sliding side door and looked inside. There was a CB radio installed under the dashboard. That was what they used to communicate with Renaldo. The van keys were on the center console.

The rest of the van was empty. He moved to Jamar's van next, cleared it and went to Benji's van.

The vehicles were empty as expected, but it was always best to verify. He opened the entry door into the garage and cleared the corner. He saw girls huddling in the cage on the far side. There were no other guards inside.

He moved quickly through the space to the rear door. He cleared the corridor, the boathouse, and returned the way he'd come since there was no other way out except the creek. The girls watched him fearfully. They thought he was one of the traffickers. He ignored them for now and went back outside.

He walked over to the bodies and frisked them. The drivers had wallets, IDs, and exactly two hundred dollars cash each. No credit cards or anything else. The names on the

IDs matched the names Renaldo had called them. They were probably genuine drivers'
licenses.

They carried flip-phones. They were so basic that they didn't have passcodes but there
was nothing on them, not even so much as a call history. There were also no house keys
or other random items most people carried around with them.

Their sidearms were still holstered, so Carver left them, but he took Renaldo's M4 and
stowed it in a van out of the way. It looked like it was in good condition and had no serial
numbers, so it was definitely a keeper.

Carver motioned Jessica over. She rose from her kneel, lowered her rifle, and jogged
over. He slung his MP5SD across his back and grabbed Benji's collar. "Help me drag these
to the other side of the garage."

Jessica slung the M4 over her back and looked down at Renaldo. He had a nice big
exit wound on the back of his head. His brains had spilled onto the dirt and were slowly
soaking in.

She gagged and shuddered, then grabbed him by the feet and tugged him toward the far
end of the garage. Carver pulled Benji around the side of the garage. He took the two-way
radio off the man's belt and clipped it on his, then tucked the body into the reeds on the
creek bank.

Jessica followed suite and then returned to get Hattie's body. Carver took Jamar next.
He was short but built like a sack of potatoes and left a trench in the sandy soil. Once the
bodies were out of the way, Carver used his foot to smooth over the sand in front of the
garage and to cover the blood.

He went back to their previous firing position and picked up the bullet casings. The
guns weren't registered and had no serial numbers, but it was best to keep things as clean
as possible. Any detective worth their salt would be able to figure out what happened, but
Carver liked making people earn their paycheck.

It was almost certain that Travis County would do their best to cover things up. Piker
had probably identified Carver and Jessica by now. All the corrupt players in the two
departments would be on the lookout.

It didn't seem likely that a general APB would be put out unless they were desperate.
They didn't want to risk a good cop finding them first. No matter how deep the corruption ran, there were almost always good folks still in the mix.

Jessica rubbed her hands together. "For my next trick, I'll make four bodies disappear."

Carver aimed the parabolic mic toward the creek and listened. He didn't hear boat
motors yet. It was taking them a while. Loading a lot of kids onto boats probably wasn't
easy even if they were all shackled together and held at gunpoint.

During his time with the SEALs, he'd once helped evacuate a village in the dead of night hours before a paramilitary force planned to come and wipe it out. Getting the damned kids to move out in an orderly fashion had been a logistical nightmare.

Jessica looked toward the garage. "What next? Can we free the girls from the cage?"

"No. We want the other guards to think everything is fine when they arrive."

Carver turned up the walkie-talkie's volume. He didn't know if the boats would radio ahead when they were on the way. It didn't matter much if they did or not, the plan was the same. The boats would arrive and presumably pull into the boathouse.

That would be the moment to strike. The central dock would provide the perfect high ground. The only trick would be eliminating the drivers quickly without shooting any of the girls.

He practiced Renaldo's voice in case he had to answer the walkie-talkie. "Copy that. Acknowledged."

"Your Spanish accent needs some work," Jessica said.

Carver kept practicing. It wasn't perfect, but it might be passable to someone sitting right next to a loud boat engine. He went to the nearest van, put the keys in the ignition, and cranked it. It started up right away. He turned it off and left the keys in the ignition.

The other vans started up just fine as well. If things went smoothly, they were going to need one more driver. If Sabrina was with the next batch of girls, she could drive, provided she wasn't drugged.

Carver doubted the girls would be drugged. It was a lot harder to herd drugged people. Keeping them sober and afraid was the best tactic for compliance.

He got out of the last van and walked over to Jessica.

She was staring at the garage. "I feel bad leaving those poor girls locked up inside. They don't even know we're here to help."

"It's better this way." Carver angled the parabolic mic toward the creek and slowly moved it back and forth. He heard the hum of boat motors this time. They were finally coming. He hurried to the creek bank and aimed the monocular toward the sound.

He didn't see anything at first. Then the first boat rounded the curve about a quarter of a mile away. The engine was loud and strained and for good reason. The boat was packed full of infrared signatures.

It was hard to count them from this angle. But if that boat was full then the others would be as well. That theory was confirmed a few seconds later when the other two boats came around the curve.

There was sudden movement on the lead boat. One of the small heat signatures jumped into the water. The boat slowed. The driver stood up and looked but didn't move from his position. The heat signature next to the one that had jumped seemed to be struggling.

Seconds later, the girl who'd jumped overboard was pulled back in by the girl she was seated next to. Carver switched to night vision and zoomed in. There were chains and cuffs securing all the girls together.

The girl who'd jumped hadn't had a chance of getting away. That was why the boat driver hadn't panicked. Now he was laughing at the girl who'd tried to abandon ship. The other two boats passed him while he had a laugh. Then he sat back down and resumed course.

"Do you hear that?" Jessica cupped a hand to her ear and angled it south.

Carver had been focused on the boats. He turned south and scanned with the parabolic mic. He heard roaring engines and the creak of suspensions on a rutted road. There were more vehicles coming this way.

Jessica cupped her other ear. "Did I hear something or is it my imagination?"

"We've got more incoming." Carver made sure the radio was turned up. It was, so he hadn't missed an incoming communication. So, who in the hell was coming down the road?

He studied the layout of the terrain. The vans were parked in front of the garage, so any other vehicles would have to park near the edge of the road. Remaining next to the creek bank wouldn't give them a good angle on the incoming vehicles.

Carver took Jessica by the hand and hurried to the scrublands across the dirt road from the garage. He found a small depression right behind some small bushes and crouched there. He scanned the area with his scope and verified that he had a clean view.

"You stay here and watch. I'll hide next to the garage." Carver turned on his earpiece. "Don't shoot unless I tell you to."

"I didn't plan on it." Jessica crouched and looked through the M4 scope. "I've got your back."

Carver jogged across the road. The engines were much closer now. They were probably just a couple of bends in the road away. He jogged to the right side of the boathouse and got a visual on the incoming boats. They were just a hundred yards away now.

He didn't need math equations to know that the boats and the incoming cars were going to get here at roughly the same time. He knew there were three boat drivers. Three men he had to put down hard and fast.

What he didn't know was who was in the oncoming cars. There was no doubt in his mind that they were Jaeger's people. Maybe they'd called in some other vans, but it didn't seem likely. The boats could carry about twenty passengers each. If they were packed full, then that was sixty girls plus the five inside the garage.

The three vans could probably hold twenty-two girls each. That was room enough for all the so-called cargo. The only reason they'd call out more vans was if there were more girls coming. None of the drivers had mentioned more vans, so the only conclusion was that these were something else.

Something unexpected.

There was still no radio communication from either the boats or the incoming vehicles. Carver opened a van and turned on the auxiliary power so the CB radio would turn on. When the digital readout appeared, he confirmed that it was on the same frequency as the walkie-talkie.

That was unusual because CB, aka citizens' band, wasn't on the same frequency as a walkie-talkie. CB radio usually operated at a frequency of around 27 megahertz. Walkie talkies generally operated on VHF, very high frequency. This CB was using 147 megahertz.

These units were probably customized and probably encrypted to keep their communications from being intercepted. At least that was his assumption.

The only thing that mattered at the moment was that an unknown number of vehicles were going to be there in seconds and he had no idea who or what they were carrying.

Carver took up position on the south side of the garage. He went to the Sprinter van they'd taken from Roy and opened the doors. He pulled three small devices from inside his equipment bag and ran back to the vans.

He magnetically attached the three devices to the three vans. They were GPS trackers. A backup plan just in case things went horribly wrong and they couldn't rescue the girls right now. If these vans didn't go to Lakeview Church, he'd know.

Carver ducked behind a van as two vehicles bounced past on the dirt road. Their headlights flashed toward the garage. Benji's van was still backed up in front of the southernmost garage door and blocked his view of the newcomers.

He slid around to the side of the van closest to the road. Keeping low, he made his way to the front of the van. The vehicle engines went silent. Car doors opened and closed. He thought about getting on his stomach and looking under the van, but then he'd only see their feet.

"Holy crap," Jessica whispered through the earbud. "It's these assholes again."

Carver slowly crept around the front of the van and looked. Benji's van still blocked his view of the newcomers. He crept toward the front of Benji's van and looked around the side of it. He saw two SUVs. Three people. They weren't ordinary people.

They were Travis County sheriff's deputies.

CHAPTER 29

Carver wasn't surprised.

Jaeger had probably called for backup just in case. Carver had seen these three deputies back in town when their buddy confronted him. There were three of them because Carver had shot their friend right in the beltline. He was probably inside the same hospital where the rescued girls were.

Bright white LEDs on top of one SUV were lighting the area in front of the garage. A tall, beefy man got out of the vehicle and looked around. "Where the hell is everyone?"

A second cop got out of the same vehicle. He was a real thin guy with a bushy mustache that made him look like a used car salesman. "Yo, Jamey. Are we getting paid extra for this?"

The first cop laughed sarcastically and looked at the third deputy who had just climbed out of the second SUV. "Extra? Man, we'll be lucky if Morton doesn't cut off our heads, thanks to Steve letting Marvin get shot."

"Ha, ha." Steve, the third deputy, pulled on a brown ball cap with the gold sheriff's badge on the front and turned it around backwards. "I told him not to go up there by himself, but he wanted to be a hero."

"Marvin is an idiot." Jamey shook his head. "I just want to know where everyone is so we can get this over and done with."

"They're probably inside." Steve spat a gob of brown saliva on the ground. His lower lip was puffed out, probably from smokeless tobacco. "Why the hell are they bringing us out here instead of hunting for that son of a bitch who shot Marvin?

"No idea." Jamey turned toward the second Deputy. "Trevor, what does the text say?"

Trevor checked his phone. "Morton says we need to coordinate with some guy named Renaldo. We have to give these vans an escort over to Lakeview."

Steve groaned. "Man, that's all the way across town. Why Lakeview?"

"No idea." Trevor patted his crotch. "They better give us a bonus. Maybe some hot little thing to play around with."

"I could go for that, but I ain't asking." Jamey started walking toward the garage entry door. "Where the hell is this Renaldo guy?"

Carver heard another engine on approach. He ducked behind Benji's van. Another silver SUV parked on the side of the road in front of the van. Carver moved through the darkness to the side of the van nearest the road so he could see the occupant of the vehicle.

The three deputies had moved from the other side of the van and were in plain view now.

"Oh, shit." Steve straightened. "What in the hell is she doing here?"

"Shut up and let me handle it." Jamey started walking toward the new vehicle.

A Latina woman hopped out. She wore the same brown sheriff's ball cap. A thick black braid hung from the hole in the back of the ball cap. "Guys, what's going on?" She walked toward the others.

Jamey approached her with a grin on his face. "Anna, what are you doing out here? Morton sent us to check out a disturbance."

"A disturbance?" Anna looked around confused. "All the way out here?" She laughed. "Who would even call that in?"

"Well, nothing is happening, so—"

Anna looked at the vans. "Whoa, why are all these church vans out here?" She read the signs. "Lakeview Church? Are they baptizing people in the creek or something?"

"Man, who knows? No one's here, so we're gonna call it in and leave."

"You already checked inside?" Anna said.

"Yeah. It's clean."

She cocked her head slightly. "Do you hear boat engines?"

The girls inside the garage must have heard something because they started shouting for help.

Anna flinched. "What the hell was that?" She started walking toward the door.

Steve shared a look with Jamey. Jamey nodded. Steve pulled a revolver from his belt and came up behind Anna. He aimed and pulled the trigger. The left side of his head caved in. The revolver fell from his grasp before he finished pulling the trigger.

Carver was already out of cover and moving. He put down Trevor with a shot to the base of the skull. Jamey went down an instant before he could shoot him.

Anna's mouth dropped open when blood and brains exploded from Jamey's head. She screamed and jumped back, nearly tripping over Steve's body. She reached for her sidearm. Carver ran up to her. "Hands up! Do not reach for your weapon!"

She froze mid-scream. Her eyes widened in terror. She looked from Carver to the bodies and back at Carver again. She shouted at him in rapid Spanish. "You killed them, you monster! You killed them!"

Carver kept his submachinegun trained on her.

"I got them, Carver!" Jessica ran from across the road. "Did you see those shots?"

He didn't reply.

Anna switched to English. "You filthy monsters! You killed them!"

"I saved your life, lady." Jessica blew out a sigh. "That guy with the porn stache was about to shoot you in the back!"

Anna looked down at Steve and the revolver next to his body. She looked from Carver to Jessica. "What? That's impossible!" Tears filled her eyes. "I can't believe you killed them!"

"Didn't you hear me?" Jessica gave her a look of disbelief. "This guy was about to kill you. They work for a pedophile ring!"

Anna went silent. "What? No, that's impossible."

"Those boat engines you heard are almost here. They're bringing human cargo from Jaeger's ranch and taking them to Lakeview Church." Carver motioned her toward the garage door. "We need to get inside right now. So, go."

Anna kept her hands raised and moved toward the door. Jessica hurried ahead and opened it for her.

"Jessica go through first and keep an eye on her." Carver didn't want Anna to try anything stupid even though she probably wouldn't once she saw the girls inside.

"Affirmative." Jessica went inside.

Anna went in and cried out almost instantly. "My God!"

Carver pushed her further in. Anna stared at the girls in the cage.

"You see?" Jessica said. "It's a massive human trafficking operation."

The boat engines sounded like they were right outside the boathouse. They'd be pulling inside any second now.

Carver looked for Anna's handcuffs, but she didn't have any on her belt. He took her sidearm and prodded her toward the back door. "I want you to go into the boathouse and smile all big and friendly at the boat drivers, okay?"

"What?" Anna looked shocked. "Why?"

"Because they're expecting your coworkers from the sheriff's department." Carver opened the back door and pushed her into the corridor leading to the boathouse. "Go, now."

Anna went down the corridor. She opened the door at the end and went into the boathouse just as the three boats were pulling inside. A short set of stairs led down to the center dock. Two steps led from the center dock to the floating docks on each side.

The men driving the boats looked up at Anna. She forced a smile. One of them winked and whistled at her. He spoke in Spanish. "Wow, look at this mamacita they sent to greet us."

Another driver stood and thrusted with his hips. "Hey mami, I can give you a ride."

Anna stared at the girls who were shackled to the boats. Tears trickled down her cheeks.

The first driver laughed. "What's wrong, baby?"

The drivers were standing. The girls were sitting down. Carver ran onto the center dock. He took out the two drivers on the right. They died with big grins on their faces. Jessica fired three times.

The lone driver on the left shouted in pain and shock as the three bullets found his chest. His body splashed into the water.

"My God!" Anna hurried down the ladder on the right and touched the nearest girl. "Oh, sweet baby, are you okay?" She started sobbing. "My sweet little angels. Who could do this to you?"

"Sabrina!" Jessica looked wildly from one boat to the other. "Sabrina!"

Carver looked the girls over. Some looked like they were in their late teens, but none of them looked like Jessica's sister.

"Sabrina isn't with them, Carver." Jessica's rifle dropped from her hands and hung by the strap. "My sister isn't here."

Carver didn't know what to say, but he knew what to do. The girls were bound together by a long chain with metal cuffs on it. The cuffs had been taken from regular handcuffs and welded to the chain. It was a real medieval torture device. Something that had no business existing in this day and age.

But it did. And devices like it were regularly used for human trafficking from all corners of the world. These girls were just a drop in an ocean of human misery. Carver knew that firsthand.

He stepped down to the right-hand dock and moored the two nearest boats since the drivers died before they could do that. Jessica secured the third boat. The girls looked up at him with a mix of shock and fear.

The younger ones were sobbing and hugging each other. Some were crying for their parents. The older teenagers watched him warily. Some asked him the usual questions.

"Who are you?"

"What are you doing?"

"I'm with the federal government," Carver said. "We're here to rescue you."

It was a lie, but relief filled their faces. The older girls relaxed and hugged each other or burst into tears of joy and relief.

Carver fished the handcuff key from the dead driver. He went to the other driver and found an identical key in his pocket. He gave that one to Jessica since the third driver had fallen into the water.

He went back to the right-hand dock and started unlocking cuffs. "It's very important that we do this in an orderly fashion. We are in the middle of nowhere, so please don't run off. There are vans outside. We will use them to transport you somewhere safe."

"There are dead bodies outside too," Jessica said. "We had to kill some crooked cops to save you."

"I was kidnapped by cops!" one of the girls shouted. "They pulled me over for a traffic stop!"

"You sweet little angels!" Anna was still sobbing. "I can't believe this. I just can't believe Steve and the others were part of this!"

Carver asked the girls some basic questions. "Were there still men or other girls at the dock when you left?"

An older girl shook her head. "No. Everyone came on the boats."

"And you came through a tunnel out of a quarry?"

"Yes." She nodded. "It was long and narrow."

Carver finished freeing them and decided further questioning could wait until they were loaded into the vans. "Once you're free, please go through the hallway behind us and stay inside the garage. We need to make sure there's no other danger before loading the vans."

"Please let any of us know if you have a medical problem or something that requires immediate attention." He helped the uncuffed girls off the boat and onto the floating dock. It took a while because there were so many of them.

There were fifty-four in total. That was less than he'd thought, probably because the older girls took up more space on the boat than the younger ones. The girls represented all body types too. Some were rail thin, and others had some extra fluff on them. Some were short, and some were tall.

Multiple ethnicities were also represented. Black, white, Asian, Middle Eastern, and probably more, though it was hard to discern at a glance who was what.

There was a reason for that. The traffickers knew that men's tastes ranged all up and down the spectrum. They wanted to cater to every deviant variable they could. That was why they usually preferred hunting in big cities because they could find diverse girls to sate diverse hunger.

The girls followed instructions well. Now that they felt safe, they remained calm and filed out in a somewhat orderly fashion. The interesting thing Carver noticed was that none of them seemed to have formed bonds while in captivity. Only a few girls seemed familiar with each other.

That made sense considering what he'd seen at the church. The girls had been kept in solitude, alone in locked rooms with sound-deadening foam on the walls so the girls couldn't communicate with each other.

Trafficking victims were usually lumped together in a single holding cell. They often bonded and leaned on each other for strength. This operation handled things much differently. It was probably because they catered to a richer clientele.

Most trafficking catered to the mass market. Jaeger's operation was clearly more refined. He was almost certainly selling what he considered a rare product to people who could afford to pay top dollar.

The clock was ticking while they freed the girls and got them outside to the vans. Carver could practically hear it in his head. Sunrise was coming and they needed to get the girls out of here before Detective Piker or someone else with the sheriff's office realized something had gone wrong.

It took eighteen minutes and some change to get the girls off the boats. Carver helped the last girl off and followed her into the garage. Jessica was already there with Anna talking to the girls. They'd already freed the five girls from the cage.

Jessica took out her phone and showed Sabrina's picture. "Did anyone see this girl while they were there?"

Most of the girls shook their heads.

"They kept me locked alone in a small room most of the time," an older teen said. "Then they drugged me, and I woke up naked on an exam table. I heard a lot of shouting and running in the hallway."

"I was in that room too," another girl said. "But I couldn't move my head or anything. They had me strapped down to a cold metal table, and my legs were up in stirrups."

"Hey, me too," a girl said in a Spanish accent. "I saw a green flag down near my feet. I heard one of the men shouting in Spanish that a girl escaped and the doctor was dead."

"I think they forgot about us for a while when they were searching for her," the first girl said. "Then someone seemed to remember us and came back in and put a needle in my arm. I woke up back in my cell. Then a long time later they piled us all into the boats."

Jessica looked desperate. "Do you know anything about the girl who escaped?"

The Hispanic girl looked sad. "I heard the men joking that she was captured and Jaeger killed her."

The younger girls started crying and wailing again.

"Who is this girl?" Anna said softly to Jessica.

"My sister." Jessica's eyes welled with tears. She wiped them away. "If anyone escaped, it's probably her. She's athletic and agile and smart." Jessica shook with sobs. "And now she's dead."

"Let's load them into the vans," Carver said. "We can't waste any more time."

Jessica's voice shook with sadness. "Yeah, you're right."

They took the girls outside. Carver just let them jump into any van they wanted and put them into another one when one was too full. They packed all three vans.

Carver was going to move the Travis County Sheriff's SUVs out of the way, but Anna was already on it. She moved all three behind the garage on the opposite side of the boathouse from the camper van Carver had borrowed from Roy.

She returned to Carver when she'd done that. "Just in case someone else comes, they won't see them right away."

"Good idea," Carver said.

She turned toward the vans. "I'll drive one of the vans."

"Thanks." Carver went to the first van and looked at the older teens inside. "Can any of you drive?"

Two of them raised their hands.

"I'm seventeen, so I have my normal driver's license."

"Me too," the other girl said.

"I just need one. You'll be responsible for driving this van."

The first girl shrugged. "I can do it. Dad lets me drive the entire family sometimes."

"Me too," the other girl said.

"Okay." Carver pointed to the first girl. "Get in the driver's seat." He pointed to the other girl. "You take shotgun just in case."

The girls squeezed past the others on the bench seat and got in. Carver gave the first girl the van keys.

"What's going on?" Jessica said. "Why is that girl in the driver's seat?" She frowned. "Oh, so you can take Roy's van back?"

Carver shook his head and motioned Anna over. "Take the girls to another county. Make sure they're safe." He turned to Anna. "Whatever you do, don't mention me. I want to be completely left out of this."

"Are you kidding me?" Anna looked shocked. "But you're a—"

"I'm not here." Carver shook his head. "It's for the best, believe me. Forget my name. Forget me."

"Who are you?"

"No one."

Jessica grabbed his arm. "Carver, what are you going to do?"

Carver patted her hand. He leaned down and kissed her forehead. "Get the girls to safety. I'm going to Jaeger's ranch to find out who that last girl was."

He was going to finish this.

CHAPTER 30

Carver couldn't walk away from that last girl.

It was clear that this was the girl Renaldo had been talking about earlier. He'd said Jaeger killed her. Maybe he had. Maybe she was dead and gone. That didn't matter. He was going to find her and bring her home.

Jessica's grip on his arm tightened. "Why are you going to the ranch? Those men said she was dead."

"We're not leaving anyone behind. Maybe she's dead, maybe she's not. I want to know for sure."

Jessica wiped tears from her eyes. "I want to tell you not to go, but I also need to know if that girl was my sister. I need closure."

Carver nodded. "I know."

"I'm coming with you."

"That's not a good idea."

"Hey, that was the original plan, remember?" Jessica gripped his hand. "Remember?"

"Yeah." Carver was perfectly comfortable going it alone. "I don't want you to risk your life. It might not be your sister."

"Aw, are you saying you care?"

Normally, Carver would ignore the question. But the truth was, he did care. It was a new feeling. Still a little alien to him. But something about this entire situation had triggered core memories that he'd suppressed or forgotten.

It was hard to say. Hard to overcome his programming. But he forced himself to say it out loud. "Yeah, I care about you."

Jessica's face sobered. "Good. I care about you too. I'm coming."

Anna watched the exchange intently. "I will make sure the girls get to safety. I have a cousin who works for the McDade police, about fifty minutes from here."

Carver nodded. "Keep them there and keep it quiet for five hours. If we're not back by then, it means we're dead."

Anna took Carver's hand in her left, and Jessica's hand in her right. "Vaya con Dios. Go with God. I will pray for you."

"Thank you, Anna."

Anna looked at Jessica. "And thank you for saving my life. I still can't believe this is real. I knew all of those men. I know their families. I've been to their houses for cookouts and played with their kids."

She shivered and wiped away tears. "To find out they are monsters is so hard to process."

"I understand." Jessica patted her hand. "Now get those little angels to safety, okay?"

"I will." Anna hugged them both quickly and went to the third van.

Carver went to the first van and opened the passenger door.

The teenage girl gave him a concerned look. "Is something wrong?"

"Looks like you get to drive after all."

She blinked. "Why? What's going on?"

"We're going to the ranch to find the girl who escaped." Carver motioned her out of the van.

"But they said she's dead."

"Maybe, maybe not. We need to know for sure."

The girl stiffened her spine. "I'll drive real good. I won't let you down."

"I know."

She hugged Carver. "I usually hate everyone, but you're all right."

Carver awkwardly patted her back. He didn't know what to say.

She backed away. "Thanks for saving us." She hurried to the van and got in.

Carver gave the thumbs up. The vans cranked up. Anna's van took the lead and pulled onto the dirt road. Then they drove off.

The sky was getting a little lighter. It was going to be daytime in thirty minutes. The radio on his belt hissed.

A man's voice crackled through the speaker. "Cargo in transit?"

Carver used his somewhat practiced Renaldo voice. "Roger."

"Okay. Over and out."

"Horrible Spanish accent." Jessica grinned at him. "You ready?"

"Yep." They already had everything they needed with them, so Carver hurried into the boathouse. The two dead drivers were still in the boats on the right, so he picked the boat on the left.

He started the engine then pushed off from the dock to back it out of the door and into the creek. He twisted the throttle and steered the boat north. He turned the throttle wide open. Without a full load, it went fast. It still wasn't a speedboat, but they would make good time.

They reached the bend in the creek in five minutes and turned north by northwest, gradually heading due west. The land rose around them, going high enough to form steep banks. They rounded another bend and reached a cliff.

A camouflage net hung over the lower portion of the wall. Carver slowed the boat and got next to the net. There was a rope hanging from a pulley that was secured to the rock face with a spike. He pulled the rope and the net slid aside like a curtain.

There was a dark tunnel on the other side. He guided the boat inside. The ceiling was low enough that his head almost touched it. There was an LED floodlamp affixed to a pole on the boat. He flicked the switch, and it illuminated the tunnel.

The tunnel stretched into the distance. If Jessica's calculations were correct, it was nearly a quarter of a mile long. The stone walls were ragged and rough. There were gaping holes in some places and small protrusions in others. The tunnel had been blasted through the rock but not smoothed or refined.

There really was no need for it. It existed to serve a simple purpose as an auxiliary exit or escape route not unlike tunnels Carver had used to get out of sticky situations. Now he was ironically using it to get into a sticky situation.

"This is creepy." Jessica shivered. "And it's cold."

Light flashed ahead where the tunnel curved slightly. It wasn't the light from their boat. It was coming from around the corner. The sun hadn't risen yet, so it wasn't being caused by daylight reflecting off the water.

Carver cut the engine. Instead of total silence, he heard the thrum of another motor. This one had a deeper pitch like it was slightly muffled. Probably because it was coming from an inboard motor.

Jessica gasped. "Is that another boat?"

"Yep." Carver switched off the floodlamp and put on his night vision goggles so he could see.

There was a ragged gap in the tunnel wall just ahead where softer soil must have been right next to the stone when it was blasted. Carver cranked the motor and gunned it in that direction. He slowed as the boat reached the wall and turned the vessel sideways, swinging the back end right at the wall.

He killed the engine and pushed his hands on the stone wall to stop the boat's momentum. He pulled the back end of the boat sideways and lined it up with the gap. It was just barely wide enough for the boat to squeeze into. He stretched his arms out to both sides of the gap and pulled the boat all the way in until the motor touched the wall.

The other motor was much louder now though it was hard to say exactly how far away it was. He turned off night vision and descended into darkness. He didn't see any light from the incoming boat yet. That meant it hadn't rounded the bend just yet.

Jessica picked up her rifle. "We'll just let it pass, right?"

"Nope. We don't want them to find the bodies and raise the alarm." Carver stepped over the bench seats and got to the front of the boat. He reached a hand toward Jessica. "Let me use the M4. It's more accurate from far off."

She handed it to him. "You didn't seem to have any problems with your little submachinegun."

Carver looked at the silencer and decided to keep it on. At this distance it wouldn't affect accuracy much. He went prone across the front benches and leaned out into the tunnel. He saw a bright light about fifty yards away.

The light was bright and blinding. He wasn't going to hit anything with it shining in his face. He'd have to wait until the boat passed by. He backed up until his head wasn't sticking out and waited.

The incoming boat wasn't going too fast, probably because the low ceiling and the occasional rock outcropping on the sides and the ceiling didn't leave much room for mistakes. One slight error would crash the boat into the wall.

Carver stayed low and waited patiently. The motor hummed at low RPMs and trolled past seconds later. Even at low speed it went past Carver's position in under a second. He glimpsed three heads, one in the driver's seat, and the other two right behind it.

They were in a small v-hulled speedboat with an inboard motor. They were probably just more muscle being sent to help with the girls. Carver hadn't seen anyone else in the boat with them, but it was best to be sure.

He braced his hands on the wall and pulled the boat out of the gap. He knelt and aimed with the night vision scope on. Without the light in his face, he clearly saw three men, or at least the backs of their heads above the backs of their seats.

They were a hundred feet away already but moving in a straight line. He held his breath, squeezed the trigger. The head on the left buckled forward. He quickly did the same with the guy on the right.

The driver must have felt or heard something because he abruptly swung the steering wheel hard left as if to juke. He crashed into the tunnel wall hard enough to throw him out of the seat and against the wall.

He recovered and ducked into the boat. A rifle came up out of the boat and started firing blindly back into the tunnel. That was bad. Real bad because it was a straight shot. All he had to do was get lucky once.

Carver braced his hands on the walls and pulled the boat back into the gap. A bullet sparked off the wall just inches from his head. Another one hit the water right behind him. The man switched to full auto and unloaded everything.

Carver stood until his head touched the tunnel ceiling and peeked around the corner with the scope. He hoped the slightly higher angle would give him sight into the boat. The speedboat was shallow like this one, offering only about two feet of coverage.

The man was ducked behind the driver console and completely out of sight. He was probably reloading. But instead of raising the rifle, the man's hand reached up from the side of the console and pushed the steering wheel slightly to the right.

The boat was still accelerating but it was stuck on an outcropping. With the steering wheel turned, it was starting to slide off the obstacle. That was smart. Real smart. The guy probably figured he could get loose and make a run for it, using his rifle to cover the retreat.

But the one thing about boats and especially speedboats, was they were usually constructed out of fiberglass, not metal. The heavy gauge metal on Carver's boat would probably stop a couple of normal slugs because they were designed to flatten on impact, not penetrate metal or armor.

Fiberglass didn't offer any sort of protection against any kind of bullet except maybe a .22 short. The console was four feet wide. Just barely wide enough to hide someone. Carver aimed to the left of the console and fired.

He fired four more times in quick succession, aiming further right each time. The man screamed in pain after the second shot. Carver put two more rounds into the same place. The man screamed again.

Now there was another problem. He needed to confirm the man was dead because he probably had a two-way radio on the boat and could call for help. It was possible his cries would go unheard because the tunnel blocked the radio signal.

But there was the possibility that the signal would make it out and someone would get the warning. He couldn't take that chance. He also didn't want to drive his boat toward the other one because the man might start shooting again.

The primary advantage Carver had was the darkness. The light on the other boat was facing away. The man in the boat didn't seem to have night vision. All he could do was fire blindly into the dark behind him.

The tunnel was barely twelve feet wide. That was just enough for two boats to squeeze past each other. A thirty round magazine had enough rounds to cover all twelve feet pretty easily. The heavy gauge steel on Carver's boat might block a couple of rounds, but that wasn't something he wanted to test. At least not if he could help it.

Carver fired two more rounds into the console. The man didn't cry out. Carver fired at the left side and then at the right. The silenced rifle coughed each time. Still no cries of pain. There wasn't much room to hide behind the console. Either the man was dead, or he was somehow not shouting in pain after being shot again.

"Is he dead?" Jessica whispered.

Carver pulled on his night vision goggles and turned them on. He couldn't see into the boat from this angle. The tunnel ceiling was too low. The other boat motor was still running. Water bubbled behind it but it wasn't moving because it was still caught on an outcropping.

He motioned Jessica to the front and handed her the rifle. "Shoot at anything that moves in the boat."

She knelt and aimed. Carver braced his hands on the tunnel wall and moved his boat out of the gap and into the tunnel. He gave a solid push off the wall and sent their boat gliding silently to the other side of the tunnel.

Carver caught the wall in time to keep the metal hull from banging against the stone. He sat on the bench seat and pulled the boat along the wall, getting them closer and closer to the other boat.

Something glinted in the night vision. A flashlight blinked on, blinding him. A rifle barked in full auto. Bullets pinged off stone and metal. Carver ducked as low as he could in the boat. He tried to grab Jessica but was still blinded and couldn't find her.

Jessica screamed in pain. The barrage of bullets abruptly stopped. Probably because the man was reloading. Carver hurried to the back of the boat and turned on the floodlight. It painted Jessica in bright light.

She was on lying on her back on the front seat. Blood trickled down across the seat and down the edge. She was bleeding from the neck.

And she wasn't moving.

CHAPTER 31

Carver saw the shooter in the other boat.

The man was lying motionless, arm outstretched. There were two puckered wounds on his head.

Carver hurried to Jessica. "Are you okay?"

Her eyes were wide open, and she wasn't moving. She abruptly flinched and looked at him. "I'm still alive?"

He sighed in relief. "So far."

Jessica winced and touched her neck. She pulled away bloody fingers. "He got me, didn't he?"

"He didn't get you good enough."

She pressed her fingers to the wound and sat up with a groan. "He nicked me. At least I hope he did. Otherwise, I'm going to bleed out."

Carver moved her hand and found the wound. The bullet had sliced into the skin rather than burning and cauterizing it. Probably because it had ricocheted off the tunnel wall and struck her. "You got lucky. Real lucky."

"When he blinded me, I panic-fired. I kept pulling the trigger even when I felt the bullet hit me." She grimaced and rubbed her neck. "It felt like getting stung by a dozen bees at once."

"Well, you got lucky twice, because you killed him and didn't die."

"I hope I haven't used up all my luck yet." Jessica closed her eyes and blew out a long, slow breath. "I just need a little more time."

"You've got plenty of time left. I'll make sure of that."

"I mean, it helps that I went prone too." She frowned. "Is it still considered going prone if I lay on my back?"

"Yes."

"Okay, well I went prone then."

"That's a good instinct to have."

She smiled. "Not bad for a programmer, huh?"

"Well, you are from Texas."

"Exactly." Jessica nodded toward the boat. "Should we turn that thing off?"

"Yeah." Carver hated to waste another moment, but he also wanted to make sure no one else was on the boat. He pulled their boat the last few feet and stepped into the other boat. He turned off the motor and looked at the men.

The men in the back seats wore business suits. He touched the suit material and checked the labels. He didn't recognize the names on the labels.

Jessica apparently did. She whistled. "Man, these guys must have money. I sat in a board room full of men who wore suits like these when I was looking for venture capital funds. One of the secretaries told me the suits cost over twenty thousand dollars."

"These aren't guards," Carver said. "They're clients." He checked their pockets and found wallets. The first guy was Derek Holland. The other man was Bruce Stafford. He didn't recognize their names.

The boat driver didn't have a wallet or any ID. He was a short Hispanic man in black jeans and a T-shirt. He was just a nobody like the rest of them. He was probably taking the clients to the girls so they could have their fun with them even while they were being evacuated.

Carver showed her the IDs. "Ever heard of them?"

She shook her head. "No, but they're rich, that's for sure."

Carver left the IDs with the bodies. It was good evidence, provided any of this ever saw the light of day. He stepped back into the other boat and helped Jessica back over. He pushed the front of the boat away from the wall to turn it around.

He went to the back of the boat and started the motor again. He aimed straight ahead and gunned it. This little skirmish had cost them twenty minutes. Since these VIPs had been on their way to the girls, it meant there might be others waiting for their turn to take a boat through the tunnel.

The tunnel entrance was several hundred feet from the dock in the quarry. It was possible they could come out unseen, provided it was still dark topside. He checked the time and saw they had eleven minutes until official sunrise.

The quarry was deep in the earth so the light might not reach inside until an hour after sunrise. He hoped that was the case, or there was no way they could approach the ranch unseen. Especially not if there were cameras.

They reached the bend in the tunnel and curled around it. The exit was just ahead, a gray semicircle of light at the end of the tunnel. Carver turned off the flood lamp and kept to the middle of the channel. He went slower to reduce engine noise, but it was still loud in the tunnel.

He cut the engine and let them drift out of the tunnel. The tunnel exit was about halfway across the quarry lake from the dock and nearly hidden from view by piles of broken limestone. The stone had probably been purposefully dumped there for that very purpose. It was interesting to note that they'd done nothing to hide it from above.

Carver let the boat drift against the pile of limestone. He got out and beached it so it wouldn't drift off then climbed to the top of the limestone and looked at the dock. No one was outside. The metal garage was closed and the window next to the entry door was dark.

He scanned the area with the monocular, looking for any obvious cameras. There were none visible. It seemed unlikely that an organization like this wouldn't have cameras anywhere. It seemed more likely that they'd have them everywhere.

Unless their high-value clientele wanted a guarantee of no cameras and no records that they were ever here. Clients like the ones in the boat wouldn't want to go anywhere they could potentially be recorded or tracked.

They didn't want to end up on a client list or have anything like flight logs showing they'd been anywhere near this place if and when the proverbial shit hit the fan. Maybe they had ways of guaranteeing that there were no cameras. Maybe they sent teams of security to scan the place and make sure there were no hidden recording devices of any kind.

With the amount of money they had, anything was possible.

Carver returned to the boat and pushed off. He started the motor and headed for the dock.

Jessica sat next to him. The bleeding on her neck had stopped and was crusting on her skin. She showed him a picture on her phone. "I found our two VIPs."

Carver glanced at the picture caption. "CEO of Wanderlust. Never heard of it."

"It's a huge social media company. The federal DOJ was investigating them for supposedly allowing child pornography to proliferate in secret groups. The last administration killed the investigation, but the new administration is looking into it again."

"Probably too late now. All they had to do was weed out the porn and delete it."

She nodded. "The other guy is some venture capitalist from Silicon Valley." She rolled her eyes. "Big surprise there."

Carver had nothing to add to the conversation, so he didn't respond. He kept a sharp eye on their surroundings. The compound was probably on full alert. They wouldn't have been transferring all their human cargo in the dead of night if they weren't.

The clients must have been scheduled to visit already and were angry when they found out all the girls were being shipped to another location. They were apparently too impatient to go to the other location and wait for them to arrive. They wanted their merchandise right away.

They'd gotten the grand prize, a one-way trip to the afterlife. It was probably more than they deserved, but it was all Carver had time to offer.

The boat bumped against the dock. Jessica hopped out and moored the boat. Carver got out and hustled to the metal shed. He tested the doorknob and wasn't surprised that it was unlocked. Probably because it had been in use moments ago when the boats were being loaded.

There was also no reason for them to lock the doors behind their front lines. It told Carver that either Jaeger ran a very loose ship, or he was supremely confident that no one could ever get in without him knowing.

Either reason improved their odds of succeeding. But what was success in this situation? If the girl who escaped was Sabrina, it sounded like she had been captured and killed. Finding her body wouldn't really be success. It would simply be closure.

The mission had been all about Sabrina. If she was dead, then Carver would have to take that out on someone. Jaeger was by far the best candidate, but he was willing to punish anyone who got in his way.

Carver stepped into the garage and shined his flashlight around. He could have used the overhead light, but this was safer. Maybe Jaeger and his men thought they were untouchable despite the events of the past few hours. Maybe this would be a cakewalk.

The best way to ensure it was a cakewalk was to play it by the numbers. To remain alert and on guard against any possibility. As Rhodes used to say, the cautious survive and the cocky die. He'd seen it proven time and time again.

His former SEALs commander, Joe Donnely, liked to tell them to keep doing what works. In other words, don't try to reinvent the wheel. Don't try to get fancy. Don't put your life on the line with a novel theory.

Carver planned to keep doing what worked. To remain as cautious and paranoid as ever. He wasn't sure if he was even capable of doing anything else. Then again, he also hadn't thought he was capable of caring about anything except the beach. Now he was running off to save people just because he considered them friends.

His flashlight picked up a row of vehicles parked against the far wall. There was nothing else stored in the garage.

"Hey, golf carts." Jessica hurried over to the vehicles. She looked at the offroad wheels and suspension. "Or would these be considered side-by-sides because they're basically ATVs?" She looked expectantly at Carver as if he might have an answer.

Carver shrugged.

She unplugged one from a charger. "These are battery powered like golf carts, so maybe they're not technically side-by-sides." She pursed her lips and shook her head. "The world may never know."

The vehicles had enclosed cabs. Carver opened the door to the one she'd unplugged. He turned the ignition key and a small LCD display lit up. The battery showed a full charge. Jessica got in on the other side.

She looked at the display. "Fancy. Do you plan on driving right up to the house?"

Carver shook his head. "The sun is coming up. We need to find the building with the wrecked garage door and start there."

Her eyes brightened. "Good idea." She forced a smile. "I'd be lying if I told you I'm doing okay. I can't stop thinking about Sabrina being dead. I feel like we're going to find her all bruised and broken and I'm going to completely lose it, you know?"

Carver reached over and squeezed her hand. Normally he'd tell her the brutal truth, that Sabrina might be the girl the others were talking about. But there were other possibilities, so he went with those instead.

"Sabrina might not even be here. They might have sold her already."

Jessica grimaced. "My God, it's like the princess is always in another castle."

Carver stared blankly at her then got out of the vehicle and lifted the middle rollup door. He got back in and looked over the controls. Putting the vehicle in drive required pressing a button on the LCD screen, so he did that and accelerated out of the garage.

Jessica patted his hand. "My God, you poor thing. You really didn't get the reference, did you?"

"What reference?"

"About the princess."

Carver glanced sideways at her and steered the vehicle onto the gravel road leading up and out of the quarry.

"Wow, were you really so deprived as a child that you didn't get to play video games or go to movies?"

Carver thought long and hard about it. He vaguely remembered something. "I went to a movie with my father once. We got a big tub of popcorn and sat down. Another man with a tub of popcorn sat next to my father. They swapped the containers and then the guy left about thirty minutes into the movie."

Jessica's nostrils flared. "What?"

"Then we left about fifteen minutes after that." Carver shrugged. "In retrospect, I think they were exchanging something hidden in the popcorn."

"Who in the hell were your parents?" She shook her head in disbelief. "No wonder you've got issues."

The quarry road had been carved right into the rock. It ascended at a steep thirty-degree gradient. The UTV handled it easily, keeping a steady thirty-five miles per hour the entire way. Carver hoped no one else decided to come down the road while they were going up it.

Though the sky was pink with sunlight, the road was still mostly in shadow because it was enclosed by steep cliff walls on either side. There was a good chance that anyone coming down the road wouldn't be able to see them clearly in passing.

He wasn't going to count on that possibility. He had his MP5 positioned in front so he could grab it quickly and fire. He considered telling Jessica to do the same with her M4, but she was rambling on about how crazy his parents must have been.

Now wasn't the best time to talk about his childhood. Now was the time to think only about discovering the fate of one child.

They reached the top of the road without incident. The road curved away from the quarry and toward the large buildings in the distance. One of those buildings was the ranch house. The other was the tall outbuilding with the concrete walls.

It was situated a good distance from the main house. It was made of concrete and stood three stories tall. There were metal shutters over all the windows. It looked like a small corporate office building, or possibly a hotel. But the metal shutters gave it a sinister vibe.

There were other outbuildings, but none of them looked anything like that one. It was obviously built to accommodate a large number of people. It was essentially a prison. It reminded Carver of a song he'd heard before.

"You think that's the place?" Jessica said.

Carver nodded. "It's built like a hotel. You can check in any time you like, but you can never leave."

"Huh?" Jessica looked confused. "I don't get it."

"It's a reference," Carver said. "It's from a song I heard a long time ago, but I don't remember the name."

She smiled. "I'm proud of you for at least trying."

Carver decided he wasn't ever going to try quoting a reference again.

The road forked ahead. One turn went to the ranch house and the other went to the hotel. The road was paved with asphalt in both directions. Carver turned toward the hotel building. The road changed into a concrete driveway and descended behind the concrete retaining wall that surrounded the building.

Carver followed the driveway around to the back and found the garage door the escapee had crashed through. The front end of a van protruded from bent and twisted metal. The van's front doors and tires were pinned. The metal door would probably need to be cut with a torch to free it. It probably wouldn't have taken someone more than ten minutes to cut the metal, but they'd apparently decided that would take too long and instead chose to ferry the girls out the back way in boats.

The van's front windshield had been kicked out. Carver pictured the scene. The girl had smashed the van through the door, kicked out the windshield, and then climbed out over the hood. She'd seen the concrete wall blocking her and hadn't known which way to go.

She'd probably been running around the building to get out when she'd been caught, because there was no way to scale the wall.

Jessica stared at the van. Tears trickled down her cheeks. "I could totally picture my sister doing this. She's strong and brave."

"I thought you didn't know her well."

"I don't. But I know her well enough after having to move back in with my parents." She wiped away her tears. "She told me to never give up, that I could do anything I wanted." Jessica turned to Carver. "I showed her your email you sent to me back when you needed my help. I wasn't going to do it, but she convinced me to at least go meet you."

"Sabrina convinced you to help me?"

"Yeah."

It was like a full circle. Jessica helped him. Now he was helping Sabrina or at least trying to. But now he felt what Jessica felt. A sense of hopelessness. There was no way for one of those girls to escape this place.

They were here, but they were too late.

CHAPTER 32

Carver steeled himself.

They'd gone through a lot to get here. They'd saved a lot of girls and killed a lot of people. He was going to see this through to the end, whatever that entailed. The next order of business was getting inside this building.

That was going to be tricky, because it looked like the only way in was through the rollup door into the parking deck or the entry door next to it. He hadn't seen any other entry doors during the ride around the building.

This wasn't a hotel. It was a prison.

He continued driving around the building. There was a dead end just around the corner. That meant the only way out was to exit the garage and turn right, then follow the driveway around to the exit.

It was a typical prison design. A rat maze with only one way in or out. Or was it? Carver noticed a manhole cover near the base of the building wall. Buildings of any size require certain things to be a functional modern living space.

Prisons need even more because they have to host large numbers of people who are never going to leave the building. Humans need to eat. They need to make waste. They sweat and produce skin oils that rub off on everything.

Supporting just a single human would require lots of food, water, waste disposal, and cleaning. In other words, the building had utilities. It had electricity, a water supply, and waste disposal. In order to have those things, it needed special spaces in the building that could accommodate wiring and plumbing.

Carver stopped the UTV and got out. He walked to the manhole cover. There were holes in the top for ventilation and to make it easier to lift. He hooked two fingers into the holes and lifted it one-handed. It was heavy, but nothing he couldn't handle.

Jessica looked down at it. "What are you doing?"

"Can you lift that?"

She bent down and hooked fingers with both hands into the holes. She crouched and lifted with her legs. She dragged it to the side. "It's not as heavy as it looks."

Carver looked into the manhole. There was a metal ladder descending into darkness. He went down it and turned on his flashlight. At the bottom was a square concrete room with lots of metal conduit and plastic pipes. Some of the pipes were for water supply and others were for sewage.

The utilities ran into two tunnels. One tunnel headed away from the building and the other went into it. The tunnels were plenty big for someone of average size. For someone like Carver, they were a real tight squeeze.

They were basically concrete tubes. The pipes and conduit ran at the top of the tube, leaving the bottom open so a worker could crawl through it. If Jaeger was really holding sixty plus prisoners in their own individual rooms, then this place needed a lot of plumbing and electrical lines.

A rotten odor exuded from the tube leading under the building and the one leading away. There were probably raw sewage leaks somewhere inside. The space was dank and humid. The sound of dripping water echoed from somewhere inside one of the tubes.

There was a light film of slime and mold in the tubes. The concrete was darkly stained where water or sewage had leaked long ago. He ran a gloved finger along the surface. It was damp and slick.

There were scuff marks in the slime. As if someone had been through here recently. Possibly the girl who'd escaped.

Carver unslung the MP5 and laid it on the floor. He got on his stomach and was able to crawl into the tube, but he didn't have space to turn around, and his sidearm holster kept wedging his leg in place. Unless he suddenly became a double-jointed contortionist, he'd have to back out the same way he came in. On the upside, the slick mold made it a little easier to slide back and forth.

He got out. Jessica went into the tube without him asking. She crawled on her hands and knees. "God, it stinks in here." She turned around without any trouble and got out. "I guess being a giant lunk has its disadvantages."

"Yeah."

Jessica looked at the tube leading away from the building. "You think Sabrina came down here and went through this tunnel?"

"It's a possibility." Carver shined the flashlight into the outgoing tube. There were scuff marks in the mold as if someone had crawled inside the tube recently. The tube went for about a hundred feet before gradually curving left.

Jessica ran a finger over the marks. "I'm going in." She gripped Carver's arm. "Do you think it's possible she escaped? That maybe all that talk about finding her and killing her was just talk?"

"We don't even know if she was here for certain." Carver gave her the flashlight. "It might be someone else entirely."

"I don't care. I'm going in." Jessica took the headlight and went into the tube. She made quick progress, reaching the curve in the tunnel in just a few minutes and vanished around the bend.

Carver slung his MP5 back on and climbed up the ladder to the surface. Once there, he listened carefully. The roar of the large air conditioning units drowned out just about anything nearby. It didn't seem likely that anyone would come back this way since it was a dead end, but it was better to be safe while Jessica was crawling to destination unknown below.

There were nothing but blank concrete walls in this section. The manhole was the only way out of here. The girl who escaped could have possibly found it, lifted the heavy metal cover, and then closed it behind her.

She could have taken the utility tube leading out. But there was one thing she probably didn't have that Carver did. A flashlight. There were no lights down there. If the girl had gone below, she would have been in pitch black.

No one in their right minds would go down there alone and into the darkness, but someone escaping this place would be desperate for any possibility, even if it meant descending into the unknown and looking for any way out.

Carver looked up at the side of the building. There were windows on the top level, but none below. He envisioned all four sides of the building. The side facing the ranch had windows on all three levels. The adjacent side also had windows. But the other two sides had none except on the top floor.

The people who came here to hunt exotic beasts also came here for other reasons. The top floor of this building might be where they stayed. Jaeger probably didn't want visitors staying in his ranch house even though it was huge.

That was why this building had windows on the top floor. They didn't want their guests to feel claustrophobic and like prisoners themselves. He imagined the girls being paraded in front of the guests. The guests choosing which girl or girls they wanted. Then they'd go to their rooms, and the girls would be brought to them.

It was interesting that this place had actual reviews on the maps app. That the reviewers talked about hunting exotic animals and how enjoyable the experience was. There were even pictures of fathers bringing their daughters and sons for the hunt.

This place existed in a dual state. Part of it was entirely legitimate, and the real money-making part of it existed in the shadows. Not everyone who came here knew about the dark side.

The other outbuildings, the smaller bungalows on the northeast side of the quarry were probably where the hunters were staged before being taken on their so-called safaris to hunt down wildebeests, bison, and other creatures.

That was why Carver hadn't seen any animals during the drive from the quarry to here. The animals were kept far away from here. The hunting side of this operation was also how Jaeger laundered all the money he made on the sex trafficking.

It was a clever setup. Carver had seen dozens of illegal operations and ways to launder money, but this was the first one he'd seen that used hunting exotic beasts to do so.

The air conditioning units were still going nonstop in the Texas heat, and he couldn't hear anything except for them. He didn't like having one of his senses blinded, but short of cutting the wires, there wasn't anything he could do about it.

Carver jogged to the corner of the building and looked around it. No one was there. That was interesting. No one was trying to pry the van out of the metal rollup door. No one was entering or exiting the garage.

An operation like this didn't require a lot of manpower. All you needed was maybe twenty men on premises to guard the merchandise. It was possible that Jaeger had sent all of his guards with the girls, and this place was now empty. If the girl who escaped was dead, then her body might be somewhere inside.

He tucked that idea away and returned to the manhole. He climbed down inside and looked into the tube. The flashlight shined in his eyes. Jessica was coming back. A few minutes later, she crawled out of the tube, dirty and breathing heavily.

"God, that thing is long." She blew out a breath. "So, I found a lot of small animal skeletons and stuff along the way. But about halfway through, there's a metal grate that only allows the utilities to go through. There's definitely no way a person could squeeze past it."

"Did it look like anyone else had been that way?"

She nodded. "There were fresh scuff marks from someone crawling through the tube. Some of the animal bones were crushed too like someone went over them." She handed him the flashlight.

Carver took it and turned it off. "This is what it was like for whoever came through here."

Jessica gasped. "I didn't even think about that. She crawled through pitch black."

Carver turned the flashlight back on. He pointed it into the tube leading under the building. "That's the only other direction she could have gone unless she climbed back out of the manhole and made a run for it."

"There's no reason to go that way." Jessica bit her lower lip. "Going into the tube under the building would be pointless."

"Maybe." Carver shined the flashlight into the other tube. There were scuffmarks from where he and Jessica had ventured a few feet inside. There were also scuffmarks beyond that. Marks that looked about as recent as the ones on the other side.

Jessica took the flashlight. "I'll go look. If she's not there, then what?"

"Then we go inside and look for her body."

"And if we find a body that isn't Sabrina?"

"Then we'll have to search the compound and find Jaeger. He probably knows what happened to her."

"You think Mateo and Antonio are here somewhere too?"

"Almost certainly." Carver wondered why they hadn't been part of the group moving the girls. Maybe there were more girls in the ranch house.

Jessica crawled into the tube and followed it around the bend. "Ew gross!" She went silent for a while and then sneezed later. The sneeze echoed from far away. She whistled three short times, from a little further away.

Carver didn't know what they meant then remembered the earbud. He turned it on. "Are you there?"

"Yes," Jessica said through the earbud. "I didn't know if you'd understand why I whistled."

"I figured it out."

"There's a ladder leading up to another manhole cover. The tube keeps going and going. There are other small tubes where the plumbing and wires go up into the building, but they're too small to climb into."

"Did you open the manhole cover?"

"No. I didn't want to risk it."

"It probably goes into a utility room with a breaker panel and other pipes. Do you hear anything?"

She went silent for a moment. "No. I hear electrical humming and water trickling."

"Open the cover and look."

"Okay." She went quiet again. Metal scraped softly and then loudly. "Crap!" She sighed. "You're right. It's a room with lots of pipes and wires and conduits. There's a door." She went quiet again. "It opens into a hallway. There's a room a few feet away from me and a door at the end."

"Any signs?"

"No, it's all blank concrete."

Carver thought it over. "You're probably on the parking garage level. Probably somewhere near the garage itself."

"I don't hear anyone or anything."

"Don't go anywhere. I'm coming in."

"How do you plan to do that?" Jessica hissed. "Don't try crawling in the tube. You'll get stuck."

"I'm coming in through the garage. Hold position."

"Affirmative, General Lieutenant Colonel."

Carver climbed up the manhole ladder. He left the cover off since it seemed doubtful anyone would come this way and hurried to the corner. He looked around it. The area was just as empty as before.

He jogged past the van and tested the entry door. It was locked as expected, but it was best to go for the simplest solution first and then work his way up the chain of difficulty. Thankfully, the next option should be just as easy as an unlocked door.

Carver went to the van. He pulled himself up and over the hood and into the cab. The side doors were pinned, so he walked past the bench seats in the back. The rear doors of the van hung open already, offering a clear view of the garage interior.

There were rows of trucks and vans inside, but no guards, so he stepped out of the van and looked around. He couldn't see the walls past the rows of vehicles, so he went left and found a door with a keypad next to it.

The door was closed and locked. "Jessica, can you open the door you saw in the hallway?"

"I'll try." There was a scrape of metal and then silence. Metal scraped again. "Okay, I opened it. There's a stairwell on the other side."

"Okay, that's not the door I was hoping it was." He took out his slim jim. "I'll try to jimmy the latch."

"What should I do?"

"Figure out where in the building you are so I can link up with you." Carver worked on the latch and finally sprung it, but the door was also magnetically locked. This place was locked down as tight as a maximum-security facility.

Cutting the power might be the only way to circumvent the magnetic doors. "Jessica, go back to the utility room and see if you can access the breaker panel."

The magnetic lock clicked, and the door swung open. Carver looked inside and saw an empty corridor.

"Hey, I found a control room with controls for the doors."

Carver didn't see any cameras, but he asked anyway. "Any video feeds?"

"No. Isn't that kind of strange?"

"Not really. Their clients require absolute privacy." Carver heard her voice through the earbud but also from somewhere down the hallway. He walked down it and found the control room.

Jessica was sitting inside. She flinched and looked at him. "Oh, there you are." She pointed to the touchscreen in front of her. On it were four diagrams, one for each level of the building. The doors on each level were color coded red or green for locked or unlocked.

The basement level where they were had only a few doors. Two led into the garage and the others led into stairwells. Levels one and two had lots of small rooms and doors. All of the doors were coded green.

The top level had larger rooms. All but one of the doors were coded green. It looked like the building had been completely emptied out.

"There are two hundred rooms on levels one and two." Jessica tapped a slightly larger room on level two. It was labeled as the exam room. "That's where the girl escaped from."

"Let's search the building. If the girl was killed, her body is probably here somewhere."

Jessica tapped on a large room located at basement level. "If there's a body, it's probably here."

Carver raised an eyebrow. "Why do you think that?"

She swiped left and the screen scrolled to reveal a label next to the room. "It's the morgue."

Carver wasn't surprised. The clients in places like this had different needs. Sometimes those needs involved violence and death. They got off on the power of snuffing out human life. Thus, the need to get rid of bodies.

"Let's go."

"One sec." Jessica tapped a gear icon and opened an options window. She typed in a code and tapped on the OK button. "I just gave us a universal passcode in case we run into any other keypad locked doors."

"What's the code?"

"You might want to write this down."

"I think can memorize whatever it is."

"Okay. It's one, two, three four."

Carver gave her a deadpan stare for a moment, then left the room. He'd more or less memorized the map, so he knew which way to go. He followed the hallway and took a right.

"Hey, sorry." Jessica hurried to catch up. "I'm trying not to freak out. Making lame jokes is how I cope." She shivered. "I don't know what I'll do if I see Sabrina's cold, lifeless body on a stainless-steel table inside."

Carver stopped and put his hands on her shoulders. "Whatever we find, you'll be okay."

Tears pooled in her eyes. "If I find Sabrina in there, I want to go kill everyone we find here, okay?"

Carver nodded. "Okay."

"Thank you." She started walking and stopped at the junction of corridors. "Um, which way?"

Carver went right. The morgue door was on the left. He gave Jessica a moment to steel herself, and then he opened the door.

CHAPTER 33

Carver looked inside the morgue.

There was a body on a stainless-steel table. It was covered by a white sheet.

Jessica gasped and ran to the table. She pulled the sheet back and burst into sobs. She backed away, stumbling and nearly falling.

Carver caught her. He hugged her tightly. "I'm sorry."

Jessica couldn't speak for a moment. She finally caught her breath. "It—it's not her. It's a little girl. Just a little girl." She could hardly breathe between her sobs. "It's horrible."

Carver pulled back the sheet. It was a girl, maybe nine or ten. Her face was swollen and black with bruises. It looked like she'd been beaten to death. There were deep bruises on her neck too. Strangulation.

The body was stiff with rigor mortis. Very stiff. This girl had been dead for a long time. Eight to ten hours at least. There were six tables in the room. Two more tables had sheet-covered bodies on them.

Carver released Jessica and looked at the next body. It was another girl of similar age. Her body was stiff too, but it was on the back end of rigor when decomposition started to set in. She had similar injuries to the first. The third girl was the same age and had the same injuries.

He covered the bodies. There were no body racks or refrigerated compartments for long-term storage of bodies like most morgues used. But there were three cremation ovens. That was a lot of ovens. The last time he'd seen that many was at a funeral home in El Fuerte.

He looked inside one. There was a metal tray that slid in and out. The body would go on that tray and be put into the oven. The oven would burn the body to ashes, leaving only bones behind. The tray would be pulled out and a powerful electromagnet on a rolling platform would extract any metals before the remains were crushed into a fine powder and disposed of.

He wondered why these bodies had been allowed to go through rigor mortis and the first stages of decomposition before burning them. He pulled the sheet down on the first girl and saw ragged cuts where her internal organs had been removed. Apparently, they didn't let anything go to waste if they could help it.

"None of these girls are the one who escaped." Carver stared at the still forms. "I think the same client killed them within hours of each other."

"How can people be so sick?" Jessica's eyes were red, but she looked more angry than sad now. "I want to squeeze the life out of them with my bare hands."

Carver felt the same. "We need to search the rest of the building."

Jessica nodded soberly. "Okay."

They left the room and entered the hallway. Voices echoed down the hallway. He went to the corner and peeked around it. Two men were standing next to the door to the parking garage. They were talking in Spanish, but he couldn't make out what they were saying.

One of them stepped through the door and pushed a gurney inside. The two men kept talking in rapid-fire sentences. They sounded angry and agitated. Like the other men he'd encountered, they had tattoos. A lot of them. They had them on their arms, necks and faces.

But these two looked familiar, even from a distance. Carver checked the pictures on his phone to confirm his suspicions. One of them wore a sleeveless V-neck tank top. The top of the number 13 was visible on his exposed chest. The other one had the number 13 tattooed on his neck.

Jessica looked from the pictures to the men. "Antonio and Mateo?"

Carver nodded. "Antonio and Mateo."

Mateo was pushing the gurney. Antonio was walking behind him and talking. They were coming toward them. A still form lay on the gurney. Probably a body. Probably the girl who'd escaped and been captured.

They were taking her to the morgue.

Carver pulled his MP5SD to the front and got ready. Jessica did the same with the M4. Carver pulled a small extendable mirror from his thigh pocket and extended it around the corner so he could see the men coming.

He caught bits and pieces of their conversation, but echoes from the concrete walls muddled the words. They were twenty feet away. Then fifteen. Then ten. Carver retracted the mirror so they wouldn't see it and waited.

The voices and footsteps grew closer and then started growing more distant. Carver extended the mirror again. The hallway was empty. He went around the corner and sidled up to the next junction. He extended the mirror around the corner and saw the men walking toward a door at the end.

The door belonged to an elevator. They weren't taking the body to the morgue. They were taking it upstairs. The elevator door didn't ding when it opened. There were no numbers above it to show which floor it was on either.

The men pushed the gurney into the elevator and the door closed behind them. They were going up, but to which floor and why? Maybe that hadn't been a body on the gurney. Maybe it was a living and breathing girl.

Carver envisioned the building layout that he'd seen on the touchscreen in the control room. Maybe he could see if one of the doors upstairs locked. Or, more importantly, unlocked. He hurried down the hall to the control room and sat down in front of the touchscreen.

He zoomed out so he could see all the floors. There was a door indicator for the elevator that showed if it was opened or closed. The elevator had probably already reached the floor that Antonio and Mateo were going to, so that indicator wasn't going to tell him anything.

He skimmed past the green doors on the first and second levels and focused on the single red door on the third floor. Apparently, not all the clients were worried enough to evacuate the compound. The clients on the speedboat had probably been going to pick out some girls and bring them back here with them.

The single locked room on the third level suggested that someone was still there. On the other hand, they might have just forgotten to unlock the door. But Carver didn't think so. He felt certain someone was in that room waiting for a special delivery.

Antonio and Mateo were making that special delivery. They sounded agitated when they were talking because they probably thought it was crazy to have to cater to a client when the entire place was on lockdown.

Carver looked at the stairwells on the map. Those doors were locked but could be opened via keypads. Only one stairwell led to the third floor. The others ended on the second floor. None of the stairwells had exterior exits.

The place broke every fire code in the book. Considering the place was mostly concrete, fires probably weren't much of a concern. But if something else happened that required an emergency evacuation, everyone would have to run all the way downstairs and exit via the parking garage.

Carver kept watching the locked door on the third floor. Nothing changed. It remained red on the screen. He began to think he was wrong. Maybe they were taking the girl to a normal room.

Then the door blinked green. It stayed green for a solid five minutes before switching back to red. The delivery had been made. The door was locked and closed again. Was the client already in there or had the two men just set up the room for him?

That didn't matter. What did matter was that the elevator door on the third level had just opened and closed. The men were back on the elevator and presumably coming back down to this floor since it was the only way out of the building.

Carver stood. "Let's go."

"What's the plan?"

"Ambush them when they step off the elevator." He jogged down the hallway and turned the corner. The elevator would probably reach the floor before he got there, so he picked up the pace and sprinted.

Jessica hurried after him. They were a few paces away when the elevator door opened. Carver took aim. He saw the gurney inside. It was empty. So was the elevator. It had been sent down with only the gurney inside.

That set his hackles on end. "Something's not right." He turned to the hallway on the right and ran all the way to the stairwell door at the end. This was the only stairwell that led to the top floor. The lock was controlled by a keypad. He punched in the code Jessica had made. A green LED lit and the door unlocked.

He went into the stairwell and listened carefully. Like everything in the building, it was all concrete. All hard surfaces. Antonio and Mateo were wearing boots. He'd heard their footsteps clearly when they'd pushed the gurney down the hallway. If they were in the stairwell, he'd hear them unless they took off their boots.

He didn't think they would do that. The only reason to send the elevator down empty was so they could run down the stairs and ambush someone waiting for them at the elevator. But how in the hell could they possibly know that Carver was here?

There were no cameras. He'd been silent and used only a small mirror to watch them in the hallway. They'd been focused on their conversation. They'd looked at the person on the gurney and at each other. If they'd noticed the mirror, then they'd done a good job of pretending they hadn't.

But Carver didn't hear boots running down the stairwell. He didn't hear anything except the click of the door closing behind Jessica. The hairs on his neck felt like they were standing up straight even though he kept his neck clean shaven. Something was off.

He went to the center of the stairwell and looked up. He had a clear view all the way to the ceiling. He aimed down the scope and scanned. He put it in infrared and looked for heat. He didn't see anything.

Carver slowly went up to the first landing. He kept his scope up and trained above. He slowly circled to the next landing and the next until he was on the landing with the door to the first level.

He kept circling slow and steady. Kept his footsteps as quiet as possible. Jessica crept behind him. Her sneakers sneaked silently. She had her rifle aimed upward too. Most importantly, she wasn't asking questions, probably because she realized Carver was concerned about something.

He reached the second level. Still nothing. The stairwell seemed quiet and empty. He didn't trust it for a second. There had been too many times things had been quiet as a whisper before gunfire thundered, bullets flew, and men screamed and died.

They reached the door at the top. Still nothing and no one. There was no window on the door so he couldn't see the other side. He knelt and aimed. He pointed to the keypad. Jessica punched in the code.

The green LED glowed. She gently twisted the door lever and pulled it open quickly. Carver swept the scope back and forth. The hallway beyond was empty. He used the mirror to look around the corner. Saw nothing.

The locked door was down the hallway to the right. It was the last door on the right. He didn't see anyone down there. The elevator was down the hallway directly ahead. That meant the men had pushed the gurney all the way down and around the corner, then sent it down the elevator alone.

Why would they do that? There was no good reason for it. None at all. Not unless they'd been called back to the room for some reason. Maybe the client was upset about something.

Carver didn't know what was happening. He just knew that something was going on behind the locked door. He kept the MP5SD at the ready and moved quickly down the hallway. Jessica moved behind him. She didn't exactly stack up properly, but she instinctively knew how to keep an eye on their six.

All the doors had keypads. Keycards would have been easier and more secure, but Carver couldn't complain. They reached the first door. The LED on the keypad was green. The door was unlocked.

The room might be empty, but what if Antonio and Mateo were hiding inside? Carver didn't like leaving uncleared rooms at his back. He stood to the side of the door and motioned Jessica to stand on the other side.

He pushed the door. It swung inward and to the right. Gunfire didn't erupt from inside the room. He didn't hear the click of rifles moving. All he heard was the rush of air from the air conditioner and the faint bump of the door touching the wall.

Carver used the mirror to look inside. There was a short hallway with a door to the right and a larger room straight ahead. Sunlight glowed through the windows. He reached inside and flicked the light switch. Overhead LED lights came on.

He slid inside. Swept his gun inside the first room. It was a small bathroom with a toilet and shower. There was a large mirror with a seat in front of it and a large array of cosmetics and skincare products.

On the left was a walk-in closet with empty hangars. There was a dress on the floor and a box with lingerie. It was obvious that this was the room where the girls were expected to get pretty before going to see the man who'd paid for their company.

He went back into the main room. It was a den, probably forty feet wide and nearly as long. A massive television stretched along one wall and a sectional couch curled around the center. There was a refrigerator with a glass door on the back wall. It contained bottled water, an assortment of beer, and champagne.

The last room in the suite was a bedroom. There was a large walk-in closet that was empty and clean. Next to it was a large bathroom with a hot tub and a shower with multiple water jets built into the walls. The shower looked large enough to host a party in. There was a small room next to the hot tub with a toilet and bidet inside. It was also empty.

There was no telling how much innocence had been destroyed in this and the other rooms on this level. No telling how many lives had also been snuffed out at the whim of powerful men. Probably more than anyone wanted to know.

Carver returned to the hallway. Jessica was still waiting there, rifle trained toward the locked door. It seemed likely that all the other rooms on this level were empty. It seemed likely that something bad was going down in the locked room.

It was against protocol. It was against Carver's deeply ingrained training and beliefs. But this was one of those times where speed was of the essence. He might forfeit his life by not clearing the other rooms in this hallway. But his gut told him he sure as hell would forfeit the life of whoever had been on that gurney if he didn't hurry.

He kept his rifle at the ready and strode purposefully ahead. He stopped briefly to push open every door they passed. All the doors were on the right. They'd all been built against the outer walls so they could have windows.

He figured pushing open the doors would trigger some kind of reaction if someone was inside and it only cost him about two seconds per door. He burned through ten seconds stopping to push open doors. Then he reached the last door. The locked door.

He put an ear to it and listened. He heard muffled shouting inside. Silence for the span of several seconds. Then the shouting resumed. Someone spoke back in a quieter voice in heavily accented English. It was hard to tell if it was either Antonio or Mateo because their English voices would be different than their Spanish voices.

Carver punched in the master code Jessica had created. The red LED blinked green. There was a very faint beep and a click. The man inside was still shouting, so it seemed doubtful anyone inside the room heard the sound.

This room was at the corner of the building. The interior might differ slightly from the other rooms, but he hoped it didn't differ too much. He pushed down the lever and gently opened the door. The shouting went from muffled to clear.

"What did you do to her? I want to talk to Jaeger right now!"

"Sir, he is very busy."

There was a short hallway like in the other rooms. There was a small dressing room and bathroom on the right. Carver saw the main room ahead, but the shouting sounded like it was coming from around the corner. He used his mirror and looked around it.

He saw three men, Antonio, Mateo, and the presumed buyer. He shouldn't have recognized the man, but he did. It was the last person he'd expected, but he realized it should have been obvious all along.

And Carver was going to kill him.

— • —

CHAPTER 34

Carver resisted the urge to rush in.

The girl was probably in the bedroom to the left, provided the layout of the room was identical to the others. He needed to know he could control the room without risking her safety. That was paramount.

He already knew who the girl was. It seemed obvious because the client was none other than her science teacher, Josh Hardin. All his doubts about the man were validated. All the puzzle pieces fell into place.

Hardin had never been invested in Sabrina's future. He wanted her for something else entirely. Jaeger's clients could put in requests for specific types of girls, so there was no reason they couldn't put in a request for a specific girl.

Jaeger's people did all the dirty work. Hardin probably couldn't have pulled it off himself, at least not without drawing attention to himself. This way he had an alibi and was above suspicion.

That was why he kept texting and calling Jessica. He wanted to know if she and Carver had made progress with their investigation. He wanted to make sure he was in the clear.

Jaeger's people would keep Sabrina here, hidden away from the world. They would take care of her so Hardin could come violate her whenever he had the urge. Sabrina had nearly escaped and probably been injured when Jaeger's men caught her.

Apparently, Hardin was very upset about her injuries, because he was still yelling at Antonio and Mateo about it. "This is unacceptable. I don't see any other recourse except to get her treatment. I don't want damaged goods."

"I'm sorry, sir, but that's not allowed." Antonio shook his head. "You can have your fun and then we will clean her up."

"No, that doesn't work for me. Look, she's bruised and bleeding!" Hardin motioned behind him, probably toward the bedroom. "I paid top dollar for a flawless girl."

Jessica stood next to Carver. She couldn't see inside the room, but she seemed to recognize the voice. Her eyes burned with fury, but she said nothing, because doing that would alert the men inside the room.

It was impossible to see where Sabrina was, but the three men stood just at the end of the hallway in the den. Carver felt certain he could get inside and take control before they could do anything.

He retracted the small mirror and chopped his hand forward. Then he counted down from three to one with his fingers. When he hit zero, he rushed inside, MP5SD aimed and ready to fire.

Killing the three men instantly would have been the optimal move, but Carver didn't want them to get out of this situation so easily. He also had some questions about Jaeger that he might convince Antonio and Mateo to answer.

Hardin saw him first. His eyes flared slightly but he didn't react with extreme alarm. He didn't shout a warning to the other men, so they didn't even know Carver was there until he prodded Mateo in the back with the MP5.

"Get on the floor, face down, hands locked behind your head," Carver shouted. He gave Mateo a love tap with the muzzle. "Get down now!"

Antonio and Mateo didn't even try to fight back. They eased down on their knees and then went prone, hands behind their heads.

"Oh, thank goodness you're here." Hardin sighed. "I thought I could handle this myself, but they weren't going to let me take her."

Jessica bared her teeth. "You're lucky I don't paint the wall with your brains. Get down now."

"No, you don't understand."

"Oh, I understand." Jessica walked past Carver and kneed Hardin in the crotch. "Get down you piece of shit!"

Hardin sank to his knees, face screwed up in pain. "Please, let me explain!"

"Get down!" Jessica screamed.

Carver cleared his throat. "Cuff them."

She blinked and looked toward the bedroom. The door was closed. She composed herself and pulled out the nylon zip cuffs. She put them on Antonio first, wrapping the cuffs around his wrists and zipping them as tightly as she could.

With his hands secured behind his back, she took out longer and wider zip cuffs and shackled his knees together with them. He could walk, but he couldn't run if given the chance.

Antonio grunted in pain. "That's too tight."

"Tough shit!" Jessica did the same to Mateo and then to Hardin.

"We have money. Lots of money." Mateo turned his head as much as he could from his awkward position. "Ten million if you just take the girl and go away. There will be no retaliation, nothing. You can just go."

Jessica ran to the bedroom door and flung it open. She gasped and ran inside to the bed. "It's Sabrina!" Tears filled her eyes. "Oh, God, what did you do to her?"

Carver backed into the bedroom, keeping his rifle trained on the men even though they were secured. Sabrina's left eye was swollen shut and her lip was split and bleeding. She was in nothing but dirty underwear.

Her knees and elbows were scraped up. She was covered in gunk and mud. Probably from crawling through the utility tube. Carver checked her pulse. It was strong but slow. She was probably drugged.

Carver went back to the three men. "What did you give her?"

"Just a little scope," Mateo said. "A tiny bit. She'll recover soon. She can hear and understand everything going on right now, she just can't respond."

"Scopolamine?" Carver said.

Mateo nodded. "Yeah."

"Twenty million dollars," Antonio said. "Just think what you could do with that kind of money."

"Please, wait." Hardin looked at Carver with pleading eyes. His voice sounded hoarse and dry. "This isn't what you think. I was trying to save Sabrina. I was trying to get her out of here."

"I don't believe you!" Jessica stormed over and pressed the muzzle of her rifle to his head. "Say that one more time and I will end you."

Carver put his hand on the top of her rifle. "No. I've got other plans."

She glared at him. "Don't try to stop me."

"I think you'll like what I have planned." Carver touched her hand. "Trust me, okay?"

"Please, just do one thing for me." Hardin squirmed. "My phone in my back pocket. Pull it out. The passcode is three, one, eight, two four."

Jessica bent down and pulled out his phone. She unlocked the screen. She opened the text messages and scrolled through them. "What am I looking for? Texts?"

"No, I had to use an encrypted app to communicate with these men." Hardin craned his neck. "Open the picture gallery and show it to these men. Ask them if they know what happened to her."

Jessica frowned and opened the image gallery. Most of the images were of a girl in her mid-teens. She had long black hair, dark eyes, and light brown skin. "Who's this?"

"My daughter." Hardin nodded his head toward the men. "Show the pictures to them."

Jessica showed Mateo and Antonio the pictures. "Do you recognize her?"

Antonio answered immediately. "I will give you this girl and twenty million if you walk away."

"Y-you know where she is?" Hardin's eyes filled with tears. "She's alive?"

"Yes, yes!" Antonio nodded. "We can take you to her."

Carver took the phone and looked at the image. He knelt next to Antonio. "How long ago was she taken?"

"A few months ago."

"What's her name?"

"I don't know. We don't exactly memorize names."

Carver knew the answers because Hardin had told them during their first meeting. He wasn't surprised that Antonio didn't know her name. There was no reason to know a name. Clients would request girls with specific body types, girls of certain ages, and were asked for specific girls.

Antonio and Mataeo would receive these requests and make them happen. They had to be very detail-oriented to keep the clients happy. They would remember when they took a girl and know exactly what she looked like unless they were snatching mass quantities of girls off the streets every month.

Hardin's daughter, Diana, had been taken three years ago. Antonio would almost certainly remember that she'd been taken years ago, not months ago. Diana was also a very pretty girl. She could probably have had a great career as a model.

In other words, she looked remarkable. Maybe Antonio just didn't remember her. Maybe his memory wasn't as great as Carver was giving him credit for. But maybe he'd never seen this girl before. And that would mean he and Mateo hadn't taken her and certainly wouldn't know where she was.

Carver knelt in front of Mateo. "Do you recognize this girl?"

Mateo nodded. "Yes. Like Antonio said, we will give her to you."

Hardin was sobbing. "Please do it, Carver. Please."

Jessica glowered at him. "Stop trying to play the pity card, you monster." She turned to Carver. "What's the plan?"

"Go get the gurney from the elevator. We'll need it for Sabrina."

Jessica bit her lower lip. "Don't kill them while I'm gone."

"I wasn't planning on it."

She jogged out of the room.

Hardin gave Carver a pleading look. "Please, just look into it. See if they really have my daughter."

"We do," Antonio said. "There's a complete record of all the girls that come through here in the doctor's office. I can unlock the computer and get you in. Just promise that if I do this, you'll take the girl, the money, and let us go."

Carver was surprised they'd keep records. "Do you really keep records? Your powerful clients probably wouldn't like that."

"Of course they wouldn't like it," Antonio said. "But Jaeger believes in covering his ass. That way if anything happens, he has dirt on all of them."

Carver shook his head. "I don't believe you."

"I'm serious!" A hint of desperation crept into Antonio's voice. "There's a desktop computer with an external hard drive connected to it. But it's set to burn if the wrong password is entered or if someone tries to disconnect it from the computer."

Carver knew such fail-safes existed, but he also knew without a doubt that Antonio would say anything to survive. Maybe he was telling the truth. Maybe he was just buying as much time as possible.

Jessica returned with the gurney. Carver lifted Sabrina from the bed and laid her on the gurney. He stopped in front of Antonio and Mateo. "Is there another way out of here besides the garage door?"

"No." Antonio shook his head. "That garage is the only way in and out unless you jump from a window."

Carver turned to Jessica. "Take Sabrina down to the garage level then come back up here."

"Okay." Jessica looked uncertainly from Carver to the other men, then pushed the gurney with her sister on it into the hallway.

Carver couldn't stop wondering if there really was a computer with records of all the girls. He knelt in front of Antonio. "You said there are records of all the girls. Is there also a client list?"

"Yes." Antonio looked up at him. "I want to live, okay? I promise this is not a setup. You can have the client list and the database. You can take it all, but promise I get to walk out of here."

Carver didn't like it one bit, but he couldn't afford to ignore it. He nodded. "Fine. You unlock the computer and give me the hard drive with everything on it, and you can walk out of here."

"My brother too."

"Sure, for twenty million dollars."

"Of course. But I'll need to get it from the vault."

"Where is this vault? Jaeger's place?"

"No. It's in the quarry hidden behind a slab of limestone."

"Jaeger is a very careful man," Mateo said.

"Your girl is going to be mad you made a deal," Antonio said. "Can you handle her?"

"My girl does what I say," Carver said. "Deliver what you promised, and I'll let you walk out of here."

"You got it, boss." Antonio nodded fervently. "It's all yours."

Jessica returned. She was panting and out of breath. "Good, you didn't kill them yet. I honestly thought you might."

"Nope." Carver put his boot under Antonio's ribs and rolled him over onto his back. He did the same with Mateo and Hardin.

"Get up."

The three men struggled into a sitting position. Mateo shifted to his knees and got up. Antonio did the same. Hardin couldn't quite manage it, so Carver yanked him to his feet.

"Jessica, you take point. Get the elevator door open."

"Okay." She left the room.

Carver prodded Antonio in the back. "Single file into the hallway now. Anyone who tries anything gets a bullet in the leg, okay?"

"You got it, boss." Antonio led the way.

Carver turned on his earbud. "Jessica, keep your rifle ready in case anyone runs."

"Okay," she replied.

They reached the elevator and filed inside. The good thing about a submachinegun like the MP5 was that Carver didn't have to switch to a handgun in the tight quarters of the elevator. Jessica had to lower her rifle because there wasn't space to use it.

She automatically drew her handgun and aimed it at the men. "Don't think of trying anything. I won't shoot you in the leg. I'll shoot you in the crotch."

"Don't worry, boss." Mateo smirked. "We'll behave."

"Where's the doctor's office?" Carver said.

Antonio nodded toward the buttons. "Second floor."

Carver hit the button. The elevator doors closed, and the elevator lurched downward.

"Doctor's office?" Jessica looked confused. "Why are we going there?"

"To see something." The elevator stopped. Carver backed off and cleared the hallway. He motioned to the prisoners to move out. "Lead the way."

Antonio turned to his right and walked to the end of the hallway. There was a long room filled with rows of stainless-steel examination tables. Each one had multiple straps and stirrups for the legs.

There were flags attached to the end of the tables and neat stacks of the flags on a table in the front of the room. They ranged from green, blue, yellow, and red. Behind the tables were large clear plastic crates.

"My God!" Jessica gaped at the tables and the boxes. "You examine the girls, rate them, and then box them for the buyer?"

Hardin shivered. His face went stark white. "Is this what you did to my daughter?"

"Hey, it's just business," Antonio said. "Your daughter got top green, man. Be proud."

Hardin roared and tried to ram into Antonio, but Carver gave him a little tap with his rifle muzzle. "Don't try that again."

Jessica glared at him. "Don't pretend to be angry, Hardin. You're just as sick and twisted as these evil bastards."

Hardin shook his head imploringly. "I was trying to save Sabrina. I promise!"

"Shut it," Carver said. He nodded at Antonio. "Where's the computer?"

"In there." Antonio nodded with his head. He shuffled forward, hindered by the knee cuffs.

Carver motioned the others to go in after him. The office was large but not ornate. The walls were concrete like everything else and there were no decorations or anything personal in the room.

There was an ultrasound machine against one wall, some other medical diagnostic devices on roller carts, and a shelf with medical tools, some of which looked like they were designed for either delivering babies or aborting them.

It was an all-in-one shop for female healthcare, but in the sickest sense of the word. In this kind of business, girls would get pregnant. They would get diseases. They would be subjected to all sorts of horrors.

For any captured girl, this place was literal Hell.

CHAPTER 35

Carver turned toward the prisoners.

"Okay, we're here."

Antonio went to the computer. "Uncuff my hands and I'll get you in."

"I don't think so." Carver glanced at Jessica, wordlessly telling her to keep an eye on everyone. She nodded.

"Tell me how to unlock it."

"Reach around the back. There's a small button there. Push it."

Carver leaned over the computer and saw a tiny black button. "If this raises an alarm, none of you are getting out of here alive."

"It doesn't. I promise. It just disables the thermite charges for thirty seconds." Antonio wasn't smiling now. "Press it and then hit the backspace key two times. No more."

Carver did as instructed. The wide monitor blinked on. There was a number on the screen, counting down from thirty to zero. Below that it said *Enter password before timer expires.*

Antonio told him the password. "Three, one, eight, Barstool with a capital 'B', asterisk, ampersand, nine, zero, exclamation point." He cleared his throat. "Don't hit enter or use the mouse. Press the button on the back of the PC again."

Carver followed his instructions. There was a physical click from inside the computer, probably the thermite charge disengaging. Thermite was a quick and easy way to roast equipment you didn't want to fall into the wrong hands.

The portable hard drive in question was a small black box sitting on top of the desktop computer. There was a small charge strapped to the side of it. A USB cable connected it to the computer, and another cable connected the thermite charge to the computer.

Carver wasn't ready to disconnect it quite yet. "How do I access the information?"

Antonio nodded at the screen. "Open the file explorer icon then open the hard drive icon."

Carver did that. There was another folder inside simply labeled *Data*. Below it was a shortcut to a program called *Decryptor*. "Do I click this?"

"Yeah."

The program opened. A page with a search bar opened. Next to it was a long list of filters. The first filter was by city. The others were all descriptors like age, race, nationality, gender, body type and so forth.

Jessica wrinkled her nose. "It's like the search function for a dating site."

"Yeah."

"Can you search for my daughter?" Hardin said. "Please?"

"Can you shut up?" Jessica went to the shelf and picked up a thick wad of gauze. She shoved it into Hardin's mouth and taped his mouth shut.

Tears trickled down Hardin's cheeks. His shoulders slumped and he finally seemed resigned to his fate.

"Will the hard drive work on any computer?" Carver asked.

Antonio nodded. "Yeah, the program is installed on the hard drive, so it works anywhere."

"No password required?"

"No."

Carver put checks in boxes that described Sabrina. He clicked the search button. A split second later, the page filled with pictures of girls matching that description. Sabrina's picture was near the top.

He clicked it. It took him to a profile page that looked exactly like something you'd find on a dating site. There were pictures of Sabrina, mostly taken of her while she was lying on a bed, probably drugged.

She was dressed in various outfits. She was described in acute detail, including that she was a virgin, athletic, and rated as a perfect specimen. The price to buy her or be the first to have her was $50,000.

"You bastards!" Jessica shuddered with rage. "You subhuman pieces of filth!"

"How do I look at the client list?" Carver said.

"There's a hidden menu," Antonio said. "Scroll to the bottom of the filters and click the box that says advanced."

Carver found the checkbox and checked it. Another checkbox appeared. There was no label next to it. He checked the box. The search screen turned from gray to black. A new set of filters appeared.

These ranged from location to net worth. Carver typed in *Austin* and hit enter. A list of clients appeared. Josh Hardin's image was at the top. He clicked on it but there was no information in the blanks.

The next client was someone named Alvin Biggs. He clicked on him. The man had a net worth of a million dollars. There were two girls listed under his profile. One was Caucasian and the other was Black. They were both ten years old.

Jessica whimpered and looked away. "Monsters!"

Carver turned off the program. "How do I disconnect the hard drive?"

"Our deal holds?" Antonio said. "We walk out of here alive and well?"

"Yes."

Jessica shivered with barely repressed rage but said nothing.

"Okay. This one is software controlled. Go to the desktop and click on the icon labeled utilities. Enter the passcode one, zero, one, zero, five, five, four."

Carver went to the desktop. It was filled with icons. He found the utilities icon and clicked it. A password prompt popped up. He entered the code. The program closed. There was a faint click from the thermite box on the hard drive.

"You can unplug it now," Antonio said.

Carver unplugged the thermite charge. "I assume the thermite would go off if the cable was disconnected without the passcode."

"Yep."

Carver unplugged the USB cable. He tucked the hard drive into his side pack. "Okay. Now, where's the vault?"

"We're walking out of here alive, right?" Antonio said. "We're square?"

"Yes." Carver stared at him. "The vault. Is it behind the metal shed somewhere?"

Antonio blinked. "How do you know about that?"

"Answer the question."

"Yes. There's big slab of limestone behind the metal garage in the quarry. It looks like a normal part of the cliff wall, but you can walk behind it. There's a tunnel with a camo net. Walk down the tunnel and you'll find the vault door." Antonio grinned. "It's Jaeger's go stash if he has to run."

"What kind of lock does it have?"

"Well, that's the thing. It needs a keycard. Jaeger's keycard, to be specific." Antonio grinned. "He trusts me and Mateo. We're his right-hand men. He'll give it to one of us, no questions asked. Just cut one of us loose and we'll go get it."

Carver grunted noncommittally. "You promised me money and can't deliver?"

"No, we can." Antonio looked worried. "Just hold one of us here and the other can go get the keycode."

"Or, we can call Jaeger here," Mateo said.

Antonio gave him a sharp look, like he shouldn't have said that.

"I like that idea," Carver said. "How would you do that?"

"He won't come," Antonio said. "We have to go get it."

"Hey now, don't lie." Carver bared his teeth. "If I don't get my money, then the deal's off."

Antonio gulped. "Get my phone out of my back pocket."

Carver reached in and pulled it out. There was a crack in the screen. "Passcode?"

Antonio rattled off a long string of numbers.

Carver entered them and the phone unlocked. "What now?"

"Open the Silent app and enter the same passcode."

Carver did that. He found several texts from the past thirty minutes, all in Spanish. Everything else had automatically deleted. The last few texts were about Hardin.

Antonio: *This guy is being a pain in the ass. He wants to still see the girl despite the lockdown.*

Jaeger: *It's fine. The man paid. Let him in.*

Moments later, another text.

Antonio: *He's complaining about the girl being a little bruised up. Wants medical treatment to make her pretty.*

Jaeger: *Not gonna happen. Not without the doc around.*

There was nothing after that. Carver looked at Antonio. "How do you plan to get him over here?"

Antonio worked his jaw back and forth. "Just say the client wants to talk to him."

Carver turned to Mateo. "Is that true? If I sense anything is wrong, you two are dying first."

"Yes." Mateo nodded. "Jaeger will come. He likes happy customers. This is a business, after all."

Jessica shuddered with rage but said nothing.

Carver typed the text in Spanish. *Customer wants to talk to you.* He tucked the phone in his pocket. "All right, let's move out."

Antonio and Mateo exchanged looks. It was obvious Antonio was angry with Mateo for suggesting Jaeger come over, but the proverbial cat was out of the bag. It was time to see how things would shake out.

The money wasn't a big deal. He could leave with or without it. But having more money was usually better than having less, so if he could pick up some easy cash on the way out, he was going to do it.

Carver marched the prisoners down the hallway and onto the elevator. They went to the parking garage level. He guided them down the hall and stopped in front of the morgue. Carver turned to Hardin. "Time to take care of you first."

Hardin's eyes bugged. He tried to talk but his words were muffled by the gauze. Antonio and Mateo smirked at each other but said nothing.

"Can you cut us free now?" Antonio said. "Everything is in motion. You're walking out of here a rich man."

"No way." Carver shook his head. "Your buddies can uncuff you when they find you after we're long gone."

"Fair enough, boss." Antonio seemed to repress a grin.

Carver prodded the prisoners through the doors and into the morgue. He grabbed Hardin by his shirt and dragged him toward the cremation oven. Hardin screamed and tried to struggle, but he couldn't stop Carver from dragging him there.

Carver opened the oven door and slid out the metal tray. Hardin was nearly six feet tall, but slim. Carver gripped him by the belt and shirt, hefted him, and slammed him onto the metal tray. He shoved it into the oven and closed the door.

Antonio and Mateo were openly grinning now.

"Damn, you don't play around, boss." Antonio laughed. "I'm glad we came to a deal."

"Yeah, we did." Carver nodded. "You walked out of that room upstairs alive just like I promised. He reached forward, put his hands on the sides of the men's heads and slammed their heads together with a loud crack.

They both cried out in surprise and pain. They staggered drunkenly, stunned by the blow to their heads. Carver opened the other two ovens. He pulled out the metal trays, then grabbed Mateo by the belt and the shirt. He hefted him like a sack of potatoes and slammed him onto the metal tray.

He shoved the tray into the oven and closed the door. Antonio was recovering from the stunning blow. He saw Carver coming for him and screamed. He tried to run, but the knee cuffs tripped him.

"You promised!"

"I promised you'd walk out of there alive." Carver pointed up. "You did walk out of that room alive. But there's not a chance in Hell you're leaving here alive." He punched Antonio in the stomach.

The other man's breath exploded from his mouth. He wriggled and screamed, but he was a short guy. His hands were tied behind his back, and his knees were cuffed together.

"This is how helpless those girls felt." Carver lifted the man easily. "I hope you enjoy the experience."

"Please, no!" Antonio screamed. "God, no! I'll give you anything!"

"Oh, you're going to give us everything," Jessica said. "Burn in hell, you monsters."

Carver shoved the tray into the oven and closed the door. He turned on the gas and hit the ignition. Flames flickered on. Antonio struggled and squirmed in vain as the flames grew larger and hotter.

He screamed in agony. Carver ignited Mateo's oven. It didn't take long for him to start screaming too.

"I want Hardin!" Jessica went to his oven. She opened the door so he could hear her. "I'm sending you where you belong you sick bastard."

Hardin's screams were muffled by the gauze, then more muffled when Jessica slammed the oven door. She turned on the gas and hit the ignitor.

"What—what's going on?" Sabrina stumbled into the room. "What's all that screaming?"

"Sabrina!" Jessica hugged her. "You're safe. We saved you from that bastard teacher of yours."

"What?" Sabrina's eyes widened slowly. "Mr. Hardin? Where is he?"

"About to burn." The flames had just started to rise in Hardin's oven. He was screaming.

"No!" Sabrina lunged toward the oven. She drunkenly scrambled to turn off the gas. "Turn it off! Get him out!" Her words were slurred but certain. She pulled open the oven door and grabbed the metal. She shouted in pain.

Carver grabbed Hardin's shirt and yanked him out, depositing him bodily on the floor. Hardin's clothes were smoking and his skin was red, but he wasn't too much worse for the wear just yet.

Sabrina knelt next to him. "Are you okay, Mr. Hardin?" She pulled the medical tape off his face and pulled out the gauze.

"Sabrina, you were drugged, so you don't know what happened." Jessica clenched her fists. "He bought you. He was going to rape you."

Antonio and Mateo were still screaming in agony. Sabrina's mouth dropped open and she looked at the other ovens. "Who's in there?"

"The men who kidnapped you."

The screams abruptly cut off. The odor of burnt flesh, hair, and clothing eked out of the ovens.

Sabrina backed up a step and looked down at Hardin. "I do know what happened. I was conscious. I could hear and see but I couldn't move. It was like I was paralyzed. I still feel so dizzy." She knelt next to Hardin and patted his arm. "I remember being pushed into a room and put on the bed. Mr. Hardin was there. He stood over me. He was crying. He said he would get me out of there. He said he would save me."

"It's true," Hardin said in a raspy voice. He tried to spit the rest of the gauze out of his mouth but couldn't.

"Oh, you poor man." Sabrina seemed to realize he was cuffed. "Set him free!"

"Are you sure?" Jessica looked from her to Carver. "He bought you."

"To save her." Hardin's eyelids fluttered. "Please, let me explain."

Carver rolled him on his side and cut the wrist and knee cuffs. He helped him to his feet.

"Water, please." Carver didn't have any water. He didn't know where any would be except back upstairs in the rooms. With the men dead any no one else in the building, he had an idea to ensure Sabrina was remembering things correctly.

He checked Antonio's phone. No response from Jaeger yet. He might not even respond. Carver lowered his gun and nodded. "There's some upstairs."

Hardin's eyes flared a little. "I don't know if I want to go back up there."

"We're going." Carver took him by the arm and guided him into the hallway.

Jessica helped Sabrina who was still staggering. They took the elevator up and went to the room where Sabrina and Hardin had been. Carver went to the kitchenette and grabbed two bottles of water from the mini fridge. He opened one and gave it to Sabrina. Opened the other and gave it to Hardin.

Carver took Sabrina gently by the arm. He wanted to have her replay everything as it had happened. "Come lay down on the bed. Make sure you remember things correctly."

Sabrina gulped the water. Nodded. "I remember everything. I'm not wrong."

"Do it anyway."

Sabrina sighed. She sat on the bed, then rotated and lay down.

"Where was Hardin?"

"Here on the right. He was crying a lot. Then he left and I heard him shouting distantly, like he went into the hallway."

"What did he say?"

"That he needed the gurney. He wanted them to bring it back."

Carver nodded. "Keep going."

"The men came back. Mr. Hardin sounded angry. He said I was injured, and he'd paid to have me in perfect condition. He wanted the gurney so he could take me to get treated." Sabrina's eyes narrowed like she was trying to remember more. "They said I had to stay here."

Carver remembered hearing that part. That was right before he burst inside. "Anything else?"

Sabrina sat up and touched the sheets. "Look, they're still wet."

Carver touched the sheets. They were damp. He looked at Hardin. The man looked like he wanted to cry again but was completely dry. Hardin had been crying hard enough to wet the bed sheets. He saw the man's reaction in a different light. Not that of a man caught doing wrong, but of a man who genuinely cared for Sabrina.

"Okay, let's go." He helped Sabrina up.

Jessica looked chagrined, but a little defiant. "I'm sorry, Mr. Hardin, but you have to understand how guilty you looked."

"I understand." Hardin finished off his water and got another bottle from the fridge. "I've been looking for Sabrina nonstop since we first met. I posted in several crime stoppers groups online and several said most rapists don't kidnap their victims."

He gulped more water. "They said this sounded like a professional kidnapping which meant she was almost certainly taken for sex trafficking."

Jessica nodded. "Sound reasoning."

"That took me down a very dark rabbit hole." Hardin shuddered. "I can hardly bear to think about it."

Carver checked Antonio's phone. Jaeger hadn't replied, but that didn't mean he wasn't coming. "No need for details now. We can discuss this later."

Hardin looked mildly relieved.

"I almost escaped," Sabrina said. "I got out of the building and couldn't find a way out, so I crawled in the utility tunnels. But there was a grate blocking the rest of the tunnel, so I had to go back. A group of men caught me when I was trying to sneak around the building."

Jessica hugged her. "I'm so sorry."

"It's okay, sis." Sabrina wiped tears from her eyes. "I should feel grateful that you and Mr. Hardin came for me." She looked at Carver. "And this soldier guy too."

"That's Carver. He's my friend."

"Okay, well he looks scary. I'm glad he's on our side."

Jessica laughed. "Me too."

Carver had heard enough. "We need to go. It's doubtful anyone else is coming, but I'd prefer we get free and clear."

"Yeah." Jessica shivered. "This place gives me the creeps."

They left the room, hurried down the hallway, and took the elevator to the parking garage level. Carver opened the door to the garage and heard loud screeching, like metal on metal. They heard men talking.

They weren't alone.

CHAPTER 36

Carver held up a fist to signal the others to hold position.

He crept up to a van and looked around the side. The van that Sabrina had rammed into the rollup door was being pushed out of the way by a mini bulldozer. The bulldozer had also ripped out the rest of the door by pushing through it.

Two other men stood in the garage watching the man in the dozer work. Those two didn't look like typical construction workers or like Jaeger's thugs. They wore slacks and oxfords. They looked like supervisors.

It hardly seemed necessary for the mini-dozer guy to have two supervisors, but maybe that was normal for construction.

A fourth guy strode into the garage. He wore skintight jeans and a black T-shirt. He looked about five feet nine or ten and had the kind of buff body that only steroids could build. He was Hispanic. His hair was neatly cut with sharp lines. His beard was neatly trimmed the same way. He had colorful tattoo sleeves but nothing on his neck or face.

He also wore glasses which was a strange juxtaposition with the rest of his appearance. It made him look less gangster and more educated. Maybe that was the goal, or maybe he really had eyesight issues.

One of the men watching the dozer at work raised a hand in greeting. "Hey, Jaeger. We'll get this door fixed in no time."

Jaeger bumped fists with him. "I appreciate it as always. You take your pick of the girls next time, okay?"

"Thanks, Jaeger. You know we appreciate it."

"I take care of my people." Jaeger patted the other man on the shoulder. "Speaking of which, did you see Antonio or Mateo come this way?"

"Yeah, like twenty minutes ago." The supervisor guy jabbed his thumb toward the door. "They wheeled a girl inside."

"Okay, good." Jaeger headed for the door. He took out a walkie-talkie and spoke into it. "Status update." He waited for a response and got none, because tons of concrete above him were blocking the signal.

He looked at the radio and cursed. It probably wasn't his preferred method of communication. Then he walked towards Carver's position. He was going inside to look for his two oven-roasted coworkers.

Carver went back inside the door. He motioned toward the security room on the left. "Get inside."

"What's happening?" Jessica said.

"We've got company." Carver stepped inside the doorway and waited. He heard the metal door scrape open. He heard Jaeger's footsteps coming down the hallway. Then he saw the man himself and stepped out in front of him, his submachine gun aimed squarely at his chest. "Hi."

Jaeger froze in place. His eyes didn't widen. He didn't gasp. He just froze and assessed Carver. Then he put the pieces into place. "You're the guy who wreaked havoc on my operation all night."

"No, he's here to talk about your car's extended warranty." Jessica stepped into the hallway, the M4 also aimed at him. "Is this Jaeger?"

Carver nodded. "Yep."

"How much money do you want?" Jaeger said. "I can give you millions if you just go away."

"From your vault in the quarry?" Carver frisked the man and pulled out a thin minimalist wallet. There were several credit cards in the pockets. At the front was a black keycard with a dragon on it.

Carver pulled it out. "I assume this is the keycard that opens it?"

Jaeger's eyes widened. "How the hell?"

"Antonio told me everything. He gave me the hard drive from the computer upstairs." Carver shrugged. "He sold you out."

Jaeger's jaw tightened. "Where is he?"

"In the morgue."

Jaeger paled slightly. "Look, we can—"

"Nope." Jessica slammed the butt of her rifle against his head.

Jaeger staggered sideways and hit the wall. Blood trickled from a wound on his temple. He tried to stand up but she'd hit him good. "Please—"

"Nope." Jessica hit him again and again. She kicked him in the crotch three times before he went down.

Jaeger groaned, but he wasn't holding his crotch which was the normal reaction from most men.

Jessica put her foot on his crotch. "Do you even feel anything or did steroids shrink your balls down to nothing?" She looked at Carver. "Put him in the oven. I want him to burn."

"Okay." Carver grabbed Jaeger's shirt and dragged him into the morgue.

Sabrina and Hardin emerged from the security room and followed them inside. They watched in silent horror as Carver heaved Jaeger onto the metal tray of the oven he'd put Hardin into earlier. The room stank of burned bodies now that Mateo and Antonio had been roasting for a while.

Jessica shoved the tray into the oven. She closed it. Turned on the gas and ignited it. Jaeger screamed. He pounded on the sides of the oven. Then he danced as the flames licked his flesh. He didn't scream much longer after that.

Jessica smiled grimly. "Do you think his rib meat will be fall-off-the-bones tender in a few minutes?"

"Gross!" Sabrina laughed. "Now I'm going to keep thinking about that."

"Now it's really time to leave." Carver left the room. The others followed close on his heels. "We've got at least three men in the garage working on the garage door. I'll recon and assess the situation. Wait behind the van next to the door while I do that."

"We could take one of the vans," Jessica said. "The keys are in the security room."

Carver nodded. "Good idea. Let me clear a path first." He went into the garage. The dozer was shoving the wrecked van to the side. The tires screeched. The diesel engine added to the noise. The two supervisors, or whatever they were, never heard him come up behind them.

He got close and shot them in the backs of their heads. They dropped like rag dolls. The man in the dozer was so focused on moving the van he didn't even look as Carver slowly walked to the side of the vehicle and put a bullet in his temple. He slumped over the controls.

The dozer kept pushing the van. He let it keep running so the noise would cover any sounds he made. He went to the edge of the rollup doorway and looked through. Didn't see anyone. He crept along the wall. Went to the corner. Looked outside. No one else was there.

He went outside and walked around the corner to the left. No one was in the dead-end. The UTV was still parked there. He hurried back inside. Jessica was waiting inside with a vehicle fob in hand.

"All clear?"

"Yeah." He looked at the number on the key. He didn't bother looking for the vehicle with the matching number and pressed the unlock button. A van in the middle row beeped. "Let's go."

They hurried to the van. Hardin helped Sabrina to the van and opened the side sliding door. They got in the second row. Carver climbed into the driver's seat and Jessica took shotgun.

"Get your sidearm out and be ready," Carver said. "I don't know if anyone else is around."

She readied her pistol. "Let's do this."

"If we do pass anyone, they might think we're one of them since we're in the van, so don't shoot unless it looks like they're going to shoot first."

Jessica nodded. "Got it."

Carver backed up the van, turned it toward the door. Shifted into drive and drove out, weaving around the bodies. He turned right and drove to the corner of the building. He nosed around it for a look and saw no one. He kept going.

No one was on the other side either. He drove up the ramp and reached the high ground. He headed for the quarry. They reached it without incident. Carver parked the van behind the garage. It took a moment to locate the limestone slab Antonio had told him about.

It looked like a solid cliff face from the front, but there was a space behind it, and a camouflage net concealing a tunnel entrance. Carver checked out the tunnel in night vision and infrared. There might be traps inside for the unwary.

He didn't see anything. He switched off night vision and looked with a flashlight. He got down on the tunnel floor and looked for the gleam of wires or obvious pressure plates. The floor and tunnel walls were ground to a smooth finish, so those things would stick out if they were present.

It didn't look like anything was there. Antonio said this was Jaeger's go stash. It's what he would take if he had to run. That made sense, given its location next to the secret backdoor out of his compound. He needed to get in and out in a hurry. Boobytraps would just slow him down, even if he knew how to avoid them.

Carver turned to Jessica. "Wait here in case something happens, okay?"

"Do you think it's booby trapped?"

"I don't think so but hang back in case."

"It's not worth risking your life over." Jessica grabbed his arm. "Carver, I don't care about the money. I care about all of us getting out of here safely."

"I really don't think it's rigged, okay?" Carver gave her a reassuring grin. "I'm just cautious."

"The word you're looking for is paranoid." She sighed. "Okay, I'll hang back. Just let me know."

"Okay." He made his way down the tunnel, slowly and carefully examining anything that looked out of place. He reached the vault door without being blown up. It was eight feet tall and thirty-six inches wide. It was a heavy slab of metal that would take serious explosives to dislodge. Using explosives would collapse the tunnel and bury the door in tons of rubble.

Thankfully, Carver didn't need explosives. He tapped Jaeger's keycard against the reader on the side of the door. There was a hum, a click, and the thick vault door swung inward. He stepped inside and swung the flashlight around.

There was a circular LED light on the wall. He pressed it and it clicked on. The vault was a tiny square space. There were three duffel bags on the floor inside. Nothing else. It was a simple grab and go. No muss, no fuss.

Carver unzipped the first bag. It was stuffed with clothing. There was a plastic packet filled with fake IDs and documents. He dumped it out and sorted through everything, but it was exactly what it looked like.

The second bag was stuffed with money. There were two handguns inside, Glock 19 gen 5 according to the etching on the side. There were six filled magazines and two silencers. Beneath them were stacks of hundred dollar bills wrapped in plastic.

The third bag was also stuffed with hundreds. He hefted the bag. It felt like it weighed two hundred pounds, easy. It might be more or less, but he guessed it had about eight to ten million in it. The other bag was just as heavy.

He knew from experience how much fifteen million in hundred-dollar bills weighed because Rhodes once made him carry a duffel bag filled with that much money to an exchange. It weighed around three-hundred and fifty pounds. Even with the shoulder strap it had been a chore carrying it.

If these weighed a combined four hundred pounds, then there was probably twenty million inside. That was nice. Real nice. He slung the straps diagonally over his shoulders and walked out. Two hundred pounds on opposite shoulders was a lot easier than carrying three-fifty on one shoulder, that was for sure.

He left the tunnel and found Jessica waiting just beyond the slab that concealed the tunnel. She sighed in relief.

"Thank God."

"No traps," Carver said. He patted the bags. "Lots of money."

"Carver, I hate to admit it, but I like you, okay? I don't like it when you scare me with talk of booby traps."

"I'm just being practical."

"There is nothing practical about the things you talk about." She leaned up and kissed him on the lips. "Can we go now?"

"Yep." The boat was where Carver had left it, so he slid the duffel bags straps off his shoulders and put the bags in the boats. They landed on the metal hull with solid thuds.

Hardin and Sabrina got out of the van and came to the dock. Hardin's gray hair was a frizzled burned mess, and he had burns on his face and hands from the oven. He hadn't escaped as unscathed as Carver had thought.

But he was alive and mostly intact. Carver didn't feel bad about tossing him in the oven. He even still felt a little suspicious of the man. But Sabrina was convinced he was trying to save her and that was really all that mattered.

He helped Sabrina and Hardin onto the boat.

Jessica hopped in and sat down next to her sister. She hugged her. "I'm sorry I'm such a bad big sister. I'm sorry I never got to know you very well."

Sabrina hugged her back. "You're an amazing big sister. You found me and saved me."

"I'm thankful too," Hardin said. "Clearly, my plan wasn't going to work. I wasn't sure what else to do."

Carver started the boat motor and took them back into the tunnel. Sabrina and Hardin stared at the motorboat with the dead men when they passed it. When Carver pulled into the boathouse, Sabrina and Hardin gaped at the dead men in the boats.

Sabrina looked at her sister. "How many people did you kill to get to me?"

"Me personally? I don't know. Maybe five." Jessica turned to Carver. "What do you think?"

Carver nodded. "At least. Your sister is a good shot."

Sabrina stared blankly at Jessica for a moment then hugged her. "I can't even imagine what you went through."

"When Carver is involved, the sky's the limit." Jessica smiled. "Let's get out of here, okay?"

Carver hefted the money bags and left the boathouse. Roy's camper van was still parked where he'd left it. He put the bags inside and got in the driver's seat.

The deputies' bodies were still where they'd left them. Vultures were circling overhead. It probably wouldn't be long before they swooped down for the free meal. Carver backed up and pulled in front of the building. The deputies' SUVs were out of sight on the other side of the building where Anna had parked them.

He put the vehicle in park, got out, and walked around to open the side sliding door.

Sabrina gasped when she saw the bodies. "The cops were involved?"

"Yeah." Jessica sighed. "The corruption runs deep. Real deep."

Jessica and Sabrina got into the camper van and sat on the couch next to the small dining table. Carver closed the door behind them and walked around to get in the driver's seat again.

Hardin climbed in the front passenger seat. He winced and groaned. "I feel so useless. I feel like everything I did was for nothing and it almost got me killed."

Sabrina leaned forward and put her hand on his shoulder. "Don't say that. I feel so grateful to everyone who came to my rescue."

"How did you find your way into the organization specifically?" Carver said. He wanted to hear more. He wanted to be absolutely convinced of the man's innocence. "People who deal in underage sex trafficking usually don't trust anyone they don't know."

Sabrina sat back on the couch. "I can't imagine what you went through."

Hardin sighed. "Do you remember Jeffery Epps, the English teacher?"

"Oh, yeah, that was my freshman year." Sabrina nodded. "He got fired for inappropriate conduct or something, right?"

"I've been teaching for twenty-five years," Hardin said. "Epps relocated from New York City schools about five years ago. I never liked him. He was always too friendly with the female students."

"Oh, I remember hearing a lot about him," Sabrina said. "Some of the older girls talked about him. One of them said they should have gotten a C, but Epps gave them an A for kissing him on the cheek or something creepy like that."

"Yes, well, I looked into him. The union at his former school said he was a model teacher. But I got in touch with some of his former coworkers and they said he was in trouble for extremely inappropriate behavior with girls. Like asking for kisses on the cheek, hugs, and other absolutely shameful things." Hardin shuddered. "The man was a disgrace, but the union protected him."

Jessica grimaced. "So, he got fired from your school system for the same kind of conduct?"

"Exactly." Hardin shuddered. "If he acted that openly around students, I could only imagine what sort of things he was doing secretly."

"So, you thought he might know a thing or two about sex trafficking?" Carver started the van and pulled onto the dirt road. He wasn't sure where to go just yet. He'd make up his mind once they reached the highway.

"Precisely." He cleared his throat. "I had no idea where Epps went after he was fired, so I asked around and found out he was living in a trailer park outside of town. Apparently, he'd been caught with a minor and is on the sex offender list. He can't go within a hundred yards of a school."

Jessica scoffed. "As if that's going to stop someone like him."

"I went to his door and told him I was interested in finding a girl," Hardin said. "He laughed in my face and said he didn't believe me. He said there was no way someone like me was interested in young girls."

"How did you convince him?" Sabrina said.

Hardin grimaced. "I told him that one of my students was kidnapped and I was desperate to find her. He said she was probably taken by the local sex trafficking ring and that he could probably find her if I paid him twenty thousand dollars."

Sabrina paled. "My god."

"I had no choice." Hardin shuddered. "I withdrew the money from my life savings and paid him. He showed me a website on the dark web that was set up like a sick dating site. I searched for Asian girls and Sabrina was near the top of the list."

"All for the low, low price of fifty thousand," Jessica said angrily.

Sabrina seemed to force a smile. "Fifty thousand is a decent price for me, right?"

Jessica shook her head. "No, you're priceless." She turned back to Hardin. "How did you pay?"

"I had to move money from my bank account to a crypto account. It was very confusing, but thankfully there are online videos that show exactly how to do it." He sipped his water. "I converted the rest of my savings to something called a stablecoin and then put a fifty percent deposit on Sabrina."

Jessica looked disgusted. "To show you were serious."

"Precisely. I told them I wanted to see her immediately, and they agreed. I met them, paid the remainder, and they took me to the room to wait for her." He swallowed hard. "I was so nervous. I thought for certain they would discover the truth and kill me. But then when they brought her to me, she was injured, and they wouldn't let me remove her from the premises."

"They seem to operate differently from most sex trafficking rings," Carver said.

"They told me that only platinum members were allowed to take their girls home." Hardin looked apologetically at Sabrina. "So, I found you, but I still couldn't save you. I planned to go to the police and bring them there."

"That would've been signing your own death warrant." Carver shook his head. "Jaeger owned people in high places."

"Technically he still does until they discover he's dead." Jessica bit her lower lip. "We don't know who we can trust. It might not be safe to go back to Austin yet."

Carver hated to admit it, but she was right.

CHAPTER 37

Carver stopped the van.

Austin wasn't a safe place to go. Not until he figured out what to do about Piker and whoever else was on Jaeger's payroll. Once they figured out Jaeger was dead, they might not do anything, or they might look for revenge now that their income stream had been disrupted.

He turned the van north toward McDade where Anna had taken the other girls.

"What about your daughter?" Jessica said. "Did you search for her on the website?"

"Yes." Hardin shook his head. "But it was like searching for the proverbial needle in a haystack and I couldn't waste time. I had to find Sabrina first."

"What did the cops do when Diana went missing?" Sabrina asked.

"The detective in charge was a woman named Piker." Hardin pressed his lips together. "She said that it was probably just a classic teen runaway scenario and that Diana would come back on her own terms."

"Piker was the detective in charge?" Jessica pounded a fist on the kitchenette table. "Of course she would say that. She's involved in all of this."

"I would say I'm shocked but in retrospect, the woman seemed more interested in making me go away than helping me." His jaw tightened. "I hired a private detective to look for Diana. I spent thousands, but he found nothing."

Sabrina leaned forward and touched his arm. "I'm so sorry, Mr. Hardin."

Hardin ran a hand down his face. "I posted signs everywhere. I looked for so long and never found anything. The only clue to her whereabouts was a statement from a homeless man. He claimed he saw a man pull Diana into the back of a gold Dodge Charger."

"A gold Dodge Charger?" Jessica frowned. "Must have been a vinyl wrap to be that color."

"It was very specific." Hardin stared silently for a moment. "The cops said the witness was a homeless drug addict who probably hallucinated the entire thing. But I followed the lead he gave me. I found other parents whose girls had been taken and asked if they knew anything about a gold Charger. One of them said yes. And it happened on the same street corner the homeless man had been at."

"Did you go back to him?" Sabrina asked.

"I did, but he'd long since died of an overdose." Hardin shook his head. "The other homeless people in the area said government agents killed him. Many might think they were crazy, but in retrospect, I think they were telling the truth."

"No doubt they were," Jessica said. She looked at the road. "Where are we going, Carver?"

"McDade for now. I have a feeling a lot of people are on the lookout for us." He glanced at the directions on the GPS. "It might be best to drop everyone off with the others and go my own way from there."

"But I'm not done with you yet." Jessica looked hurt. "I don't want you just running off. You helped me save my sister, for God's sake."

"It's for the best."

"No, it's not for the best. Not even a little bit. We still have some unresolved issues, like Piker."

"Jaeger is dead. His operation is finished." Carver shrugged. "Once Piker discovers Jaeger is dead, she probably won't do anything."

"Maybe you're right." Jessica pursed her lips. "Or maybe she and the others will be pissed and come looking for whoever killed Jaeger."

"I'll think about it."

McDade was a tiny blip on the map. Carver almost drove through it before realizing it was the destination. The police station was a tiny building. He'd expected to see several vans parked out front, but the place looked deserted. He immediately got an uneasy feeling.

"Where are they?" Jessica looked up and down the highway. "Those vans have to be here somewhere."

Carver looked at the map. He zoomed in to see what was what and decided to drive up and down the streets. There weren't many of them and it wouldn't take much time at all. He turned the corner, drove down the road, and saw the vans in front of a large red metal building.

The sign outside said it was the volunteer fire department. It was a much larger building than the police department. The local police chief probably took one look at three vanloads of girls and decided to take them somewhere they could all fit.

Carver drove around the building. He hadn't planned on going in because showing his face to more cops didn't seem like a good idea even if they were on his side. But he'd wanted to make sure the girls made it safely and they were being taken care of.

He saw Anna's police cruiser parked on the side of the building. He saw an old Ford Crown Victoria with the McDade PD badge on the side. He also saw an old brown GMC with a Bastrop County Sheriff's Department star on the side. Apparently, they'd called for all the help they could get.

"Are we going in?" Jessica asked.

Carver shook his head. "No need to. We'll find a motel and execute my plan and then everything should be good."

She frowned. "What plan?"

"Easy." He turned right and began circling back towards the highway. "You upload the Jaeger files, the client list, and everything else to the internet for all to see."

"You make it sound so simple."

"Use a VPN to upload it anonymously to a website where it can be downloaded by everyone and maybe email links to a few people who will get the word out."

"I can make that happen, but I'll need time to set up."

Sabrina's face brightened. "That's an amazing idea. Expose all those horrible people who bought and sold us like cattle."

Hardin nodded. "It's the next best step. And done anonymously, there will be no threat of retaliation."

"I'll whip up a press package." Jessica tapped her bottom lip. "I'll need to look into the data and see exactly what we've got first. It'll take a day or two if I'm being realistic."

"That's fine."

"So, we'll lay low in a hotel for a few days?" Sabrina said. "Shouldn't we tell Mom and Dad that we're okay?"

"At this point, I don't trust anyone in Austin except for them." Jessica shook her head. "You need to hear the entire story. Then you'll understand how crazy things are."

"Yeah, I'd like to hear how my big sister pulled this off."

Jessica touched Carver's arm. "With a lot of help."

"Ooh, you've got a thing for him, don't you?"

Jessica laughed. "I mean, he's got the irresistible charm of a honey badger."

Sabrina burst into laughter. "I can't decide if that's a compliment or an insult."

"Oh, it's both." Jessica grinned. "Definitely both."

Carver didn't get it. "Another reference?"

"Yeah, but also a honey badger is a wild animal. Don't you know anything about them?"

"I've never needed to." Carver took another right and headed toward the highway. He reached the intersection and hit the brakes. Something had been gnawing at him since seeing the fire department building and now he knew what it was.

Anna's police cruiser.

Anna had driven a van and left the cruiser behind. She hadn't had time to go back and get it. If she had, she would have crossed paths with them when they were coming here. Which meant that cruiser wasn't Anna's.

It belonged to someone else in the Travis Sheriff's department.

"What's wrong?" Jessica leaned forward. "Carver?"

He backed up the van and parked it where it wouldn't be seen. "Wait here." He took the M4 because he wanted accuracy. "We might have unwanted company."

"Huh?"

"There's a Travis County Sheriff's car in front of the fire department, and I'm positive Anna didn't drive it there."

"I'm coming too." Jessica patted her sidearm.

He shook his head. "Not this time. Just be ready to run if things go south."

"Oh, God." Hardin's face hardened into anger. "Can I help?"

"Nope." Carver got out of the van. He dodged through some trees and crossed the road. The metal building had no windows on the sides. There were large doors for the trucks on the front, but they were closed.

There was a rear exit for fire safety, and a front entry door. He chose the rear door. It was a simple fiberglass door. There was no window so he couldn't see what was on the other side without opening it.

Carver tested the door handle. It was unlocked. He gently eased open the door. The rear of a large yellow fire truck was on the other side. Sounds echoed in the metal building. He heard talking. He heard crying. He heard someone talking loudly over the noise. He knew that voice, unfortunately. He knew that it meant nothing good for the girls.

Carver eased around the side of the fire truck and saw exactly who he'd expected to see. Detective Piker. She wasn't alone. She was with four armed men he also recognized. They were from Ramona's protest group. One of them was Ramona's guitar-playing boyfriend.

Apparently, protesting was only one of their day jobs.

He went to the other side of the fire truck. There was a longer fire engine parked next to it. He got behind it and went to the edge. From there, he saw everything. He saw all the girls huddling in a corner. He saw Anna standing with them.

A Hispanic man in jeans, a button-up shirt, and a cowboy hat stood next to Anna. That was probably her cousin, the local cop. There was a body on the floor. A man in a brown sheriff's uniform lay on his side. A small puddle of blood was on the concrete beneath him.

Carver didn't see any firemen. That made sense because they were volunteers. They didn't live here full time. Anna's cousin probably had the key to the place.

Piker didn't have her gun drawn, but the four men with her had sidearms. They were holding them down by their sides. They didn't seem worried about the girls making a run for it. They were also blocking the front entrance.

They obviously hadn't realized there was a back entrance or hadn't bothered securing it. That was their mistake. Probably their last mistake. Carver detached the silencer from the M4. He didn't care about making noise now and he wanted a little extra accuracy and power.

The men were lined up in front of the girls, all nice and neat. Piker stood behind them. She kept checking her phone like she was expecting a call from someone. Maybe from Jaeger. She didn't know he was dead yet. She probably thought recovering his merchandise would lead to a big bonus.

She and her men were right in Carver's sights.

But he didn't act. Not yet. There was a small office in the front corner. The door was closed, and he couldn't see through the window. Was it empty? Was someone in there? No way to tell.

He hadn't seen anyone outside of the building when passing by earlier or when he approached the back. That meant no one was patrolling outside. Everyone was inside.

Always assume you don't see everyone.

Someone told him that once and he'd taken it to heart. Someone might be inside the office. He had some information, but not all the information he needed. Barring a miracle, that was all he was going to get.

He practiced the shots in his head. He'd done this countless times before. The men didn't have their weapons aimed at the girls. They were low and not ready. They assumed they had everything under control.

They also didn't have all the information they needed. They hadn't secured the back door. They hadn't secured the area behind the fire truck or engine. It was amateur hour. All things considered, Carver had the upper hand.

It was time to act.

He braced his shoulder on the fire engine and slid around it nice and slow. The man closest to him was about twenty feet away. The man flinched like he saw something out of the corner of his eye. It was the last thing he saw.

Carver fired once, twice, three times. He hit the first guy in the head. The second guy in the neck. The third guy was turning, his weapon coming to bear. A shot took him just below the base of the throat. The second shot hit him in the bridge of the nose.

Ramona's boyfriend looked completely taken by surprise. He seemed to barely register that shots had been fired. His first instinct was to freeze and watch with wide eyes while his comrades went down.

Yeah, this was definitely amateur hour.

Ramona's boyfriend lost the ability for rational thought. Not just because he was surprised by the sudden gunfire, but because Carver vacated the brain matter from his cranial cavity with a well-placed bullet.

Piker was suddenly all alone.

She wasn't staring like a deer caught in the headlights, but her gun was still snapped into her holster. She was in full panic mode, tugging uselessly on her holstered sidearm.

Carver rushed Piker's position. He kept his eye on the office door waiting for someone else to come out. Piker managed to yank her gun from the holster and started to raise it.

Carver shot her in the shoulder.

She screamed and dropped her gun. "Wait!" she shouted. "Wait! I'm a cop!"

If Jessica were here, she'd probably have a witty parting comment. Carver couldn't think of anything and figured it was a waste of breath. He put a bullet in Piker's stomach. She squealed like a wounded animal and pressed her hands to the entrance wound.

The echoes of the last booming shots faded. Carver's ears were ringing. M4 carbines were loud. Every shot sent ripples in the air you could feel all the way through your body like a shockwave.

The girls were screaming. They were huddled on the floor their hands over their heads. Anna was on top of some of them shielding their bodies with hers.

Piker was still squealing like a stuck pig. She slowly keeled over on her side. It would take hours for her to die. She would be in terrible pain for the entire time. Carver kicked her gun away and figured she deserved to suffer for as long as possible.

Then Piker started coughing. Bloody foam sprayed from her mouth. The bullet had probably bounced and nicked a lung. It looked like she was going to suffocate in minutes instead. Carver could live with that.

Carver turned to Anna. "Is anyone in the office?"

Anna didn't seem to hear him. He shouted it again.

She looked up. Shook her head. "No, that was all of them."

Carver rushed to the office and opened the door. He cleared the room anyway. No sense in taking her word for it. It was empty.

The downed sheriff twitched. He was still alive. Carver jogged over to him. Saw the wound in his stomach. He was bleeding, but he might be okay. It depended on how much the bullet had bounced around his insides.

The local cop ran over. He checked the sheriff too. "Hang on, Ralph, we've got paramedic gear in the truck." He ran to the truck and began pulling out equipment.

Anna disentangled herself from the distraught girls and knelt next to Ralph. Tears streamed down her face. "My God. I can't believe this is happening! I thought I worked with good men, not criminals!"

It was loud inside the fire station. There was lots of crying, shouting, and screaming. Apparently, the nightmare still wasn't over for the rescued girls.

Carver gripped Anna by her arm and pulled her to her feet. "What happened? How did Piker find you?"

"She just walked right in with those men." Anna still seemed to be in shock. "She's a detective! A damned detective!"

"Yes, but how did she find you?" Carver led her away from Ralph and out of the back door where it was quieter.

Once outside, she blinked and seemed to recover some of her wits. "She walked in and told me, Pedro, and Ralph to throw down our weapons. Ralph went for his and one of those men shot him." She took a deep breath to calm herself. "She said the vans have GPS trackers on them and they were supposed to be heading in the opposite direction. She went to the boathouse and found the bodies, then she and her men took my cruiser because I left it there with the keys."

Anna shook her head. "She thanked me for leaving it because she didn't have room in her car for transporting the men."

Carver didn't know how he'd missed seeing Piker's car at the boathouse. She must have parked it on the other side of the building where Anna had parked the SUVs. He hadn't driven to the other side of the building to verify the vehicles were still there.

Jessica hurried across the road to them. "What happened?"

"A few more bumps in the road." Carver laid out the details. "They're still not safe."

There was no telling how many more people would come for the girls since the vans had trackers on them. Thanks to specialized gear he'd appropriated during his time in Washington DC, he could probably get rid of them.

He went to the camper van and dug out an RF inspector from the equipment bag. It was a general-purpose detector, good for finding bugs, wireless cameras, and GPS trackers. He went to the first van and found the tracker in the engine compartment behind the windshield washer fluid reservoir. It was wired straight into the battery and was screwed down tight.

He went inside the fire station. They had a large toolbox. He found a screwdriver and went back to the vans. After some grunting and swearing he managed to get the tracker loose. He disconnected the wiring harness that powered it, rendering the tracker dead and useless.

He removed the other ones. He checked Roy's camper van just in case and didn't find one. Anna's police cruiser had one, so he disabled it too. They needed to be as off the radar as possible.

A diesel engine roared. A big Dodge Ram with dual rear wheels squealed around the corner and headed for the fire station. Carver ducked behind one of the vans. He slung the M4 back around to the front and got ready.

This wasn't over yet.

CHAPTER 38

Carver aimed his rifle at the truck.

Anna ran outside and waved her hands. She was grinning. She looked relieved. There were four Hispanic men in the back of the pickup. Five more climbed out of the pickup truck. They were all in jeans, button-up shirts, cowboy boots and cowboy hats.

They had the weather-beaten skin of ranch hands and the serious eyes of men who knew how to handle themselves. They were armed with M4 style rifles and sidearms holstered on their thighs.

Anna greeted some of them with hugs. She was laughing and crying, probably in relief. These weren't new enemies, they were reinforcements.

Carver approached them.

Anna introduced the driver of the pickup. "This is my brother, Carlos."

"I'm Carver." Carver shook his hand. "I assume you can take over security?"

"Wow, you're big." Carlos looked up at him. "Anna says you saved her life. I'm eternally grateful. Mainly because our mother would kill me if something happened to her."

"Understood."

"My ranch is a few miles outside of town. We can take the girls there for safekeeping until this is sorted."

"I'll tag along too," Carver said. "There are some things that need to be sorted out."

"Sounds good. My wife, Lorraine, is already preparing food and rooms. It'll be tight, but I think we can accommodate everyone."

One of the men behind him said something in Spanish and the others nodded seriously.

Carlos patted the man on the shoulder. "The men will gladly give up their bunks in the ranch hand house, so everyone has a place to stay."

Anna wiped her tears away. "Thank you, little brother."

Carlos smiled and clapped his hands together. "Should we round everyone up and head out?"

Anna nodded enthusiastically. "Yes, please!"

Pedro came out of the fire station and greeted Carlos with a brief handshake. "Ralph will be okay. That fat belly of his redirected the bullet down and out of his side." He smiled. "I told him all those empanadas Lorraine makes him were going to save his life someday."

Carlos flashed a quick smile. "Thank God. What would we do without Sheriff Ralph around the picnic table?"

Anna went inside and organized the girls again. She told them what was happening. Some girls cried for their parents. Others accepted it quietly. Others looked like they hardly heard her at all.

"I know you want to go home, but there are very bad people still looking for you," Anna said. "We will keep you safe until we figure this out."

That seemed to quiet most of the girls. Several of them ran up to Carver and hugged him around the legs on their way to the vans. Carver didn't know how to respond. He knew how to fake a response by mussing their hair or smiling and patting their backs, but this was something far different than he'd ever experienced before.

Jessica watched from a distance. She was all smiles at his discomfort and didn't do a thing to help him out of it.

The girls were loaded into the vans again. Anna drove one. Two of Carlos's men were going to drive the other vans, but the teenaged girls who'd driven the vans to the fire station told them they were plenty capable of driving the vans to the ranch.

The men backed away, hands up in surrender and smiling. One of them spoke in Spanish to the other. "They're as bossy as my daughter."

The other man laughed.

They drove out to the ranch. It was on a big plot of land with lots of cows. A large white brick house sat on a rise. There were two large metal garages next door, and another long brick building that was probably where the ranch hands stayed with their families.

Lorraine was waiting out front with three girls and two boys who looked excited to meet their new guests. Carver parked the camper van and went into the back of it. He was dead tired and just wanted to sleep. It had been a long night and a long day.

Sabrina and Hardin went inside.

Jessica lingered behind. "Not coming inside?"

He shook his head.

"There's food inside."

"I want sleep more than I want food."

She kissed him long and hard. "Thank you, Carver. I don't even know how to convey what I'm feeling and thinking. I just want you to know that you're a true friend. A real man. A good guy."

"I can only handle so much praise," Carver said in a deadpan voice.

She laughed. "I know. I just wanted to tell you how I feel. And also, I don't want you to go when this is all over. I'd like you to stick around. Nothing serious, or anything, but I've kind of gotten attached to you."

Carver blew out a breath.

"Don't say no." She put a finger over his lips. "Just enjoy the moment, okay?"

He didn't want to admit it, but he was enjoying the moment. It was strange not being on a beach and feeling somewhat content with life despite everything they'd been through. Unfortunately, there was still a lot to worry about.

Jessica took out her laptop. "I'm not going in just yet. I'm going to look through the hard drive so we can figure out how to put this information out there with maximum impact."

"If anyone can, it's you." Carver pushed her long black hair behind her ear and kissed her. "Good night."

"It's only early afternoon, Carver."

He took off everything but his underwear and lay down on the camper bed. It was surprisingly large enough to accommodate him. He closed his eyes and didn't even have to go through his relaxation routine to fall asleep.

He woke up around eighteen hundred hours. Jessica was still working on her laptop. She had an empty paper plate next to her and was sipping what looked like iced tea. She turned around when he sat up.

"You slept like the dead."

"That's the best way to sleep." Carver stretched. The camper van was nice and spacious.

Jessica smiled. "You like the van, don't you?"

"Maybe I should buy it from Roy."

She laughed. "He probably won't even notice it's missing."

"Better to buy it from him and keep it under his name rather than get caught in a stolen vehicle."

Jessica's eyes brightened. "Maybe we could frame him for a crime."

"The sky's the limit."

Her smile faded. "I exported the client list into SQL, linked the tables, and created a simple web app front end to make it easily searchable. All the clients are now listed with their victims. There are at least a dozen millionaires in the Austin area alone who are platinum members. And that's not all. The client list contains people from all over the country."

"Do all the platinum members keep girls offsite?"

"Some do, yes. Others elected to leave the girls at Jaeger's ranch. They pay a maintenance fee to keep them there." She shook her head. "It's like a subscription for sex slaves.
It's the worst thing I've ever seen in my life!"

Carver had seen worse, but it was all bad. It was the worst humanity had to offer no
matter what other horrible things happened in the world.

"I found a guy with three girls in his mansion." She pulled up a profile. There was a face
shot of a light-skinned male, maybe Middle Eastern if Carver had to guess. The name,
Abdul, confirmed that he was probably right.

Abdul's net worth was fifteen million. He had a mansion right on banks of the Colorado River. He'd bought his first girl three years ago, and two more since then.

"Can you believe they even have a disposal service?" Jessica clenched her fists. "If you
want to get rid of a girl, they'll do it for a fee. Either find her a new buyer, or you know..."
Jessica slashed a finger across her throat. "It's pure evil."

Carver looked at the girls Abdul had purchased. He pointed to the second one Abdul
had bought. "Is that why you singled him out for me?"

She nodded. "According to the database, she's still alive. I don't know how current the
information is, but we need to find out."

Carver opened the blinds on the back of the camper. It was still light outside but dusk
would settle in soon. "I'm going to eat. Then I'll look into it."

"I'm going with you."

He nodded. "I know."

Carver walked around the back of the ranch house where steaks, ribs, and more were
slow cooking over a large barbeque grill. There was a long table set up with a wide variety
of foods. He picked up several of the empanadas that Ralph liked so well, got himself a
thick ribeye, and went back to the camper van to eat before anyone noticed him.

After he ate, he and Jessica drove back to Austin. He drove past Abdul's address and
looked it over. It was a mansion by any definition of the word. It had a stone wall, a large
iron gate, and a brick-paved driveway leading to a four-car garage.

Satellite view on the maps app showed an Olympic sized swimming pool, a long dock
in the river, and even a tennis court.

The house was constructed of pale limestone. The roof had lots of gables and peaks
and even a square watchtower rising from the middle. The house looked like the modern
equivalent of a medieval castle.

There were cameras next to the gate but none along the perimeter. The stone wall
didn't have spikes or anything on the top, so scaling it wasn't going to be a problem. There
were no guards and no signs of security either at least on the front side.

There might be more cameras inside and outside, but Carver wasn't worried about them. Unless there was a squad of guards inside, this was going to be a quick in and out mission.

He drove to the other side of the river. There was a public marina right across from Abdul's house. He used it to scout the house with his monocular. He didn't see anyone through the large windows in the back of the house or outside.

Maybe no one was home. Or maybe Abdul didn't have a family and didn't come outside much. There really was no telling.

Carver went back to the other side of the river and parked down the street from Abdul's mansion. "Let's get some sleep. I'll go in at zero two hundred."

"Good idea. I'm dead on my feet right now." She seemed to realize she was sitting down. "Well, dead on my ass anyway."

Carver's nap had helped some, but he could use a few more hours of shuteye. He fell asleep and woke up a little before his internal alarm did. He shook Jessica awake.

She shouted in alarm and sat up. "Sorry, bad dreams. I keep seeing all those people I shot." She sighed. "I don't feel bad about it, but it's not something I'll ever forget."

"That's a natural reaction," Carver said.

She nodded. "Yeah, I know. It's just a weird feeling to know that I killed another human, no matter how evil they were."

Carver didn't have any advice about that. "Stay here and let me know if you see anything." He put the earbud in his ear and tested it. "Testing."

"I don't hear anything." Jessica checked hers. "We forgot to recharge them."

Carver put the earbud down. "I think I'll be fine."

"Be careful." Jessica kissed him.

Carver exited the van. He was wearing all black from head to toe. He pulled up his mask and slung the MP5SD over his back. He pulled himself up and over the stone wall then looked for cameras.

He saw one near an entry door. It was angled to see anyone approaching from the paved pathway, so he might be in its sights. He went right up to it and sprayed the lens with black paint. The house almost certainly had an alarm system complete with motion detection, so covering the cameras probably wouldn't do much good.

The house also probably had a panic room and an escape route if Abdul needed to flee for his life. If the girls were being kept here, they'd be locked somewhere safe, secure, and probably hidden. Probably somewhere near the panic room.

Entering the home on the ground floor without setting off the alarm or being recorded by a camera would be hard. It would be better to go in on the second floor because homeowners typically didn't put security upstairs. They figured criminals wouldn't be able to access the higher floors very easily.

That was normally true. Run of the mill criminals didn't typically carry ladders with them. But in this case, they didn't need to. The top of the stone wall was level with the first floor roof and was barely five feet away from it.

Carver pulled himself on top of the wall and made the short leap to the roof. He walked across it to the nearest second-floor window. It was an expensive steel-framed vertical window, but Carver made short work of the latches with his slim-jim.

He opened the window and looked for motion detectors on the second floor. As suspected, there were none. Carver stepped inside onto a tile floor. He lowered his night-vision goggles and followed the hallway, clearing rooms as he went. The bedrooms were large, well furnished, and empty of human occupants. In fact, it didn't look like anyone had ever lived in any of the rooms.

The master bedroom was the exception. It was a big room with a California king against one wall. The covers were rumpled and unmade. No one was in the bed. He went into the walk-in closet.

There was a large painting of Abdul on one wall. He sat on a giant golden throne, wore a crown, and held a golden scepter. Clearly, he thought of himself as a king even though he was living like a pig.

There was clothing on the floor and in baskets. The furniture was covered in dust. There was dirt and food stains on the floor. It looked like King Abdul didn't even have a maid, and not because he couldn't afford one.

Abdul didn't let anyone into his mansion because he didn't want to risk exposing his dark secret. A maid might stumble across wherever he kept the girls or might hear them. Allowing someone to freely roam the house was dangerous.

Since Abdul wasn't here, finding the girls was going to be a problem. This place was huge and could have any number of secret rooms. Most of the time hidden rooms were in the basement.

That meant he'd have to circumvent motion sensors and alarms on the first floor. There was probably a keypad or a remote of some kind in the bedroom. He was about to start looking when he thought of something else.

The painting of Abdul and the design of the house gave Carver all the clues he needed to find the girls. Abdul thought of himself as a king and his house was built like a castle. There was one place where kings kept special prisoners.

Prisoners named Rapunzel, for example. At least Carver knew that reference. He looked out of the bedroom window. The tall square tower was right in the middle of the house. It had windows, but they were all blacked out.

Carver left the bedroom and took a left into the hallway. He took another left at the next junction and saw an iron door at the end of it. It looked like heavy iron, with large rivets and ornate hinges. There were heavy iron barrel bolts on the outside, but they weren't engaged.

The barrel bolts were dead giveaways, but why weren't they latched?

He went to the door and gently pulled on the large pull handle. It opened silently on well-oiled hinges. There was a short stone stairway ahead. He slowly made his way to the top. There was a single large room at the top.

In the middle of the room was a four-post canopy bed with heavy carved timbers for posts and an ornate metal canopy. It was a king's bed, no doubt about that. And right in the middle was King Abdul.

CHAPTER 39

Carver walked closer to the bed.

Abdul lay in the middle of the bed between four females. Apparently, he'd required a fourth girl from somewhere besides Jaeger. All four females were on the petite side. Abdul was a small guy himself, so he probably didn't want a female who could overpower him.

The females also wore collars with long, slender chains that were bolted to the stone wall. Carver stalked over to the bed for a better look. Everyone was dead asleep. There were two empty bottles of wine next to the bed, and it smelled like everyone had been drinking.

The collars on the girls' necks were metal with padding on the inside. They weren't tight enough to rub the skin raw, but there was no getting them off without a key to the small padlocks on the back.

There was also a slender wire running from the collar, down the chain, and into the wall. It was a low-voltage wire. It was probably a signal wire that would trigger an alert if broken or if the circuit from the metal collar was broken.

The alert probably texted Abdul or caused his phone to make a specific sound. The keys to the collars were probably kept somewhere in Abdul's bedroom. That explained how this man was able to keep four girls locked up in his tower for years.

If they tried to overpower him, there was no escape from the collars. The windows were blacked out and there was probably heavy insulation in the walls to deaden their screams for help. Without Abdul, they would starve or die from dehydration.

He never took them from the room. He probably rarely slept in his own bed, opting to sleep with his sex slaves instead.

There was a treadmill and an elliptical on one side of the room. There was a large-screen television and entertainment on the other side. It looked like he required the girls to stay in shape for his pleasure.

There were windows on three sides of the tower. They were all normal sized, all blacked out, and upon closer inspection, seemed to be made of thick bulletproof glass. Even pounding on them wouldn't make much noise.

The steel frames were welded shut on two of them. The one facing the same side as the pool wasn't. The two heavy latches were locked and required a key to open them.

Carver didn't feel like hunting for the padlock keys, so he took the direct route. He yanked down the covers, grabbed Abdul by the arm, and jerked him up and out of the middle of the girls. Freed from the covers, Abdul was naked as the day he was born.

Carver dropped him on the hard stone floor and pinned him down by his neck. Abdul was a small man, maybe 5'5" with thin arms, skinny legs, and a large round belly packed with fat. His face was pockmarked with acne scars, and his hair was thin and wispy with a large bald spot on the top. Abdul had money, but he sure as hell didn't have good looks or much of anything in the manhood department either.

Abdul woke up with a high-pitched scream. One of the girls screamed. That woke the others who added to the chorus of screams. Carver flipped up his night vision goggles and shined a flashlight in Abdul's face.

"Where are the keys to the collars?"

"Who are you?" Abdul wriggled but he wasn't going anywhere. "Do you know who I am?"

"That doesn't really matter," Carver said. "What matters is that you tell me where the keys to the collars are before I get angry."

"Let me go!" Abdul struggled like a madman, but he obviously hadn't used the exercise equipment in the room. He was panting after just a few seconds. "I have money."

"Save the bribes," Carver said. "I've got plenty of money. What I don't have are the keys to the padlocks."

"They're in a safe in my bedroom closet." Abdul whimpered. "I'll give them to you if you promise to let me go."

"I'll let you go." Carver yanked him to his feet and pushed him toward the door.

"What's happening?" one of the girls said. It was pitch black and they couldn't see Carver.

Carver didn't answer. He guided Abdul down the stairs, down the hallway, into his bedroom and the closet. Carver turned on the closet light and stared at the giant painting of Abdul.

If Carver was a betting man, he'd bet the safe was right behind that painting. He would have lost that bet because Abdul wasn't that stupid. Abdul went to a shelf, moved a stack of shirts, and pulled down on the back of the shelf. It slid down to reveal a safe with a keypad.

He punched in the code. The door clicked open.

"Is there a weapon inside?" Carver said.

"Yes."

"Don't reach for it and you'll be just fine."

"The keys are next to the gun."

"That's fine. Get the keys, leave the gun."

Abdul opened the safe. There was a compact pistol inside. Next to it was a small rose gold box. Abdul took it out. He opened it and showed five keys to Carver. Four looked like normal padlock keys. The fifth one was different.

"What does this one go to?"

"The window in the tower."

"Why did you weld the other windows shut but leave that one functional?"

Abdul shrugged. "I reward the girls with a look outside sometimes if they are especially good."

"Define especially good."

Abdul touched his tiny manhood. "If they can take me without wincing in pain at the size."

The man was clearly delusional, but Carver figured that was normal for people like him. "Do you have an alarm system?"

Abdul nodded. "But I'm the only one who monitors it. It doesn't automatically call the police."

Carver wasn't surprised. "Good. Because me and the girls are walking out of here after I let you go."

Abdul nodded. "Okay. Will you tell the police about me?"

"I don't trust the cops in this town."

"They are owned by a very powerful man."

Carver prodded Abdul out of the closet, through the bedroom, and into the hallway. "You're talking about Jaeger."

"Yes. He's very powerful. I'm almost as afraid of him as I am of my own family. It's best if you don't go to the police. You're likely to end up dead."

"He's dead now, so you don't need to be afraid anymore."

Abdul stopped walking. A horrified expression spread across his face. "He's dead? How?"

"He stuck his head in an oven." Carver prodded him onward. "No more questions. Just do what you're told."

Abdul walked down the hallway and up the stairs into the tower. Carver turned on the lights to reveal the girls huddled under the blankets. They didn't look scared. They looked uncertain but hopeful.

"I was abused as a child," Abdul said. "My uncle did terrible things to me. Please don't blame me for what I've done."

Carver ignored him. He went to the functional window and unlocked it. It was a casement window, so it swung outward like a door. He looked down. The pool lights were on and there was dim outside lighting revealing a wide concrete pool deck and furniture.

The tower was tall enough to make it a four-story drop to the ground. There was no way out even if the girls got free of their collars and managed to open the window. They could only scream for help and hope the neighbors heard them.

He turned back to Abdul. "Unlock the collars."

The girls hopped out of bed. They were all just as naked as Abdul, but some of them had bruises and scars, evidence that Abdul hadn't exactly treated them like princesses.

Abdul hesitated but complied, releasing them one at a time. One of the girls kneed him in the crotch. She screamed and flung herself at him, slapping and kicking. Abdul bared his teeth and clenched his fists, but a warning look from Carver stopped him from retaliating.

"Take it like a man," Carver said. "Then I'll let you go."

"Really?" One of the girls looked cautious. "We can beat the hell out of him?"

Carver nodded. "Knock yourselves out." He leaned back against the wall and watched the girls beat Abdul until he screamed for mercy.

The girls pounded on him for several solid minutes. They'd obviously been using the treadmill and elliptical because they weren't even breathing hard when they stepped back. Abdul was curled into a ball and whimpering. He was also bleeding from dozens of cuts and scratches.

"I think you broke my rib." Abdul was crying. "It's agonizing."

"Good," Carver said. He looked at the girls. "Finished?"

One of the girls stepped towards Carver. None of them seemed even aware or concerned about being naked. Judging from the lack of clothing in the room, it seemed that Abdul kept them naked all the time.

"Are you really letting him go?"

Carver nodded. "I promised."

"But he's a monster."

"I know." Carver lifted the bruised and bloodied Abdul from the floor.

Abdul groaned and grasped his bleeding crotch. "Please let it end."

"I will." Carver didn't want to, but he grabbed Abdul by the crotch and throat, squeezing hard. Abdul squealed and struggled. Carver carried him to the window and as promised, let him go.

Abdul screamed briefly before his head hit the pool deck.

One of the girls laughed hysterically.

Carver brushed his hands together. "See? I let him go."

"Is this really happening?" One of the girls asked. "Or did he drug us again?"

"It's happening." Carver looked around the room. "Do you have clothing anywhere?"

"No." They shook their heads.

"I haven't worn clothing in years." Another girl said.

Carver nodded. "Let's find something and leave." He took them to Abdul's bedroom. He washed the blood off his hands while the girls found something to wear. Abdul's shirts and pants fit them just fine. They left via the front door and Carver helped them over the stone wall.

They hurried to the van. Jessica hopped out and opened the side door. "That was fast."

"Abdul was very cooperative." Carver got into the driver's seat.

"Who are you people?" One of the girls said. "How did you find us?"

"Oh, that's a long story," Jessica said. "But I can tell you on the way."

"On the way to where?"

"To a safe place for now." Jessica turned to one of the girls. "I know someone who will be very happy to see you."

She frowned. "You do?"

"Yes." Jessica teared up. "I'm happy we found you, Diana."

"You know my name?"

"Yes, and we know your father, Josh Hardin."

Diana gasped. "This is really happening, isn't it?"

"Yes," Jessica said. "It is."

The girls shouted in joy, hugging each other and crying.

It was a long drive back to the ranch. Jessica talked to the girls about their years-long ordeal. About the horrors of being Abdul's sex slaves. Carver had heard it all before. And despite everyone they'd saved, this was just a drop in the bucket.

When they reached the ranch, Jessica took Diana to her father. He was overjoyed. Then Jessica told him about Abdul and the joy morphed to anger and anguish over what his daughter had suffered all these years.

"I can't thank you enough," Hardin said. "Words can never express how I feel."

Carver just nodded. "I figured the local cops wouldn't do anything."

"What about others like me?" Diana said. "Can we save them?"

"Hopefully when this information gets out, the authorities will actually do some-thing," Jessica said. "There are too many victims for one man to handle."

"Yeah." Diana looked at the other girls, many of whom were sleeping in the den. "I can't believe you saved so many already."

"It's easier when they're all in one place," Carver said. He went to the van and got the duffel bags of cash. He didn't take any for himself. He still had plenty from his time in Washington DC. He took the bags inside.

Anna was sitting in the kitchen talking to her brother and sister-in-law. She looked at Carver when he entered and smiled wearily. "Taking care of so many people is exhausting, but we couldn't sleep."

"We saw what you did for Hardin," Carlos said. "That's unbelievable."

Carver dropped the duffel bags on the floor. "There's millions in here. I trust you can distribute the cash to the victims." He turned to leave.

"Wait." Anna hugged him. "Thank you for saving my life."

Carver patted her back. It felt a little more natural after all the hugs he'd been getting. "Sure."

"A man of few words." Carlos grinned. "Thank you for saving my sister. We'll figure out how to hand out the money."

"We'll need to use some to pay for food," Lorraine said. "It's like feeding a small army."

"Okay." Carver shook Carlos's hand. "You have beer around here?"

"Yeah!" Carlos opened the refrigerator and took out a bottle.

"Three ought to do it," Carver said.

Carlos laughed and handed him the entire six-pack. "Whatever you want, it's yours."

Carver took the beer and left.

Jessica was in the den talking to her sister. She looked up at Carver and smiled sadly. "We're going to be okay."

"Good. I'm going to the van." Carver went outside and decided the porch was better. It was zero four hundred, but his two naps had refreshed him. This far out in the country without lights, the stars looked like dust overhead.

He sat in a rocking chair and twisted the cap off a beer. He took a deep swig and sighed in contentment. There was still a lot to do, but Jessica could handle it. He'd stick around for a while and maybe return to the beach.

Or maybe he'd stick around for a little longer. He really wasn't sure. Somehow, all of this felt right. It felt like he'd been trying to escape from responsibility for too long. Felt like he'd been running from destiny, not that he really believed in all of that.

He wasn't ready to follow Leon's path. Maybe it was time to forge his own. Time to put his skills to good use with purpose rather than being dragged into things. Thinking like that normally bothered him. But not this time. This time he felt fine.

Just fine.

EPILOGUE

It took several days, but everything was finally ready.

Jessica had created a website linked to the client list and anonymously hosted it on various cloud servers. That way there was no single point of failure if powerful people tried to shut it down. Then she anonymously sent out press packets to thousands of digital media companies and a few traditional news companies.

She simultaneously sent packets to federal and local law enforcement agencies all over the southwestern United States so they could immediately take action before the people on the list had time to cover their crimes. Some people would naturally be protected by the system because it was run by political allies, but others would not.

The client list spread like wildfire. The feds and other local authorities had no choice but to act. News agencies reported on arrests every day. Some of Jaeger's clients tried to run. They were arrested in other countries and would be sent back to the states to face their crimes. Some chose to end their own lives rather than face justice.

The client list ran the entire gamut of income earners, ethnicities, and nationalities. Most were naturally in the top brackets because they could afford Jaeger's prices. There were lots of wealthy politicians on his client list. Lots of top executives too.

Companies and governments were rocked by the allegations. Hundreds of politicians and high-ranking law enforcement officials were caught up in the scandal. So many resigned that the local governments became dysfunctional and had to be taken over by the state.

Two weeks after the scandal rocked the nation, it seemed safe to start reuniting the victims with their families. It would be a long, slow painful process. Some would recover and go on to live normal lives. Others would not.

There had been a little more than thirty million dollars in the duffel bags Carver took from Jaeger's vault. Anna divided it up as equally as she could among the victims, so they all ended up with around five hundred thousand dollars each.

It was a tiny amount that could in no way make up for what they'd been through, but it was immediate relief. The state government seized all of Jaeger's assets and promised to create a fund for the victims. Whether that would really happen was anyone's guess.

Carver stuck around and worked on Carlos' ranch. He was in no hurry to get to the beach and wanted to make sure Jessica's master plan went off without a hitch. If he was being honest with himself, he also didn't mind Jessica's company.

When he got the itch to move on and find another beach, maybe he'd ask her to come along. But that was a decision for another day. For now, he was content.

And that was good enough for now.

BOOKS BY JOHN CORWIN-

PSYCHOLOGICAL THRILLERS
The Family Business
AMOS CARVER THRILLERS
Dead Before Dawn
Dead List
Dead and Buried
Dead Man Walking
Dead by the Dozen
Dead Run
Dead Weather Days
Dead to Rights
Dead But Not Forgotten
Dead Reckoning
CHRONICLES OF CAIN
To Kill a Unicorn
Enter Oblivion
Throne of Lies
At The Forest of Madness
The Dead Never Die
Shadow of Cthulhu
Cabal of Chaos

Monster Squad

Gates of Yog-Sothoth

Shadow Over Tokyo

Into the Multiverse

THE OVERWORLD CHRONICLES

Sweet Blood of Mine

Dark Light of Mine

Fallen Angel of Mine

Dread Nemesis of Mine

Twisted Sister of Mine

Dearest Mother of Mine

Infernal Father of Mine

Sinister Seraphim of Mine

Wicked War of Mine

Dire Destiny of Ours

Aetherial Annihilation

Baleful Betrayal

Ominous Odyssey

Insidious Insurrection

Utopia Undone

Overworld Apocalypse

Apocryphan Rising

Soul Storm

Devil's Due

Overworld Ascension

Assignment Zero (An Elyssa Short Story)

OVERWORLD UNDERGROUND

Soul Seer

Demonicus

Infernal Blade

OVERWORLD ARCANUM

Conrad Edison and the Living Curse

Conrad Edison and the Anchored World

Conrad Edison and the Broken Relic

Conrad Edison and the Infernal Design

Conrad Edison and the First Power

STAND ALONE NOVELS
Mars Rising
No Darker Fate
The Next Thing I Knew
Outsourced
Seventh

ABOUT THE AUTHOR

John Corwin is the bestselling author of the Amos Carver Thrillers, Overworld Chronicles, and Chronicles of Cain. He enjoys long walks on the beach and is a firm believer in puppies and kittens.

After years of getting into trouble thanks to his overactive imagination, John abandoned his male modeling career to write books.

He resides in Atlanta.

https://www.facebook.com/groups/overworldconclave

Join the Overworld Conclave for all the news, memes and tentacles you could ever desire!

https://www.facebook.com/groups/overworldconclave

Or get your fix via email: www.johncorwin.net

Fan page: https://www.facebook.com/johncorwinauthor

Printed in Dunstable, United Kingdom